2/97

TRAVELLERS
IN MAGIC

TRAVELLERS
IN MAGIC

LISA GOLDSTEIN

A TOM DOHERTY ASSOCIATES BOOK / NEW YORK

TRAVELLERS IN MAGIC

Copyright © 1994 by Lisa Goldstein

This book is printed on acid-free paper.

A Tor Book
Published by Tom Doherty Associates, Inc.
175 Fifth Avenue
New York, N.Y. 10010

Tor ® is a registered trademark of Tom Doherty Associates, Inc.

Library of Congress Cataloging-in-Publication Data

Goldstein, Lisa.
    Travellers in magic / Lisa Goldstein.
        p.   cm.
    "A Tom Doherty Associates book."
    ISBN 0-312-85790-X
    1. Science fiction, American.   I. Title.
PS3557.O397T7   1994
813'.54-dc20   94-31310
                                                      CIP

First edition: December 1994

Printed in the United States of America

0 9 8 7 6 5 4 3 2 1

"Alfred"—*Asimov's Science Fiction*, December, 1992.

"Cassandra's Photographs"—*Isaac Asimov's Science Fiction Magazine*, August, 1987.

"Ever After"—*Isaac Asimov's Science Fiction Magazine*, December, 1984.

"Tourists"—*Isaac Asimov's Science Fiction Magazine*, February, 1985.

"Rites of Spring"—*Asimov's Science Fiction*, March, 1994.

"Midnight News"—*Isaac Asimov's Science Fiction Magazine*, March, 1990.

"Preliminary Notes on the Jang"—*Isaac Asimov's Science Fiction Magazine*, May, 1985.

"A Traveller at Passover"—*Pulphouse*, Winter, 1991.

"Infinite Riches"—*Asimov's Science Fiction*, April, 1993.

"Death Is Different"—*Isaac Asimov's Science Fiction Magazine*, September, 1988.

"Breadcrumbs and Stones"—*Snow White, Blood Red*, edited by Ellen Datlow and Terri Windling, AvoNova/Morrow, 1993.

"The Woman in the Painting"—*Fantasy & Science Fiction*, July, 1993.

"Daily Voices"—*Isaac Asimov's Science Fiction Magazine*, April, 1986.

"A Game of Cards"—*Sisters in Fantasy*, edited by Susan Shwartz, forthcoming.

"Split Light" is original to this collection.

To Larry,
brother *par excellence*.

CONTENTS

TRAVELLERS
IN MAGIC

ALFRED

A lison walked slowly through the park near school. Usually she went to Laura's house after school let out, but on Fridays Laura had a Girl Scout meeting. She passed a few older boys playing basketball, two women pushing baby strollers. Bells from the distant clock-tower rang out across the park: five o'clock, still too early to go home.

A leaf fell noiselessly to the path in front of her. The sun broke through the dark edge of the clouds and illuminated a spider web on one of the trees, making it shine like a gate of jewels. A spotted dog, loping alone down the path, looked back and grinned at her as if urging her on. She followed after it.

An old man sat on a bench ahead of her, his eyes closed and his face turned toward the sun.

If Laura had been here they'd be whispering together about everyone, laughing over their made-up stories. The two women would have had their babies switched at the hospital, and they would pass each other without ever knowing how close they were to their true children. The old man was a spy, of course.

As Alison walked by the man she saw that his face and

hands were pale, almost transparent. At that moment he opened his eyes and said, "I wonder—could you please tell me the time?"

He had a slight accent, like her parents. Her guess had been right after all—he *was* a spy. "Five o'clock," she said.

"Ah. And the year?"

This was much too weird; the man had to be crazy. Alison glanced around, acting casual but at the same time looking for someone to run to if things got out of hand. You weren't supposed to talk to strangers, she knew that. Her mother told her so all the time.

But what could this man do to her here, in front of all these people? And she had to admit that his question intrigued her—most adults asked you if you liked school and didn't seem to know where to go from there. "It's 1967," she said. Somehow his strange question made it all right to ask him one in return. "Why do you want to know?"

"Oh, you know how it is. We old people, we can never remember anything."

She tried to study him without being obvious. She'd been right about his accent: it sounded German, like her parents'. He had a narrow face and high forehead, with thinning black hair brushed back from his face. He wore glasses with John Lennon wire frames—very cool, Alison thought.

But other than the glasses, which he'd probably had forever, there wasn't anything fashionable about him. He had on a thin black tie, and his coat was nearly worn through in places.

He pushed back his sleeves. Nothing up my sleeves, Alison thought. Then she saw the numbers tattooed on his arm, and she looked away. Her parents had numbers like that.

"What is your name?" he asked.

She shook her head; she wasn't going to fall for that one. "My mother told me never to talk to strangers," she said.

"Your mother is a very smart woman. My mother never told me anything like that. My name is Alfred."

"Aren't you supposed to offer me candy now?" Alison said.

"Candy? Why?"

"That's the other thing my mother said. Strangers would try to give me candy."

He rummaged in his pockets as if searching for something. Alison saw with relief that his coat sleeves had fallen back over his arms, covering the tattoo. "I don't have any candy. All I have here is a pocket-watch. What would your mother say to that?"

He brought out a round gold watch. The letter "A" was engraved on it, the ends of the letter looping and curling around each other. Her initial, his initial. She reached for the watch but he moved it away from her and pressed the knob on top to open it. It had stopped hours ago.

"Aren't you going to wind it?" she asked.

"It's broken," he said. "I can tell you an interesting story about this watch, if you want to hear it."

She hesitated. She didn't want to hear about concentration camps; people—adults—got too strange when they talked about their experiences. It made her uncomfortable. Terrible things weren't supposed to happen to your parents; your parents were supposed to protect you.

On the other hand, she didn't want to go home just yet. "Okay," she said. She was almost certain now that he was harmless, but just to be safe she wouldn't sit on the bench next to him. She could probably outrun him anyway.

"My parents gave this watch to me a long time ago," he said. "I used to carry it with me wherever I went, and bring it out and look at it." He pried open the back and showed her a photograph of a dark-eyed boy and girl who looked a little like her and her brother Joey. But this back opened as well, revealing a small world of gears and springs and levers, all placed one over the other in careful layers, all unaccountably stopped.

"I took the watch down to the river once. I had my own

place there where no one could find me, where I would sit and think and dream. That day I was dreaming that someday I would learn how to make a watch like this. Someday I would find out its secrets.''

He fell silent. The sun glinted over the watch in his hand. ''And did you?'' she asked, to bring him back from wherever he had gone.

He didn't seem to hear her. ''And then the angel came,'' he said. ''Do you know, I had thought angels were courteous, kind. This one had a force of some sort, a terrifying energy I could feel even from where I sat. His eyes were fierce as stars. I thought he asked me a question, asked me if I desired anything, anything in the world, but in that confused instant I could not think of a thing I wanted. I was completely content. And so he left me.

''I looked down at the watch, which I still held in my hand, but it had stopped. And no one in the world has ever been able to make it start again.''

He looked at her as if expecting a reply. But all she could think of was that her first thought had been correct; he was crazy after all. No one in her family believed in angels. Still, what if—what if his story were true?

''But I think the angel granted my desire,'' he said. He nodded slowly. ''Do you know, I think he did.''

The shadows of the trees had grown longer while he'd talked to her; it was later than she'd thought. ''I've got to go now,'' she said reluctantly. ''My parents are expecting me.''

''Come again,'' he said. ''I'm in the park nearly every day.''

The bus was just pulling out when she got to the bus stop; she had to wait for the next one and got home just as her father and Joey were sitting down to dinner. Her mother carried plates filled with chicken and potatoes into the dining room. She frowned as Alison came in; it was a family rule that everyone had to be on time for dinner.

Her mother sat and her parents began to eat. Joey looked from one parent to the other uncertainly. Finally he said, "What happens to planes when they crash?"

Alison could see that he was trying to be casual, but he had obviously been worrying about the question all day. "What do you mean?" Alison's father said.

"Well, like when they fall. Where do they land?"

Her mother sighed. Joey was six, and afraid of everything. He refused to get on an elevator because he thought the cable would break. When they went walking he tried to stay with their parents at all times, and would grow anxious if he couldn't see them. Sometimes at night Alison heard screams coming from his room, his nightmares waking him up.

"I mean, could they land on the house?" he said. "Could they come through my bedroom?"

"No, of course not," Alison's father said. "The pilots try to land where there aren't any people."

"Well, but it could happen, couldn't it? What if—if they just fall?"

"Look," Alison's father said. "Let's say that this piece of chicken is the plane. Okay? And your plate here is where the plane comes down." Speaking carefully, his accent only noticeable as a slight gentleness on the "r" and "th" sounds, he took his son through a pretended plane crash. "Past where all the people live, see?" he said.

Joey nodded, but Alison saw that the answer didn't satisfy him. Their father was a psychologist, and Alison knew that it frustrated him not to be able to cure Joey's nightmares. He had told her once that he had studied to become a rabbi before the war, but that after he had been through the camps he had lost his faith in God and turned to psychology. It had made her uncomfortable to hear that her father didn't believe in God.

"He had another nightmare last night," her mother said softly.

"I don't know what it is," her father said. "We try to make a safe place here for the kids. They're in no danger here. I don't understand why he's so frightened all the time."

"Eat your dinner before it gets cold, Alison," her mother said, noticing for the first time that Alison had not touched her food. "There was a time when I would have given anything to have just one bite of what you're turning down now."

The next day, Saturday, Alison called Laura and told her about the old man in the park. She wanted to go back and talk to him again, but Laura said she was crazy. "He's some kind of pervert or something, I bet," Laura said. "Didn't your parents tell you not to talk to strangers?"

"He's not—"

"Why don't you come over here instead?"

Alison liked going to Laura's house, liked her parents and the rest of the family. They were Jewish, the same as her family, but Laura's grandfather had come to America before the war. To Alison that made them exotic, different. They seemed to laugh more, for one thing. "Okay," she said.

The minute Alison stepped into the house Laura's mother called Laura to the phone, then disappeared on some errand of her own. No one had invited Alison farther in than the living room. She looked around her, hoping the call wouldn't last long. In the next room Laura laughed and said something about the Girl Scout meeting.

The furniture in the living room was massy and overstuffed: a couch, two easy chairs, a coffee table and several end tables. A grandfather clock ticked noisily in the corner of the room, and opposite it stood a clunky old-fashioned television that Alison knew to be black and white.

For the first time she noticed the profusion of photographs, what looked like hundreds of them, spread out over the mantelpiece and several end tables. All of them had heavy, ornate frames, and doilies to protect the surfaces under them. Curious, she went over to the mantelpiece to get a closer look.

Most were black and white, groups of children bunched around a stern-looking mother and father. Everyone stared straight ahead, unsmiling. The fathers wore fancy evening clothes Alison had never seen outside of movies, and sometimes a top hat and even a walking cane. The mothers wore dresses covering them from head to foot, yards and yards of flowing, shiny material. In one of the pictures the children were all dressed alike, the girls in dark dresses and bows and the boys in coats and shorts.

A trembling hand came over her shoulder and pointed to a small boy in the front row. She turned quickly. Laura's grandfather stood there, leaning on his cane, his eyes watery behind thick glasses.

"That's me," he said. Alison looked back at the photograph, trying to see this ancient man in the picture of the young boy. The shaking finger moved to another kid in the same picture. "And that's my brother Moishe."

He looked down at her, uncertain. His face was flushed now, suffused with blood, a waxy yellow mixed with red. His eyes were vacant; something had gone out of them.

The clock sounded loud in the room. Finally he said, "Which one are you?"

"What?"

"Which one of these are you? You're one of the cousins, aren't you?"

"No, I'm—I'm Alison—"

"Alice? I don't know an Alice. That's me in that picture there, and that's my brother Moishe. Or did I already tell you that?"

Should she tell him? She was unused to dealing with old people; all her grandparents had died in the war. But just then he seemed to pull himself together, to concentrate; she could see the man he used to be before he got old.

"Moishe played the trombone—it was a way of getting out of the army in Russia. If you played an instrument you could be in the marching band. He played for anyone, Moishe did, any army in the world. He didn't care. The only army he ever quit was the White Russians. You know why?"

Alison shook her head.

"Because they made their band march in front of them in the war," the old man said. He laughed loudly.

Alison laughed too. "What happened to him?"

The old man started to cough.

"Hi, Alison," Laura said. Alison turned; she hadn't heard Laura come in. "Let's go to my room. I got a new record yesterday."

As they walked up the stairs Laura said, "God, he's embarrassing. Sometimes he calls my mother by her maiden name—he thinks she's still a kid. My dad wants to put him in a nursing home but she won't let him. I hope he didn't bother you too much."

"No," Alison said. She felt something she couldn't name, a feeling like longing. "He's okay."

She didn't get a chance to go back to the park for another week, until Friday. Laura had remained firm about not wanting to meet Alfred. But when she finally got there she couldn't see him anywhere. Her heart sank. Why had she listened to Laura? Why hadn't she insisted?

No, wait—there he was, sitting on the same bench, his head tilted back toward the sun. He looked thin, frail, even more transparent than the first time she'd seen him. She hurried toward him.

He opened his eyes and smiled. "Here she is—the child without a name," he said. "I was afraid you would not come again. I thought your mother might have told you not to talk to me."

"She doesn't know," Alison said.

"Ah. You should not keep secrets from your mother, you know that. But if you do, you should make sure that they are good ones."

Alison laughed. "Got any candy?"

"No, no candy." He looked around him, seeming to realize only then where he was. "Do you want to take a walk?"

"Sure."

He stood and they went down a shaded path. Alison shuffled through the fallen leaves; she wondered how Alfred managed to walk so quietly. Ahead of them, where the path came out into the sun, she saw a man with an ice cream cart, and she thought for a moment that Alfred might have intended to buy her a sweet after all. But they passed the cart without stopping, and she realized, ashamed, that he probably didn't have much money. "Do you want some ice cream?" she asked.

He laughed. "Thank you, no. I eat very little these days."

The path fell back into shade again. At the end of the path stood the old broken carousel, with a chain-link fence around it so that children could not play on it. Alfred stood and looked at it for a long time. "I made something like this once," he said.

"Really? Carousel animals?"

"No, not the animals. The—what do you call it? The mechanism that makes the thing go around." He moved his hand in a slow circle to demonstrate.

"Could you fix this?"

"Could I?" He looked at the carousel for a long time, studying the tilting floor, the cracked and leaning animals, the proud horse on which someone had carved "Freddy & Janet." Dirt and cobwebs had dulled the animals' paint. "How long has it been broken?"

"I don't know. It's been like this since I started coming to the park."

"I think I can fix it, yeah," he said. He pronounced it "Yah," just like her parents. "Yah, probably I could. Mostly I made large figures that moved. A king and a queen who came out like this—" he moved his hands together "—and kissed. And a magician who opened a box, and there was nothing inside it, and then he closed it, and opened it again, and there was a dove that flew away. I made that one for the Kaiser. Do you know who the Kaiser was?"

She shook her head.

"He was the king. The king of Germany."

"Did you have any kids?" she asked, thinking how great it would be to have a father like this man, and remembering the photograph of the two children in his watch. But almost immediately she wished she hadn't said anything. What if his children had died in the war, like so many of her parents' relatives?

"I did, yah," he said. "A boy and a girl. I wanted them to take over the business when I retired. It was a funny thing, though—they didn't want to."

"They were nuts," Alison said. "I would have done it in a minute."

"Ah, but you would have needed more than an interest in the figures. You would have had to understand electricity, and how the mechanisms work, and mathematics. . . . Both my children were terrible at mathematics."

She was terrible at mathematics too. But she thought that if she had been given a chance at the kind of work Alfred did she would have studied until she understood everything there was to know.

She could almost see his workshop in front of her, the gears and chains and hinges, the tall wooden cabinets filled with hands and silver hair, tin stars, carved dogs and trumpets. The king and queen lay on their sides like fallen wooden angels, wearing robes of silk and gauze, and wooden crowns with gaudy paste jewels. The bird hung from the ceiling, waiting for its place inside the magician's box. All around Alfred apprentices were cutting into wood, or doing something incomprehensible with pieces of machinery. She thought that she could even smell the wood; it had the elusive scent of great trees, like a forest from a childhood fairy tale.

She turned back to Alfred. What had happened? The day had grown cold; she saw the sun set through the trees, dazzling her vision. "I've got to go home," she said. "I'll be late for dinner."

"Oh. I hope I have not bored you terribly. I don't get much of a chance to talk."

"No," she said. "Oh, no."

She hurried down the path, shivering in the first real cold of the year. Once she looked back but Alfred had vanished among the shadows of the trees and the carousel.

Her parents and Joey were already eating dinner when she got home. "Where do you go on Fridays?" her mother said as she sat down. "Doesn't Laura have her Girl Scout meeting today?"

"I don't go anywhere," Alison said.

"You know you're not supposed to be late for dinner. And what about your homework?"

"Come on, Mom—it's Friday."

"That's right, it's Friday. Remember how long it took you to do your math homework last week? If you start now you'll have it done on time."

"We didn't get very much. I can do the whole thing on Sunday."

"Can you? I want to see it after dinner."

Her father looked at her mother. Sometimes Alison thought her father might be on her side in the frequent arguments she had with her mother, but that he didn't feel he had the right to interrupt. Now he laughed and said to her mother, "What would you know about math homework? You told me you didn't understand anything past addition and subtraction."

"Well, then, you look at it," her mother said. "I want to make sure she gets it done this time. And maybe you can ask her where she goes after school. I don't think she's telling me the truth."

Alison looked down at her plate. What did her mother know? Sometimes she made shrewd guesses based on no evidence at all. She said nothing.

"Mrs. Smith says she saw you talking to an old man in the park," her mother said.

Alison didn't look up. Didn't Mrs. Smith have anything better to do than spy on everyone in the neighborhood?

"When I was your age I knew enough not to talk to strangers," her mother said. "The Gestapo came after my father—did I ever tell you that?"

Alison nodded miserably. She didn't want to hear the story again.

"They came to our house in Germany and asked for my father," her mother said. "I was twelve or thirteen then, just about your age. This was before they started sending Jews to the camps without a reason, and someone had overheard my father say something treasonous about Hitler. My mother said my father wasn't home.

"But he was home—he was up in the attic, hiding. What do you think would have happened if I'd talked to the Gestapo the way you talk to this man in the park? If I'd said, 'Oh, yes, Officer, he's up in the attic'? I was only twelve and I knew enough not to say anything. You kids are so stupid, so pampered, living here."

It wasn't the same thing, Alison thought, realizing it for the first time. Germany and the United States weren't the same countries. And Alfred had been in the camps too; he and her mother were on the same side. But she felt the weight of her mother's experience and couldn't say anything. Her mother had seen so much more than she had, after all.

"We escaped to Holland, stayed with relatives," her mother said. "And eight years later the Nazis invaded Holland and took us to concentration camps. My father worked for a while as an electrician, but finally he died of typhus. All of that, and he died anyway.''

Her mother's voice held the bitterness Alison had heard all her life. Now she sighed and shook her head. Alison wanted to do something for her, to make everything all right. But what could she do, after all? She was only twelve.

She took the bus back to the park the next day. Alfred sat on his usual bench, his eyes closed and turned toward the sun. She dropped down on the bench next to him.

"Tell me a story," she said.

He opened his eyes slowly, as if uncertain where he was. Then he smiled. "You look sad," he said. "Did something happen?"

"Yeah. My mother doesn't want me to talk to you anymore."

"Why not?"

This was tricky. She couldn't say that her mother had compared him to the Gestapo. She couldn't talk about the camps at all with him; she never wanted to hear that note of bitterness and defeat come into his voice. Alfred was hers, her escape from the fears and sadness she had lived with all her life. He had nothing to do with what went on between Alison and her mother.

He was looking at her with curiosity and concern now, expecting her to say something. "It's not you. She doesn't trust most people," Alison said.

"Do you know why?"

"Yeah." His eyes were deep brown, she noticed, like hers, like her mother's. Why not tell him, after all? "She—she has a number on her arm. Like yours."

He nodded.

"And she—well, she went through a bad time, I guess." It

felt strange to think of her mother as a kid. "She said last night the Gestapo came after her father when she was my age. She said he had to hide in the attic."

To her surprise Alfred started to nod. "I bet it was crowded in that attic too. Boxes and boxes of junk—I bet they never threw anything away. Probably hot too. But then who knew that someday someone would have to hide in it?"

At first his words made no sense whatsoever. Then she said, slowly, "You're him, aren't you? You're her father. My—my grandfather." The unfamiliar word felt strange on her tongue.

"What?" He seemed to rouse himself. "Your grandfather? I'm a crazy old man you met in the park."

"She said he died. You died. You're a ghost." She was whispering now. Chills kept coming up her spine, wave after wave of them. The sun looked cold and very far away.

He laughed. "A ghost? Is that what you think I am?"

She nodded reluctantly, not at all certain now.

"Listen to me," he said. "You're right about your mother—she went through a bad time. And it's hard for her to understand you, to understand what you're going through. Sometimes she's jealous of you."

"Jealous?"

"Sure, jealous. You never had to distrust people, or hide from them. You never went hungry, or saw anyone you loved killed. She thinks it's easy for you—she doesn't understand that you have problems too."

"She called me stupid. She said I would have talked to the Gestapo, would have told them where my father was. But I never would have done that."

"No. It was unfair of her to say that. She wants you to think of the world the way she does, as an unsafe place. But you have to make up your own mind about what the world is like."

She was nodding even before he had finished. "Yeah.

Yeah, that's what I thought, only I couldn't say it. Because she's been through so much more than I have, so everything she thinks seems so important. I couldn't tell her that what happens to me is important too."

"No, and you might never be able to tell her. But you'll know it, and I'll know it too."

"What was your father's name?" Alison asked her mother that night at dinner. Joey stopped eating and gave her a pleading look; he was old enough to know that she was taking the conversation in a dangerous direction.

"Alfred," her mother said. "Why do you ask?"

There were probably a lot of old men named Alfred running around. Did she only think he was her grandfather because she wanted what Laura had, wanted someone to tell her family stories, to connect her with her past?

"Oh, I don't know," she said, trying to keep her voice casual. "I was wondering about him, that's all. Do you have a picture of him?"

"What do you think—we were allowed to take photographs with us to the camps?" The bitterness was back in her mother's voice. "We lost everything."

"Well, what did he look like?"

"He was—I don't know. A thin man, with black hair. He brushed it back, I remember that."

"Did he wear glasses?"

Her mother looked up at that. "Yah, he did. How did you know?"

"Oh, you know," Alison said quickly. "Laura's grandfather has glasses, so I thought. . . . What did he do?"

"I named you after him," her mother said. "I wanted a name that started with A." To Alison's great astonishment, she began to laugh. "He told that story about the attic all the time, when we lived in Holland. How crowded it was. He said my mother never threw anything away." She took a deep breath and wiped her eyes. "He made it sound like the funniest thing that ever happened to him."

Alison walked slowly through the park. It was Sunday, and dozens of families had come out for the last warmth of the year, throwing frisbees, barbecuing hamburgers in the fire pits. Joey held her hand tightly, afraid to let go.

She began to hurry, pushing her way through the crowds. Had she scared Alfred off by guessing his secret? She knew what he was now. He had drifted the way Laura's grandfather sometimes drifted, had forgotten his own time and had slipped somehow into hers. Or maybe this was the one wish the angel had granted him, the wish he hadn't known he wanted. However it had happened, he had come to her, singled her out. She had a grandfather after all.

But what if she was wrong? What if he was just a lonely old man who needed someone to talk to?

There he was, up ahead. She ran toward him. "Hey," Joey said anxiously. "Hey, wait a minute."

"Hi," Alison said to the old man, a little breathless. "I've decided to tell you my name. My name's Alison, and I was named after my grandfather Alfred. And this is my brother Joey. Joey's afraid of things. I thought you might talk to him."

AFTERWORD

A lfred'' is in some ways sheer wish fulfillment. My grandfather's name was Alfred, and he looked like the man in the story; he escaped from Germany to Holland with his family, my grandmother and my father. He was a mechanic, though he didn't have the glamorous profession I gave him here. I find, reading the story over, that I even made the character who stands in for me a year younger than I am, though that was mainly to get in the reference to John Lennon glasses.

The pocket watch was my grandfather's and is now mine, the only thing I have of his. It sat on my desk while I wrote the story.

In another sense, of course, "Alfred" is not wish fulfillment at all. It's about the healing power of history and family and imagination.

CASSANDRA'S PHOTOGRAPHS

The best car to smuggle reptiles in is a Subaru station wagon," Aurora said at the wheel of the car. "Because it's got four-wheel drive, and great brights so you can see them on the road at night, and because the panels come out easy. So you can hide the snakes and stuff behind them. I'm gonna get one when I can afford it."

I was sitting in the back seat of the car (which was, unfortunately for Aurora, only an old VW squareback) wondering how things had progressed this far. We had been on our way to get burgers when Aurora decided that, since it was such a nice summer day and everything, we should go down to Mexico and see if we could find some snakes to round out Aurora's collection. After all, she said, it was only a few hundred miles away. So we made a stop at the corner J.C. Penney's to buy pillowcases to put the snakes in, and headed out on Highway 5 to Baja California.

Cassie, Aurora's sister, was sitting up front next to Aurora. Cassie was the reason I was on this trip in the first place. I had noticed her the minute she walked into my class in beginning calculus at the college. Everyone says you shouldn't date your students, and everyone is probably right, but within a month we were going out two or three times a week. And since I was just the teaching assistant, and not responsible for grades, we had nothing to quarrel about at the end of the semester when Cassie got a C in the class. She didn't even seem to mind all that much.

I sat still and looked at Cassie's orange-red hair flying out the window and tried to figure out if there was something I needed to do in the next few days. School was over, so I didn't have classes. I badly wanted to take out my small pocket diary and flip through it, but I knew what Cassie would say if I did. "Stop being so responsible all the time," she'd say. "We're on vacation. Put that book away."

Lately all our arguments had been about how obsessive (her word) I was, and how childish (my word) she was. She was constantly late, not just once or twice but every single time. I hadn't seen the beginning of a movie since I started going out with her. So I didn't say anything when Aurora suggested going to Mexico. I wanted to prove that I could be as open to adventure as the rest of Cassie's crazy family. It occurred to me that Cassie had to go in to work tomorrow (she cleaned up at a day care center), but I said nothing and looked at her hair, brilliant in the sun. The sight of her hair made it all worthwhile.

"Did you bring the book?" Chris said. Chris was in Aurora's grade in high school and, like half the class (if the phone ringing day and night was any indication), found it impossible to resist Aurora's manic energy, her wild schemes. If Aurora was going to collect and trade illegal reptiles then she, Chris, was going to collect and trade illegal reptiles too. The book, *The Field Guide to North American Reptiles and Amphibians*, had become Chris's bible.

"No, it's at home," Aurora said. "But don't worry. I know the ones we want."

On the other side of Chris sat Alan. Alan had said nothing

for the past ten miles. Later it turned out that he was deathly afraid of snakes. But he was in love with Aurora, so what could he do? Poor boy. I knew exactly how he felt.

We stopped just this side of the Mexican border for our last hamburger and fries. It was 7:30. "We're making good time," Aurora said when we sat down to eat. "We should be at this place I know in a few hours. And we can spend the night driving up and down, and be back by tomorrow afternoon."

"What about sleep?" I said. Immediately I cursed myself. Someone setting out on the grand adventure wouldn't think of sleep.

"Who needs sleep?" Cassie said. I thought she looked a little disappointed in me.

"Certainly not you," I said, trying to make a joke of the whole thing. "Or the rest of your crazy family."

"What makes you think we're crazy?" Cassie said.

I thought she was being reasonable. That was my first mistake. I looked across the table at her red hair and brown eyes, both tinted with the same shade of gold, and I started to relax and enjoy the trip for the first time. If I could be with her it didn't matter where we were going. Anyway her eccentricities were only part of her charm. "Well, you know," I said. "Your great-uncle, what's-his-name, the one who thinks he's an Egyptian."

"He doesn't think he's an Egyptian," Cassie said. Alan was watching us glumly. Chris drew pictures of snakes on her napkin. "He's an Osirian. The cult of Osiris. He explained it all to you when you were over at the house."

"He didn't explain anything," I said. "He asked me questions. 'Knowest thou the name of this door, and canst thou tell it?' And then the lintel, and the doorpost, and the threshold—"

"You weren't listening," Cassie said. She still sounded reasonable. "If you know all the names you can get past the door into the land of the dead. And if you don't you're stuck. He's got to keep all that in his head. It's a long list."

"And you don't think that's a little strange," I said. "That he believes all this."

"Well, what if he's right?" Cassie said. "I mean, millions of people used to believe in it. Maybe they knew something."

"Well, what about your grandmother?" I said. "She stays in her room for weeks on end and then she comes out and makes these cryptic utterances—"

"Look, Robert," Cassie said. Something passed between the two sisters then, something I was too much of an outsider to understand, and Aurora turned to Chris and started talking rapidly. The gold seemed to leave Cassie's eyes; they became flat, muddy. "Just because you came from a boring home doesn't give you the right to pass judgment on other people's families. Okay? I mean, I know your parents belonged to the right kind of religion and had the right kind of jobs and never said anything unusual or anything that would make you think, but that doesn't mean that everyone's family is like that. Some of us wouldn't want to be like that, okay? So you can just keep your stupid opinions to yourself."

"I'm sorry," I said. "I didn't mean—I was just joking around. I'm sorry."

Cassie turned away from me to talk to Aurora and Chris. Alan looked at me sympathetically, but I refused to catch his eye.

The rest of the trip was a nightmare. To my surprise we made it past the border guards with no problems. Sometime in the middle of the night we reached the place Aurora had heard about with two snakes we had picked up along the way. Aurora and Chris were ecstatic, I didn't know why. I'm afraid one snake looks like another to me. Alan, rigid and wild-eyed, was starting to look like a speed freak. We found one more snake, put it in a pillowcase, put the pillowcases in the trunk and headed back. Then Aurora fell asleep at the wheel.

The car swerved, bounced over a few rocks and stalled. Aurora hadn't woken up. "Aurora?" Cassie said, shaking her. "Aurora?"

"Hmm. Mf," Aurora said.

We pulled her out and set her in Cassie's seat. I was hoping she didn't have a concussion. Naturally no one in the car was wearing a seat belt. Cassie drove a few more miles and then said, "God, I'm sleepy," and came to a dead stop in the middle of the one lane road.

"I'll drive!" Alan said, a bright note of desperation in his voice. Then he looked over Cassie's shoulder and leaned back, but not too far back. Ever since we put the snakes in the trunk his body hadn't made contact with the back of the seat. "Oh. Stick shift. I can't do it."

"Look," I said. "There was a big city just a few miles back. We'll find a hotel or a motel or something and get some sleep. All right?"

No one said anything. "Do you want me to drive?" I asked Cassie. "Or can you handle it? It's only a few more miles, I think."

"Sure, I can do it," Cassie said. She never stayed angry at anything for long. This always confused me; I come from a long line of grudge-holders.

The city was more than a few miles away, but we made it. Aurora, wide awake now, cheerfully told us about a man who had been bitten by a cobra and was immobilized just as he picked up the phone and started to dial the hospital. In the street outside a seedy one-story hotel we counted our money and discovered that between us we had eleven dollars and ninety-two cents. Wearily I went inside and found to my absolute amazement that they would take my charge card. I motioned Alan inside. We had already decided that the two men would rent the room and we would sneak the three women in later. I wanted as little trouble as possible. As I was stretching out on the floor, prepared to offer someone else the sagging double bed, I noticed Cassie and Aurora come in. Cassie lay on the floor next to me. In my sleep-fogged mind I thought the sacks Aurora was carrying were her luggage.

Cassie and I were the last ones up. We went outside and found the others at a restaurant down the street. None of them, it turned out, knew Spanish, and they had ordered in gestures and pidgin English. Despite all the warnings and jokes, each of them was drinking a glass of Mexican water. I wondered how they thought they were going to pay for the meal.

Aurora picked up one of the pillowcases scattered around her and looked inside. "Damn," she said. "One of the snakes escaped. I wonder if it's back at the hotel. Alan? Alan!" The poor kid's eyes had rolled up under his fluttering eyelids. "Well if you're afraid of snakes you should have said something when we started out."

I hadn't had any water, but I was sick for a week after we got home. Lying in bed with a hundred-and-two-degree temperature I had time to think about the trip, go over the details, figure out how one thing led to another. I felt as though it had happened to someone else, someone who had far less of a grip on reality than I did.

That trip clarified things for me. Life just wasn't lived that way, the way Cassie and her family lived it. You didn't just jump in a car and drive to Mexico because you felt like it. What if I hadn't been there with my credit card? What if Aurora had gotten a concussion? I wanted something more for my life—order, sanity. I wanted to complete my studies, get my doctorate in math and get a job in industry.

I recovered, got busy with fall classes and stopped calling her. I didn't consciously think that we had broken up, but I'd think of her or her family from time to time with nostalgic regret. There was a guy who hung around their house—I don't know if he was part of the family or what—who had been in films as a saxophone player. The only thing was, he couldn't play the saxophone. He just *looked* like a saxophone player. So there'd be these close-ups of this guy and someone else on the soundtrack. I used to watch him practice, moving the saxophone this way and that without making a sound. It was eerie.

And I'd remember her great-uncle, asking Cassie to name some part of a doorway in ancient Egyptian. Sometimes she'd know the answer, and he'd beam with satisfaction. Other times she wouldn't, and he'd shake his head sadly from side to side and say, "Cassandra, my pet, what will become of you?" Once I caught myself shaking my head with regret just thinking of him.

I probably would have called her eventually, but one day my office-mate's sister came wandering into the office looking for him, and I ended up taking her out for coffee. Her name was Laura, and she was very sensible.

I was home, a few weeks after I'd started seeing Laura, when I heard a loud pounding at the door. I set down the *Journal of Multivariate Analysis* and got up. Once I'd unlocked the door to the apartment I wished I hadn't. It was Cassie.

"You want order in your life!" she said with no preamble. Her face was twisted and ugly, her brown eyes hard and flat. I tried to stop her but she pushed her way into the room. "Goddamn it, you want everything to be dull and predictable, you want to know what's going to happen in your life at every minute. Don't you?"

I couldn't think of anything to say.

"Well, don't you?" she said loudly. I knew enough about her to tell that she was on the verge of tears. "The way I live is too unpredictable for you, right? If somebody gave you a timetable of your life that told you everything that was going to happen from now until you die you'd welcome it, wouldn't you? Well?"

She reached into her purse and took out a small manila envelope. "Cassie, I—" I said.

"Well, here!" she said, thrusting the envelope at me. "I hope you're happy!"

A little dazed, I took it. It seemed too slight to be a timetable of my life. I reached inside and took out—photographs. Photographs of me.

She was turning to go. "Cassie," I said. "Where did you get these?"

"My grandmother!" she said, and broke away and ran loudly down the hall.

I took all the photographs out and looked at them after she had gone. There were only five of them. The first one showed me at my graduation walking across the stage in a cap and gown to receive my diploma. But I hadn't been at either of my graduations, not the one at my high school or the one at college where I received my B.A. degree. I turned the picture this way and that, trying to figure out how it had been done. There were these odd details—the guy in front of me was in a wheelchair, for example—but on the whole it was very believable. The person on stage looked a lot like me.

The next picture showed me in an unfamiliar kitchen, pouring myself a cup of coffee. In the third one I was running down the street in the rain, a briefcase flying out from one hand. I looked harassed, and older too, in some indefinable way. The next one was a picture of me and a woman I had never met. We were in a tight embrace and I had a look of perfect peace on my face. The picture ended just below the neck, but I had the impression we were both naked. And in the last picture I was definitely older—at least thirty—and bending down to talk to a five- or six-year-old boy.

I ran the pictures through my hands, shuffling them like a deck of cards. So that's what Cassie's grandmother had been doing all those months in her room. She must have had a darkroom in there. I could see her bent over the photographs, cutting a head from this one, a background from that one, maybe re-touching them, arranging them so that they looked like actual photographs. What a strange hobby. No wonder when she came out of her room she would say things like "The wind blows the skeleton of his lips."

I looked at the photographs again. Very nice, but I didn't see what the hell I was supposed to do with them. I put them back in the envelope, stuffed the envelope in a drawer and forgot about them.

There was a man in a wheelchair in front of me at my graduation. I felt vaguely uneasy when I saw him—he reminded me of something unpleasant, but I couldn't remember what—but I managed to put him out of my mind. My parents had come out from Chicago to see me graduate—otherwise, I suppose, I wouldn't have gone to this graduation either—and at the reception afterward I introduced them to Laura and my friends without thinking too much about the ceremony. It was only when we were out to dinner that I remembered the photograph.

"What is it?" Laura said. "Is something wrong?" Later she told me that until she saw me that night she had never believed in the cliche "his jaw dropped."

"Nothing," I said uneasily, and, I guess, closed my jaw. Amazing, I thought. An amazing coincidence. I wondered what Cassie's grandmother would make of it. Cassie. I shook my head. I hadn't thought of her in months. "I just remembered something, that's all."

When I got home that night I pulled out all my drawers looking for the photographs. I found them at last, buried under the first few drafts of my dissertation. My fingers were shaking when I pulled the photographs out of the manila envelope.

The scene in the photograph matched point for point with the scene on stage. It might almost have been a picture taken by someone in the audience. There was Dr. Miller, who had been hastily invited to speak when Dr. Fine became ill. There was my friend Larry walking across the stage behind me. You could see his sneakers under the edge of his gown; he hadn't had time to change his shoes. There was the guy in the wheelchair, rolling down the ramp off stage.

I felt as though someone had opened a window and let in a blast of cold air. I was shivering and had to sit down. How had the old lady done it? How on earth had she known?

I looked at the other photographs more intently than I'd ever looked at anything before. My hands were trembling badly. So that's what Cassie had meant. This was to be my life. Someday I'd live in a house with a kitchen like the one in the photograph. I'd have a job that involved carrying a briefcase. And in about ten years I'd talk to a boy about five or six years old. Could the boy be my son? At the thought I felt another chill wind through the room and I shuffled that photograph to the end of the pile.

The picture I looked at the longest, though, was the one of me and the woman embracing. Her face was just under my chin and turned in slightly toward my chest, but from what little I saw I thought that she was beautiful. She had blond, almost gold, hair cut very short, and fine, delicate features. The one eye visible in the picture was closed. I thought she looked happy.

Surprisingly my trembling had stopped. I accepted—somehow—that I was seeing scenes from my future, but the idea no longer frightened me. I saw nothing bad in these pictures, no death or grief or pain. In fact, the future seemed to hold only good things for me. A job, a house, a beautiful woman, perhaps a child.

If Cassie had hoped to frighten me with these photos,

hoped somehow to win me back, she had badly miscalculated. It was with a feeling of profound satisfaction that I put the photographs in the manila envelope and put the envelope carefully back in the drawer.

After graduation I got a job with an aircraft company in a suburb of L.A. Feeling a little foolish, I carefully studied the briefcase in the photograph and then went out and got one just like it. I was looking at the photos about two or three times a week now, noting small details. The woman seemed to have small freckles scattered like stars across her face. The boy looked vaguely familiar, though if he were my son that wouldn't be surprising. A car was parked directly in back of him. There was a poster on the wall of the kitchen on which, after a week of effort, I could read the words "Save the Whales."

Laura and I had several arguments around this time. None of them was very serious—I had thrown out a pamphlet she had given me without reading it, for example, or she disapproved of my choice of restaurants—but each time I would think, "The woman in the photograph wouldn't act this way." The woman in the photograph, I thought, was wise and loving and giving. After a while Laura and I drifted apart.

I began to date women for a week or a month and then drop them, secretaries from the aircraft company or women I'd pick up in singles bars in the Marina. One morning I woke up in an unfamiliar bed next to a woman I could barely remember and saw by her alarm clock that I had to be at work in an hour. I staggered out to her kitchen and poured myself a cup of coffee. It was only after I drank the coffee that I turned around and saw the Save the Whales poster tacked up on the wall.

I was buoyant all that day. Several people at work even asked me what I was smiling about. If another one of the pictures had come true, I thought, the rest couldn't be that far behind.

The next few months were probably the happiest in my life. I lived in a state of almost constant anticipation. At any moment I might see her, turning the corner or buying a pair of shoes. I invented names for her, Alexandra, Deirdre. I fantasized taking her home and showing her the photograph, telling her the story and seeing her eyes open wide in amazement. I worked hard, dated some, and spent long evenings running the photographs back and forth through my hands.

You can only anticipate for so long, though. Gradually, so gradually I barely noticed it, the photos became less and less important. I only looked at them once or twice a week, then once a month. I stopped holding my breath whenever I saw a woman with short blond hair. I still felt that my future held something wonderful, that my life was more intense than most people's, but I no longer thought about why I felt that way.

After about five years I quit the aircraft company and went into consulting. I had saved some money, but the first year on my own was very rocky. Then I began to make a reputation for myself and in the second year earned almost twice what I would have with the company. I bought a house in the suburbs. I was working very hard now, so hard I had almost no time to date or entertain friends. It didn't matter, because I knew that sooner or later I would see the blond woman and my life would change. Sometimes, working late into the night, I caught myself wondering what she would think of the way I'd decorated the spare bedroom, or whether she'd like it if I had a pool put in the back yard.

One day I locked my keys in my car and hurried to a phone booth to call the automobile club. It was raining lightly, and suddenly I recognized the scene from the photograph. I felt vindicated. My life was on the right track.

Ten years after I graduated I saw Cassie again. I had gone

to a firm in an unfamiliar part of town, and on my way to the car I remembered that I didn't have any food in the house. I crossed the street to the supermarket, and in the parking lot, holding a bag of groceries in one hand and a child's hand in the other, was Cassie. It took me a few minutes to recognize her. By that time she had already turned to me. She knew who I was immediately. "Robert?" she said, grinning widely. She looked as though she'd hardly aged.

"Cassie!" I said. "How you doing?"

"Fine, just fine," she said. "How are you?"

"I'm fine. How's Aurora? When did you get married?" I nodded at the kid, now pulling hard on Cassie's arm and humming to himself.

"I'm not married," she said. Of course. Same old Cassie.

The kid said something I couldn't catch, and I squatted down to hear him better. "My mommy's a singing parent," he said, talking around the largest piece of candy I had ever seen.

"A singing parent?" I said.

"Single parent," Cassie said, and I stood up, feeling foolish. "So I guess you graduated, huh?"

People in school or at the aircraft company sometimes talked about inspiration, about suddenly solving a problem that had bothered them for weeks, seeing the problems that their solution brought up and going on to solve them too, on and on, effortlessly. I had always envied them profoundly. That sort of thing had never happened to me. But now, as I stood up, I realized that Cassie's son was the boy in the photograph; that he looked familiar because he looked like Cassie, though without her red hair; that since I was the oldest in the photograph with the child all the other scenes must have happened to me already. All this took a fraction of a second, and I was able to say, "Yeah, I did," before the realization hit me and I said, "You cheated me!"

The boy, so familiar now, looked up, alarmed. "What do you mean?" Cassie said.

"Those photographs," I said. "Those goddamn photographs you gave me, you little bitch. You wanted to get my hopes up, you wanted me to think that some day I'd meet a woman I'd fall in love with, and all this time it was a lie. All the scenes have happened, including the one with your stupid son just now, all except the one with that woman. And I'm too old for that one now. You put it in there just to—to—"

"I remember now," Cassie said, looking thoughtful. The boy started to pull her hand again. "I gave you those photographs, that's right. I was mad at you, because you never called me. I got them from my grandmother. But all the scenes were true, she told me. All of them. If they said you were going to meet a woman then you'll meet her. I didn't really look at the pictures all that closely. Wait. You're right—there was one with a woman in it. I asked my grandmother who she was and she said she worked in a department store. Was my son in one? I don't remember that."

In a department store, I thought, feeling bereft. Now I remembered a woman I'd taken home about five years ago. Halfway though the evening I'd realized she looked a little like the woman in the photograph, but she had turned to face me and the illusion was broken. Her name was Irma, and she had worked in a department store, I thought, amazed that I could remember so much. She'd left in the middle of the night because she'd been worried about her dog. I never called her back.

"You mean I've been waiting—" I said. "Waiting ten years for a woman, and all this time—"

Cassie shrugged. "I don't know," she said. "Look, I'm sorry if—"

"Sorry," I said numbly. "Somehow that doesn't seem to cover wasting ten years of my life. I guess you got your revenge after all."

"I wasn't out for revenge," she said. "I wanted to show you something. To show you that life isn't as much fun when you know what's going to happen. To make you loosen up a bit."

"Yeah, well, you did just the opposite," I said, turning away.

"Robert?" she said, tentatively. I didn't look back.

When I got home I took the photographs out and spread them across my desk. I was surprised to see how worn they were, how frayed at the edges. How many hours had I spent looking at them, planning a future that never existed? I lit a match and held it up to one photograph, then threw them in the fireplace. Five seconds later they had all burned.

Now, in the evenings, mostly I sit and think. I feel lost, as though I've survived a great tragedy. I neglect my work, and my answering service has one or two messages every day from irate clients. I think about my wasted ten years, about Cassie and her crazy family, and their strange ability to charm. I think that sooner or later it will be time to call Cassie back, to start a life that was stopped—that I stopped—ten years ago. I'm pretty sure Cassie will turn me down. But for the first time in a long time, *I don't know for sure.* And that excites me.

Afterword

Sometimes two separate story ideas combine to make one story. The idea of photographs that show the future had come to me about three or four years before I'd started this story; I'd tried writing it then but it hadn't worked out. And I knew a few reptile smugglers and thought that they might be interesting to write about. It was only when I tried putting these two things together, when I came up with the character of Aurora the reptile fanatic, that the story started to work.

EVER AFTER

T he wedding ceremony had been very tiring. Of course
they'd rehearsed it—rehearsed it over and over until she
thought she'd fall asleep during the actual ceremony—but
they had never gone through it while she was wearing the
wedding gown. The gown had been made in a hurry, and
made wrong: the bodice pinched so tightly she thought she
wouldn't be able to breathe.

The gown. The princess felt a wave of embarrassment
thinking about it, glad that the inside of the coach was so
dark that he couldn't see her blush. Of course she couldn't
afford a wedding gown, she had known that, and she had expected that something had been arranged. But when she'd
found out that it hadn't been, she'd had to go to the prince
and haltingly, stuttering on almost every word, explain her
problem. And the prince had had to go to his father, the
king, and the king (who was very kind, everyone had said so)
had laughed and said, Well of course, buy her a gown. Only
make it green, to match her eyes.

It had been a joke, she knew that. Only when the king
made a joke everybody took it as an order, because they were
never sure when it wasn't going to be a joke. And her eyes

were blue, not green, but the king, being very near-sighted, hadn't known that. So she had to stand through the ceremony horribly self-conscious, knowing that all around her people must be whispering, "The fairest in the land? She certainly doesn't look it."

And the reception afterwards had been, if anything, even worse. "You're very fortunate," people told her, over and over again. "Very fortunate." The princess had smiled and nodded, thinking, But what about him? Don't they know how fortunate he is to have me? Because I do love him, more than any of these people ever would. And once she had said, "Yes, very fortunate," and the woman she had been talking to laughed, and she had blushed a deep red, wondering if she had said the wrong thing.

"It's your accent, dear," the woman said. "We can barely understand you."

I can understand you just fine, the princess had wanted to say, but of course she had been hearing aristocratic speech, and following aristocratic orders, ever since she was a small child. "It's very quaint," another woman had said, clearly anxious to make her feel better, and then had said, "Oh, look, she's blushing."

In the darkness of the coach she tugged at the bodice, trying to straighten it. She had only worn one other fancy gown in her life, and that one had fit so perfectly she had thought they all would be like that. "Is something wrong, dear?" the prince said, reaching over to squeeze her hand. "We'll be there soon."

"Oh no, nothing," she said. How could she act this way, so ungrateful? As if she hadn't just been given the most exciting day of her life? She smiled at him. "I'm just tired, that's all."

An hour later the coach stopped. She had thought, when the prince had told her they were going to his country estate, that it would be a small house hidden among trees. Through the windows of the coach she could see an enormous building, to her eyes almost the size of the castle in the city. All the lights were blazing.

The servants were ready to take the coach, to feed them if they wanted food, to undress them and take them up to bed. She lay in the large, canopied bed, waiting for him, feeling bereft. When he finally came to her she recognized the sensation: she wanted to cry.

The prince took her very gently, stopping often to whisper reassurances. At times she almost wanted to laugh. Did he really think she knew nothing about what went on between a man and a woman? There had been nights, at home, when her stepsisters would talk of nothing else. Still, she couldn't help feeling a tenderness towards him. He did love her, after all.

He was gone when she woke the next morning. She remembered he had said something about fox-hunting the night before. She sat up, wondering what happened next. After a while she stood up, padding about the stone floor in her bare feet. One door she opened led to a closet filled with men's clothing. The next door should be—Yes, it was. She took out a simple white dress, very much like the one she had worn to the ball, and put it on.

One of the servants, a woman, looked in the door for a minute. The servant began to laugh. The princess could hear her running down the hall, laughing. After a few minutes another servant—much younger, about her age—came in the room.

"Good morning, my lady," the servant said.

"Hello," the princess said nervously.

"Please come with me, my lady," the servant said. She led her to an adjoining room. "Here. I'll help you undress."

What's that? the princess wanted to say, but she recognized a bath just in time. She had never seen one so large and so white. Did these people bathe every day then? She stepped out of the dress and the servant hung it up for her.

When she got out of the bath the servant had another

dress ready. Was the other one dirty? Or wasn't it appropriate for today, for whatever she was going to do today? Without questioning, she put the dress on.

The prince was already at the table when she came down for breakfast. "Lessons," he said, popping a muffin into his mouth. "You're going to have lessons, starting today. You can't do everything the way you've always done it." He looked at her fondly.

"Yes, my lord," she said, bowing her head to cover her blushes. He had heard, then. Someone had told him about what had happened this morning. Still, he thought she was capable of learning. And if he thought so then she was capable. She would live up to his trust in her. She was eager to learn. "What sort of lessons?"

"Mmm," the prince said. "Etiquette. Manners. What else? What do ladies have to know? Embroidery. Oh, and we'll have to correct your pretty little accent. We'll start here, on our honeymoon. That way when we get back to the palace you won't feel so out of place."

She looked at him, puzzled. He did love her, didn't he? Then why was he so anxious to keep her out of his way during the day? "And you, my lord?" she said. "What will you be doing?"

"Oh, the usual thing," he said. "Fox hunting, falconry. I have my lessons too. I'll have to learn to be a king someday. But you don't have to worry about that."

She smiled at him. Of course not. Of course he would have more important things to do.

And so it started. Monday, Wednesday and Friday in the morning was etiquette. She learned how to address people, and she learned how they should address her. She learned where to seat them at dinner. She learned what to wear to which occasions and what the latest fashions were. In the afternoons she learned how to speak like an aristocrat. Her Tuesdays and Thursdays were free, which meant that in the morning she had to embroider with the ladies-in-waiting and in the afternoon she had to deal with the day to day problems of running an estate. Your neighbor Lord So-and-so has just had a son, what should we get the baby? The coachman wants the day off to see his mother. The downstairs maid is sick. On weekends she got to see the prince, but on Saturdays there was usually a dinner or a dance to go to, and on Sundays there was church.

And she had insomnia. Of course that was to be expected after nearly a lifetime of sleeping on hard stones, but she hadn't thought that it would happen, and it worried her. She tossed and turned in the large bed, trying to get comfortable, trying not to wake the prince. The prince must never know, never suspect that she was ungrateful. The prince would rise early to go hunting, and she would fall asleep at dawn and be awakened, hours later, by the young servant, her personal maid. "Come, my lady, it's time to go to breakfast."

She never got enough sleep. She was tired doing her lessons, tired doing her embroidery, tired talking to the cooks and cleaning women. "You look very pale," they would tell her, and shake their heads. She once overheard two of the kitchen maids wonder if she was pregnant.

Of all her lessons she liked embroidery the best. She was good at it, having had to sew and mend for her stepmother and stepsisters all her life. She liked working with the silk threads and good linen and bright, sharp needles. But the conversation of the ladies-in-waiting, even of the ones who made an effort to be kind to her, flowed over her. She didn't know the people they talked about, didn't know why it was important that Lord So-and-so's cousin had married Lady Such-and-such or that Lord So-and-so's son had come down with a mysterious disease. She had asked the woman who taught her court etiquette, but the woman, an old distant relative of the king's, hadn't been to the palace for years, and all her gossip was thirty years out of date. And once or twice it seemed that the ladies-in-waiting laughed and talked about her. But there was nothing she could do about that.

Every day the princess improved, everyone told her so. She made fewer and fewer mistakes. The servants hadn't laughed at her since that first day. Her accent still wasn't perfect, but she never said anything at the major functions, and nobody seemed to notice. (She noticed that the women hardly talked until after dinner anyway, and then only among themselves.) Still, when the prince told her that they had to be back at the palace in a few days she felt apprehensive.

The palace was far more confusing than the country house. There were hundreds of people, each one with a different name and a different function, and she was supposed to remember them all. Some of the more important servants looked like nobility, and some of the least important of the nobility looked like servants, so that she could barely keep them straight. And the king was here, the king who seemed jolly enough but who always made her nervous. How did he really feel about his son marrying a commoner?

Here people were always whispering to her, warning her about other people. "Do you see that woman there, leaning against the pillar?" a minor prince said to her one night at a dance. She nodded. "That's the Lady Flora. She was the prince's sweetheart, before he met you. You'd better watch out for her." She nodded again, puzzled. What could either one of them do? The princess was married, the Lady Flora was not: what did the man mean by "watch out for her"?

One night after a concert in the small dining room (the one that sat twenty-four people) the young woman who played the harp came up to her and slipped a note into her hand when no one was looking. The princess looked up, startled, but the harpist had already crossed the room. She took the note to bed with her and got up to read it after the prince was asleep. She had had some schooling before her father died so she knew how to read. She laughed to think that she might have had to ask someone to help her read a note that was so obviously intended to be private.

"We are in desperate need of your help," the note said.

"If you love liberty and justice—and we know that you do, being of the people yourself—please respond to us through the harpist. Your friends."

She crumpled the note and burned it with the candle she had used to read by. What did it mean? Who were these people who called themselves her friends? They were working against the king, that much was clear. Did they expect her to betray her king, her husband the prince?

She could not sleep at all that night. In the morning, instead of going to her lessons, she sent for the young harpist.

"Yes, my lady?" the harpist said, coming into her room.

"I want to talk to you," the princess said. She stopped, immediately at a loss. What did she want to talk about? "About your note."

"Yes, my lady?" The harpist was clearly nervous.

"You can't—surely you can't expect me—" The princess stopped for a moment, silent.

"I had nothing to do with it, my lady!" the harpist said, alarmed. "They just asked me to deliver the note, because they knew I'd be safe. I'm not a revolutionary—I just play the harp. Truly, my lady."

"I believe you," the princess said. "I—What's your name?"

"Alison, my lady."

"Well, Alison," the princess said. "I—I just wanted to know who it was who gave you the note. No, no, I don't ask you to betray anyone!" she said hastily, seeing the girl become alarmed again. "I'm curious, that's all. Who are they?"

"They?" Alison said. For a moment the princess thought the girl might be half-witted. "I know—I only know one of them, the—the leader, I guess. He asked me to deliver the note."

"And what's he like?"

"Oh, he's very handsome, my lady," Alison said. "He's—

I don't know—very persuasive. A personality like sparks flying. You should meet him, my lady.''

The princess said back, satisfied. It was clear now. A young woman in love with a handsome young man who persuades her to deliver a note. Perhaps there was no revolution at all, perhaps there was just this young man. There was no threat to the palace, she could be sure of that. She had done her duty. She could let the harpist go.

And yet—and yet there was something else, something that intrigued her. "How old are you, Alison?''

"Nineteen, my lady.''

"Nineteen," the princess said. "How long have you been playing the harp?''

"Oh, all my life, lady," Alison said, laughing. "I got my first harp as a child, for my sixth birthday.''

"But to play for the king—young women generally don't—''

"I've been playing for my supper since I was ten, my lady," Alison said.

"Yes?'' the princess said, hoping the girl would go on, unable to ask more questions.

"I'm from the north, my lady," Alison said. She spoke flatly now, without emotion. "My house was burned by the king's armies when I was ten years old. I'm an orphan, my lady.''

"So—so am I!'' the princess said, delighted to have something in common with her.

"I know, my lady," Alison said.

The princess stopped. Of course Alison knew. No doubt the whole country knew. No doubt Alison had even sung songs about the orphan who had married a prince. When would she stop being so stupid?

And Alison—things had not gone as well for her. She was very plain, flat face, flat nose, her green northern eyes too wide and too far apart. Not even the revolutionary would be interested in her. "And then?" the princess said. "What happened then?"

"I dressed as a boy and made my way here," Alison said. "To the capital."

"A boy?" the princess said.

"Oh, yes," Alison said. "I've done it—I've had to do it—many times since then, to travel. A boy or a man. It's not very difficult."

"Listen," the princess said suddenly, impulsively. "Could you—I mean, would you like to give me harp lessons? That's something a lady should know, isn't it? How to play the harp?"

Alison smiled for the first time. "Yes, my lady," she said. "I would love to."

Somehow the harp lessons were fit into the princess's schedule. The prince made no objection. Alison told her about her life, about the time she had sailed on a merchant ship because she had no money, the time she had played in an alehouse and spotted in the audience the man who had burned her house, the time she had lived in the woods and hunted to stay alive. Gradually the lessons on the harp stopped and the two women would talk instead. Alison learned to stop calling her "my lady."

And gradually the princess began to tell Alison about herself. The prince's eyesight was failing, like the king's, and he was coming back from the hunt in worse and worse temper. She felt, she told Alison, as if she should know what to do, as if there were some court pleasure that would keep him occupied but she had never learned what it was. She could not confide in any of the ladies-in-waiting. When the prince was away she would remember how he had loved her, remember the look in his eyes when he had found her after all his searching, and she would try not to cry.

Alison continued to see the revolutionary and to tell the princess a little about his plans. The princess felt as if she should be telling the prince what she was learning, but somehow the bond between Alison and her had grown too strong. And she never really believed the revolutionary could be a threat. He had raised followers, he was living in the forest beyond the city, he still wanted her to join him and "the people." She still would not go to him.

One evening the princess dressed and went down to dinner. The prince was already there, along with the king and the court. "Good evening, my lord," she said. "How are you?"

"As if you care," the prince said. He lifted his goblet and drank. "As if you care about anything but that damned harpist friend of yours."

She sat, stunned. Around the table people were averting their eyes, pretending not to listen. She knew this would be the major piece of gossip among the ladies-in-waiting the next day. "How—how was the hunt, my lord?" she asked softly.

"You know damn well how the hunt was!" he said. "I can't see a damn thing. Never could. Never could even back when I thought you were the fairest in the land. The fairest. Hah!"

"My lord?" she said.

"You know what they say about you?" the prince said. "They laugh at you! They laugh at you and they make fun of your accent and they think I'm just about the funniest fellow since my great-great-great-grandfather, the one they had to lock away, for bringing you here. If only I had known! If only I had thought before bringing you here, instead of being seduced by a pretty face. My life is ruined. Ruined!"

"I'll leave, my lord," she said with great dignity. "I wouldn't want to be the cause of your unhappiness."

"No, no, that's all right," he said. He took another sip of wine and patted her hand. "You stay. You stay and tell me all about what you did today. What did you and that harpist talk about, hm? Did you talk about me?"

"You? No, my lord."

"No," he said. "Well, what then? Plots, conspiracies? What do you talk about behind my back?"

For a moment she thought he had heard about the revolution and that they were lost. Her fingers twisted under the table. "I don't feel well," the prince said suddenly. "I don't feel well at all."

"Quick!" the princess said, motioning to one of the soldiers standing at the door. "The prince is unwell. Take him to his room."

The prince lay back in his chair, gone very pale. Two soldiers came and escorted him out of the room. "Very good, my dear," the king whispered to her. "Very good indeed. You handled that very well."

And the princess thought that she had handled it well, too. She went to bed that night and slept till dawn, woke and bathed and dressed. It was only when one of the clerks came to see her about a minor problem, a dedication ceremony at one of the churches, that she began to cry.

"My lady?" the clerk said.

"Go away," she said. "Oh, please, go away."

She went to bed. She cancelled all her lessons and engagements, and she stayed in bed, crying. The prince came in to see her and said that he was very sorry, that he had been drinking and that he would never go hunting again but would stay and take care of her, but she told him to go away, and he moved into another room. She cried for her dead parents, for all the years she had spent sleeping on the hard floor and being taunted by her stepmother and stepsisters, for all the months locked away in a stone castle, her happy ending. And, after a while, after a month or so, she stopped.

She sat up in bed. Her first feeling was surprise, surprise that there were no more tears. Sun came in through the high windows. She stood up, pleased to feel the hard stone floor under her feet, and went to her closet. None of the maids was around, and she dressed herself carefully, feeling pleasure in the act of doing something for herself. Things weren't so bad, after all. There was nothing that she couldn't live with. She sat on the edge of the bed, looking at the room.

There was a broom in one of the corners that a careless maid had left. Without even thinking about what she was doing she took the broom and began to sweep, a slow, pleasant motion that drove all thoughts from her mind. It was good to be up again, good to be doing something besides lying in bed. . . .

A sudden movement at the door made her look up. One of the maids stood at the doorway, looking in. The maid turned and ran down the hallway. The princess wasn't sure, but the woman at the door had looked like the maid who had laughed at her on the first day of her honeymoon, that day long ago when she hadn't known what to expect.

Dinner that night was a disaster. Somehow everyone in the court had heard that she had swept her room like a common kitchen girl that morning. The gossips stood in the corner and laughed, glancing at her often from behind their fans. Once she even heard her old nickname, the one she had hated, spoken in whispers—Cinder Girl. She looked up sharply and saw Flora watching her coolly. She looked away quickly and tried not to cry.

After dinner she went straight to her room, speaking to no one. As she left the dining-room she saw the prince and Flora deep in conversation. Flora was laughing. She told her maid she wanted to see Alison in the morning and went to bed. She turned on the soft mattress all night trying to get comfortable, trying to forget the sound of Flora's laugh.

Alison came to her room the next day. "I'm glad to hear you're better," she said.

"I wasn't really ill," the princess said. "Just—I don't know—disappointed."

Alison nodded sympathetically. "I know what that's like," she said.

"I'm sorry," the princess said, feeling stupid again. "You must have had much worse disappointments in your life—I mean—I'm sorry. If only I wouldn't complain so much."

Alison nodded again.

"But why are people so cruel to each other?" the princess said. "That maid who laughed at me my first day here—why does she hate me?"

"She hates you because you didn't sack her," Alison said. "That was your mistake. You should have gotten rid of her immediately."

"Because—but why?" the princess said. "I don't understand." But she did understand, or was beginning to. She had been a peasant long enough to know that an aristocrat who let you take advantage, an aristocrat who was easy, was someone to be hated. You hated him or her just because you could.

"Oh, God," the princess said. "What a mess. Should I get rid of her now? She's got friends now, the Lady Flora—What do I do?"

"I don't know," Alison said. "I've never been a princess."

"I'm sorry," the princess said. "I just said I wasn't going to complain. How's your revolutionary?"

Alison laughed. "Oh, he's fine," she said. "I think he's gotten enough men to start the uprising." She looked around exaggeratedly and laughed again. They had both long since decided to trust each other. "I'm staying there now, sometimes, though luckily I wasn't there when you sent me your message. He's hiding out in that abandoned fortress near the forest. But—I don't know—I think if he ever decides to go through with it I won't be there. It's time to travel again."

"You won't?" the princess said. "But—I thought—"

"You thought I was a revolutionary too," Alison said. "So did I. But I've watched him for a while now, and I think— well, I think he doesn't love the people so much as he loves himself. That if he does win a war he'll set himself up as king and start all over again. And I've had all the dealings I want with kings."

"Oh," the princess said. "I'm almost ready to think that's too bad."

"My lady!" Alison said, laughing again. "You weren't going to join the revolutionaries, were you? He still asks about you, you know."

"No," the princess said. "Not after what you've told me. Still, it's a disappointment. Just one more disappointment. How do you live with it?"

"Oh, I don't know," Alison said. "You just keep going, that's all. You do the best you can."

After Alison left the princess went down to join her ladies-in-waiting to do embroidery. If everything ended in disappointment then one disappointment was just as good as another. If this was her fate, to sit and sew and wait for her husband to come home from the hunt, then so be it. It could be worse. It had been.

There was a hush when she came in the room, and she knew immediately that they had been talking about her. "Sit down, my lady," someone said, and they moved to make a place for her. "I'm glad to see that you're feeling better."

"Thank you," she said.

The talk started up again, words weaving like thread. Stories were taken up, tapestries displayed, the whole panoply of names and dates and countries she had never learned. "And then I said to Lady Flora, I said—" one of the ladies said.

"Hush!" someone else said, with a meaningful look at the princess.

"Oh," the first lady said, as if to say, It doesn't matter what you say in front of her, she won't be here much longer anyway. And a few minutes later the two had started up again, talking in low tones, and once again the princess heard the hated nickname, Cinder Girl.

Something snapped. The princess excused herself and stood up, pretending that her work was finished. She went upstairs to the prince's room and opened his closet, taking out an old vest, a pair of riding-breeches, a shirt that needed mending. She went back to her room and dressed in the prince's clothes, her heart pounding loudly. Then she opened the door and looked out.

The corridor became hazy. Something shimmered like water boiling. A woman dressed in blue the color of a summer evening formed out of the haze. "Good day, my lady," the woman said in a low, beautiful voice.

"Hello, Godmother," the princess said. "You're not going to stop me."

"I don't want to stop you, my child," the fairy godmother said. "I'm only here to make you happy. I guess you can't be very happy here—I should have seen that. But you wanted it so badly. What would you like now—the brave young revolutionary?"

"No, Godmother," the princess said. "I don't want anything—I only want to be left alone. When I went to the ball you promised me I'd live happily ever after. Well, there's no such thing. Nothing lasts forever, not even a prince and a castle and all the jewels I could ever dream of. This time I want to make it on my own."

"But where will you go?" the godmother asked. "What will you do?"

"I'm going to join Alison in the abandoned fort," the princess said. She was calm now, despite the pounding of her heart. "I think I'd like to travel with her, learn to play a harp for my supper. That reminds me—I should probably take the jewels." She overturned her jewel case and stashed the rings and necklaces and brooches in the vest pockets. "I wish these things had bigger pockets," she said, almost to herself. "And after that," she said to her godmother, "who knows?"

"But—But happily ever after—" the godmother said.

"I don't want it," the princess said. "Give it to someone else. Give it to Flora, she could probably use it. Oh, don't look so sad. You've done all you can for me, and I'll always be grateful. But right now—" The bell rang for dinner. "I've got to go. Good-bye." She kissed her fairy godmother on the cheek. "Good-bye, and give my love to Flora." She ran down the corridor lightly, happy as she'd been in years.

AFTERWORD

I 'd had the idea for "Ever After" for years and years, and one day on a long walk I worked the whole thing out in my mind. Were Prince Charming and Cinderella at all suited to each other? What would a peasant woman have in common with the aristocracy? Now, rereading the story, I see that I wrote it around the time of the marriage of Prince Charles and Princess Diana; perhaps that was at the back of my mind. I've always been suspicious of happy endings.

I'm fond of this one because it was my first published story. I'd already sold two novels, but it seemed as if I was under some sort of short-story curse until Shawna McCarthy bought it for *Isaac Asimov's Science Fiction Magazine.*

TOURISTS

H e awoke feeling cold. He had kicked the blankets off, and the air conditioning was on too high. Debbie—Where was she? It was still dark out.

Confused, he pulled the blankets back and tried to go to sleep. Something was wrong. Debbie was gone, probably in the bathroom or downstairs getting a cup of coffee. And he was—he was on vacation, but where? Fully awake now, he sat up and tried to laugh. It was ridiculous. Imagine paying thousands of dollars for a vacation and then forgetting where you were. Greece? No, Greece was last year.

He got up and opened the curtains. The ocean ten stories below was black as sleep, paling a little to the east—it had to be east—where the sun was coming up. He turned down the air conditioning—the soft hum stopped abruptly—and headed for the bathroom. "Debbie?" he said, tentatively. He was a little annoyed. "Debbie?"

She was still missing after he had showered and shaved and dressed. "All right then," he said aloud, mostly to hear the sound of his voice. "If you're not coming I'll go to breakfast without you." She was probably out somewhere talking to the natives, laughing when she got a word wrong, though she had told him before they left that she had never studied a foreign language. She was good at languages, then—some people were. He remembered her saying in her soft Southern accent, "For goodness sake Charles, why do you think people will understand you if you just talk to them louder? These people just don't speak English." And then she had taken over, pointing and laughing and looking through a phrasebook she had gotten somewhere. And they would get the best room, the choicest steak, the blanket the craftswoman had woven for her own family. Charles's stock rose when he was with her, and he knew it. He hoped she would show up soon.

Soft Muzak played in the corridor and followed him into the elevator as he went down to the coffee shop. He liked the coffee shop in the hotel, liked the fact that the waiters spoke English and knew what an omelet was. The past few days he had been keeping to the hotel more and more, lying out by the beach and finally just sitting by the hotel pool drinking margaritas. The people back at the office would judge the success of the vacation by what kind of tan he got. Debbie had fretted a little and then had told him she was taking the bus in to see the ruins. She had come back darker than he was, the blond hairs on her arm bleached almost white against her brown skin, full of stories about women on the bus carrying chickens and temples crumbling in the desert. She was wearing a silver bracelet inlaid with blue and green stones.

When he paid the check he realized that he still didn't know what country he was in. The first bill he took out of his wallet had a 5 on each corner and a picture of some kind of spiky flower. The ten had a view of the ocean, and the one, somewhat disturbingly, showed a fat coiled snake. There was what looked like an official seal on the back of all of them, but no writing. Illiterates, he thought. But he would remember soon enough, or Debbie would come back.

Back in his room, changing into his swim trunks, he

thought of his passport. Feeling like a detective who has just cracked the case he got out his money belt out from under the mattress and unzipped it. His passport wasn't there. His passport and his plane ticket were missing. The traveller's checks were still there, useless to him without the passport as identification. Cold washed over him. He sat on the bed, his heart pounding.

Think, he told himself. They're somewhere else. They've got to be—who would steal the passport and not the traveller's checks? Unless someone needed the passport to leave the country. But who knew where he had hidden it? No one but Debbie, who had laughed at him for his precautions, and the idea of Debbie stealing the passport was absurd. But where was she?

All right, he thought. I've got to find the American consulate, work something out. . . . Luckily I just cashed a traveller's check yesterday. I've been robbed, and Americans get robbed all the time. It's no big thing. I have time. I'm paid up at the hotel till—till when?

Annoyed, he realized he had forgotten that too. For the first time he wondered if there might be something wrong with him. Overwork, maybe. He would have to see someone about it when he got back to the States.

He lifted the receiver and called downstairs. "Yes, sor?" the man at the desk said.

"This is Room 1012," Charles said. "I've forgotten—I was calling to check—How long is my reservation here?"

There was a silence at the other end, a disapproving silence, Charles felt. Most of the guests had better manners than to forget the length of their stay. He wondered what the man's reaction would be if he had asked what country he was in and felt something like hysteria rise within him. He fought it down.

The man when he came back was carefully neutral. "You are booked through tonight, sor," he said. "Do you wish to extend your stay?"

"Uh—no," Charles said. "Could you tell me—Where is the American consulate?"

"We have no relations with your country, sor," the man at the desk said.

For a moment Charles did not understand what he meant. Then he asked, "Well, what about—the British consulate?"

The man at the desk laughed and said nothing. Apparently he felt no need to clarify. As Charles tried to think of another question—Australian consulate? Canadian?—the man hung up.

Charles stood up carefully. "All right," he said to the empty room. "First things first." He got his two suitcases out of the closet and went through them methodically. Debbie's carrying case was still there and he went through that too. He checked under both mattresses, in the nightstand, in the medicine cabinet in the bathroom. Nothing. All right then. Debbie had stolen it, had to have. But why? And why didn't she take her carrying case with her when she went?

He wondered if she would show up back at the office. She had worked down the hall from him, one of the partners' secretaries. He had asked her along for companionship, making it clear that there were no strings attached, that he was simply interested in not travelling alone. Sometimes this kind of relationship turned sexual and sometimes it didn't. Last year, with Katya from accounting, it had. This year it hadn't.

There was still nothing to worry about, Charles thought, snapping the locks on the suitcases. Things like this probably happened all the time. He would get to the airport, where they would no doubt have records, a listing of his flight, and he would explain everything to them there. He checked his wallet for credit cards and found that they were still there. Good, he thought. Now we get to see if the advertisements are true. Accepted all over the world.

He felt so confident that he decided to stay the extra day at the hotel. After all, he thought, I've paid for it. And maybe Debbie will come back. He threw his towel over his shoulder and went downstairs.

The usual people were sitting out by the pool. Millie and Jean, the older women from Miami. The two newlyweds who had kept pretty much to themselves. The hitchhiker who was just passing through and who had been so entertaining that no one had had the heart to report him to the hotel management. Charles nodded to them and ordered his margarita from the bar before sitting down.

Talk flowed around him. "Have you been to Djuzban yet?" Jean was saying to the retired couple who had just joined them at the pool. "We took the hotel tour yesterday. The marketplace is just fabulous. I bought this ring there—see it?" And she flashed silver and stones.

"I hear the ruins are pretty good out in Djuzban," the retired man said.

"Oh, Harold," his wife said. "Harold wants to climb every tower in the country."

"No, man, for ruins you gotta go to Zabla," the hitchhiker said. "But the buses don't go there—you gotta rent a car. It's way the hell out in the desert, unspoiled, untouched. If your car breaks down you're dead—ain't nobody passing through that way for days."

Harold's wife shuddered in the heat. "I just want to do some shopping before we go home," she said. "I heard you can pick up bargains in leather in Qarnatl."

"All we saw in Qarnatl were natives trying to sell us decks of cards," Jean said. She turned to Millie. "Remember? I don't know why they thought Americans would be interested in their playing cards. They weren't even the same as ours."

Charles sipped his margarita, listening to the exotic names flow around him. What if he told them the names meant nothing to him, nothing at all? But he was too embarrassed. There were appearances to keep up after all, the appearance of being a seasoned traveller, of knowing the ropes. He would find out soon enough, anyway.

The day wore on. Charles had a margarita, then another. When the group around the pool broke up it seemed the most natural thing in the world to follow them into the hotel restaurant and order a steak, medium-rare. He was running low on cash, he noticed—he'd have to cash another traveller's check in the morning.

But in the morning when he awoke, cold sober, he knew immediately what he'd done. He reached for his wallet on the nightstand, fingers trembling a little. There was only a five with its bleak little picture of a shrub left. Well, he thought, feeling a little shaky. Maybe someone's going to the airport today. Probably. The guys in the office aren't going to believe this one.

He packed up his two suitcases, leaving Debbie's overnight bag for her in case she came back. Downstairs he headed automatically for the coffee shop before he remembered. Abruptly he felt his hunger grow worse. "Excuse me," he said to the man at the desk. "How much—Do you know how much the taxi to the airport is?"

"No speak English, sor," the man said. He was small and dark, like most of the natives. His teeth were stained red.

"You don't—" Charles said, disgusted. "Why in God's name would they hire someone who doesn't speak English? How much," he said slowly. "Taxi. Airport." He heard his voice grow louder; apparently Debbie was right.

The man shrugged. Another man joined them. Charles turned on him with relief. "How much is the taxi to the airport?"

"Oh, taxi," the man said, as though the matter were not very important. "Not so much, sor. Eight, nine. Maybe fifteen."

"Fifteen?" Charles said. He tried to remember the airport, remember how he'd gotten here. "Not five?" He held up five fingers.

The second man laughed. "Oh no sor," he said. "Fifteen. Twenty." He shrugged.

Charles looked around in desperation. Hotel Tours, said the sign behind the front desk. Ruins. Free. "The ruins," he said, pointing to the sign, wondering if either of the men could read. "Are they near the airport?" He could go to the ruins, maybe get a ride. . . .

"Near?" the second man said. He shrugged again. "Maybe. Yes, I think so."

"How near?" Charles said.

"Near," the second man said. "Yes. Near enough."

Charles picked up the two suitcases and followed the line of tourists to the bus stop. See, he thought. Nothing to worry about, and you're even getting a free ride to the airport. Those taxi drivers are thieves anyway.

It was awkward maneuvering the suitcases up the stairs of the bus. "I'm going on to the airport," Charles said to the driver, feeling the need to explain.

"Of course, sor," the driver said, shrugging as if to say that an American's suitcases were no business of his. He added a word that Charles didn't catch. Perhaps it was in another language.

The bus set off down the new two-lane highway fronting the hotels. Soon they left the hotels behind, passed a cluster of run-down shacks and were heading into the desert. The air conditioning hummed loudly. Waves of heat travelled across the sands.

After nearly an hour the bus stopped. "We have one hour," the driver said in bad English. He opened the door. "These are the temple of Marmaz. Very old. One hour." The tourists filed out. A few were adjusting cameras or pointing lenses.

Because of the suitcases Charles was the last out. He

squinted against the sun. The temple was a solid wall of white marble against the sand. Curious in spite of himself he crossed the parking lot, avoiding the native who was trying to show him something. "Pure silver," the small man said, calling after him. "Special price just for you."

In front of the temple was a cracked marble pool, now dry. Who were these people who had carried water into the desert, who had imprisoned the moon in pale marble? But then how much had he known about the other tourist spots he had visited, the Greeks who had built the Parthenon, the Mayans who had built the pyramids? He followed the line of tourists into the temple, feeling the coolness fall over him like a blessing.

He went from room to room, delighted, barely feeling the weight of the suitcases. He saw crumbling mosaics of reds and blues and greens, fragments of tapestries, domes, fountains, towers, a white dining hall that could seat a hundred. In one small room a native was explaining a piece of marble sculpture to a dozen Americans.

"This, he is the god of the sun," the native said. "And in the next room, the goddess of the moon. Moon, yes? We will go see her after. Once a year, at the end of the year, the two statues—statues, yes?—go outside. The priests take outside. They get married. Her baby is the new year."

"What nonsense," a woman standing near Charles said quietly. She was holding a guidebook. "That's the fourth king. He built the temple. God of the sun." She laughed scornfully.

"Can I—Can I see that book for a minute?" Charles said. The cover had flipped forward tantalizingly, almost revealing the name of the country.

The woman looked briefly at her watch. "Got to go," she said. "The bus is leaving in a minute and I've got to find my husband. Sorry."

Charles' bus was gone by the time he left the temple. It was much cooler now but heat still rose from the desert sands. He was very hungry, nearly tempted to buy a cool drink and a sandwich at the refreshment stand near the parking lot. "Cards?" someone said to him.

Charles turned. The small native said something that sounded like "Tiraz!" It was the same word the bus driver had said to him in the morning. Then, "Cards?" he said again.

"What?" Charles said impatiently, looking for a taxi.

"Ancient playing set," the native said. "Very holy." He took out a deck of playing cards from an embroidered bag and spread them for Charles. The colors were very bright. "Souvenir," the native said. He grinned, showing red-stained teeth. "Souvenir of your trip."

"No, thank you," Charles said. All around the parking lot, it seemed, little natives were trying to sell tourists rings and pipes and blouses and, for some reason, packs of playing cards. "Taxi?" he said. "Is there a taxi here?"

The native shrugged and moved on to the next tourist.

It was getting late. Charles went toward the nearest tour bus. The driver was leaning against the bus, smoking a small cigarette wrapped in a brown leaf. "Where can I find a taxi?" Charles asked him.

"No taxis," the driver said.

"No—Why not?" Charles said. This country was impossible. He couldn't wait to get out, to be on a plane drinking a margarita and heading back to the good old U.S.A. This was the worst vacation he'd ever had. "Can I make a phone call? I have to get to the airport."

A woman about to get on the bus heard him and stopped. "The airport?" she said. "The airport's fifty miles from here. At least. You'll never find a taxi to take you that far."

"Fifty miles?" Charles said. "They told me—At the hotel they told me it was fairly close." For a moment his confidence left him. What do I do now? he thought. He sagged against the suitcases.

"Listen," the woman said. She turned to the bus driver.

"We've got room. Can't we take him back to the city with us? I think we're the last bus to leave."

The driver shrugged. "For the tiraz, of course. Anything is possible."

If Charles hadn't been so relieved at the ride he would have been annoyed. What did this word tiraz mean? Imbecile? Man with two suitcases? He followed the woman onto the bus.

"I can't believe you thought this was close to the airport," the woman said. He sat across the aisle from her. "This is way out in the desert. There's nothing here. No one would come out here if it wasn't for the ruins."

"They told me at the hotel," Charles said. He didn't really want to discuss it. He was no longer the seasoned traveller, the man who had regaled the people around the pool with stories of Mexico, Greece, Hawaii. He would have to confess, have to go back to the hotel and tell someone the whole story. Maybe they would bring in the police to find Debbie. A day wasted and he had only gone around in a circle, back to where he started. He felt tired and very hungry.

But when the bus stopped it was not at the brightly lit row of hotels. He strained to see in the oncoming dusk. "I thought you said—" He turned to the woman, hating to sound foolish again. "I thought we were going to the city."

"This is—" the woman said. Then she nodded in understanding. "You want the new city, the tourist city. That's up the road about ten miles. Any cab'll take you there."

Charles was the last off the bus again, slowed this time not so much by the suitcases as by the new idea. People actually stayed in the same cities that the natives lived. He had heard of it being done but he had thought only young people did it, students and drifters and hitchhikers like the one back at the hotel. This woman was not young and she had been fairly pleasant. He wished he had remembered to thank her.

The first cab driver laughed when Charles showed him

the five note and asked to be taken to the new city. The driver was not impressed by the traveller's checks. The second and third drivers turned him down flat. The city smelled of motor oil and rancid fish. It was getting late, even a little chilly, and Charles began to feel nervous about being out so late. The two suitcases were an obvious target for some thief. And where would he go? What would he do?

The panic that he had suppressed for so long took over now and he began to run. He dove deeper into the twisting maze of the city, not caring where he went so long as he was moving. Everything was closed, and there were few street-lamps. He heard the sounds of his footfalls echo off the shut-tered buildings. A cat jumped out of his way, eyes flashing gold.

After a long time of running he began to slow. "Tiraz!" someone whispered to him from an abandoned building. His heart pounded. He did not look back. Ahead was a lit store-front, a store filled with clutter. The door was open. A pawn shop.

He went in with relief. He cleared a space for himself among the old magazines and rusty baking pans and child's beads. The man behind the counter watched but made no comment. He took out everything from the two suitcases, sorted out what he needed and repacked it and gave the other suitcase to the man behind the counter. The man went to a small desk, unlocked a drawer and took out a steel box. He counted out some money and offered it to Charles. Charles accepted it wordlessly, not even bothering to count it.

The money bought a meal tasting of sawdust and sesame oil, and a sagging bed in an old hotel. The overhead fan turned all night because Charles could not figure out how to turn it off. A cockroach watched impassively from the corner.

The city looked different in daylight. Women in shawls and silver bracelets, men in clothes fashionable fifty years ago walked past the hotel as Charles looked out in the morning. The sun was shining. His heart rose. This was going to be the day he made it to the airport.

He walked along the streets almost jauntily, ignoring the ache in his arms. His beard itched because last night, in a moment of panic, he had thrown his electric razor into the suitcase to be sold. He shrugged. There were still things he could sell. Today he would find a better pawn shop.

He walked, passing run-down houses and outdoor markets, beggars and children, automobile garages and dim restaurants smelling of frying fish. "Excuse me," he said to a man leaning against a horse-drawn carriage. "Do you know where I can find a pawn shop?"

The man and horse both looked up. "Ride, yes?" the man said enthusiastically. "Famous monuments. Very cheap."

"No," Charles said. "A pawn shop. Do you understand?"

The man shrugged, pulled the horse's mane. "No speak English," he said finally.

Another man had come up behind Charles. "Pawn shop?" he said.

Charles turned quickly, relieved. "Yes," he said. "Do you know—"

"Two blocks down," the man said. "Turn left, go five blocks. Across the hospital."

"What street is that?" Charles asked.

"Street?" the man said. He frowned. "Two blocks down and turn left."

"The name," Charles said. "The name of the street."

To Charles's astonishment the man burst out laughing. The carriage driver laughed too, though he could not have possibly known what they were talking about. "Name?" the man said. "You tourists name your streets as though they were little children, yes?" He laughed again, wiping his eyes, and said something to the carriage-driver in another language, speaking rapidly.

"Thank you," Charles said. He walked the two blocks, turned left and went five blocks more. There was no hospital where the man had said there would be, and no pawn shop. A man who spoke a little English said something about a great fire, but whether it had been last week or several years ago Charles was unable to find out.

He started back toward the man who had given him directions. In a few minutes he was hopelessly lost. The streets became dingier, and once he saw a rat run from a pile of newspapers. The fire had swept through this part of the city leaving buildings charred and water-damaged, open to the passersby like museum exhibits. Two dirty children ran toward him, shouting, "Money, please, sor! Money for food!" He turned down a sidestreet to lose them.

Ahead of him were three young men in grease-stained clothes. One of them hissed something at him, the words rushing by like a fork of lightning. Another held a length of chain which he played back and forth, whispering, between his hands. "I don't speak—" Charles said, but it was too late. They were on him.

One tore the suitcase from his hand, shouting "El amak! El amak!" Another knocked him down with a punch to his stomach that forced the wind out of him. The third was going through his pockets, taking his wallet and the little folder of traveller's checks. Charles tried feebly to rise, and the second one thrust him back, hitting him once more in the stomach. The first one yelled something and they ran quickly down the street. Charles lay where they left him, gasping for breath.

The two dirty children passed him, and an old woman balancing a basket of clothes on her head. After a few minutes he rolled over and sat up, leaning against a rusty car up on blocks. His pants were torn, he noticed dully, torn and smeared with oil. And his suitcase with the rest of his clothes was gone.

He would go to the police, go and tell them that his suitcase was gone. He knew the word for suitcase because the young thief had shouted it. Amak. El amak. And suddenly he realized something that knocked the breath out of him as surely as a punch to the stomach. Every word in English, every word that he knew, had a corresponding word in this strange foreign language. Everything you could think of—hand, love, table, hot—was conveyed to these natives by another word, a word not English. Debbie had known that, and that was why she was good at languages. He hadn't. He had expected everyone he met to drop this ridiculous charade and start speaking like normal people.

He stood up gingerly, breathing shallowly to make the pain in his stomach go away. After a while he began walking again, following the maze of the city in deeper. At last he found a small park and sat on a bench to rest.

A native came up to him almost immediately. "Cards?" the native said. "Look." He opened his embroidered bag.

Charles sighed. He was too tired to walk away. "I don't want any cards," he said. "I don't have any money."

"Of course not," the native said. "Look. They are beautiful, no?" He spread the brightly colored cards on the grass. Charles saw a baseball player, a fortune teller, a student, some designs he didn't recognize. "Look," the native said again and turned over the next card. "The tourist."

Charles had to laugh, looking at the card of the man carrying suitcases. These people had been visited by tourists for so long that the tourist had become an archetype, a part of everyone's reality like kings and jokers. He looked closer at the card. Those suitcases were familiar. And the tourist—He jerked back as though shocked. It was him.

He stood quickly and began to run, ignoring the pain in his stomach. The native did not follow.

He noticed the card sellers on every corner after that. They called to him even if he crossed the street to avoid them. "Tiraz, tiraz!" they called after him. He knew what it meant now. Tourist.

As the sun set he became ravenously hungry. He walked around a beggarwoman squatting in the street and saw, too late, a card seller waiting on the corner. The card seller held out something to him, some kind of pastry, and Charles took it, too hungry to refuse.

The pastry was filled with meat and very good. As though that were the signal the other card sellers he passed began to give him things—a skin of wine, a piece of fish wrapped in paper. One of them handed him money, far more money than a deck of cards would cost. It was growing dark. He took a room for the night with the money.

A card seller was waiting for him at the corner the next day. "All right," Charles said to him. Some of the belligerence had been knocked out of him. "I give up. What the hell's going on around here?"

"Look," the card seller said. He took his cards out of the embroidered bag. "It is in here." He squatted on the sidewalk, oblivious to the dirt, the people walking by, the fumes from the street. The street, Charles noticed as he sat next to him, seemed to be paved with bottle caps.

The card seller spread the cards in front of him. "Look," he said. "It is foretold. The cards are our oracle, our newspaper, our entertainment. All depends on how you read them." Charles wondered where the man had learned to speak English, but he didn't want to interrupt. "See," the man said as he turned over a card. "Here you are. The tourist. It was foretold that you would come to the city."

"And then what?" Charles asked. "How do I get back?"

"We have to ask the cards," the man said. Idly he turned over another card, the ruins of Marmaz. "Maybe we wait for the next printing."

"Next—" Charles said. "You mean the cards don't stay the same?"

"No," the man said. "Do your newspapers stay the same?"

"But—Who prints them?"

The man shrugged. "We do not know." He turned over another card, a young blond woman.

"Debbie!" Charles said, startled.

"Yes," the man said. "The woman you came with. We had to convince her to go, so that you would fulfill the prophecy and come to the city. And then we took your pieces of paper, the ones that are so important to the tiraz. That is a stupid way to travel, if I may say so. In the city the only papers that are important to us are the cards, and if a man loses his cards he can easily get more."

"You—you took my passport?" Charles said. He did not feel as angry as he would like. "My passport and my plane tickets? Where are they?"

"Ah," the man said. "For that you must ask the cards." He took out another set of cards from his bag and gave them to Charles. Before Charles could answer he stood up and walked away.

By midday Charles had found the small park again. He sat down and spread out the cards, wondering if there was anything to what the card seller had said. Debbie did not appear in his deck. Was his an earlier printing, then, or a later one?

An American couple came up to him as he sat puzzling over the cards. "There are those cards again," the woman said. "I just can't get over how quaint they are. How much are you charging for yours?" she asked Charles. "The man down the street said he'd give them to us for ten."

"Eight," Charles said without hesitation, gathering them up.

The woman looked at her husband. "All right," he said. He took a five and three ones from his wallet and gave them to Charles.

"Thank you, sor," Charles said.

The man grunted. "I thought he spoke English very well," the woman said as they walked away. "Didn't you?"

A card seller gave him three more decks of cards and an

embroidered bag later that day. By evening he had sold two of the decks. A few nights later, he joined the sellers of cards as they waited in the small park for the new printing of the cards. Somewhere a bell tolled midnight. A woman with beautiful long dark hair and an embroidered shawl came out of the night and silently took out the decks of cards from her bag. Her silver bracelets flashed in the moonlight. She gave Charles twelve decks. The men around him were already tearing the boxes open and spreading the cards, reading the past, or the present, or the future.

After about three years Charles got tired of selling the cards. His teeth had turned red from chewing the nut everyone chewed and he had learned to smoke the cigarettes wrapped in leaves. The other men had always told him that someone who spoke English as well as he did should be a tour guide, and finally he decided that they were right. Now he takes groups of tourists through the ruins of Marmaz, telling them about the god of the sun and the goddess of the moon and whatever else he chooses to make up that day. He has never found out what country he lives in.

Afterword

The idea for "Tourists" came to me as I woke up on a bus in Mexico, somewhere between Cancún and Mérida. I had a moment of disorientation, of absolutely not knowing where I was, and I imagined someone who continued in this state for his entire vacation. This dislocation seems to me the essence of the tourist experience, that sudden shock when you realize, My God, we're really *not* in Kansas anymore.

I liked visiting this imaginary country so much that I wrote two more stories (both in this volume) and a novel about it. The novel is also called *Tourists* but has little in common with the story except the title and setting. I gave them the same title because I liked it, and because I wanted to confuse bibliographers, but bibliographers turn out not to be as easily confused as one would wish.

RITES OF SPRING

I 'm sitting at my desk catching up on paperwork when there's a knock on my office door. "Come in," I say.

The door opens and a woman steps inside. "Have a seat," I say, filing one last piece of paper.

"Are you Ms. Keller?" she asks.

"Liz Keller. And you are—"

"Dora Green." Wisely, she picks the more comfortable of the two office chairs. "I want you to find my daughter."

I look across the desk at her. She has an oval face, dark gray eyes. Her hair is medium-length and black, with a little gray at the temples. She doesn't look much like a parent of a missing child. She doesn't play with the handles of her purse, or light a cigarette. I nod, encouraging her to go on.

"My daughter's name is Carolyn—Carolyn Green," Ms. Green says. "At least it was. I suppose her husband's made her change it."

I try not to frown. In most missing children cases the child is much younger. "Are you sure she wants to be found?" I ask.

"I'm certain. Her husband forced her into the marriage, you see."

"Was she pregnant?"

She doesn't flinch. "No."

I look over this possible client for a moment. She's very well dressed—she wears a soft green pullover and a skirt with a print of entwining leaves and vines and flowers. I remember that it's St. Patrick's Day today, though I would bet that she's not Irish. She smells a little like some flower too, a subtle, expensive perfume. Golden earrings dangle from her ears.

"Look," I say. "Before I can take your money I need you to be clear about some things. I can promise to do my best to find your daughter. Whether she wants to be found is up to her. I'll give her a message from you, whatever—"

"She has to get away from him."

"I can't do that. Your daughter's of legal age—She is of legal age, isn't she?"

"Yes."

"All right then. If she tells me herself that she wants to end the marriage—"

"She does—"

"Then I'll help her. But not otherwise. If she won't leave him I can give her the name of a women's shelter, in case she changes her mind. I know a counselor there. Do you understand?"

"Yes."

"Okay. I need to know some things about your daughter—her husband's name, their last address if you know it. Do you have a picture of them?"

She does. The photograph she shows me must have been taken shortly after the two eloped: The daughter is wearing what looks like a bridal wreath, a circlet of flowers. She is beautiful, with light brown hair and blue eyes. I can't tell what she's thinking; she has the vacant expression of the very young. Her mother seems to have gotten all the wisdom in the family.

Her husband looks nearly twice her age. He is unsmiling, almost grim. He has long, greasy hair, a short beard, and wears a black leather vest over a t-shirt. He stands a little in front of her, casting her partly in shadow. "What does she do?" I ask.

"Nothing, as far as I know," Ms. Green says. "He won't let her leave the house."

"What about him? He looks like a Hell's Angel."

"I wouldn't be surprised." For the first time she looks away from me, down toward her lap. She smooths her busy skirt. "I don't like to think about it."

"How long has she been with him?"

"About four months. They got married right after they met."

"Where did she meet him?"

Ms. Green looks away again. "She says it was in a park."

We talk a little more, and then I give her my standard contract and explain about my fees. She signs the contract and writes a check for my retainer.

As soon as she leaves the nausea I've been fighting the past few weeks returns. I run down the hallway to the bathroom and make it just in time to throw up into the toilet. As I stand and catch my breath I wonder why the hell they call it morning sickness. Mine seems to go on all day.

I make my way back to the office. I've got to do something about this, I think. I've got to decide. I flip through the calendar on my desk. The doctor's appointment is in two days, on March 19.

Dora Green had given me the last address she had for Carolyn and her husband, and had told me that her daughter had been taking classes at the university. It's past four o'clock, though, and in this sleepy northern California town the university is probably closed for the day. I decide to visit Carolyn's neighborhood.

Before I leave I call a contact in the Department of Motor Vehicles and ask her to run a check on Jack Hayes, Carolyn's husband; on Carolyn Green; and on Carolyn Hayes. Then I pick up my coat and purse, lock the office door, and step out into the hallway.

The landing smells even worse than usual, frying grease and floor polish. They say that your sense of smell improves when you're pregnant, but in the past few weeks I've discovered that this doesn't nearly go far enough. What I think actually happens is that your entire skin becomes a giant olfactory gland.

The temperature outside is in the thirties, and the sun is barely visible through the clouds. It's the coldest March people in this town can remember. Wind burns my ears. My well-dressed client, I remember, wore a plush padded overcoat. I wrap my thin cloth coat around me and get into my car.

The car's heater kicks in just as I drive up to Carolyn's address. I sit in the car a moment longer before going out to face the cold. Iron bars front the windows of some of the houses around me; other houses are boarded up or burned out or covered with graffiti. Five or six teenage boys walk down the street, drinking something from a paper bag and laughing loudly. An old man stands at a bus stop, talking angrily to himself.

I turn off the car and step outside. The wind chills me almost instantly, and I huddle into my coat. The address Ms. Green gave me is an apartment building, and I see the apartment I want facing the landing on the second floor. I climb the outside stairs and knock. Music plays from the first floor.

There is no answer. I knock again, louder. The door to the nearest apartment opens and a man steps out. "What the hell do you want?" he asks. "Can't a man get a little sleep around here?"

Despite his words he is not angry—he sounds weary, as if he has been certain something would wake him up sooner or later. His blonde hair is lank and greasy, his face an unhealthy white. People pay a lot of money to get jeans as scuffed as his are, with just those holes at the knees. He might—just might—have a night job, but the odds are against it.

"Do you know Jack Hayes?" I ask. "Or Carolyn Hayes?"

"No. Who the hell are they?"

"They live here, in this apartment. Or they did."

"Oh, those guys." He leans against his door-jamb, suddenly disposed to talk. I see now that he is younger than I first thought, in his early twenties. A child somewhere in the building cries, and someone shouts for quiet. "Those guys were weird, let me tell you. They belonged to some cult or something. Satanists."

"Satanists?"

"Yeah. They had all these people coming and going at all hours of the day or night, all of them wearing black. Lots of chanting, lots of strange smells. Incense, maybe."

I sniff the air. There is a whiff of something, though it's harsher than incense. My stomach roils.

"You said 'had,' " I say. "Past tense. Are they gone?"

"I don't know, man," he says. "Now that you mention it I haven't seen them around for a couple of days. Weeks, maybe. You a bill collector?"

I give him one of my cards. He squints at it, as though he has grown unused to reading. "Private investigator, huh?" he says. "Isn't that dangerous, you being a woman and all?" He smiles, as if he thinks he's said something witty.

"Asking personal questions is always dangerous," I say. He squints again; he knows that I've insulted him, but for the moment he doesn't get how. "Call me if they come back, all right?"

He mumbles something and retreats back into his apartment. I try Carolyn Green's doorknob, but the door is locked.

I drive back to the office. There is a message on my machine from my contact at the DMV: She can find nothing for any of the names I gave her. I frown. It's hard to get around in this town without a car, though it is just barely possible. So much for the Hell's Angel theory—I had specifically asked her to check for motorcycle licenses. Maybe they're using aliases, I think, and I frown again.

I had been looking forward to finding Carolyn, to discovering why she had run away with such an unsuitable man. One thing I learned in this business is that people are far stranger than you would ever think, that they almost never do what you would expect. Now I wonder if I'll ever get to meet her.

The next day I wrap myself in my coat and two scarves and head out toward the university. It's even colder than yesterday, and a heavy rain begins while I'm driving. The rain turns into snow as I pull up to a parking garage. It hasn't snowed in this town since I moved here ten years ago.

I show the woman at the registrar's office my PI's license and ask about Carolyn Green. "I'm sorry," she says, shaking her head. "It's against university policy to give out information on students."

She doesn't look sorry at all; she seems delighted to be able to enforce a rule and cause trouble at the same time. Her face is unremarkable, with faded blue eyes and sprayed straw-colored hair, but her glasses are unfortunate—narrow and black, with upswept tips. She must have been in a terrible mood the day she visited the optometrist.

The office is overheated; I shed first one and then the other scarf, and open my coat. I try an appeal to the woman's emotions—missing daughter, frantic mother—but she is unmoved.

It feels good to leave the office, to walk down the hall and push open the door to the cold outside. The snow has stopped. Students are scraping up the thin snow and trying to make snowballs. Someone slips on the grass and goes down; his friends laugh. I'm not foolish enough to think that

I'll run into Carolyn Green, but just in case I stop several people and show them her picture. No one recognizes her.

I go to the student store to buy a pair of gloves, and then return to the registrar's office. I'm in luck—Ms. University Policy has left, probably for lunch, and a young woman who looks like a student has come in to replace her. Her eyes widen as I show her my license, and before I even finish my story she is calling up Carolyn's name on the computer.

"Here—I'll give you a print-out of her schedule," the young woman says. "And here's her address, at the top."

The address is the one Ms. Green gave me, but the list of classes could be useful. I thank the woman and leave.

The first class on Carolyn's schedule is Classical Literature, taught by a Professor Burnford. Once again I am amazed at how strange people are, how complex. Who would have thought that the woman in the photograph would be interested in such a thing?

I find the building where Carolyn studies Classical Literature and go inside. Professor Burnford's office is on the third floor; a sign on the door says that his office hours are from 12:00 to 2:00. It's five to twelve. I lean against the wall to wait.

A few minutes later the professor comes toward me, followed by a student who tries in vain to keep up with his long strides. Burnford says something over his shoulder to the student following him. "Rabbits!" I hear him say as he reaches the door. "Rabbits are fertility symbols!"

Burnford nods to me as I step forward, and without stopping he says, "I can see you after I talk to Joe here. Late Etruscan burial customs, isn't it?"

It isn't, but before I get a chance to tell him so he's unlocked his door and ushered poor Joe inside. I wait a bit more, and then wander down the hallway and read the notices and cartoons posted on office doors. It's all fairly interesting, in a sort of anthropological way. I never finished college myself.

Five minutes later Professor Burnford's door opens and Joe emerges, looking wrung out. He does not meet my eyes as he leaves.

"Sit down," Burnford says as I enter. His hair, eyes and skin are very nearly the same sandy color, and he wears a sand and black houndstooth coat. I wonder if he matched his coat deliberately to his face or if it's just a coincidence.

"I hope you don't mind if I eat my lunch while we talk," he says. He opens a brown paper bag and takes out a plastic-wrapped peanut butter sandwich. "I have no time otherwise."

The mention of lunch, and the smell of peanut butter, make my stomach turn again. The doctor's appointment is tomorrow, I think.

"I'm sorry," he says, taking a bite of the sandwich. "I don't remember your name."

"I'm not a student here, Dr. Burnford," I say. I take out my license and show it to him. "I'm looking for one of your students. Carolyn Green, or Carolyn Hayes."

He nods, his mouth full of peanut butter.

"Do you know her?" I ask.

"Of course I know her. Brilliant girl. You don't get too many undergraduates that good in ancient Greek."

Brilliant? I show him the photograph. "Yes, that's her," he says, taking it from me. "Don't know who the man is, though."

"That's her husband," I say. "Jack Hayes."

"Husband?" He puts down his sandwich, for which I am grateful, and wipes his mouth with a napkin. "So that's what happened to her. I'm sorry to hear it."

"What do you mean?"

"She stopped coming to class a few months ago. I don't usually stick my nose in my students' business, but I was worried about her and I went to the registrar's office to get her phone number. She doesn't have a phone, it turns out."

I nod. I had already noticed that.

"So I thought, that was that," he says. "Husband, you say. Sometimes you get a man who'll pull his wife out of school, even in this day and age."

I say nothing. He'd be surprised if he knew what goes on in this day and age.

He gives me the photograph back. "Shame," he says, shaking his head.

"Do you know anything about her?" I ask. "Any friends you might have seen her with? Acquaintances?"

"No. I never saw her outside of the classroom or my office."

I thank him and leave. The professors of her other two classes aren't in, so I scribble something on the backs of two business cards and push them under the doors. As I drive back to the office I turn on the radio; someone is explaining how to put on snow-chains.

There are two messages waiting for me at the office. A company I've worked for before asks me to run a credit check, and a friend wants to go see a movie tonight.

I should call both of them back. Instead I take out a legal pad and write down columns of numbers. Stroller, car seat, crib, play-pen. So much for clothing, so much for medical expenses. College, and classes in Classical Literature with Professor Burnford. I'm staring at the pad of paper when the phone rings.

I let the machine catch it. "I'm sorry I was angry with you the other day," a voice says, much to my surprise. "We should talk. Please call me."

It's my mother. She's wrong, though; we have nothing to talk about.

"Your test results came back," the doctor says. "They're positive."

I take a deep breath. "That was quick," I say.

"Oh, we're very efficient these days," she says. She smiles;

I guess she's trying to put me at ease. "We don't have to kill rabbits anymore."

For some reason this makes me think of Dr. Burnford, shouting at his student about rabbits and fertility symbols.

"Can I ask—" The doctor pauses. "Is this welcome news?"

I've checked the box marked "Single" on the intake form. "I don't know," I say slowly. "It was a one-night stand, really. A friend came into town unexpectedly. I don't—"

The vastness of what I've gotten into hits me; I have to stop and take another breath. I'm not going to break down in front of this woman, though; I'm not going to treat her the way my clients sometimes treat me, as if she's a wisewoman capable of solving all my problems. If I start I'll end up telling her about the screaming fight with my mother, about all my doubts, about God knows what else. "I'd just like some time to think about it," I say.

The doctor nods. She puts me up in those awful cold stirrups and examines me, and then, when I'm dressed, gives me some vitamins and a list of foods I should and shouldn't eat, and a pamphlet on abortion. "Do you need to talk to someone?" she asks. "I can recommend a good counselor."

I can't remember the number of times I've said the same thing to my clients. I've always prided myself on my ability to manage my own life, to stay out of the kinds of messes my clients seem to get into. I shake my head.

Dora Green is waiting for me in front of my office. I nod to her and unlock the door. "I wanted to know if you made any progress," she says.

I feel very weary. It's far too early for her to expect results. I motion her inside the office and sit at my desk. "I'm sorry," she says, taking the chair opposite me. Today she's wearing a green print dress that's even busier than her skirt, more leaves and flowers and what looks like little animals peering through the foliage. "I should have waited."

"Your daughter seems to have moved, and she's stopped

going to classes," I say. "Other than that, I can't tell you anything yet."

She nods. Her calm expression does not change. I wonder if she's had the same thought I had, that her daughter is dead, killed by her husband. Satanic rituals, I think.

"I'm meeting someone for lunch," she says. "You must be hungry too. Can I get you something to eat?"

You're supposed to eat enough for two when you're pregnant, but at the same time you're usually sick to your stomach. Just another example, I think, of how impossible the whole thing is. "I've already eaten," I say.

For a moment I think she knows I'm lying; worse, that she knows everything about me, including where I went this morning. I have never felt this way about any of my clients; usually it's the clients who feel the need to justify their behavior.

"Come with me anyway," she says, smiling a little.

The animals on her print dress are moving. I shake my head, trying to focus, but the hallucination doesn't go away. A badger or something shoulders aside a flowering vine and pads forward, its nose twitching.

I look away. I'd better eat something. "All right," I say, and we head out into the street.

She stops at a restaurant a few blocks from my office, and we go inside. I have never seen this place before; probably it's new. There are posters of flowers on the walls, and vases filled with bright flowers at the table.

Her friend is already there. "This is Mickey," Ms. Green says as we sit down. "Mickey, this is Liz Keller."

Mickey nods at me, amused at something. He is slender, with curly blond hair and light gray eyes. There is a slight family resemblance, and for a moment I think he is Carolyn's brother. But surely Ms. Green would have told me if there were others in the family. I wonder who he is, how they know each other.

The waitress comes soon afterward. I study the menu, trying to remember the list of food the doctor gave me. I could use a cup of coffee, but I'm almost certain the doctor would disapprove. "I'll have some tea," I say.

The waitress takes the rest of the orders and leaves. "How do you know Ms. Green?" I ask Mickey.

"We're related," he says. "Cousins. What about you? How do you know her?"

"She's hired me in a professional capacity," I say. It's all I can tell him without breaking my client's confidentiality.

"Ah," Mickey says. "You're the new detective."

"New detective?" I say, looking at Ms. Green. The animals on her dress are motionless now, thank God. "You didn't tell me about this. What happened to the old one?"

"She wasn't very good," Ms. Green says.

"And time is running out, isn't it?" Mickey says.

"What do you mean?" I ask.

We're interrupted by the waitress, bringing food for Mickey and Ms. Green and a teapot and cup for me. "So," Mickey says. He reaches over and pours me some tea. "What have you found so far?"

"I can't discuss it without my client's permission," I say.

"Oh, Mickey's family," Ms. Green says. "You can tell him anything you tell me."

I sip my tea, enjoying the warmth. My stomach feels fine now. I remember the first time I met Ms. Green, when she came to my office to hire me, and how the nausea had disappeared then too.

I tell Mickey about my trip to Carolyn's old apartment, my visit to the university. He's still smiling. I'm almost certain he's hiding something, that Ms. Green is wrong to trust him. He seems to feel very little concern for his missing cousin.

He pours me another cup of tea. "What do you plan to do now?" he asks.

It's a good question. I've pretty much run out of leads, but it doesn't do to say so in front of the person paying your salary. I take a sip of tea. "Did you know her husband?" I ask him.

"A little," he says.

"Did you like him?"

Mickey laughs. "Like him? The boyfriend from Hell?"

"Why do you think she married him?"

He shrugs.

"They seem very different," I say, pushing him.

He pours more tea. I look at the small teapot; it can't possibly hold that much. I lift the lid. It is filled to the brim.

I look up quickly at Mickey. He's grinning, as if daring me to confront him. "How did you do that?" I ask.

"Do what?" he says.

He must have switched teapots somehow, maybe while I was looking at Ms. Green. "Got to fly," he says. He stands and kisses Ms. Green on the cheek. "It was good seeing you."

I watch him go. My earlier suspicions of him become a certainty: he knows something he's not telling. "I've got to go too," I say. I stand and hurry through the restaurant, trying to keep him in sight.

He hasn't gotten that far ahead of me. He turns left out the door and heads east. A few miles farther on is Carolyn's old apartment. I drop back a little, keeping him in sight. Surely he doesn't intend to walk the entire distance.

He continues on for about a mile. The neighborhood slowly changes: the shopfronts here are dingier, and several of them are boarded up. Some of the buildings are painted three or four colors in a vain attempt to cover the graffiti; they look as if they have mange. A man moves to block me, his hand held out. "Spare change?" he asks.

I sidestep him and continue on. Mickey is still in front of me. He is hurrying a little, as if he's getting closer to his destination.

He comes to a corner. He stops for a moment, as if trying

to make up his mind. Then he turns and looks directly at me, grins, and goes right.

I take the corner after him. I've never had anyone spot me, never, not in any of the dozens of tails I've done. How had he known?

There is no one at all on the street. Grimy warehouses face each other, some protected by corrugated doors or iron gratings, all of them locked. One warehouse has rows of tiny windows on the second floor; about half of them are broken, as if they'd been the target in some game. Trees with branches like sticks line the street. No one seems to work here.

I walk up and down the street for over an hour, looking for Mickey in likely and unlikely places, but he is gone.

I go back to my office to get Ms. Green's phone number. I need Mickey's address, need to ask him a few questions.

The phone rings as I'm paging through my files. I pick it up. "Liz Keller, Private Investigations," I say.

"Liz?" the voice at the other end asks.

It's my mother. I don't need this right now. "What?" I say.

"Did you get my message?"

"Yeah."

"I want to talk to you. I want—I changed my mind. I had no right to interfere with anything you do. It's your life."

"I've always thought so."

"Did you see a doctor?"

She promises not to interfere, and then the first thing she says is interfering. "Yeah," I say.

"What did—"

"The test was positive." Even over the phone lines I can feel her straining to ask a question. "I haven't decided what to do yet."

"Did you think about what I said?"

"No."

"If you're going to have a child—"

"I thought you said you weren't going to interfere."

"Well, I just thought that you could take less dangerous work for a while. At least until the child is born."

"I've told you before. This is what I want to do."

"I know that. I'm not saying you should stop being a detective. But maybe you could take different cases—"

I sigh loudly. My mother has never held a job in her life, and yet she thinks she knows everything about everything. If she meets a jeweler she'll talk with great authority about gemstones. If she meets a car mechanic she'll go on about what the best makes of cars are. You can't correct her misconceptions; she feels absolutely no embarrassment when she finds out she's wrong.

Now she wants to tell me how to run a detective agency. "There are no safe cases," I say. "You can never tell how a case will turn out."

"Well, then, maybe you can stop—"

"No."

"I've talked it over with your father—we can afford—"

I hang up. Next thing she'll suggest I move back in with her and my father, into the old bedroom they've kept for me all these years.

Angry now, I pull Dora Green's file. I start to dial her number and then change my mind. I'm going to go visit her. If Mickey's been hiding something then who's to say she hasn't been? What do I really know about her anyway?

I put on my coat and two scarves and leave the office, slamming the door behind me. My stomach has started to feel queasy again.

There are huge plants on Ms. Green's lawn, pushing up against her outside wall. Somehow they have managed to put forth a few leaves, though the trees on the sidewalk are bare.

I ring her doorbell, wondering what it is about this woman and flowers.

Her house is light and warm, with wooden beams and hardwood floors, and, of course, pots of plants placed to catch the sun. Red and green and blue weavings cover the backs of white couches and hang from the walls. She leads me to one of the couches and sits across from me.

Once again I notice how calm she is, how composed. There is a stateliness to her that I don't associate with the parents of missing children. "Have you found my daughter?" she asks.

"No, not yet. But I have found—Well, I wonder how much you know about Mickey."

"Mickey?"

"Yes, your cousin. He didn't seem very concerned about Carolyn at the restaurant. I wonder if he's holding something back."

"Mickey." She sits back on the couch and smooths down the edge of the weaving. "I've been thinking the same thing myself. I think that's one of the reasons I asked you to lunch, so you could meet him and form your own impressions. I don't think he's telling me everything he knows."

"Do you have his address?"

"Yes, of course." She recites his address from memory. It's in a very mixed part of town, with apartment buildings and middle-class houses and small neighborhood shops all jumbled together. It's miles from the warehouse district he led me to this afternoon.

I thank her and start to leave. "Take care of yourself," she says.

Once again I get the unsettling feeling that she knows all about me. For a moment I want to tell her everything, to pour out the things I held back from my mother and the doctor. Why on earth did Carolyn Green run away from a mother like this?

Suddenly I realize that it's not the financial aspects of having a child I'm worried about. That would be tough, but I can handle it. What I'm terrified of is being the kind of mother my own mother was, interfering, small-minded, unable to let go. What other example do I have?

As I go back to my car I see that the streetlights are starting to come on. I've wasted more time than I thought following Mickey. I go home, and turn the heat up as high as it will go.

The next day I am parked across the street from Mickey's house. There is a car in the driveway, a late model Mercury. He might be out on one of his long walks, but I gamble that the car means he's still home.

Time passes slowly. My car is freezing, but I can't risk turning on the engine to start the heater. Finally the front door opens, and Mickey steps out. He passes the car in the driveway and heads for the sidewalk. Another walk today, I think.

I let him get a half a block ahead of me and then ease open the car door. This time I am certain he hasn't seen me. He walks slowly, as though he has no destination in mind; it is easy enough to keep him in sight.

He continues this way for several miles. He shows no sign of stopping. Finally he turns down a main street, and I see that he is heading toward the warehouse district he visited yesterday. He is moving faster now.

I follow, hurrying to keep him in sight. He comes to the corner at which I lost him and turns. I take the corner after him. He is still in front of me, moving very fast now, almost running.

The rain starts again, lashing the bare trees. He goes halfway down the street and pushes on one of the warehouse doors. I run after him, but by the time I get there the door is closed. I try it; it opens with only the slightest squeak of rusty metal.

I step inside and close the door quickly. The first thing I notice is the smell of corroded metal. I can see nothing; even minutes after I have shut the door the warehouse is pitch dark. I can hear nothing either, not Mickey, not anyone he has come to meet. After a few minutes I make out the distant sound of water dripping on metal.

A flare burns suddenly across the room, too dim to reach me. I move toward it cautiously, keeping close to the shadows by the wall.

As I get nearer I see two huge chairs made of rusted metal. One is empty; a man sits in the other. It is too dark to tell, and I am too far away, but I am almost certain he is the man in the photograph, Carolyn's husband. The sight of the empty chair makes me uneasy.

The light flares higher, and now I see Mickey among the shadows, standing before the man in the chair. The man wears a crown made of iron; its points catch the flames and glow red.

I feel the nudge of an elusive memory, a story I once heard or a lesson I learned in school. I know this place: the dark hall, the two chairs, the harsh smell of rusting metal. But before I can remember it fully the man in the chair speaks.

"Greetings, cousin," he says. "What news do you bring me from the upper world?"

"She know nothing," Mickey says. "She is unable to find her daughter."

"Good. Her daughter is mine, gained by lawful means."

"Of course," Mickey says.

The red light erupts again. The shadows fall back. The man in the chair looks up and sees me. "Who is that woman?" he asks.

I turn and run. I find the door to the outside, but it is stuck, locked. I am still pulling on it when Mickey comes up behind me.

"Come, Liz," he says. "This is no fit way to greet the King of Hell."

I turn and face him, look beyond him to Jack Hayes. "King of Hell," I say scornfully. "Is that King Jack, or King Hayes?"

"Hades," he says. It is a while before I realize that he is correcting my pronunciation.

"Where is Carolyn?" I ask.

"My wife is safe."

"Where is Carolyn?" I ask again.

"She is not Carolyn," Hayes says. "Her name is Kore. Some call her Persephone."

"I don't have time—"

"I will tell you where she is," he says. "I first saw her many years ago. She was gathering flowers, and she had wandered too far from her companions. I fell in love with her then—I saw that she would bring light to my dark lands. I rode my chariot up from Hell, and I seized her and bore her down to my kingdom. Her mother Demeter searched all the earth for her but could not find her, and in her sorrow called down the chilling winter. It was Hermes who led Demeter to her daughter, that first winter so long ago."

"Hermes?"

Mickey bows toward me mockingly. "The Romans called me Mercury. The messenger, the quick-witted one, the god of commerce. And also—" he grins "—the trickster, the god of thieves."

I wonder if they are both crazy. But it doesn't really matter; the important thing is making sure that Carolyn is safe. "Where is she?"

"You *are* persistent," Mickey says. "She chose well for a change, Demeter did."

"What do you mean?"

"Demeter searches every year for her daughter. She will not end her winter until Kore is found, and we made the search more difficult than usual this year." Mickey shakes his head, almost in admiration. "This is the first time she's hired a private investigator, though. I made sure that the one she found was incompetent, but apparently she tried again without my help."

"Why didn't you just tell her where her daughter is?"

"Some years I do, some years I don't. You can't trust me, really." He grins engagingly. "You know the Little Ice Age, during the Middle Ages? That was my doing. And now—she should have gone to you sooner. She's left it far too late."

"Where—"

Jack Hayes raises his hand to stop me, then waves to a corner of the room still in shadow. Carolyn comes toward us. She is very pale; even her blue eyes seem paler, and there are dark circles under her eyes. Her long white dress is torn and dirty.

Suddenly I remember the rest of the Greek legend. "You've had your time with her," I say to Hayes. "She ate four pomegranate seeds—that gave you four months with her. It's spring now—it's time for her to go home."

Hayes nods. The foul light slowly diminishes. Before he can change his mind I grab Carolyn by the wrist and hurry toward the door.

Mickey is standing there, blocking my way. I didn't even see him move; I would have sworn that he was still behind me. "No," he says. He's still smiling; it's all a game to him. "Let's have another Ice Age. The last one was such fun."

I let go of Carolyn and turn to look at Hayes. It's a mistake; Mickey shoves me toward the throne and tries to force me to the floor.

I sidestep him, sliding to one side and crouching down. He is still lunging forward, and as he moves in front of me I punch him in the kidney.

He doubles over. Before he can get up I run for the door, taking Carolyn with me. The door opens easily.

We step outside. It's raining hard; we are drenched within seconds. I slam the door behind me and run down the street, taking Carolyn with me. As we reach the corner a taxi comes toward us. I hail it and we get inside.

I give the driver Dora Green's address and sit back. Carolyn stares through the wiper blades at the streets outside. There is a trace of sadness on her face, and—what seems worse to me—resignation. What does she think, having been delivered from the terrors of that warehouse? Has it happened before, as Mickey said? For how many years has she had to take this ride home?

A few minutes later we drive up to Ms. Green's house. I pay the driver and we walk up to the front door. I ring the bell.

The door opens. Dora Green steps outside and sees her daughter. She goes toward Carolyn and holds her close; they stand motionless for a long time. I cannot read the expression on her face.

The rain stops. A warm wind courses from somewhere, heavy with the scents of flowers and oranges. Tiny green leaves are budded on the branches of the trees; I hadn't noticed them before. They open as I watch.

After a long moment Dora releases her daughter and turns the full regard of her gaze to me. The air burns around her, bright as gold. She seems to read my entire life in an instant, both my past and what is to come. Her expression is perfectly balanced between joy and sorrow.

I want to fall to my knees before her. The goddess of earth, of fertility. "I thank you," Demeter says.

I am taking a leave of absence from my job, at least until the child is born and is old enough for daycare. Demeter has been more than generous in settling up her bill, and Hermes, the god of commerce, seems to have shrugged off the incident in the warehouse and has offered me a loan. He is also, as he was good enough to warn me, the god of thieves, but I've dealt with crooks before. I am very glad not to have to take money from my parents.

The doctor tells me the child will be a girl. I am going to call her Demetra.

AFTERWORD

I 've always liked the story of Demeter and Persephone. Partly this is because it's one of the few Greek myths to deal with women, with the primal relationship of mother and daughter. And partly it's because around about January winter starts to seem horribly oppressive, and I long for spring. (My novel *Summer King, Winter Fool,* which I wrote around the same time as this story, deals with a prolonged winter as well.) I tried writing a story based on this myth three separate times—as science fiction, as mainstream, and as fantasy, which finally seemed to work.

Thanks are due to David Cleary for the title.

Midnight News

S tevens and Gorce sat at the hotel bar, watching television. Helena Johnson's face nearly filled the entire screen. Snow drifted across her face and then covered the screen, and five or six people in the bar raised their voices. The bartender quickly switched the channel, and Helena Johnson's face came on again, shot from the same angle.

She had told the reporters she was eighty-four, but Stevens thought she looked older. Her face was covered with a soft down and her right cheek discolored with liver-colored age spots, and the white of one eye had turned as yellow as an egg yolk. The hairdressers had dyed her hair a full, rich white, but Stevens remembered from earlier interviews that it had been dull gray, and that a lot of it had fallen out.

"I lived at home for a long long time," Helena Johnson was saying in her slow, scratchy voice. The reporters sat at the bar or at round tables scattered throughout the room and watched her raptly. The bar, which the hotel called a "lobby lounge," had once been elegant, but two months of continuous occupancy by the reporters had changed it into something quite different. Cigarette butts had been ground into the lush carpet, drinks had been spilled, glasses broken.

"Well, it was the Depression, you know, and I couldn't move out," the old woman said. "And girls weren't supposed to live on their own back then—only loose girls lived by themselves. My father had been laid off, and I got a job as a stenographer. I was lucky to get it. I supported my family for two years, all by myself."

She stopped for a moment, unwilling or unable to go on. The camera pulled back to show her seated on the bed, then cut to the small knot of reporters standing in her hotel room. Stevens saw himself and Gorce and all the rest of them. He remembered how tense he'd been, how worried that she wouldn't call on him. One of the reporters raised his hand.

"Yes, Mr.—Mr.—" Helena Johnson said.

"Look at that," Stevens said in the bar. "She's senile, on top of everything else. How can she forget his name after two months?"

"Shhh," Gorce said.

"Capelli, ma'am," the reporter said. "I wondered how you felt while you were supporting your family. Didn't it make you feel proud?"

"Objection," Gorce said in the bar. "He's leading the witness."

"Shhh," Stevens said.

"Well, of course I was proud," Helena Johnson said. "I was putting my younger brother through college, too. He had to stop after two years, though, because I lost my job."

Her manner was poised, regal. She reminded Stevens of nothing so much as Queen Victoria. And yet she hadn't even finished grade school. "Look at her," he said in disgust. He raised his glass in a toast. "This is the woman who's going to save the world."

No one knew how the aliens had chosen Helena Johnson. A month after they had appeared, their round ships like gold coins above the seven largest cities in the world, they had jammed radio frequencies and announced their terms for a meeting. One ship would land outside of Los Angeles, and only twenty reporters would be allowed to board.

Stevens's first surprise was that they looked human, or at least humanoid. (After the meeting scientists would speculate endlessly about androids and holograms and parallel biology.) Stevens sat on an ordinary folding chair and watched closely as the alien stepped up to the front of the room. Near him he saw reporters looking around for clues to the aliens' technology, but the room was bare except for the chairs and made of something that might have been steel.

"Good afternoon," the alien said. Its voice sounded amplified, but Stevens could see no microphone anywhere. "Hello. We are your judges. We have judged you and found you wanting. Some of us were of the opinion that you should be destroyed immediately. We have decided not to do this. We have found a representative of your species. She will make the decision. At midnight on your New Year's Eve she will tell you if you are to live or die."

No one spoke. Then a bony young woman, her thin black hair brushed back and away from her face, jumped up from her seat. It was the first time Stevens saw Gorce in person, though he had heard of her from his colleagues. He held his breath without knowing it. "Why do you feel you have the right to sit in judgment over us?" she asked. Her voice was level.

"No questions," the alien said. "We will give you the name of the woman who is to represent you. Her name is Helena Johnson. She lives in Phoenix, Arizona. And there is one more thing. Brian Capelli, will you stand please?"

Capelli stood. His face was as white as his shirt. The alien made no motion that Stevens could see, but suddenly there was a sharp noise like a backfire and Capelli's chair burst into flames. Capelli moaned a little and then seemed to realize where he was and stopped.

"We have power and we will use it," the alien said.

Not surprisingly, with every state and federal organization mobilized to look for her, Helena Johnson was found within two hours. She lived in a state-sponsored nursing home. She was asleep when the FBI agent found her, and when she woke she seemed unable to answer the simplest question. "What is your name?" the agent asked. Helena Johnson gave no sign that she had heard him.

But within a month she seemed to have accepted the situation as her due. The government put her up in the best hotel in Washington and hired nurses, hairdressers, manicurists, companions. She had an ulcer on her leg that had never been seen to at the home, and the government sent out a highly-paid specialist to treat it. Another specialist discovered that she wasn't so much disoriented as hard of hearing, and she was fitted with a hearing aid.

She granted interviews with the twenty reporters daily, then screened the tapes and deleted anything she didn't like. The world discovered to its dismay that Helena Johnson's life hadn't been an easy one, and everything possible was done to make it easier. Television programs now played for an audience of one: stations showed *The Nutcracker* over and over again because she had talked about being taken to see it as a child. Newspapers stopped reporting crime and wars—crime and wars had, in fact, nearly disappeared—and ran headlines about the number of kittens adopted. She got an average of ten thousand letters a day: most of them came with a gift, and about a third were marriage proposals.

"So my co-worker, Doris, she said the boss would let you stay on if you would, well, do favors for him," Helena Johnson was saying. "You know what I mean. And I decided that I'd rather starve. But then the next day I thought, well, it's not just me that's depending on the money I earn. It's my parents, and my brother who I was putting through college—did I tell you about that?—and I decided that if he asked me I'd

do it. I'm not ashamed to tell you that that's what I thought."
The camera cut to the reporters again. Most of them were
nodding sympathetically. "So the next day I was called into
his office. I was called alone, so I thought, here it comes. Usually when he fired you he called you in in a group. He was
standing behind his desk—I can see it now, as clear as day—
and he opened his mouth to say something. And then he
shook his head, like this, and he said, 'Forget it, girl, go
home. You're too ugly.' "

"I wonder if that guy's still alive," Stevens said in the bar.

"I hope for his sake he's dead."

"Gone to the grave never knowing he doomed the world
with one sentence."

"She doesn't seem too bitter."

"Who knows what she seems? Who knows what she's
thinking? Look at her—she looks like the cat that ate the ca-
nary. She's going to play this for all it's worth."

"I got married at the beginning of the war," Helena
Johnson said. "World War Two, that was. I was thirty, a bit old
for those days. My husband met one of those female soldiers
over there in Europe, one of those WACs, and left me for
her. Left me and our baby son."

"Is that when you went back to your maiden name?"
Gorce asked.

"Yes, and that's a very sharp question, young lady,"
Helena Johnson said.

"I don't see why," Stevens said, in the bar.

"Because she wants to talk about herself, that's why,"
Gorce said.

"My husband's name was Furnival," Helena Johnson
said. "Isn't that a dreadful name? It sounds just like funeral,
that's what I always thought. I went back to my maiden name
as soon as I heard about him and that WAC. They tell me he's
dead now. Died in 1979. I lost track of him a long time ago."

"And then you had to raise your baby all by yourself,"
Gorce said.

"That's right, I did," Helena Johnson said, smiling at her. "And he left me too, soon as he could get a job. He was about seventeen. Seventeen, that's right."

"Have they found him yet?" Stevens asked in the bar.

"They traced him to that trailer camp in Florida," Gorce said. "He left last April, and they haven't been able to pick him up from there. Probably on the run."

"You'd be too."

"I don't know. This could be just what she needs, an emotional reunion with the prodigal son. Make great television."

"The prodigal son has a record as long as your arm—assault, armed robbery, breaking and entering. . . ."

"Do you think the Feds will grant him that pardon?"

"Probably."

On the screen the interview was coming to an end. "Anything else you want to say, Miss Johnson?" the hired companion asked.

"No, I'm feeling a little tired," she said. "Oh, I did want to thank—what was his name? Oh, dear, I can't remember it. A young man in Texas who sent me this ring." She held the back of her hand to the camera. The diamond caught the light and sparkled. "Thank you so much."

Her face faded. "The Dance of the Sugar-Plum Fairies" came on over the credits and several people in the bar groaned loudly. The bartender turned the sound down and then turned it back up for the nightly news.

"Good evening," the anchorman said. "Our top story today concerns the daily interview with Helena Johnson. During the course of the interview Miss Johnson spoke once again about her childhood and growing up during the Depression, about her marriage and son. She had this to say about her husband."

"Good God, she's the most boring woman in the world!" Stevens said. "Why do we have to sit through this drivel again?"

"You know why," Gorce said. "In case she's watching."

"In other news, the government reported that the number of survivors of the Denver fire-bombing stands at two," the anchorman said. "Both the survivors are listed in stable condition. Both have burns over fifty percent of their bodies. Skin grafts are scheduled to begin tomorrow."

"God, that was stupid," Gorce said. "I wonder whose idea it was to attack that ship."

"Well, how the hell could we know? All we'd seen them do was burn a chair, and any special-effects man could have done that. What if they were just bluffing?"

"And now we know," Gorce said.

"Now we know."

"Government sources say the bombs were not nuclear weapons," the anchorman said. "There is no radioactive fallout at all from the bombing. Miss Johnson has sent both the survivors a telegram expressing her wishes for their speedy recovery."

"Bully for her," Stevens said.

"Come off it," Gorce said. "She's not that bad."

"She's a horror. She hasn't called on me once the last three days, and you know why? It's because I accidentally called her 'Ms.' "

"I feel sorry for her. What a hard life she's had."

"Sure you do—she loves you. Look at the way she beamed at you all through the interview today. But I guess you're right. I guess she's been lonely. She was only married a year before her husband was called up."

"I didn't mean just her marriage—"

"Now don't go giving me that feminist look," Stevens said, though in fact Gorce's steady gaze hadn't changed. "You know what I meant. If they're not married they usually have a career, something they're interested in. Like you. But this woman had nothing."

"Were you ever married, Stevens?"

"No." He looked at her, surprised by the question. "Relationships don't work out for me. Too much travelling, I guess. How about you?"

"No," she said.

On the screen a scientist was summarizing the latest attempt to communicate with the ships, and then the news ended. "Stay tuned for *Cinderella* following tonight's news," the announcer said over the credits.

"Cinderella!" Stevens said, disgusted. "Come on, guys. She can't be awake this late."

"Shhh."

"What—you think she'll hear me? She's on the top floor."

The bartender turned the television off. Stevens and Gorce ordered another round. "You know what I was thinking?" Gorce said. "Have you thought about these aliens? I mean really thought about them?"

"Sure," Stevens said. "Like everyone else in America. I've got a new theory, too. I bet it's a test."

"A what?"

"A test. It doesn't matter what the old bitch chooses, whether she wants us destroyed or not. It's like a laboratory experiment. They're watching us to see how we act under pressure. If we do okay, if we don't all go nuts, we'll be asked to join some kind of galactic federation."

Gorce said nothing for a while. The dim light in the bar made her face look sallow, darkened the hollows under her eyes. "You ever read comic books when you were a kid, Stevens?"

"Huh? No."

"That's what it always turned out to be in the comic books. Some kind of test. All these weird things would happen—the super-hero might even die—but in the end everything returned to normal. Because the kids reading the comics never liked it when things changed too much. The only explanation the writers could come up with was that it had all been a test. But I don't think these tests happen outside of comic books."

"Okay, so what's your theory?"

"Well, think about what's happening here. These guys have set themselves up as the final law, judge, jury and executioner all rolled into one. Sure, they picked the old woman, but that's just the point—*they* picked her. They probably know how she's going to vote, or they have a good idea. What kind of people would do something like that?"

"I don't know."

"Pretty sadistic people, I'd say. If there was some kind of galactic federation, wouldn't they just observe us and contact us when we were ready? I mean, we were on our way to blowing ourselves up without any outside help at all. Maybe these people travel around the galaxy getting their jollies from watching helpless races cower for months before someone makes the final decision. These aliens are probably outlaws, some kind of renegades. They're so immoral no galactic federation would have them."

"That's a cheerful thought."

Gorce looked around. "Hey, where's Nichols?"

"I don't know. He said something this morning—"

"What?"

"He was going to try to talk to her alone."

"He can't do that."

"You're damn right he can't. Look at all the security they've got posted around her."

"No, I mean he can't get a story the rest of us don't have. We've got to go up there."

"Forget it."

"Come on. We can stop by for a visit or something. Play a game of cards. She'll be happy to see us."

"You're crazy."

"All right, you stay here. I'm going up and talk to her. She won't mind—she likes me."

"Gorce—"

Gorce stood up. "Gorce, don't do that. For God's sake—Melissa!"

He wouldn't have remembered her first name if they hadn't done interviews with each other for their respective news stations. "This is Melissa Gorce, reporting from Washington," she'd said, and he'd thought that he couldn't have come up with a name less like her. Using it seemed to work. She stopped, and the mad light in her eyes went out. "Okay," she said. "Maybe you're right."

The next day, at the daily interview, Stevens found out how right he'd been. The number of FBI guards at the door had been doubled, and when his ID had been checked and he'd finally been let in he saw that Nichols was gone.

"He tried to get inside her room last night," Capelli said. "The guards said they were reaching for their guns when they saw this bright flash of light go off. He was practically unrecognizable—they had to check his dental records to make sure it was him."

"He'd been Denverized," another reporter said, trying to laugh.

"He wanted to commit suicide, you ask me," Capelli said. His hands were shaking.

"You see?" Stevens couldn't resist saying to Gorce. "You see what I mean?"

The two cameramen finished setting up, and Helena Johnson's companion opened the floor to questions. No one brought up the dead reporter and Helena Johnson didn't mention him; maybe, Stevens thought, she didn't know. To Stevens's relief she called on him for the first time in four days.

"I was wondering," he said, "how you spend your time. What are your hobbies?"

She smiled at him almost flirtatiously. He was surprised at how much hatred he felt for her at that moment. "Oh, I keep busy," she said. "I look through my mail, though of course I don't have time to answer all my correspondence. And I watch some television, I watch videotapes people send me, I have my hair done . . . I enjoy mealtimes especially, though there's a lot of food my stomach can't take. Do you know, I'd never eaten lobster in my life until last week."

Gorce was right, he thought. She does like talking about herself. If they survived New Year's Eve he'd have to keep in contact with Gorce—she was one smart woman.

Someone asked Helena Johnson a question about her father, and the old woman droned on. She's already told us this story, Stevens thought. There were a few more questions, and then Gorce raised her hand. Helena Johnson smiled at her. "Yes, dear?"

"What do you think of the aliens, Miss Johnson?"

"Gorce!" Capelli whispered behind her. The other reporters thought he'd lost his nerve at the first press conference, when his chair had burst into flames behind him.

"I suppose I'm grateful to them," Helena Johnson said. "If it wasn't for them I'd still be in that dreadful old age home."

"But what do you think of the way they've interfered with us? Of the way they want to make our decisions for us?"

Capelli wasn't the only reporter who became visibly nervous at this question. Stevens felt he could have cheerfully strangled her.

"I don't know, dear. You mean they want to tell us what to do?"

"They want to tell you what to do. They want to force you to make a choice."

"Oh, I don't mind making the choice. In fact—"

Oh, Lord, Stevens thought. She's going to tell us right now.

The companion stepped forward. "Our hour with Miss Johnson is almost up," she said smoothly. "Do you have anything else you want to say, Miss Johnson?"

"Yes, I do," the old woman said. "I wanted to say—Oh, dear, I've forgotten."

The companion moved to the desk and brought her a slip of paper. "Oh yes, that's right," Helena Johnson said, looking at it. "I wanted to tell everyone not to get me a Christmas present. I know a lot of people have been worrying about what to get me, and I just want to tell them I have everything I need."

So give a contribution to charity instead, Stevens thought, but Helena Johnson seemed to have finished. Did she neglect to mention charity because she knew there would be no charities, or anything else, in a few weeks? It was amazing how paranoid they had all become, how they analyzed her slightest gesture.

The companion ushered everyone out of the room. The reporters went downstairs to stand in front of the hotel and tape a short summary of the interview for their stations. Upstairs, Stevens knew, Helena Johnson and the cameramen were going over the footage, editing out parts where she thought she looked too old, too vulnerable or too uncertain.

He felt depressed by the interview, by Nichols's death. The old lady hadn't given them any hope at all this time. What would he be doing a few weeks from now? If she said no, he could probably have his pick of assignments. But if she said yes he'd be charred bones and ashes, like poor Nichols, like all the people in Denver. God, what a horrible way to die. She had to say no, she had to.

On New Year's Eve everyone was either watching television, getting drunk or doing both at once. The last show would be broadcast live. Stevens had taken a sedative for the final interview, and he knew he wasn't the only one. There had been no commercials on any network for the last five hours; if the old lady said no, Stevens had heard, there would be commercials every three minutes.

They were let into the room for the last time at exactly midnight. "Hello," Helena Johnson said, smiling at all of them. The smell of fear was very strong.

"I have been chosen by the aliens to decide Earth's future," she said. "I don't understand why I was chosen, and neither does anyone else. But I have taken the responsibility very seriously, and I feel I have been conscientious in doing my duty."

Get on with it, Stevens thought. Yes or no.

"I have to say I have enjoyed my stay here at the hotel," she said. "But it is impossible not to think that all of you must consider me very stupid indeed." Oh, God, Stevens thought. Here it comes. The old lady's revenge. "I know very well that none of you were interested in me, in Helena Hope Johnson. If the aliens hadn't chosen me I would probably be at the nursing home right now, if not dead of neglect. My leg would be in constant pain, and the nurses would think I was senile because I couldn't hear the questions they asked me.

"So at first I thought I would say yes. I would say that Earth deserves to be destroyed, that its people are cruel and selfish and will only show kindness if there's something in it for them. And sometimes not even then. Why do you think my son hasn't come to visit me?" The yellow eye had filled with tears.

Oh, shit, Stevens thought. I knew it would come to this. He had heard her son was dead, killed in a bar fight.

"But then I remembered what this young lady had said," Helena Johnson said. "Miss Gorce. She asked me what I thought about the aliens interfering with our lives, with my life. Well, I thought about it, and I didn't like what I came up with. They have no right to decide whether we will live or die, whoever they are. All my life people have decided for me, my parents, my teachers, my bosses. But that's all over with now. My answer is—no answer. I will not give them an answer."

No one moved for a long moment. Then one of the

agents stationed outside the door ran into the room. "The ships are leaving!" he said. "They're taking off!"

Suddenly everyone was cheering. Stevens hugged Gorce, hugged Capelli, hugged the FBI agent. The reporters lifted Gorce and threw her into the air until she yelled at them to stop. I hope the camera's getting all this, Stevens thought. It's great television.

The reporters, quieter now, came over to Helena Johnson to thank her. Stevens saw Gorce kiss the old woman carefully on the cheek. "You'd better leave now," the companion said. "She gets tired so easily."

One by one the reporters went downstairs to the bar. Helena Johnson and Gorce were left alone together. Stevens went outside and waited for Gorce near the door. He wanted to tell her she'd been right to ask that question.

Gorce seemed pleased to see him when she came out. "What'd she want to talk to you about?" he asked.

"She wanted me to ghostwrite her autobiography."

Stevens laughed. "No one would read it," he said. "We know far too much about her as it is."

"It don't matter—they've already given her a million-dollar contract."

"So what'd you say?"

"Well, she offered me ten percent. What do you think I said? I said yes."

"Congratulations," he said, happy for her. Outside he heard police sirens and what sounded like firecrackers.

"Thanks," she said. "Do you want t-t-to go out somewhere and celebrate?"

He looked at her with surprise. He had never known her to stutter before. She wasn't bad-looking, he thought, but too bony, and her chin and forehead were too long. She had to have gotten her job through her mad bravery and sharp common sense, because she sure didn't look like a blow-dried TV reporter. "Sorry," he said. "I told my girlfriend I'd call her when this whole thing was over."

"You never told me you had a girlfriend."

"Yeah, well, it never came up," he said. "See you, Gorce."

She looked at him a long time. "You know, Stevens, you better start being nicer to me," she said. "What if the aliens pick me to save the world next time?"

AFTERWORD

I t seems to me that there aren't nearly enough old women in science fiction. Or in real life, for that matter. When we put these people in nursing homes, send them to the margins of society, we are depriving ourselves of an extraordinary amount of accumulated wisdom. I wanted to write a story in which a neglected old woman has power.

A very minor reason for writing this story is that I wanted to call both men and women by their last names: Stevens and Gorce. Read almost any book on any subject and you'll find that the men are referred to by their last names and the women are called Joan and Betty Ann. Even feminists do this; even Douglas Hofstadter, in an essay *about* sexism in language ("A Person Paper on Purity in Language," *Metamagical Themas*) ends by calling William Safire "Safire" but Bobbye Sorrels "Ms. Sorrels." Once you start noticing this sort of thing you find it all over; it's weirdly insidious.

PRELIMINARY NOTES ON THE JANG

Simon stood in front of the door, panting a little from the climb up three flights of stairs, wondering if he had come to the right place. He checked the piece of paper in his hand again—3460C, the same as the address painted in cracking numbers over the peephole. The sound of an instrument—a sitar?—could be heard faintly through the door, and the hallway smelled like ginger. Why would his advisor want to live here? He shrugged and knocked. There didn't seem to be any bell.

The door opened—the sound of the instrument grew louder—and a man with an enormous black mustache stood in front of him. "Yes?" the man said. A threadbare oriental rug lay on the floor of the hallway behind him.

"I—I'm sorry," Simon said, stepping back. The man was standing too close, he felt his space being violated. "I have the wrong—That is, I'm looking for—I don't suppose Dr. Glass lives here."

"No, no doctors here," the man said. He wore loose green trousers and a yellow tunic. Simon couldn't place his accent. "You are sick?" He studied Simon intensely from under jet-black eyebrows. Eyes and eyebrows were the same color.

"No, he's not—not a medical doctor—" Simon said. "Never mind. Thanks anyway."

"No one here but my family," the man said. "We celebrate. My wife, my second wife, her husband, my cousins and their children, my wife's cousin, you have no word for it in English . . ."

Simon had started to draw kinship diagrams in his mind. The smell of spices was making him a little dizzy. He thought he could hear feet stamping beyond the hallway, bells shaking. His second wife's *husband*?

"Where—Where are you from?" Simon said, unable not to ask. He had probably transgressed somehow, broken some taboo, at the very least irritated his informant. His informant? Who was he kidding? But his textbooks had never mentioned how to deal with a situation like this.

"We are the Jang," the man said. He bowed courteously and began to close the door. "Good day." Simon turned away, aware that he had been dismissed. His mind was humming by the time he reached the street.

"Dr. Glass!" Simon said, running into his advisor's office.

"Hello, Simon," Dr. Glass said, looking up from his desk. "You missed a good party Saturday."

"I—Listen, I tried to find it, I ended up in this place—"

"Place?" Dr. Glass said. "Sit down, I've never seen you so excited. What do you mean?"

"I went to your house," Simon said. He fished out the scrap of paper from his pocket. "Here—3460, right? Only the guy who answered the door—"

"Twenty-four sixty," Dr. Glass said.

"What?"

"You went to the wrong place," Dr. Glass said. "You missed a great party."

"Oh," Simon said. "Well, listen. This guy who answered the door—he was foreign, right?—he said he was—his people were—the Jang. And then I went to the anthro library, and I did some research, and, well, I couldn't find them. Anywhere. And so I thought—So I'm going to do my thesis on them." He was out of breath when he finished.

Dr. Glass watched with amusement, one eyebrow lifted. For the past year Simon had led discussion groups and graded papers and kept office hours and done research when it was required and not done much of anything else. He had been a graduate student for four years, time enough to find a thesis topic and move on. Only nothing seemed to interest him—everything was either boring or had already been researched to death. Some days he had just given up and gone to the beach.

"How do you know this is what you want to work on?" Dr. Glass said. "What do you know about these people anyway?"

Simon sighed, running his hand through his already unruly hair. "Well, their kinship system—their kinship system is incredibly complex," he said. The door to the office opened and he looked up, grateful for the interruption.

"Hello, Dr. Glass," Linda said, coming in. Linda was another of Dr. Glass's students. "Hello, Simon. You missed a great party Saturday."

"I know," Simon said.

"All right," Dr. Glass said. "Write up some notes and bring them to me. I'll let you know what I think."

Simon stood again in front of the door of 3460C, a briefcase in his hand and a tape recorder draped over his shoulder. His heart pounded loudly as he knocked. The same man—he looked to be about fifty, Simon thought, athletic for his age—opened the door. This time the hallway smelled strongly of garlic.

"Yes?" the man said. "You find your doctor?"

Simon was surprised the man remembered. "Look I'd like to ask you a favor. I'd like to—to ask you a few questions. You and your family."

The man was unperturbed. "You are a cop, yes?" he said.

"No!" Simon said. "No, I'm—I'm a student. From UCLA. The university." He brought out his wallet and showed the man his registration card.

"Very nice," the man said dryly. "And if you were a cop you would have one of these cards also, yes?"

"No, listen," Simon said. "I'm a student. I study different cultures, peoples. I'd like to know more about you. About the Jang."

The man hesitated, then seemed to come to a decision. "All right," he said. "Come in. But we don't talk about our criminal pasts, all right?" In the dim light of the hallway he seemed to wink.

The room the man led him into had no furniture except four or five fat pillows arranged in a half circle. Rugs covered the old wood floor and hung from the walls, their colors mostly dark red, black or yellow. Portraits and yellow photographs of dark people Simon didn't recognize stood over the fireplace, and candles in glass cups were placed in front of them. Simon could smell cooking coming from another part of the apartment.

The man sat on one of the pillows and took out a pipe from his trousers. Simon sat next to him, sinking into the pillow with difficulty. He moved to turn his tape recorder on but the man stopped him with an upraised hand. "No," he said. "Not that. We think it steals our souls."

"Okay," Simon said. He took a pen and notebook out of his briefcase and wrote, "Recorder steals souls." "To begin with, what is your name?"

"What is yours?" the man said.

Simon blinked. "What?" he said.

"A custom among the Jang," the man said. "The stranger among us gives us his name first."

"Oh," Simon said. "Simon Montclair."

"I am called Mustafa," the man said. He bowed a little, from the waist.

"And your last name?" Simon said.

Mustafa shrugged. "What is a good last name in your country?" he said. "Smith. I am called Mustafa Smith."

Simon looked up sharply but Mustafa had not smiled. "And the rest of your family—are they called Smith as well?"

"If you like," Mustafa said.

"But you—What do you call yourselves?"

"Oh, you know," Mustafa said. "This and that. It depends on the country."

"Well, then what—" Simon began.

Mustafa said, interrupting him, "I will introduce you to the rest of the family. Would you like?"

"Of course," Simon said. Mustafa clapped his hands. Immediately the room seemed full of people. "My second wife, Francesca. And her husband, Tibor. And these are my cousins, these her brothers." Simon soon stopped trying to make sense of the names. "And my daughter, Clara."

Simon was looking at a young woman with long black hair and deep black eyes and skin that looked like silk. She wore an embroidered blouse and a flowing red skirt, and chains of coins fell from her earlobes. "Hello," Simon said weakly.

"Hello," she said.

There was an awkward silence. Then Simon recalled his purpose and took up his pen and notebook once more. "Your names," he said. "They're from different parts of the world, aren't they? I mean how—"

"We take the names of the country we are born in," Mustafa said. He dismissed the family with a wave of his hand. Simon watched Clara as she left the room.

"But where are you from?" Simon asked. "I mean originally."

Mustafa shrugged. "Who knows?" he said. "We are from

all over. The Jang are from every country on earth. There are Chinese Jang and New Guinea Jang. We are the travellers."

The session was a long one, and very satisfying for Simon. He made three charts of kinship before he got it right and saw Mustafa nodding in approval. These people seemed to marry whenever and wherever they liked: Once Mustafa surprised Simon by mentioning his wife in Spain. Simon learned that Mustafa had been a horse trader, a carpenter, a guitar player. He learned that the festival he had interrupted last week celebrated the birth of a saint and lasted three days, that Mustafa believed the king of Hungary could cure any illness, that white was the color of mourning and red the color of marriage.

At the end of the session, after they had agreed to meet every week, Mustafa said, "You go home and tell the police now, yes?" This time Simon definitely saw him wink.

"I'm going home and writing all this up," Simon said.

"Ah," Mustafa said. "And then what will you do with it?"

"I'm writing a—a dissertation," Simon said. "When I'm finished I'll be able to graduate. To leave school. Finally."

"And then?" Mustafa said. "What will you do?"

"Get a job," Simon said. He shrugged. "Probably teach somewhere."

"So this dissertation," Mustafa said thoughtfully. "It is important to you, yes?"

"Oh, yeah," Simon said fervently. "Listen, you guys saved my life."

Mustafa drew on his pipe and leaned back on the pillows, looking satisfied.

"Hi, Linda," Simon said, coming into Dr. Glass's office. "Where's Glass?"

Linda shrugged. "Don't know," she said. "I've been waiting an hour."

Simon looked at papers on Dr. Glass's desk, walked to the

window and looked out. "I hear you've found a thesis topic," Linda said.

"Oh, yeah," Simon said. He laughed. "Finally." He turned to face her.

"Sounds exciting," Linda said. "Imagine stumbling on a tribe here in Los Angeles." Linda was going to the Australian outback in summer. "What are they—gypsies?"

"No," Simon said. His caution about revealing his information fought with his need to tell someone and lost. "They call themselves the Jang. Means the People, of course. They know the gypsies, they've travelled with them, but they don't consider the gypsies part of the people."

"That's great," Linda said. "I wonder why no one's ever heard of them. You couldn't find anything in the library?"

Simon shook his head.

"What does Dr. Glass say?" Linda said. "Hey, it's too bad you missed his party Saturday. It was lots of fun."

"I know," Simon said. "And it doesn't look good for me to miss my advisor's party. I got lost."

"Don't worry," Linda said. "There'll be another one."

"I still don't know where the man lives," Simon said.

"Well, next time I'll show you," Linda said. "We can go together."

"Okay," Simon said. Linda smiled at him and he realized that somehow the idea of the two of them going to a party together had turned into a date in her eyes. What have I gotten myself into? he thought. She wasn't bad looking, shoulder-length brown hair, face too thin, chin maybe a little too pointed. Unbidden, the face of Clara rose in his mind.

"Listen, I'm tired of waiting," Linda said. "Do you want to go to Westwood for a cup of coffee?"

"Sure," Simon said.

Once at the coffee shop it seemed the most natural thing for Simon to offer to pay for the coffee and for Linda to accept. Mating rituals of North American peoples, Simon thought. But when he took out his wallet he found he had no money. He remembered getting twenty dollars from an automatic teller just that morning, and remembered too Mustafa's face, eyes gleaming, white teeth showing in a smile.

"You stole from me," Simon said.

"What?" Mustafa said. He lit his pipe and offered it to Simon.

Simon refused, too angry to care about the significance of the ritual. "Listen, you people stole from me. When I got here last week I had twenty dollars. And when I left it was gone. I don't like that. There has to be trust between us, Mustafa."

Surprisingly, Mustafa laughed, showing clean white teeth. "Of course," he said. "And I will tell you what it is. We had to learn if you were from the cops, yes? And so Luis, my first wife's cousin's boy, looked in your wallet. It is hard work, stealing a man's wallet and then replacing it so that he suspects nothing. And so Luis probably thought he deserved something for his trouble. That's the way it is in your country, is it not, hard work is rewarded?"

"Yes, and stealing money is rewarded by jail," Simon said, still angry.

Mustafa laughed again. "But now," he said. "We know now that you are not from the cops, we know that we can trust you. Surely that was worth twenty dollars?"

Despite himself Simon began to laugh too. What was twenty dollars, after all? Hundreds of ethnologists paid their informants. And now, as Mustafa said, these people knew they could trust him. He would just keep a closer watch on his wallet from now on.

"I will tell you what," Mustafa said. "In exchange for the twenty dollars I will read your palm. All right? All right!"

Bemused, carried away by Mustafa's enthusiasm, Simon held out his palm. "Ah!" Mustafa said. "I see—I see a woman. Hair to her shoulders, blond hair or brown. A beautiful woman." Linda? Simon thought. He would have never called Linda beautiful. "You know her, yes? She will be important to you, very important. I see you leaving school, you and her together. You are finished with school. And you are ready to start a new life." Mustafa looked up. "That is all I can see today," he said. "Is it helpful to you?"

Simon shrugged. "I don't know," he said.

"Maybe it will be helpful later," Mustafa said. "And maybe I can be helpful today. Today is a feast day. And you, since you are now worthy of trust and not a cop, are invited along. We celebrate."

"A feast day?" Simon said, beginning to get excited, not quite believing his luck. "For what?"

"Our saint," Mustafa said. "Ana, the mother of all the Jang. It is her birthday today." He offered his pipe to Simon and this time Simon took it. "You will stay for dinner, of course."

Simon coughed. "I'd be honored," he said, wiping his eyes. He followed Mustafa into the dining room.

Simon tried to take notes during the meal, but his pen and notebook got in the way and he gave up. Everything was delicious. "What is this?" he asked, having noticed that the Jang talked with their mouths full.

"Hedgehog," someone said, one of the brothers or cousins or husbands.

Simon nearly stopped eating. And yet it was good. Everything was good. He took a second helping and washed it down with wine.

Everyone was talking loudly. Simon thought he heard bells again, and someone dancing, but when he looked around all he saw were the people at the table. The room was growing dim, the candleflames spiraling up to the ceiling. His notebook fell off his lap to the floor and he realized he had dozed off for a minute. Clara's face shone across the table and he smiled at her.

Then it seemed as if they had gone outside and into

brightly-painted caravans smelling of hay. The horses (Horses? Simon thought. In Los Angeles? But he was too tired to look outside) brought them to a grassy field surrounded by tall trees standing like sentinels. A stream splashed somewhere in the distance. The men got out their guitars and began to play. Men and women danced, feet stamping. Bells jangled.

The full moon was rising. In the empty space above the meadow the sky looked like a banner filled with stars. Simon looked from the moon to Clara's face and to the moon again. I should be taking notes, he thought, and struggled to rise. "Hush," Clara said. "Rest. Everything is all right." He trusted her voice. The music wove through his dreams.

He woke the next day in his room, though he did not remember coming home. He groaned and rolled over. The notebook lay open beside his bed. "Preliminary Notes on the Jang," the notebook said in his handwriting.

He sat up carefully. His head seemed heavy, about to fall off. There were pages and pages of notes, most of them illegible, citing almost every anthropologist he had studied or heard of. "Trickster god—see Amer. Indian myth," one of the notes said. Then a scrawl, then "Mercea Eliade," then a page and a half of scrawls, and then what looked like "cf. Jim Henson's Muppets." He squinted, hoping the words would say something else, but they stayed the same.

Pieces of the night before were coming back to him. He remembered dreaming, remembered that they had all dreamed, that they had all had the same dream. It was the dream of the tribe's origins, how Ana, mother of the Jang, had disobeyed her mother the moon and was sent out to wander the world forever.

His headache was gone. He was trembling with excitement now. *They had all had the same dream.* What had he discovered? This was bigger than he had thought. He would be the next Carlos Casteneda, legend of the UCLA anthro department. Best-sellers, lecture tours, his paper on "The Collective Unconscious of the Jang" considered seminal in the field. . . . He dressed slowly, organizing his notes in his mind.

He dreamed of the feast in the meadow nearly every night that week. Clara was there, bending over him in the moonlight, kissing him. Sometimes it was Linda instead of Clara, and then he would wake dissatisfied, feeling that something had been taken from him. He began to avoid Linda, stopping by Dr. Glass's office only when he knew Linda would not be there. He visited Dr. Glass every day now, excited, hardly able to wait for the next session with Mustafa, but he said nothing about the feast night. He wanted to save that for later.

Clara, not Mustafa, answered his knock at the next session. "Where—Where's your father?" Simon said.

"I don't know," Clara said.

"I was supposed to meet him today," Simon said, a little impatient. "At—" He looked at his watch. "At three o'clock."

Clara laughed. "And you expected him to be here?" she said. "You don't know much about the way we figure time."

"Well," Simon said. "Can I wait for him? Or could you— Would you answer some questions?" He wouldn't mind getting to know Clara better. And her answers would give him insight into the customs of the women of the tribe.

Clara shrugged. "All right," she said.

"Great," Simon said. She led him into the room with pillows and sat down.

Simon sat and took out his notebook. "To begin with—" he said.

"Why don't you use a tape recorder?" Clara asked.

"I—" Simon stopped, confused. "Your father told me you think it steals your souls."

"He told you that?" Clara said.

"Here," Simon said, showing her the page in the notebook as if that would prove something. Was she laughing at him? "My first entry. 'Recorder steals souls.' You mean he wasn't telling me the truth?"

Clara leaned back in the pillows. "Everything we say is a lie," she said. Simon sat upright and started to say something, but she wasn't finished. "Our native tongue is quite different from yours. Everything we say must be translated, put in sounds foreign to us. What would be pure truth in my language comes out muddy and unclear in yours. We cannot help but lie, you see. We are exiles, and all exiles lie."

What was she telling him? How many of his notes were wrong? He chose a question at random. "Why did your father tell me the recorder would steal his soul?"

"I don't know," Clara said. "You'd have to take that up with him."

Simon paged nervously through his notes. "Trickster god—see Amer. Indian myth," he read. He wondered what he had gotten himself into. "Where—Where did you learn to speak English?" he asked, to gain time. "You speak very well."

"I was at the university," Clara said. She tucked her legs inside her long skirt. "Same as you."

"The university?" Simon asked. Clara looked at him impassively. "I—Well, I'm surprised. It doesn't seem like the Jang would send their children to the university. Especially the daughters."

"Why not?" Clara said. Simon winced a little under her even gaze. "It's the daughters, the women, who have to make a living, after all."

"You—You do?"

"Well, of course," Clara said. "The men's status depends on how well their women support them. The more money his wives make the more prestige the man has. Men aren't expected to work."

"They aren't?" Simon asked. He was aware he sounded stupid, unprofessional. "But Mustafa told me—" He looked through his notes. "Mustafa was a horse trader, a carpenter, a guitar player."

Clara laughed. "He plays the guitar, certainly," she said. Then, aware that something more was being asked of her, she said, "I don't know why he told you that. You'd have to ask him."

The session went a little better after that. Clara told him about burial customs, superstitions, the organization of the tribe. Toward the end Simon put away his notebook, and they talked a little about UCLA. Clara had even had a beginning anthropology class with Dr. Glass and she did an excellent imitation of him raising one eyebrow and looking out at his students. Simon was so charmed by her he forgot to ask about the dreams, about what really happened in the meadow the night of the feast of Ana. He wondered how he could ask about courtship rituals without offending her.

Finally he looked at his watch. "It's getting late," he said. "I've got to go. Listen, when I come back next week could we pick up where we left off? I've still got a few questions to ask you."

"Sure," Clara said. "I don't see why not." She walked him to the door. "Good night," she said, and added a phrase in her language. She had told him it meant "Luck travel with you."

Simon stopped at a fast food place on the way home and got a burger. Then he went straight to his room to look through his notes. He felt as if he were glowing, as if people on the street could see him radiate light. His thesis was turning out far better than he'd expected, and he'd met a dark exotic woman who seemed to like him. *Maybe that's why I got interested in anthropology,* he thought, remembering whole afternoons spent looking through his parents' copies of *National Geographic. I wanted to meet dark exotic women.*

A half an hour later he had to stop, aware that something was wrong. Mustafa had told him the Jang believed in an afterlife, but Clara had mentioned reincarnation. Mustafa had said the Jang didn't eat beef, but Clara had given him a recipe with beef in it. Mustafa had told him about a long and beautiful wedding ceremony, but Clara had said two people were considered married if they'd simply shared a meal and a bed.

Could there be two sets of customs, one for men and one for women? No, not with this much disparity between them. His agitation grew the more he compared Clara's and Mustafa's sessions. He knew he couldn't wait until next week. Angry now and a little frightened, he got into his car and drove to Mustafa's apartment.

He could hear voices raised in argument as he climbed the stairs. A man and a woman were shouting in the Jang's dark rolling language, exchanging insults like thunder. Simon hesitated a little before the door, but his anger overcame everything else and he knocked loudly.

The argument stopped in mid-sentence. Mustafa opened the door, his face flushed, his eyebrows lowered. Clara stood behind him in the hallway.

Simon had never seen Mustafa so angry. It terrified him, made him want to turn around and leave. Then he remembered his thesis, his future, and summoned up the courage to stay. "You lied to me," he said to Mustafa.

"Did we?" Mustafa said. His voice was dangerously low.

"Your information is totally different from Clara's," Simon said. "It's like two different cultures. One of you lied."

Abruptly Mustafa's expression changed. "Well, come in," he said. "Our guests do not stand out in the hall. Perhaps we can discuss this, yes?"

Simon followed them into the room with the pillows. A fire was lit in the fireplace, and candles glowed in front of the dark portraits on the mantelpiece. Clara sat down and looked at her nails, almost bored. She would not look at him.

"We would not like to mislead you," Mustafa said. "This thing you write, it is very important to you, yes?"

Simon nodded, still too angry to speak.

"Well then, perhaps we can come to an agreement," Mustafa said genially. "Is it worth, say, a thousand dollars? A thousand dollars for the correct information, for the truth about the Jang?"

"What?" Simon said weakly. He felt as if he'd been hit. He looked at Clara for reassurance but she did not look up. At least, he thought, she has the decency to be embarrassed.

"Come now, a thousand dollars," Mustafa said. "That's not so much. And then your future is secure, you have a teaching job, you are all set."

"Don't be ridiculous," Simon said. "I don't have a thousand dollars. And anyway I don't have to do my thesis on the Jang. There are millions of topics, millions of cultures."

"Yes, but are you willing to spend another four years waiting for one of them?" Mustafa said. How did he know that? Simon thought. "Another four years at the university, waiting for a topic of interest? Come, we will be reasonable. Eight hundred dollars. In a few months it will be time for the Jang to travel again, maybe to cross the water. Think of your notes, your work, all wasted. We can finish our sessions before we leave, and then you can teach, you can settle down, you can marry Linda—"

"Marry Linda?" Simon said, shocked. "Why?"

For the first time Simon saw Mustafa look confused. "Why? You are in love with her," Mustafa said. He sounded uncertain.

Simon laughed. He felt as if he were pressing his advantage, but he had no idea what his advantage was. "What gives you that idea?"

"Because of the dreams," Clara said suddenly. Mustafa said something to her in the language of the Jang but she ignored him. "Because of the dreams we gave you."

"You gave me dreams?" Simon said. "Those dreams about Linda? And about Clara?"

Clara looked at Simon for the first time. He found it impossible to translate her expression. Surprise? Gratitude?

"You—You dreamed about Clara?" Mustafa said. It was easy to recognize Mustafa's expression, not so easy to find an explanation for it. It was defeat.

"Yes, I did," Simon said. "Now will someone please tell me what's going on?"

Mustafa was silent. "We are the Jang," Clara said finally. "We worship Ahitot, son of the moon, brother of Ana, our brother. The trickster god, you would call him. He tells us to defy authority and to aid lovers. He teaches us to dream together, and we dream the stories of the tribe. Like the story of Ana, that you dreamed with us. And he tells us to aid lovers. We were to help you and Linda."

"Me and—and Linda?" Simon said. "But what gave you the idea we were lovers?"

"Ahitot told us in our dreams," Clara said. "But then you met me. My father wanted to meet you. He called you and you came to learn about us. My father wanted to make money." She looked at her father accusingly, as if to say, You see where your scheming gets you?

"Your father—called me?" Simon asked.

"Yes," Clara said. "That is another thing Ahitot has taught us to do. We can change reality by our dreams."

This was too much. This was worse than the conflicting information he had been given earlier. They were laughing at him, mocking him. "You can stop it now," he said. "I give up, all right? I'm going home. I'm not going to listen to any more. This is crazy."

"You do not believe me?" Clara said. Once again she looked at him impassively, incapable of being contradicted. Her eyes shone in the firelight. "Who do you think it was who changed the address on your piece of paper so that you would come here and not to your advisor's? It changed because we dreamed it."

Simon could not move. He felt he was being called upon to assimilate too much, to believe too many impossible things at once. Mustafa spoke into the silence. "My daughter would like to share a meal with you," he said.

Clara looked at her father, horrified. He had wanted to embarrass her, that much was clear, but Simon understood nothing else of what was happening. "A meal and a bed," Mustafa said, clarifying.

Had Clara told him the truth about the significance of sharing a meal and a bed? "You want—you want to marry me?" he asked, and as he asked it it did not seem so absurd.

Clara looked into the fire. "That is what we were arguing about, my father and I, when you came," she said. "It is rare—very rare—for a Jang to marry someone from outside the tribe."

Simon thought of the wild music, the dancing in the moonlight. He thought of his years as a graduate student, four years of sterility, with more to come. Clara was asking him to live with the Jang, to share their dreams, travel to far countries with them and become involved in the weave of the tribe in a way impossible for any anthropologist. He walked over to the fireplace and looked at Mustafa. "I'm sorry if it disturbs you, sir," Simon said. The blaze consumed his notebook. "But I would like very much to accept your daughter's offer."

AFTERWORD

J ang" was written around the same time as "Tourists" and
shares many characteristics with it—a puzzled young man,
a strange and magical society, an abandonment of a former
life. If there is a theme to the stories in this volume it is seen
most clearly in these two, which are about the ways in which
magic makes its presence felt in the mundane world, erupt-
ing through the rime of everyday life like a flower pushing its
way through pavement.

   I have to admit to a heresy here: I've never agreed with
Arthur C. Clarke's dictum that any sufficiently advanced
technology is indistinguishable from magic. Magic is something utterly different from technology; it has a very different
feel to it. A magician is part scholar, part poet, part warrior,
part priest or priestess. Any idiot can turn on a light switch.

A TRAVELLER AT PASSOVER

T he phone rang the minute Emily got home from work. She hung up her coat and yelled for Heather—"You home, kid?"—and finally answered it on the fourth ring.

"Hello?" the person at the other end said, as if uncertain she had reached the right number. And for a moment Emily didn't recognize the voice, it had been that long.

"Hello," she said.

"Emily." She heard relief in her mother's voice, but something more as well—trepidation, probably. "I was wondering—well, we'd like to know—that is, Passover starts next week." She was silent, waiting for Emily's reply. When it didn't come she said, "Well, we'd like it if you came over for the first night."

"We?" Emily said. "Or you?"

"Please. He misses you."

"Does he? He's got a funny way of showing it. Why can't he tell me so himself?"

"It's hard for him, you know that—"

"Actually I don't know it. I never noticed that it was hard getting him to talk. The problem was always shutting him up."

She heard her mother's in-drawn breath, and then the sound of static on the line. She'd gone too far. Or maybe not—how far were you allowed to go if your father had more or less disowned you? It was an interesting question. Probably the etiquette books didn't cover it.

"I called to ask you to dinner," her mother said. "Heather deserves to get to know her grandparents."

"And whose fault is it that she doesn't?" Emily said. Anger and resentment flared up so strongly she shook as she said it.

"I thought that for Heather's sake—"

Somehow her mother had hit on the only argument that would carry any weight at all. She had never been so good at getting her own way when Emily was growing up. Her father had been the one Emily had had to watch out for. What else had changed in six years?

Emily forced her anger away. She owed it to Heather to try to lay aside old wounds, old scores. "All right," she said reluctantly.

"And please—don't argue with him."

That was the way she remembered her mother. It had been so easy to disobey her as a child, almost a game. "Did you ask him not to argue with me?"

"He never starts it—"

"He *does*. He's just cleverer about it than I am. Watch him if you don't believe me."

"All right, I'll ask him."

For a moment Emily felt sorry for her mother, for the way she and her father had used her as a game-piece in their skirmishes. "Okay, I'll be there," she said. "Should I bring something?"

"Oh, no." Her mother sounded hurt. If Emily brought anything it would mean that her mother had been lacking in some way, that all bounty did not flow from her mother's kitchen. She was remembering all the ways her family interacted now, and she sighed. What had she gotten herself into? Would Heather be able to hold her own? "We're looking forward to seeing you," her mother said.

Emily sat by the phone for a while after she had hung up, thinking about her family. She was fourteen, and had brought home a boy from school. She had thought about this boy every day for the past month and having him so close to her now made her breath hurt. Everything seemed sharper, more filled with meaning, around him, so that she felt that she had never really noticed anything until this moment. And her father had laughed and joked with him, and told him a story about being captured by gypsies as a child.

"Your father is so great," the boy had said. "I wish mine was like that."

She couldn't describe what she felt until much later. It was jealousy, pure and simple. Jealousy, and anger that someone she loved had spent two hours talking to her father when he should have been paying attention to her. "You know that nothing he said was true," she said.

"So what?" the boy said.

She was eighteen, and the family car she had been driving had been hit by a van which had then driven off before she could get the license number. She arrived home shaking, terror at what had nearly happened to her mingling with anger at whoever had hit her. And her father, instead of comforting her, instead of saying that she was fine and that was the important thing, had told her a story about being a truck driver, and the strange people he had met on the road.

Over the years she had learned that very few of his stories were true. The process had been slow and painful, like coming to terms with a chronic but non-fatal illness. He might have been a construction worker and a truck driver, and maybe he had even ridden the rails as a young man, but everything else had been elaborations, fantasies. In place of the conversations most kids had had with their fathers she had gotten stories. Endless stories.

But the stories had ended when she'd married Andy, who

wasn't Jewish. Tales of carnivals and princesses and magicians and pirates had suddenly given place to silence. And she wasn't at all sure that the silence hadn't been welcome, a space in which she could sort out who she really was, what was true and what was lies.

She and Andy had gotten divorced six months ago. It had been a friendly divorce; they still talked on the phone, and she had met him for lunch once when his business took him close by. How typical of her parents that they called after the divorce, that now she was their daughter again. But her anger had gone for good; she wondered only how she would survive an evening with her family.

At first, as she stepped into the entryway with Heather, she thought that nothing had changed. The house still smelled of tea and chicken. The bulky furniture of her childhood, the hi-fi cabinet and end tables and coffee tables, stood in their old places. The same worn trail on the rug led from the living room to the kitchen.

Her mother, coming forward shyly to kiss her, as if entertaining royalty, seemed the same too: small and worried and smelling of cosmetic creams and dish detergent. But when she moved back Emily saw the lines in her mother's face and the thickness of her new glasses. She'd changed the color of her hair, too; it was redder now. "Hello, Emily," she said. "I'm so glad you came. Your father's out in back."

Of course, Emily thought. I've got to go to him. I wonder if he set it up that way.

"Heather!" her mother said. "I didn't see you at first. Look at how you've grown."

Heather had never been shy. "Yes, I have," she said gravely.

"You were only two years old the last time I saw you. I bet you don't recognize me, do you?"

"Sure I do."

Emily wondered if that was true. She still remembered the time her mother had stopped by the house, furtively, as if scouting out enemy terrain. There had been an argument about, of all things, whether she could have Sinclair the dog. "He's *my* dog!" Emily had screamed as her mother hurried toward her car. "I raised him. He's not yours. Or Dad's either!" The entire block must have heard her. Since then they had communicated through Emily's brother David.

"Just leave Heather with me," her mother said. "We have a lot to catch up on. Your father's looking forward to seeing you."

Was that true? Emily made her way down the hall and past her parents' bedroom. Her old room was at the back of the house but she didn't look inside. From the kitchen she heard laughter: David and his wife and their two children.

The light was going from the sky as she stepped out onto the back porch. Her father looked up from his weeding. He had always been a stocky, vital man, with powerful shoulders and black eyes and curly black hair. It came as a shock to see that his hair had turned almost pure white. But when she got closer she noticed that aside from his hair he had not changed at all. Just for a moment she had hoped he had become smaller, shrunken. But she couldn't wish that of anyone, even him. And he would stay the same until he died; he was too stubborn for anything else.

Why hadn't she stayed in the house? She couldn't think of anything to say to him. Or maybe she had too much to say, and no way to manage it. Why didn't you visit for six years? Are your stupid principles more important than your daughter, your grandchild?

Just as he filled any space he entered he filled her silence with words. Anyone watching wouldn't have guessed that six years had passed since they'd last seen each other. "Emily! I hope you've brought Heather. She'll have to say the Four Questions, your brother's boys are older than she is. We've got eight people tonight—that's the largest Passover we've had since Aunt Phyllis and Uncle Moe moved away. Your mother's been cooking all week."

"Sure, Heather's a great reader," Emily said. You'll like her, she wanted to add, but she didn't know if that was true. He hadn't even visited when she was born, she thought, and, suddenly angry, she nearly said something she would regret. I won't argue if he doesn't, she thought, remembering the promise she had given her mother. "How've you been?"

"Fine, just fine. Your mother wants to go to Canada to see Phyl and Moe, and we're going to visit Quebec while we're there. I've always wanted to go someplace they speak French. I took a class at the local college. *Comment allez-vous?*"

She didn't understand him. "Listen, I think I hear Ma. I'd better go see if she needs any help."

He waved at her and returned to his weeds. Going inside felt like surrender, but she didn't think she could stay outside another minute. What did I expect? she thought. An apology?

In the house she helped set the table with David's wife Janet. "This is so great," Janet said. "My family never celebrated Passover when I was growing up."

"Wait till it's over before you say anything," Emily said.

Janet looked at her oddly. She wondered what her brother David had been saying about her. Did they think of her as the black sheep of the family, the one who had never fit in?

She went back into the kitchen to see what else needed to be done. David and his two sons had gone out to the backyard, and the family was now divided the way she remembered it from her childhood: the men standing and talking, the women working in the kitchen. Heather watched while her grandmother lifted a platter from the oven. Wonderful, Emily thought. What terrific role models we're showing her. The kitchen windows had steamed over from all the cooking.

"I think we're done here," her mother said. "Oh—Elijah's cup. Could you reach it, Emily? It's in the top cupboard there. Heather, go tell your grandfather we're ready.''

Emily would have wanted to be there when Heather met her father but she thought that her daughter could take care of herself. And maybe it would work out better this way; she knew she could hardly act neutral around him. Carefully she took down the goblet of cut crystal and filled it with wine.

She had been fascinated by the cup as a child, that something so weighty could be fashioned into such airy beauty. She remembered how the candlelight would shine from its facets. And sometime during the evening the wine in the goblet would disappear. Her father would tell her and David that Elijah had come, that they had missed him again this year. She had been eight or nine when she realized that her father had been the one to drink the wine, and then she'd felt angry and embarrassed, as if she'd been taken in by a confidence trick.

She took Elijah's cup to the table and set it in front of Heather. If her daughter got bored by the service at least she would have something to look at. Everyone except her father was already sitting down at the table: the chair at the head was empty. Finally he came into the room. He had washed and changed, but Emily could see the dirt beneath his fingernails.

Her father looked at the family with great satisfaction and made the blessing over the wine. ''The youngest child reads the Four Questions,'' he said when he had finished. ''Bob read them last year and Mike the year before, and now it's Heather's turn.''

Emily showed Heather the Four Questions in the Haggadah. She looked nervous but pleased by everyone's attention. ''Why is this night di—diff—''

''Different,'' Emily said.

''Different. Different from all other nights.'' Her voice, which had started out breathy, grew louder, more confident.

"Very good," Emily said when she had done.

"You have asked me the four questions and now I will answer you," her father said solemnly, exactly as he had said to her and her brother twenty and thirty years before. He began to read from the Haggadah in his sing-song old-fashioned Hebrew. *"Avadim hayenu l'Paro b'Mizraim."* We were slaves of Pharaoh in Egypt. . . .

She barely listened as her father told the story of Passover. The plagues God sent to Pharaoh. The flight of the Jews in the night. The parting of the Red Sea. Manna in the desert. Stories and miracles; no wonder her father enjoyed Passover so much. It was rooted in his blood and stretched back thousands of years. But no more; it would end here, with her and Heather. Heather would not be raised on this superstitious nonsense.

She watched Heather and wondered what her daughter made of it all. She couldn't be following it very well, even in the English translation printed alongside the Hebrew in the Haggadah. But Heather wasn't even trying to understand. She was watching her father as he read, a look of wonder on her face.

Damn! Emily thought. He's doing it to her, just like he used to do it to all my friends. She's fascinated by him, she's under his spell. What on earth did he say to her outside? I'd better set her straight about him before it's too late. It was Andy her grandfather had snubbed, after all. We're only here because of the divorce—I'll have to tell her that. And even then he didn't even have the courage to invite me back—he had to get my mother to do it.

She was so angry she didn't notice her father had stopped reading. That was quick—they must have shortened the ceremony considerably during the years she'd missed. The shorter the better, as far as she was concerned. She had to get Heather home and tell her a few things, the difference between truth and lies, for one.

Her mother and Janet got up and went into the kitchen

for the food. Her father had embarked on one of his stories. She had missed the beginning; he was somewhere in Prague, arguing with someone. She would bet any amount of money he had never been to Prague. He had been too young for World War Two and too old for Korea; he had probably never left the country in his life.

"So I said to the rabbi, I said, I know you have him there, up in your attic. And the rabbi says no, but he's smiling, so I think, you know, he's not telling me everything. I've heard the stories, I tell him, I know there's a golem in the attic in this synagogue in Prague. You know what a golem is?"

Bob and Mike and Heather watched him closely, as if he might turn into something magical and strange before their eyes. Their mouths were half-open. "A golem is a man made out of clay. A wise man had made this particular golem, the golem of Prague, and he put a verse from the Bible in its mouth, and the clay man got up and walked. And then the wise man put another verse in his own mouth, and he could fly."

"Which verse?" David asked.

"How do I know which verse? If I knew that I'd do it myself."

"People can't fly," Heather said.

Good for you, Emily thought.

Her father looked at Heather. Emily remembered that look from her childhood; it was as if he'd chosen you for something special. It felt terrifying and exhilarating at once. To her credit Heather looked back at him, unblinking.

"How do you know that, young lady?"

"Well, they can't. If you want to fly you have to get in a plane. I have to take a plane to visit my father."

"It's just a story," David said.

"That's the point," Emily said. "When you're a kid you don't know that. I don't want Heather growing up to believe all this mystical nonsense."

"But she knows what's real and what isn't. You heard her. She's not stupid."

"She doesn't know. That's why she had to say something, to make sure. He's confusing her." And now I'm talking about my child in the third person, something I swore I'd never do, Emily thought.

"Oh, come on, Emily. We knew, when we were kids."

"No, we didn't. We *believed* it. You don't remember."

"Maybe you believed it. I didn't."

She knew he was wrong. He had forgotten it all; he thought their childhood had been idyllic because he had been the pampered one, the son. Sometimes she wished she could talk to him about growing up, wished they could compare maps of the country of their childhood. She thought she might like getting to know him. But it was probably too late: he had had six years of hearing their father recreate their past just as he had fabricated his own. David was beyond knowing what had happened and what hadn't. The gulf between them was too great for her to cross.

Her mother and Janet came in with the last two plates, piled high with chicken and salad and potatoes, and the family started to eat. As always her mother waited until everyone else had started before she would begin. "Emily," she said. "Please don't argue."

"I—" Emily said.

"You either, David," her mother said. She had learned a few things over the years.

Heather reached out in front of her to play with Elijah's cup. "Uh uh, don't touch that, young lady," her grandfather said. "Do you know whose glass that is?"

"No," Heather said.

"That's Elijah's glass. Do you know who Elijah is?"

Heather shook her head.

"A prophet," Mike said.

"That's right, a prophet. But more than that. When the Messiah comes, Elijah will come before him, announcing him. And tonight he visits every Jewish house in the world, drinking from the glasses we set out for him. What do you think of that? He must get awfully drunk, don't you think?"

Bob and Mike laughed. Heather, more serious, said, "Have you ever seen Elijah, Grandfather?" Emily thought she might be trying to get at the truth of this story too.

"Me? No. But my grandfather, your great-great-grandfather, he saw him once, when he was a small child."

Bob and Mike put down their forks, intrigued, hoping for another story. All around the table the rest of the family stopped eating and looked up expectantly. Satisfied that he had everyone's attention her father took a sip of his wine and began.

"My grandfather lived in Russia, a long time ago. They didn't treat the Jews very well in Russia, you know, they were very anti-Semitic. Do you know what that means?"

Heather shook her head. Emily remembered her father explaining the word to her when she was young, remembered the same tinge of sadness in his voice, so that she knew that whatever the word meant it was bad, very bad.

"It means they didn't like the Jews. Every so often they would sweep though a Jewish village and beat people, and steal things, and smash everything that was left. And when we celebrated Passover they would tell each other that we drank the blood of Christian babies, and then they would break into our houses and even kill a few people.

"This particular Passover, the father of the house came back from the synagogue with a stranger, an old man. 'He's travelling by himself and he doesn't have anyone to celebrate with,' he said to his wife. 'I told him he was welcome at our house.'

" 'Of course,' the mother said, even though they were very poor and hardly had enough food for themselves.

"So they put another chair at the table and sat down, and just as they'd started the service they heard a knock at the door. The father opened the door but there was no one there. The flames of the candles nearly blew out in a sudden gust of wind. The father looked down and saw a young boy slumped on the doorstep. He looked closer and saw that the boy was dead.

"Sometimes, you see, the Russians would kill children, Christian children, and leave them on the doorsteps of Jewish homes. And then they would come by and look for this child, and the whole family would be blamed. They'd be arrested, or worse. So the father felt frightened, terribly frightened. He didn't know what to do. There was no time to bury the boy, or take him away. The mother was saying, 'Who is it?' and he stepped in front of the body so she wouldn't see it.

"But the stranger had come up behind him, and he knew what to do. 'Quick!' he said. 'This boy is about the same size as your youngest.' That was my grandfather. 'Dress him in his clothes and seat him at the table. When they come looking we'll say this boy is one of your children.' "

Her father took another sip of wine. Emily looked at Heather and wondered what she would make of all this. Whenever her family got together they would tell stories of atrocities against the Jews. She felt they were showing her little training films, and the lesson she had to learn was that to be Jewish was to suffer. But she had never encountered any anti-Semitism in her life, though she knew her father had. Did she want Heather to grow up knowing this long and bloody history?

Her father continued the story.

"The father didn't like that, but he could see he had no choice. So they carried the boy inside and dressed him in my grandfather's clothes, and they sat him at the table, his head down. And no sooner had they done this then there was another knock on the door.

"The father went to answer it, and another gust of wind came inside and shook the candle flames. Five or six soldiers stood outside on the doorstep. 'A woman reported her boy missing,' one of them said. 'We're checking all the houses in the area.'

"Well, the father couldn't say anything, but the stranger waved them in. 'Of course, of course,' he said. 'Anything we can do to help.' He showed them around the house, which was very small, only three or four rooms. 'As you can see, the boy isn't here. I hope you find him.' And he led the soldiers back to the door.

"But one of them stopped and looked at the dead child, sitting face down at the table. 'He's been ill,' the stranger said. 'We didn't want to wake him for the service.'

" 'He looks like the one reported missing,' the soldier said.

"The father watched as he moved toward the table. He couldn't move, couldn't do anything. What would they do when they discovered the dead boy? His family, his children, would all be killed. He knew how the mother of this boy must feel. It's a dreadful thing to lose a child, the worst thing in the world."

Her father looked at Emily as he spoke. There it was again, that intense black gaze, the feeling of being singled out. He wanted her to understand something.

"The stranger went to the table. 'Rise, my child,' the stranger said. 'The time has come to say the Four Questions.' "

No one at the table spoke. They had forgotten to breathe. And suddenly Emily knew what it was her father wanted her to understand, though it had taken her a lifetime to learn it. He had never told her how he felt because he couldn't; the only way he knew was to tell stories. When he'd talked about losing a child he'd meant her. That was the only apology she would ever get for six years of silence, but it was enough. More than enough.

"There was silence in the room," her father said, finishing the story. "Some silences are terrible. Then the young boy stood, and in a clear voice he said, 'Why is this night different from all other nights?' "

Everyone at the table sighed at the same time, a pent-up breath of relief. "The traveller, the old man," her father said. "That was Elijah."

"Was that a true story, Grandfather?" Heather asked.

"True?" her father said, looking at Emily. She nodded to show she understood. Some silences are terrible. "That's the way my grandfather told it to me, and I believed it. Not that I don't believe it now, on the first night of Passover, when everything is possible."

—For Amy and Alex Galas

AFTERWORD

When Kristine Rusch asked me to write a story for the holiday issue of *Pulphouse* I misunderstood the assignment. Her letter asked for stories about holidays "from Halloween to Valentine's Day." She meant, of course, that she wanted stories that took place between October 31 and February 14, but I thought she wanted writers to deal with themes running the gamut of holidays, everything from Halloween to Valentine's Day.

So I wrote about Passover. I've never been very good at writing to editorial order.

I've always felt that there's a mystic quality to Passover. It seems to lend itself to fantasy more than any other Jewish holiday. It is, after all, a night of recounting of miracles.

When I went to Los Angeles for Passover the year I wrote this story my uncle, without knowing it, gave me some of the best lines. It is to him and to my aunt that "A Traveller at Passover" is dedicated.

INFINITE RICHES

H e heard the key turn in the lock: after so many years he
could pick out that sound from a hundred other noises.
He looked up from his books, heard the muffled conversation and laughter outside his cell. Then, suddenly, his small
room filled with men.

There seemed to be hundreds of them; he was not used to
seeing so many people at once. He had to blink to allow his
vision to accommodate them all.

"Sir Walter," one of them said. He spoke a little scornfully, as if Raleigh's knighthood no longer meant anything.

"Aye?" Walter said.

"The king is considering granting you a pardon."

"Is he?" Walter heard the dry, sardonic tone in his words,
but he could not bring himself to beg, not even now.

"Aye. He wants to know the location of El Dorado."

"Ah," he said, not allowing his expression to change. He
had heard rumors of the King James's financial problems
and had seen immediately how he could use those problems
to his advantage. He had written several people, bribed several more. His heart beat faster. Could it be that after twelve
years he would finally be allowed his freedom?

Now he noticed the fine clothes of the men who had come to deal with him, all of them the king's courtiers and favorites. He stood; he topped the tallest by nearly a head. "Aye," he said. "Tell the king I'll find him El Dorado."

They exchanged courtesies and then the finely-dressed men—there were only half a dozen of them, after all—took their leave. He had not recognized any of them: a whole generation had come to power since he had been imprisoned. He wondered how much his lack of knowledge of court life would hurt his cause.

He would have to be cautious now, very cautious. He would have to plan carefully, to call in favors from all the men he had helped over the years. But he was too excited to sit still. He began to pace his small cell, thinking of the strange history that had brought him to the Tower.

It was true that he had served the old queen, Elizabeth, for so long that the accession of King James had caught him unprepared. And his first meeting with the new king had hardly been propitious: "On my soul, man, I have heard rawly of thee," James had said. He knew then that while he had been mourning his queen his enemies had been busy with the old charges, the accusations of atheism, treason, Machiavellian policy. He was unready, his defenses down. In a very short time he had been sentenced to imprisonment.

They were afraid of him, he understood that. "Damnably proud," they had called him, even before his fall from favor. And all the men from the old reign had died, Leicester and Drake and Essex; he alone had survived into this drab, petty age. It was no wonder James hadn't known what to do with him, that the king had taken the path of cowardice and sent him to prison.

Not that his confinement had been as harsh as some. He had been allowed a small garden, and a shed filled with retorts and copper tubing in which to conduct chemical experiments. He had had leisure enough to begin to write a book called *The History of the World;* if he was not to be freed perhaps he would continue with it and take it beyond the year 168 B.C., where he had left it. Two years after he had come to the Tower of London his friend the Earl of Northumberland had been imprisoned as well, and together they had carried out experiments, talking long into the night. But he would not be sorry to leave—nay, he would not. If the king wanted him to find El Dorado he would be ready. Perhaps his entire life had been spent in preparation for this voyage.

The king's men returned a few days later. He was pacing his cell again when they came; he knew its measurements to within an inch on every side. This time they seemed cautious, unwilling to promise anything. "How can we be certain there is such a place as El Dorado?" one of them said.

"You know that I've visited Guiana once before," he said, and then stopped. Did they, in fact, know anything at all? Gone were the days when his doings furnished gossip for all of London. "In 1595, over twenty years ago. All along the river we heard stories about the city of gold, and its tall golden towers and streets of silver. The little children there use precious stones to play with. And in their ceremonies their chieftain covers himself with oil and his men take hollow canes and blow powdered gold over his body. The Golden One, they call him."

He saw how eagerly the men looked up at the mention of gold. He would have to play variations on that tune, find ways of introducing the subject again and again.

"Why did your expedition turn back?"

"We were hungry and tired, and many of us were sick. We had spent most of our time trying to find our way out of the Orinoco delta. And I expected to be back within the year. Certainly I did not think so much time would have passed before I could return."

He realized he spoke as if the king had already granted him his pardon. Perhaps he should be more circumspect. Nay, why should he be? It was the king who had humbled himself and come to entreat with him; these men were the supplicants, not he.

"Why do you think you'll find El Dorado this time?"

"Because we learned how to navigate the delta. When I return I'll be able to sail directly up the river, toward the city of gold."

"Will you take treasure from the Spaniards?"

He grinned. "Certainly. How else could I raise funds for the expedition?"

"The king forbids it. He wants to make peace with Spain."

Peace with Spain, Elizabeth's old enemy? It was nearly unthinkable. What else had happened at court while he had been imprisoned?

They kept him talking for hours, circling him so that he was never sure who would speak next. Days later they came back with more questions, and they returned often after that. When they left he would review what they had asked, how he had answered. Had he seemed confident, but not so confident that James would have reason to fear him? Could they trust him to remember a voyage he had made over twenty years ago? He tried to find out from them what the king thought, but he could discover nothing.

Then, on a day like every other day, so that he had had no warning, no time to plan, they signaled to the jailer and let him go free.

He sent a messenger to his wife Bess in Sherbourne immediately, telling her about his release. Then, while the king and his men waited anxiously for him to meet with navigators, sailors, shipbuilders and merchants, he spent days doing nothing but walking the streets of London. The skies that week were overcast, but to him everything seemed too bright, as if he'd stepped out into a summer's day at noon. He had to squint to take it all in. He laughed a little to himself. Why should he hazard his life to travel half a world away? Here in front of him lay El Dorado, the city of gold.

London had changed as if with a wave of a sorcerer's wand. Streets that had been mud when he had gone into the Tower were paved over with cobblestones. New buildings had gone up or been magicked out of recognition; in the Strand his own former house, Durham House, had become part of a two story arcade of shops.

But the hardest thing of all to understand was Westminster Abbey, where Queen Mary and Queen Elizabeth, Catholic and Protestant, now lay side by side in their carved tombs. How could they have forgotten the half-sisters' enmity in so short a time? Was he the only one who remembered? Could it be that he was unfit to live in this world?

And always, wherever he walked, he saw the walls of his prison cell, hemming his vision in. His heart would pound, and he would have to turn quickly to make sure this was not some evil dream, that he had truly left the Tower. Then the outlines would fade and he would be back in London, a traveller from the fantastic past.

After a few days Bess arrived in London. She had visited him often in the Tower—his son Carew had even been conceived there—but there was a world of difference between seeing her as a prisoner and as a free man. They spent long hours talking over his plans and the voyage ahead. She was worried for him, of course, but she understood that he had no choice. It was only by finding El Dorado that James would grant him his freedom. Neither one said what they both thought, that if he failed he would at best be sent back to the Tower to rot. At the worst he would lose his life.

"Why don't you take the ships and set sail for another country?" she asked him. "You did good service in France— they would certainly remember you there, and treat you well."

"I can't, Bess," he said. "I have a commission from the

king.'' But he wondered if he was telling her the truth, or if it was only his famous pride that kept him from doing as she suggested. He was an old man of sixty-three now, and he felt every one of his years. How could he be certain he would succeed? But nay—he could not let himself think that way.

And then, to the great relief of the king's informer who had been despatched to follow him, he began finally to ready himself for the voyage. His son Wat, who was to sail with him, came to London from Sherbourne. He met with captains, and saw shipbuilders in Deptford, and arranged for the sale of everything he owned to pay for the fleet. On June 12, 1617, he and his men set sail for Guiana.

His return to Guiana was marked by one disaster after another. Most of his crew became ill on the voyage, and one of the ships went down in a storm; not enough of his sailors had remained well enough to man it. And he caught the fever as well; when they reached the island of Trinidad he had to stay behind and recover while his son and others went on.

Two months later they returned with the worst possible news: against all orders the men had attacked the Spanish fort of San Thome. Two had died, one of them his impetuous son Wat.

It seemed to signal the end of all his hopes. He returned to his cabin and stayed there for days, thinking and writing in his journal. How could he break the news about their son to Bess? And what would James say when he returned without the location of El Dorado?

By the third day he came to a decision. He would not think about failure. He had hazarded much on this last great expedition, and he would succeed. Fortune's wheel would turn for him: he would come home in triumph, his ships heavy with the gold they carried. It would be his enemies, all the small-minded men who had gleefully predicted his failure, who would be laid low. He grinned and rubbed his leg, which had stiffened with sitting too long. By God, he would show them something about pride.

He chose men hastily and led them on board a wherry, and they set sail for El Dorado.

The journey down the Orinoco River was uneventful. They passed the Spanish fort and landed near the junction of the Orinoco and Caroni Rivers, and then went inland, following the landmarks Walter remembered.

As they walked Walter felt memories of his last voyage come flooding back. The bright birds, colorful as any fashionable court, crimson and purple and green. The strange smell in the air, half rottenness and half the odor of new growth. The grass as short as that of any parkland, cropped by the deer that walked over it unafraid.

But the plains seemed too vast; the grassland opened out like the sea in front of him. As he walked he saw the walls of his old prison rise up to contain it. He felt a prisoner's fondness for his cell, where he had had everything he needed, books and plants and chemicals. Infinite riches in a little room, he thought, remembering a line from a play by his old friend Christopher Marlowe. But Kit Marlowe was dead now, like too many others.

One of his men, Francis Molyneux, had come up beside him and said something to him. "What?" Walter asked.

"Look, sir," the man said.

He looked. Hundreds of tiny gold pebbles lay on the ground, sparkling in the sun. A few of the men were bending eagerly to pick them up. "Leave them," Walter said. "There'll be far more than this when we get to the mine."

He tilted his head to study the sun, trying to gauge how much longer they would be able to march. Afternoon had come while he had been deep in thought. Gold swam before his eyes.

They walked a few hours more. As the sun set they began to look for a place to make camp. Birds sang. On his last voyage he had seen termites and ants, snakes and the small boars called peccaries, and now he studied the ground carefully, trying to find a place where they would be safe.

"Sweet God," someone said in a high, terrified voice.

He looked up quickly. A group of people were heading for the camp, their shapes indistinct in the fading light. As they came closer he felt his heart turn cold. A premonition, he thought, terrified to his soul. An apparition. A warning of what might happen to me. For the men who approached the camp were headless.

Nay, not headless. He almost laughed with giddiness. Their eyes were in their shoulders, and they had mouths in the middle of their breasts. The Ewaipanoma. He had heard of them on his last expedition and had believed the stories, though some had doubted. He motioned to a man who knew some Spanish. "Hugh," he said, not taking his eyes from the strange beings in front of him. "Come here. I need you to translate."

Hugh moved next to him. "We greet you in the name of James, king of England by grace of God," Walter said.

The men listened gravely to Hugh's translation. One of them began to speak. For a moment Walter could not hear Hugh beside him or anything else, fascinated by the sight of the man's mouth moving in his breast. The two eyes in the shoulders blinked.

He forced himself to pay attention. "They greet you and ask you why you've come," Hugh said.

"Tell them we've come to find the city of gold."

To look at Walter the Ewaipanoma had to turn his entire body. He spoke directly to him, as if he understood that Walter was the leader of the company. "They say they've heard of it, but have never seen it," Hugh said. "They think it's to the east."

"I thank you very much for this information," Walter said. He could not keep his eyes away from the space above the man's shoulders, where he expected to see a head and found only a flat covering of skin. He forced himself to look at the man's chest; the eyes were too far apart to take both of them in at once. "Would you care to take your supper with us?"

Behind him he heard one of the men vomit on the ground. The thought of seeing a man eat through his breast had proved too much for him, probably.

"He says he thanks you, but they will not be able to eat with us," Hugh said. Now Walter saw that some of them carried birds tied to their backs. They were heading back after a hunt, no doubt. He felt disappointed; he would have liked to have learned more about the tribe. Already he was thinking of writing a second part to his book about Guiana; he felt certain it would prove even more popular than the first.

The Ewaipanoma took their leave. The company foraged for food and then stretched out on the ground to sleep. Soon they had all dropped off except Walter. He stared up at the unfamiliar stars, thinking of the mine. They were close indeed, if the Ewaipanoma had heard of the city. Soon he would have all he had worked for: freedom and riches, everything he desired. He watched the fiery stars wheel overhead. Toward dawn he slept.

He woke first and roused his men, and they set off. Though it was still early morning the sun burned fiercely overhead, and midges bit them on every uncovered surface. The pleasant grass gave way to rough outcroppings of granite. A few of the men grumbled as they walked over the rough ground but he barely noticed the discomfort.

Toward noon he saw another company riding toward them. He squinted against the sun, trying to make them out. Spaniards, or more of the Ewaipanoma? The strangers stopped their horses as they approached the company, and he saw the men were Indians, though slightly built. Nay, not men. Women. Amazons.

The women dismounted. One of them spoke. "They ask

who it is who rides through their country without leave," Hugh said.

Walter nearly grinned; he knew all about flattering queens. "By your leave, Your Majesty, we did not know that this was your country. We are looking for—"

The queen had apparently heard enough of Hugh's translation. "Who on this earth does not know about the country of women?" she said. "You must be strangers indeed."

"Aye, strangers from a very long way off. From across the ocean. I am Sir Walter Raleigh, knight. I served my queen until she died, and now serve James, king of England by grace of God."

He had hoped to impress her with talk of his queen, but she seemed more puzzled by his speech than anything else. She remained silent for a moment, and he had leisure to observe her and her tribe. They wore the breeches and shirts of men, but they grew their black hair long and braided it behind them. All carried bows nearly as tall as themselves and quivers of arrows. Behind one of the women, mounted on her horse, rode a small child. Some of them wore jewelry fashioned out of green stones and gold, bracelets and pins to tie up their hair. He had heard that they traded with El Dorado, these stones for gold. His eyes moved involuntarily to their breasts.

"Nay, Sir Walter, we do not cut off our breasts," the queen said. "Why should we do such a thing? That is a story men put out about us—we do not know why."

He flushed. The women strode closer to him and he backed away, confused. They were too bold, he thought. In all his life only one woman had acted so, as an equal with men, and she had been a queen.

One of his men laughed lewdly. Walter turned quickly. The man took a step toward the woman nearest him, grinning, but before he could reach her all the women around him had set arrows to their bows.

Francis Molyneux unsheathed his dagger and put it at the throat of the man who had laughed. "Not one step closer," he said. He twisted the man's arm behind him for emphasis.

"Nor will we choose among you for men to lie with," the queen said. She had not dropped her bow, or taken her eyes off the man she aimed at. "We choose only strong men, so that our daughters will be strong."

Angry now, Walter nearly made a retort he would regret later. Why should these foul harridans think he would lie with them? He searched for a neutral reply and finally said, "What do you do with the sons?"

"We send them to their fathers."

"Ah," he said. "My lady, we hope not to inconvenience you further. We are looking for El Dorado, the city of gold, and beg leave to ride through your country."

"Very well," the woman said. She returned the arrow to her quiver and mounted her horse. "Our country extends a half a day's walk in that direction. You must not kill any of our animals for food, or eat from any of our trees, or cut down our trees for your fires. If you do we will know it, and we will hunt you down and kill you."

"Have you seen El Dorado?" he asked.

"We have heard stories, no more."

He didn't believe her. Where had they gotten the gold he saw on their arms and in their hair? If it came to that, though, he didn't believe the Ewaipanoma either. No one could live so close to the city of gold and remain in ignorance of it. But he bowed courteously and led his men away.

His spirits began to rise soon after they left the Amazons, and he strode quickly over the stony ground. Sun glittered over the chips of gold. The men behind him panted as they walked, and he grinned harshly; he was twice as old as they were and could still outpace any of them.

He looked back at the company and laughed. Aye, the Amazons had done well to refuse this sorry crew. And why had he thought they would want him, old and gray and nearly lame? Bess, he thought, you never had worse cause to fear for my loyalty.

Francis Molyneux pushed ahead of the rest of the company and walked beside him. He frowned. Something about the man's behavior with the Amazons had been wrong; he had acted just a moment too late, after the women had already aimed their bows. Or had he thought the Amazons would not be able to defend themselves?

"Nearly there, sir," Francis said. "Have you noticed the way the ground shines with the stones?"

"Aye," Walter said. Nay, why should he suspect this man, the only one who had acted while the others had stood like sheep? Only Francis seemed to understand what this voyage meant to him, only Francis had shown excitement at the prospect of discovering El Dorado. The others were merely interested in the gold; he had seen them collecting pebbles when they thought his attention was elsewhere.

"What will you do with the riches you find?" Francis asked.

"The riches belong to the king, of course. If we are strong enough we will take El Dorado in his name. If not I will return later with an army, if the king grants me leave."

"But surely the king will allow you to keep some of the gold."

"I hope so, Francis. And you hope the same for yourself, I'm sure."

Francis fell silent. Walter saw that he had embarrassed him in some way. But why else had he come, if not for riches? Perhaps he had come for the thrill of discovery. Perhaps Walter had misjudged the man.

He looked ahead to the granite plains before him. The walls of his prison returned to hem him in, but by an effort of will he forced them outward, widened them to take in more of the plain. No man in history, he thought, had gone so quickly from such a little room to such infinite riches.

The sun began to set. The men complained of hunger but he forbade them to eat anything; he had no doubt that the Amazons would do as they had threatened. He looked to the west and saw a shining path stretching back the way he had come: the sun illuminating the gold on the ground.

The sky grew darker. Now the men wanted to stop for the night, but he pushed them onward, anxious to reach his goal. In a few moments he was rewarded. He topped a rise and in front of him, lit by the last rays of the setting sun, he saw the golden towers of El Dorado.

The men came up behind him and stood without speaking. The city shone like a beacon. At the feet of the proud towers lay the lake he had heard of, Manoa. In the glow of setting sun the lake seemed on fire.

The men needed no encouragement now to press on. They came to the lake and found boats lying at the docks, as if they were expected. Did these people fear no one, then? The city would be easier to take than he had thought: he could do it with the few men he had.

The company divided into two parts and rowed toward the towers. Francis had followed him onto his boat. Suddenly he understood Francis's behavior: the boy worshiped him as a hero. He had seen this from men he had commanded before, but it had been so long ago he had forgotten.

The boats rowed smoothly toward the towers. In the sky the sun began to set, taking the color from the lake. He heard no sound but the creak and splash of oars.

Docks waited for them on the other side too. Walter disembarked first. He stood and rubbed his bad leg, which had stiffened in the chill from the water. Then he said, "I claim this, the city of El Dorado, in the name of James, king of England by grace of God."

Someone placed cold steel at his throat. He tried to turn but the man held him deftly. "Did you think the king would allow you to get this far?" Francis said. His breath was hot in Walter's ear. "He knows your plans, how you would set yourself up as king of El Dorado and return with your wealth to challenge his throne."

"I—" Walter said.

"Do not speak, traitor. He cautioned me against your honeyed words, told me you could make a man swear black was white if suited your purposes. He said I was to thank you for your services, and then make certain you died once we reached El Dorado."

Walter twisted but could not get away. Francis was in his twenties, young and strong. Walter had only his cunning to get himself free, and it had not served him well so far.

The company stood by the boats, unmoving. He had chosen them poorly indeed: these men were the scum of the earth. Then, to his great surprise, he felt the arm holding the dagger grow lax. Francis slumped to the ground.

He turned and saw a man as tall as himself move softly out of the shadows. The man held a blow-tube of the kind he had seen before among the native tribes. "Welcome to El Dorado, Sir Walter Raleigh," he said in perfect English. "We were expecting you. Do not be alarmed—he is not dead. Come—we have planned a great feast."

Moving as if in a dream, he followed the man away from the lake. Other men came out of the shadows, lifted Francis and carried him away. Behind him he could hear his company arguing fiercely among themselves but he did not look back; he could not bring himself to care if they came or stayed. Finally the arguments stopped and he heard them follow.

The sand surrounding the lake gave way to grass. The tall man—the chief, Walter supposed—led them onto a small winding path. Trees grew on both sides of them. Night had fallen, and he could see very little, but he smelled lemon and some kind of perfumed flower. The air around them was still warm.

The path broadened, became smoother. He wondered if it was paved with silver or gold, as in the stories. Certainly it felt more level than the London streets he knew.

Towers rose up above them: in the night he felt their bulk rather than saw them. Light spilled from windows directly in front of him. The chief led them inside.

They passed through several rooms. Fires burned in the hearths, and by their lights he could see intricate tapestries, vases of colored glass, golden figurines. Men and women passing through looked up from their tasks and nodded to them graciously. Finally they came to a room which held nothing but benches and a long table. Each of his men was led to a place set with silver plates and goblets of fragile colored glass. He heard the men murmuring among themselves, exclaiming softly over the finery.

Six men and women brought out a huge platter, nearly staggering under the weight of it. "The peccary—you would call it a small boar," the chief said, sitting beside Walter. "I hope you enjoy it."

He did. They hadn't eaten anything in the Amazons' territory, and he saw his men fall on the food as if they had been starving for weeks. More courses appeared after the peccary: fish and birds and fruit, each more delicious than the last. Servants came and poured wine in the goblets, filling each glass before it became empty.

The men grew quiet, sated. Even the wine failed to rouse them. For the first time Walter considered poison, and cursed himself for a fool. These people had proven they knew how to manufacture sleeping draughts. What had been in the potion that had felled Francis Molyneux?

Walter turned and studied the chief carefully. He was an old man, but time had sharpened rather than dulled his features, so that his face looked carved out of stone. He wore a long flowing skirt and nothing else; the skin of his chest and arms and face seemed to glow with rich health. Was that how the rumors of the Golden One had started?

"Are you enjoying our hospitality, Sir Walter?"

"I don't know," Walter said. "The food, at least, is excellent. But does your hospitality extend to answering a few questions?"

The chief laughed. "Of course."

"Well, then, how do you know my name? What did you mean when you said that you were expecting me? Are you the chief of these people?"

"I am the king, yes. My name is Tuala. I—"

"Where is Francis? What have you done with the rest of my men?"

"I'll explain everything, I promise you. But first I have to tell you a story. Will you listen?"

Walter nodded grudgingly.

"We are an old people," Tuala said. "Many, many years ago we travelled the world and saw strange sights, as strange as anything you have seen here. After we had mapped the globe we realized that nowhere in the world had we come across anything as fair as the country you see around you. We had found nothing so fertile, so rich, so pleasant. And so we made the decision, which some have criticized, to turn inward, to contemplate philosophy. We have not gone travelling in a very long time."

Walter stirred impatiently. His bad leg hurt from the walking he had done that day.

"One of the places we saw on our journeys was London," Tuala said. "But it was a London you would not recognize, a collection of huts by the river. Many years later we heard rumors of you, Sir Walter, and of the inquiries you made about us, and we remembered the tiny village on the banks of the Thames. We were amazed that you had come so far in so short a time."

Was he being patronized? Angrily he said, "I don't see what—"

The chief continued as though Walter had said nothing. His voice was low, sonorous, and he spoke English well, though with a slight musical accent. "We knew then that nothing would stop your people, the English, that you would not rest until you found us. And we felt certain that it would be you, Sir Walter, who would return and make the discovery. We were only surprised that it took you so long to do it."

He seemed to be waiting for an answer. "I was in prison," Walter said. "For twelve years."

A look of disgust passed over the chief's face. "Ah," he said. For a moment it seemed he could not go on. He gazed at Walter with something like pity. "Well," he said, "we planned for your return. We learned all we could about your people. We found a Spaniard who would teach us English."

That was the slight accent he heard, then—not the chief's own language but Spanish. "Did you wonder, Sir Walter," Tuala said, "why it was so easy for you to find us? Why the Spanish, who have been here for decades, have never conquered us?"

Suddenly Walter understood. It had been a trap—they would kill him here. They had already killed Francis, probably, and poisoned his other men. He had been a fool, he had allowed these men to gull him with their fine food and wine. He rose from the bench. "What—"

"Sit, Sir Walter, please. We have done nothing to your men, you have my word on that. Would you be surprised if I told you that many people have found us, that we have played host to dozens, perhaps hundreds, of Spaniards?"

"No more riddles, please. Tell me what you plan to do with me."

"You are our guest—tell me first what you planned to do with us."

"We wanted to—to trade with you."

"Nay, it does not become you to lie. I have been honest

with you in all things so far, and I hope you will do the same for me. We heard you claim our city for your king.''

''Very well. We intended to conquer you.'' It sounded foolish, a child's boast. ''We did not understand—I did not know what you were like. We thought you were barbarians.''

''Ah. So you have given over your plans of conquest?''

Walter nodded.

''Can I believe that? It was just a moment before that you lied to me. Or should I believe that you will return to your King James and lead his army to our city?''

Walter said nothing. He could not lie to this man—he knew that now. But the chief did not know about the bargain he had made with James. He could not return without the location of the mine.

''You see that we cannot allow you to leave,'' Tuala said.

''Ah. And so I am to be your prisoner.''

The chief's look of distaste returned. ''We do not like to imprison people. There is another way. We can make you forget everything you have seen here. You will leave without ever knowing you have discovered the city you sought.''

''Nay—''

''Aye. How else do you think we have kept our location a secret for so long? We made the Spaniard who taught us English forget. And the Amazons we trade with, and the Ewaipanoma.''

''And if I refuse to forget?''

''Then, my friend, we will have to keep you here.''

Walter looked up in surprise. He had guessed from Tuala's reaction to his talk of prison that the chief would not hold anyone against his will.

''Oh, yes, Sir Walter. But we will not put you in prison. You'll be allowed to go anywhere you like, anywhere but back to your country and King James. And who knows? Perhaps you'll come to like it here.''

Walter said nothing. ''We will give you leisure to think,'' the chief said.

"To think! How am I to think—what am I to think in this place? Everything I thought I knew has proven false. How do I know I didn't meet you twenty years ago, on my first voyage?"

The chief laughed. "Nay, we did not meet. I have looked forward to this moment for a long time. You have proven yourself every bit as clever as I had heard."

Walter rubbed his forehead. "I don't feel very clever. And I don't like the idea of you doing something to my memories. I have nothing in the world, nothing. I sold everything I owned to raise the money for this voyage. My mind and what is in it are all I have left."

"We have no choice. We must have you return to King James and tell him—tell him honestly—that there is no such land as El Dorado."

And lose my head, Walter thought. What would this man say if he knew all that is at stake here?

"Think about what I have said," the chief said. "You are free to explore any part of the city, but you will not be allowed to go beyond our borders."

Music began to play in another room. "You are tired, Sir Walter," Tuala said. "You and your men must rest. We will talk later."

He fought against sleepiness. What had been in the wine? Would all his long journey end here, sometime in the night, as he finally succumbed to slow-acting poison?

Servants came to lead them to their rooms. He tried to hold to coherent thought, to ask an intelligent question. He must have said something, because he heard a servant laugh. Then, somehow, he was in the bed, drifting off to sleep.

He awoke feeling refreshed, clear-headed. The servants had provided him with a wash-basin, and he cleaned himself as best he could. When he was done he saw that clothes had been set out on a chest at the foot of the bed. He dressed himself slowly, marveling at the textures of the doublet and hose. And how did they know the kinds of clothes he was accustomed to wear? The men here wore—what did they wear? He couldn't remember. Had it all been a dream?

He went outside. Tuala had given him the liberty of the city, and he decided to take the other man at his word. He strode the lawns with their riotous profusion of flowers, so different from a formal English garden. He walked by the canals that fed the lake, looking with interest at the boats drawn by horses on the towpath. He moved through the golden streets and saw children using markers of precious gems— ruby, sapphire, emerald—in their games.

He entered the towers with their banners of silver and green, red and gold, and came finally to a library crowded with ancient volumes. Tuala and a younger man stood by a table weighted down with scrolls. They spoke in low, urgent voices. The younger man seemed to be arguing, demanding something from the chief. They had not yet noticed Walter.

Finally Walter heard his name. What were they saying? But the two men had seen him, and the chief broke off to come over and greet him. The other man moved toward the door. Before he left he gave Walter a look that seemed heavy with malice.

"Did I interrupt something?" Walter asked.

"We were discussing matters of state, nothing more," the chief said smoothly. "It is not your concern."

It was his concern, though; he had heard his name. That day and in the days that followed he continued his explorations, walking with a tireless intensity. He chose a different direction each time, hoping to make Tuala think his walks were aimless. But he had a purpose, a method. He wanted to find the mine, or, failing that, the storehouse where the gold was kept.

And what then? Could he escape and return to England? He would have to cross the country of women, and the Amazons seemed to be allied in some way with Tuala's people. And then he would have to pass by the Spanish fort, and somehow sail alone down the Orinoco, because he couldn't trust the men he had brought with him. But these things seemed unimportant in the face of his urgency. All that mattered was finding the mine.

One day he followed a road and found himself, to his surprise, in an English countryside. Men were hurrying to bring in the crops before the rainy season, which in this upside-down country started in April. Beyond the fields he saw a low weathered building. It looked out of place, and he realized with surprise that it was the first structure he had seen that reminded him of England. A barn, probably, he thought, but his heart beat faster as he approached it.

The door opened to his touch. Surely they would not be so foolish as to keep their gold here, unprotected. But a shaft of light came through the cracks in the walls, and it illuminated all the riches he had sought, gold and silver and precious gems. He could not help reaching out his hand to touch, to hold. A sane part of his mind whispered, Are we turning thief, then? but he ignored it.

Someone shouted. He turned, dropping the emerald he had taken. The man he had seen arguing with the chief stood behind him in the strange cathedral light, speaking angrily and moving toward him. Walter raised his hands in a gesture of surrender. Did they all understand English, or only Tuala? "I was exploring, nothing more," Walter said, backing away carefully.

The man made a fist. Walter tried to block him but it was too late—the blow hit his face, cutting his lip. The man made as if to strike again, but this time Walter was ready, landing his own blow on the man's stomach. The other man doubled over with a cry of pain and rage.

Walter grinned. Age had not slowed him down, then—it had only made him more cunning, more capable of finding another man's weaknesses. The young whelp remained bent over, more stunned than hurt, probably. Finally he stood and said through clenched teeth, "The king will be told about this."

"Certainly. I'll tell him myself. What will he say about an unprovoked attack on one of his guests?"

"Unprovoked! I caught you in the middle of committing a crime. He'll put you on trial."

"What crime?"

"We don't have a word for it," the man said. "But in your language I think it's called theft."

"Is it true you were in the storehouse?" the chief asked Walter. The man who had attacked him stood at the chief's side, smiling maliciously.

"Aye. You said I could walk wherever I pleased."

"And is it true you stole an emerald?"

"Nay. I stole nothing."

"Only because I stopped you," the other man said. "He had the emerald in his hand—I saw it."

The chief sighed. "Nuad thinks we cannot trust you. He thinks you've come to rob us."

Walter said nothing.

"He says our only choice is to kill you now."

"Nay, tell him all of it," Nuad said angrily. "Kill him, aye—but that will solve the problem for only a little while. We must strike at the root."

"Do you understand, Sir Walter?" Tuala said.

"We'll attack England," Nuad said. "We made a mistake all those years ago, when we decided to turn inward. We must wake up and look around us, see what is happening in the world. Sooner or later your people will come to destroy us. We must destroy them before that happens."

For the first time Walter thought the chief looked tired, defeated. "Do you understand?" Tuala said again. Walter nodded—he had seen struggles for power before. "You did not arrive at the best of times for us. Somehow we must resolve this question before you return home."

"Resolve the question?" the young man said scornfully. "Kill him now!"

"Nay!" Tuala said. For the moment the chief seemed to grow, to gain stature.

"Then put him on trial."

"For what? We have no laws against theft in this country. The children come to the storehouse to take gems for their games."

"But this man is not a child," Nuad said, becoming angrier as he saw the chief about to decide against him. "He is not one of us. Sooner or later he will lead his king to our mine."

"Will he?" Tuala said.

"Of course he will! Or do you place all your hopes in this man's honor? I tell you he has none!"

The chief said nothing. Nuad took it as a dismissal. "Remember my words," he said as he left. "He'll return with an army at his back."

That evening after dinner Tuala escorted them to a room filled with musicians and dancers. To Walter's surprise the chief took to the floor and danced a wild and complex measure with a young woman. "Come, Sir Walter, join us," Tuala said when the dance had ended.

His leg was bad that night—he should not have walked so long and so hard. "Nay, I thank you," he said. Some of his company, he saw, were choosing up partners for the next dance.

"Then we will talk awhile," the chief said.

He sat easily, not even winded from the dance. In the candles on the table the golden glow of his skin was very pronounced. How old was Tuala? He had spoken of the huts of London as if he had seen them personally. For a heart-stopping moment, a moment in which it seemed as if he hung, dizzyingly, over a precipice, Walter wondered if these folks were immortal. "How old are you?" Walter said.

Tuala smiled. "Nearly a hundred."

Not immortal then, Walter thought, feeling both relieved and disappointed. "Tell me about your king," the chief said.

Walter shrugged. "I barely know him. I served Elizabeth, who was queen before him."

"Ah. And what was she like?"

"Wise and beautiful, virtuous and kind," he said. He put aside his memories of her last days, her back gone crooked and her teeth rotted to blackness in her mouth. A lady whom time had surprised, he had called her once.

"And James? Is he wise as well?"

"I don't know."

"Was it he who sent you to prison?"

Walter nodded.

"Then he cannot be so very wise, I think."

"Nay, he is a coward." The words burst from him before he was aware of them. "He wears a thick padded jerkin, summer and winter, because he fears the assassin's knife. He sent a man to spy on me, a coward like himself, who would only fight when he saw the odds were on his side, or when he could attack from behind."

"Then why do you serve him?"

"Because he is king. Because God appointed him king."

Tuala said nothing. Walter thought over what he had said, wondering how it would appear to this strange man before him. It was true that he would have preferred to serve Elizabeth to the end of his days. Like a feudal serf he gave his loyalty to few, and always to a person rather than an institution. James had never earned his trust; perhaps that was why he had been sent to the Tower.

"The dances are ending," the chief said. "We had best go to bed."

That night Walter dreamed of Wat. He had hardly thought of his son in the past few days, had put out of his mind the letter he would have to write to Bess. Yet when he woke he thought he saw the boy standing in front of him, like an avenging ghost in a play.

Wat was dead, and the other man who had been shot by the Spanish—sweet God, he didn't even know his name! By what right did he think he could command men to do as he ordered, to send them even to their deaths? God had not appointed him king. He had been driven only by personal ambition and his hope for gain.

Nay, it was worse than that. Nuad had been right—he was nothing but a common thief, a man without honor. What was the difference, after all, between robbing a man and plundering a country? The latter had been sanctioned by a king, true, but what was the word of James worth?

He stayed in his room the next day, thinking and writing in his journal. Toward evening he went out and walked through the gardens to the plains beyond. He must not have come to the borders of the chief's country, because no one made as if to stop him. He had the sense he was being watched.

The walls of his cell widened outward to take in the entire plain. Then it seemed as if they widened still further, that his mind grew to encompass all he had learned in the past few weeks. He thought of the Ewaipanoma, and the Amazons, and the folk of El Dorado.

He turned and went in search of the chief.

"I have another plan," Walter said to Tuala. "I do not choose to forget the beauties of your country. But I won't stay in any prison, no matter how fair. I'll go back to King James and say of my own free will that I have not found El Dorado."

"And what will the king do then? What happens when you return without the treasure you promised him?"

"I don't know."

"I daresay you have some idea. We have spoken to some of your men—they tell us you will be killed if you return without the location of the mine."

So the old chief knew that as well. Was there nothing of his life hidden from this man?

"Can we trust you to keep our secret in the face of death?" the chief asked.

Walter nodded slowly. "I promise you I will do it. You have my word on it."

"You surprise me. And yet I find I believe you. But if that's true then we can't allow you to go back—we won't have your death on our hands. Stay here, Sir Walter. You'll find that your prison will be very fair indeed. We'll give you the liberty of our city—you'll study the old books with us and learn our philosophy."

"Nay—I've had enough of prisons. And what of my wife? What will she think when I don't return?"

"What good can you do her under a sentence of death?"

"Very well, then, what will happen to you? Someone will guess where I am and come after me. What will you do then?"

"We cannot keep our city a secret much longer. The world is opening up to travellers and explorers—sooner or later we will be discovered. Already stories about us are spreading throughout the land. We need another hundred years or so, and then we will be ready."

"What do you mean?"

"I mean that when this plain is finally explored there will be no trace of us left. We will have gone away, into the heart of the jungle. People will think the stories of El Dorado a myth, nothing more."

"Then let me grant you the time you need. Let me tell the king there is no El Dorado."

The chief sighed. "I'll have to think about it. But I will tell you this, Sir Walter—you have more courage than any man I have ever met. Your king was a fool to keep you imprisoned."

"Aye, he was," Walter said, and grinned. Somehow he had transferred his loyalty to this chief who sat before him.

Nay, not a chief—he had wanted to be called king. And why not? He had earned the title, unlike James.

One of Tuala's men led Walter through the main tower to a room he had never seen before. Something Tuala had said made Walter think the man might be some sort of surgeon, but one who practiced a medicine unlike any Walter had ever known. The surgeon stopped at a doorway and took out a key. Walter looked on in surprise—he had not seen any locked rooms since he had come to El Dorado, not even his own.

The surgeon opened the door. Francis lay on a bed inside. He sat up when the surgeon came in and began to speak angrily. "Why am I imprisoned here? When am I to be released?" His eyes widened when he saw Walter, and he had the grace to look afraid.

"I would not have killed you," Francis said quickly. "I was to make certain you claimed El Dorado for King James, nothing more."

"Of course," Walter said evenly. Did the man's treachery have no end? Was this fool typical of the men James liked to have around him? Elizabeth would have taken Francis's measure in minutes, and then dismissed him forever.

The surgeon gave Francis food and drink, and the man ate and drank hungrily. "You'll get me out, won't you, Sir Walter? When the king finds out how I've been treated he won't be pleased. He'll return with an army, won't he, sir? Tell this fool what the king will do to him."

His words grew slower, disjointed. Finally he lay back on the bed, his eyes unfocused. "I put the potion in his drink," the surgeon said. "Watch."

Fascinated, Walter listened as the surgeon described a journey Francis had never taken. The surgeon led Francis over the plains and beyond, to the forests and highlands of the lower Orinoco. Francis nodded in agreement, his eyes glazed. "When you return to your ship you will remember nothing of this city," the surgeon said. "You will be able to tell your king you could not find us. El Dorado is a pretty story, nothing more."

Francis nodded. "A pretty story," he said, and slept.

Three months later, at dawn, King James's men led Sir Walter from the Gatehouse to the scaffold at Westminster Hall. Someone kindly gave him a cup of sack and asked how he liked it. "It's a good drink," Walter said, "if a man might tarry at it," and was pleased to see that the old jest still had the power to make men laugh.

He felt very nearly content. The fever that had infected him on the way to Guiana had returned, and his limp was worse than ever. He was an old man, his life over. Yet he had one act more to play out, one final secret to carry to the grave.

All during the voyage home, while around him his men slowly forgot the gardens and golden towers, while they spoke of a voyage that had never happened, a dream-voyage, he had torn out pages from his journal and substituted another story. Anyone who found his journal would think that he had never left Trinidad. He wrote a letter to Bess and thought about Wat, his impetuous son who had been so much like him. His life was over. He had lost, and won. He had found quite another sort of riches.

In the dawn air he shook from cold and from his fever. He hoped that the crowd would not take his shivering for fear. For there was a crowd, and a large one, although King James had scheduled the execution on the same day as the Lord Mayor's pageants and shows. It was important that all of London talk about his execution, and that there be no mention of the gold mine he had gone to find. His death would buy King Tuala and his people the hundred years they needed.

He mounted the scaffold and looked out over the crowd. In spite of himself he felt gratified that so many people had come to see him, all his old friends and enemies, even folks who knew him only as a legend. "I thank God that He has sent me to die in the sight of so honorable an assembly and not in the darkness," he said.

His listeners expected to hear a defense of the charges of treason and atheism brought against him, and so he spoke a little more. He saw their upturned faces, listening raptly. Aye, he had not lost the ability to move a crowd. London would talk about nothing else for a very long time to come.

Finally he lay himself down on the block. The executioner hesitated, and he heard someone say into the silence, "We have not another such head to be cut off." He closed his eyes and saw before him the high towers of El Dorado, and then the shadow of the axe. Then he saw and heard nothing more.

AFTERWORD

I nfinite Riches" grew out of research I did for my Elizabethan novel *Strange Devices of the Sun and Moon*. Most Elizabethans, I found, led lives as compelling as novels; some days I gave up the pretense of research entirely and just read where my fancy took me. What fascinated me about Sir Walter Raleigh was how he was able to go from a tiny room in the Tower of London to vast open seas and uncharted countries. What on earth could that have been like?

If you read any history at all you find yourself taking sides, favoring one person over another. This is bad for historians, but perfectly acceptable behavior for a writer. I have to count myself as one of Raleigh's supporters—because he spoke his mind in an age when most people thought it politic to dissemble; because he succeeded at so many different things: courtier, poet, historian, explorer, philosopher; because, perhaps alone among Elizabethan husbands, it seems that he was faithful to his wife.

Gardner Dozois, who bought this story for *Isaac Asimov's Science Fiction Magazine,* had me take out fifteen pages of fairly tedious up-the-Orinoco travelog. If "Infinite Riches" works at all it is at least in part due to him.

DEATH IS DIFFERENT

She had her passport stamped and went down the narrow corridor to collect her suitcase. It was almost as if they'd been waiting for her, dozens of them, the women dressed in embroidered shawls and long skirts in primary colors, the men in clothes that had been popular in the United States fifty or sixty years ago.

"Taxi? Taxi to hotel?"

"Change money? Yes? Change money?"

"Jewels, silver, jewels—"

"Special for you—"

"Cards, very holy—"

Monica brushed past them. One very young man, shorter even than she was, grabbed hold of the jacket she had folded over her arm. "Anything, mem," he said. She turned to look at him. His eyes were wide and earnest. "Anything, I will do anything for you. You do not even have to pay me."

She laughed. He drew back, looking hurt, but his hand still held her jacket. "All right," she said. They were nearly to the wide glass doors leading out into the street. The airport was hot and dry, but the heat coming from the open glass doors was worse. It was almost evening. "Find me a newspaper," she said.

He stood a moment. The others had dropped back, as if the young man had staked a claim on her. "A—a newspaper?" he said. He was wearing a gold earring, a five-pointed star, in one ear.

"Yeah," she said. Had she ever known the Lurqazi word for newspaper? She looked in her purse for her dictionary and realized she must have packed it in with her luggage. She could only stand there and repeat helplessly, "A newspaper. You know."

"Yes. A newspaper." His eyes lit up, and he pulled her by her jacket outside into the street.

"Wait—" she said. "My luggage—"

"A newspaper," the young man said. "Yes." He led her to an old man squatting by the road, a pile of newspapers in front of him. At least she supposed they were newspapers. They were written in Lurqazi, a language which used the Roman alphabet but which, she had been told, had no connection with any Indo-European tongue.

"I meant—Is there an English newspaper?" she asked.

"English," he said. He looked defeated.

"All right," she said. "How much?" she asked the old man.

The old man seemed to come alive. "Just one, mem," he said. "Just one." His teeth were stained red.

She gave him a one (she had changed some money at the San Francisco airport), and, as an afterthought, gave the young man a one too. She picked up a paper and turned to the young man. "Could you come back in there with me while I pick up my suitcase?" she said. "I think the horde will descend if you don't."

He looked at her as if he didn't understand what she'd said, but he followed her inside anyway and waited until she got her suitcase. Then he went back outside with her. She stood a long time watching the cabs—every make and year of car was standing out at the curb, it seemed, including a car she recognized from Czechoslovakia and a horse-drawn carriage—until he guided her toward a late model Volkswagen Rabbit. She had a moment of panic when she thought he was going to get in the car with her, but he just said something to the driver and waved good-bye. The driver, she noticed, was wearing the same five-pointed star earring.

As they drove to the hotel she felt the familiar travel euphoria, a loosening of the fear of new places she had felt on the plane. She had done it. She was in another place, a place she had never been, ready for new sights and adventures. Nothing untoward had happened to her yet. She was a seasoned traveller.

She looked out of the car and was startled for a moment to see auto lights flying halfway into the air, buildings standing on nothing. Then she realized she was looking at a reflection in the car's window. She bent closer to the window, put her hands around her eyes, but she could see nothing real outside, only the flying lights, the phantom buildings.

At the air-conditioned hotel she kicked off her shoes, took out her dictionary and opened the newspaper. She had studied a little Lurqazi before she'd left the States, but most of the words in the paper were unfamiliar, literary words like "burnished" and "celestial." She took out a pen and started writing above the lines. After a long time she was pretty sure that the right margins of the columns in the paper were ragged not because of some flaw in the printing process but because she was reading poetry. The old man had sold her poetry.

She laughed and began to unpack, turning on the radio. For a wonder someone was speaking English. She stopped and listened as the announcer said, "—fighting continues in the hills with victory claimed by both sides. In the United States the President pledged support today against what he called Russian-backed guerrillas. The Soviet Union had no comment.

"The weather continues hot—"

Something flat and white stuck out from under the shoes in her suitcase, a piece of paper. She pulled it out. "Dear Monica," she read, "I know this is part of your job but don't forget your husband who's waiting for you at home. I know you want to have adventures, but please *be careful.* See you in two weeks. I love you. I miss you already, and you haven't even gone yet. Love, Jeremy."

The dinner where she'd met Jeremy had been for six couples. On Jeremy's other side was a small, blond woman. On her other side was a conspicuously empty chair. She must have looked unhappy, because Jeremy introduced himself and asked, in a voice that sounded genuinely worried, if she was all right.

"I'm fine," she said brightly. She looked at the empty chair on the other side of her as if it were a person and then turned back to Jeremy. "He said he might be a little late. He does deep sea salvaging." And then she burst into tears.

That had been embarrassing enough, but somehow, after he had offered her his napkin and she'd refused it and used hers instead, she found herself telling him the long sad chronology of her love life. The man she was dating had promised to come, she said, but you could never count on him to be anywhere. And the one before that had smuggled drugs, and the one before that had taken her to some kind of religious commune where you weren't allowed to use electricity and could only bathe once a week, and the one before that had said he was a revolutionary. . . . His open face was friendly, his green eyes looked concerned. She thought the blond woman on his other side was very lucky. But she could never go out

with him, even if the blond woman wasn't there. He was too
. . . safe.

"It sounds to me," he said when she was done (and she
realized guiltily that she had talked for nearly half an hour;
he must have been bored out of his mind), "that you like
going out with men who have adventures."

"You mean," she said slowly, watching the thought surface as she said it, "that I don't think women can have adventures too?"

The next day she applied to journalism school.

She didn't see him until nearly a year later, at the house
of the couple who had invited them both to dinner. This time
only the two of them were invited. The set-up was a little too
obvious to ignore, but she decided she didn't mind. "What
have you been doing?" he asked between courses.

"Going to journalism school," she said.

He seemed delighted. "Have you been thinking of the
conversation we had last year?" he asked. "I've thought
about it a lot."

"What conversation?"

"Don't you remember?" he asked. "At the dinner last
year. About women having adventures. You didn't seem to
think they could."

"No," she said. "I'm sorry. I don't remember."

He didn't press it, but she became annoyed with him anyway. Imagine him thinking that a conversation with him was
responsible for her going to journalism school. And now that
she was looking at him she realized that he was going bald,
that his bald spot had widened quite a bit since she'd seen
him last. Still, when he asked for her phone number at the
end of the evening she gave it to him. What the hell.

It was months later that he confessed he had asked their
mutual friends to invite them both to dinner. But only after
they were married would she admit that he might have been
right, that she might have enrolled in school because of him.

For a while, since he didn't seem to mind, since he neither praised nor blamed, she told him about her old lovers. The stories became a kind of exorcism for her. The men had all been poor (except, for a brief time, the drug smuggler, until his habit exceeded his supply), they had all been interesting, they had all been crazy or nearly so. Once he mixed up the revolutionary who had stolen her stereo with the would-be writer who had stolen her stereo, and they laughed about it for days. After that the chorus line of old lovers had faded, grown less insistent, and had finally disappeared altogether. And that was when she knew something she had not been certain of before. She had been right to marry Jeremy.

The radio was playing what sounded like an old English folk song. She turned it off, read and re-read the short letter until she had memorized it, and went to sleep.

The young man was on the sidewalk when she stepped out of the hotel the next morning. "What can I do for you today, mem?" he asked. "Anything."

She laughed, but she wondered what he wanted, why he had followed her. She felt uneasy. "I don't—I don't really need anything right now," she said. "Thanks."

"Anything," he said. He was earnest but not pleading. "What would you desire most if you could have anything at all? Sincerely."

"Anything," she said. You mean, besides wanting Jeremy here with me right now, she thought. Should she confide in him? It would get rid of him, anyway. "I want," she said slowly, "to talk to the head of the Communist Party."

"It will be done," he said. She almost laughed, but could not bear to damage his fragile dignity. "I will see you tomorrow with your appointment," he said, and walked away.

She watched him go, then opened her guide book and began to look through it. A travel magazine had commissioned her to do a piece on the largest city in Amaz, the ruins, the beaches, the market-place, the famous park designed by

Antonio Gaudí. How was the country holding up under the attack by the guerrillas, under the loss of the income from tourists which was its major source of revenue? "Don't go out of the city," the magazine editor had said. "Be careful. I don't want you to get killed doing this." Five hours later, when she'd told him about the assignment, Jeremy had repeated the editor's warning almost word for word.

But she had other ideas. As long as the magazine was paying her travel expenses she might as well look around a bit. And if she could find out if the Russians were arming the guerrillas or not, well, that would be a major scoop, wouldn't it? No one had seen the head of the Communist Party for months. There were rumors that he was dead, that he was with the guerrillas in the hills, that the party itself was about to be outlawed and that he had fled to Moscow. She laughed. Wouldn't it be funny if the young man could get her an interview?

She began to walk, stopping every so often to take notes or snap a picture. The morning was humid, a portent of the heat to come. Her blouse clung to her back. She passed fish stalls, beggars, a building of white marble big as a city block she supposed was a church, a used car lot, a section of the city gutted by fire. On the street, traffic had come to a standstill, and the smells of exhaust and asphalt mingled with that of fish and cinnamon. Cars honked furiously, as though that would get them moving again. The sidewalk had filled with people moving with a leisured grace. Silver bracelets and rings flashed in the sunlight. Once she came face to face with a man carrying a monkey on his shoulder, but he was gone before she could take his picture.

She took a wrong turn somewhere and asked a few people in Lurqazi where the Gaudí Park was. No one, it seemed, had ever heard of it, but everyone wanted to talk to her, a long stream of Lurqazi she could not understand. She smiled and moved on, and looked at the map in the guide book. Most of the streets, she read, were unnamed, so the guide book had rather unimaginatively called them Street 1, Street 2 and so on. After a long time of walking she found the park and sat gratefully on a bench.

The benches were wavy instead of straight, made of a mosaic of broken tile and topped with grotesque and fanciful figures. The park looked a little like Gaudí's Guell Park in Barcelona, but with harsher colors, more adapted, she thought, to this country. She was trying to turn the thought into a caption for a photograph, and at the same time wondering about the structure on the other side of the park—was it a house? a sculpture of flame made of orange tile and brass?—when a small dirty boy sat on the bench next to her.

"Cards?" he asked. "Buy a pack of cards?" He took a few torn and bent cards from his pocket and spread them out in the space between the two of them.

"No thanks," she said absently.

"Very good buy," he said, tapping one of the cards. It showed a man with a square, neatly trimmed beard framing a dark face. His eyes, large with beautiful lashes, seemed to stare at her from the card. He looked a little like Cumaq, the head of the Communist Party. No, she thought. You have Cumaq on the brain. "Very good," the boy said insistently.

"No," she said. "Thanks."

"I can tell time by the sun," the boy said suddenly. He bent his head way back, farther than necessary, she thought, to see the sun, and said gravely, "It is one o'clock."

She laughed and looked at her watch. It was 11:30. "Well, if it's that late," she said, "I have to go." She got up and started over to the other side of the park.

"I can get more cards!" the boy said, calling after her. "Newer. Better!"

She got back to the hotel late in the evening. The overseas operator was busy, and she went down to the hotel restaurant for dinner. Back in her room she began to write. "Why Antonio Gaudí accepted the old silver baron's commission in 1910 no one really knows, but the result—"

The phone rang. It was Jeremy. "I love you," they told each other, raising their voices above the wailing of a bad connection. "I miss you."

"Be careful," Jeremy said. The phone howled.

"I am," she said.

The young man was waiting for her outside the hotel the next morning. "I did it," he said. "All arranged." He pronounced "arranged" with three syllables.

"You did what?" she asked.

"The interview," he said. "It is all arranged. For tomorrow."

"Interview?"

"The one you asked for," he said gravely. "With Cumaq. The head of the Communist Party."

"You arranged it?" she said. "An interview?"

"Yes," he said. Was he starting to sound impatient? "You asked me to and I did it. Here." He held out a piece of paper with something written on it. "For tomorrow. Ten o'clock."

She took the paper and read the ten or twelve lines of directions on it, what they had in this crazy place instead of addresses, she supposed. She didn't know whether to laugh or to throw her arms around him and hug him. Could this slight young man really have gotten her an interview with the man everyone had been trying to find for the past six months? Or was it a hoax? Some kind of trap? She knew one thing: nothing was going to keep her from following the directions the next morning. "Thank you," she said finally.

He stood as if waiting for more. She opened her purse and gave him a five. He nodded and walked away.

But that night, listening to the English news in her hotel room, she realized that there would be no interview, the next day or ever. "Government troops killed Communist Party head Cumaq and fifteen other people, alleged to be Communist Party members, in fighting in the Old Quarter yesterday," the announcer said. "Acting on an anonymous tip the troops surrounded a building in the Old Quarter late last night. Everyone inside the building was killed, according to a government spokesman."

She threw her pen across the room in frustration. So that was it. No doubt the young man had heard about Cumaq's death this morning on the Lurqazi broadcasts (But were there Lurqazi broadcasts? She had never heard one.) and had seen the opportunity to make some money off her. She thought of his earnest young face and began to get angry. So far he had sold her a sheet of poetry she couldn't read and some completely useless information. If she saw him again tomorrow she would tell him to get lost.

But he wasn't in front of the hotel the next day. She went off to the Colonial House, built in layers of Spanish, English and Dutch architecture, one layer for each foreign occupation. The place had been given four stars by the guide book, but now it was nearly empty. As she walked through the cool, white stucco rooms, her feet clattering on the polished wooden floors, as she snapped pictures and took notes, she thought about the piece of paper, still in her purse, that he had given her. Should she follow the directions anyway and see where they led her? Probably they were as useless as everything else the young man had given her, they would lead her into a maze that would take her to the fish stalls or back to her hotel. But time was running out. Just ten more days, ten days until she had to go back, and she was no closer to the secret of the rebels. Maybe she should follow the directions after all.

She got back to the hotel late in the afternoon, hot and tired and hungry. The young man was standing in the marble portico. She tried to brush past him but he stopped her. "Why were you not at the interview this morning?" he asked.

She looked at him in disbelief. "The interview?" she said. "The man's dead. How the hell could I have interviewed him? I mean, I know you don't read the papers—hell, you probably don't even have newspapers, just that poetry crap—but don't you at least listen to the radio? They got him last night."

He drew himself up. He looked offended, mortally wounded, and at the same time faintly comic. She saw for the first time that he was trying to grow a mustache. "We," he said, gesturing grandly, "are a nation of poets. That is why we read poetry instead of newspapers. For news we—"

"You read poetry?" she said. All her anger was spilling out now; the slightest word from him could infuriate her. How dare he make a fool of her? "I'd like to see that. There's ninety percent illiteracy in this country, did you know that?"

"Those who can read read the poems to us," he said. "And then we make up new poems. In our villages, late at night, after the planting has been done. We have no television. Television makes you lazy and stupid. I would have invited you to my village, to hear the poems. But no longer. You have not followed my directions."

"I didn't follow your directions because the man was dead," she said. "Can't you understand that? Can't you get that through your head? Dead. There wouldn't have been much of an interview."

He was looking offended again. "Death is different in this country," he said.

"Oh, I see," she said. "You don't have television and you don't have death. That's very clever. Someday you should tell me just how you—"

"He will be there again tomorrow," the young man said, and walked away.

She felt faintly ridiculous, but she followed the directions he had given her the next day. She turned left at the statue, right at the building gutted by fire, left again at the large intersection. Maybe what the young man had been trying to tell her was that Cumaq was still alive, that he had somehow survived the shooting in the Old Quarter. But every major radio station, including those with Communist leanings, had reported Cumaq's death. Well, maybe the Communists wanted everyone to think he was dead. But then why were they giving her this interview?

The directions brought her to an old, sagging three-story building. The map in the guide book had lost her three turns back: according to the guide book the street she was standing on didn't exist. But as near as she could tell she was nowhere near the Old Quarter. She shrugged and started up the wooden steps to the building. A board creaked ominously beneath her.

She knocked on the door, knocked again when no one came. The door opened. She was not at all surprised to see the young man from the airport. Here's where he beats me up and takes my traveller's checks, she thought, but he motioned her in with broad gestures, grinning widely.

"Ah, come in, come in," he said. "It is important to be in the right place, no? Not in the wrong place."

She couldn't think of any answer to this and shrugged instead. "Where is he?" she asked, stepping inside and trying to adjust her eyes to the dim light.

"He is here," he said. "Right in front of you."

Now she could see another man in a chair, and two men standing close behind him. She took a few steps forward. The man in the chair looked like all the pictures of Cumaq she had ever seen, the neat beard, the long eyelashes. Her heart started to beat faster and she ignored the peeling paint and spiderwebs on the walls, the boarded over windows, the plaster missing from the ceiling. She would get her scoop after all, and it was better than she ever thought it would be.

The young man introduced her to Cumaq in Lurqazi. "How did you survive the shooting in the Old Quarter?" she asked the man in the chair.

Cumaq turned his head toward her. He was wearing the same earring as the young man and the taxi driver at the airport, a gold five-pointed star. "He does not speak English," the young man said. "I will translate." He said something to Cumaq and Cumaq answered him.

"He says," the young man said, "that he did not survive. That he came back from the dead to be with us."

"But how?" she asked. Her frustration returned. The young man could be making up anything, anything at all. The man in the chair had no wounds that she could see. Could he be an imposter, not Cumaq after all? "What do you mean by coming back from the dead? I thought you people were Marxists. I thought you didn't believe in life after death, things like that."

"We are mystical Marxists," the young man translated.

This was ridiculous. Suddenly she remembered her first travel assignment, covering the centenary of Karl Marx's death. She had gone to Marx's grave in Highgate Cemetary in London and taken pictures of the solemn group of Chinese standing around the grave. A week later she had gone back, and the Chinese group—the same people? different people? the same uniforms, anyway—was still there. Now she imagined the group standing back, horrified, as a sound came from the tomb, the sound of Marx turning in his grave. "What on earth is a mystical Marxist?"

The man in the chair said two words. "Magicians," the young man said. "Wizards."

She was not getting anywhere following this line of questioning. "Are the Russians giving you arms?" she asked. "Can you at least tell me that?"

"What is necessary comes to us," the young man said after Cumaq had finished.

That sounded so much like something the young man would have said on his own that she couldn't believe he was translating Cumaq faithfully. "But what is necessary comes—from the Russians?" she asked. She waited for the young man to translate.

Cumaq shrugged.

She sighed. "Can I take a picture?" she asked. "Show the world you're still alive?"

"No," the young man said. "No pictures."

An hour later she was still not sure if she had a story. Cumaq—if it really was Cumaq—spoke for most of that time, mixing Marxist rhetoric about the poor downtrodden masses with a vague, almost fatalistic belief that the world was working on his side. "You see," he said, "it is as Marx said. Our victory is inevitable. And our astrologers say the same thing." She wondered what they made of him in Moscow, if he had ever been to Moscow.

"You must go now," the young man said. "He has been on a long journey. He must rest now."

"How about some proof?" she asked. "Some proof that he isn't dead?"

"He spoke to you," the young man said. "That is proof enough, surely."

"No one will believe me," she said. "I can't sell this story anywhere without proof. A picture, or—"

"No," the young man said. "You must leave now."

She sighed and left.

The next day she rented a car and drove to the beaches, took pictures of the white sand, the tropical blue water, the palm trees. The huge air-conditioned hotels facing the water were nearly empty, standing like monuments to a forgotten dynasty. In one the elevators didn't run. In another the large plate glass window in the lobby had been broken and never replaced.

She stayed at one of the hotels and took the car the next day to the ruins of Marmaz. Even here the tourists had stayed away. Only a few were walking through the echoing marble halls, sticking close together like the stunned survivors of a disaster. A man who spoke excellent English was leading a disheartened-looking group of Americans on a tour.

She and the tour finished at the same place, the central chamber with its cracked and empty pool made of white marble. "Tour, miss?" the guide asked her. "The next one starts in half an hour."

"No, thank you," she said. They stood together looking at the pool. "Your English is very good," she said finally.

He laughed. "That's because I'm American," he said. "My name's Charles."

She turned to him in surprise. "How on earth did you end up here?" she asked.

"It's a long story," he said.

"Well, can you tell me—" she said.

"Probably not," he said. They both laughed. Ghosts of their laughter came back to them from the marble pool.

"How do people get news around here?" she said. "I mean, the only broadcasts I can find on the radio are foreign, the United States and China, mostly, and what I thought was a newspaper turns out to be poetry, I think. . . ."

He nodded. "Yeah, they're big on poetry here," he said. "They get their news from the cards."

"The—cards?"

"Sure," he said. "Haven't you had half a dozen people try to sell you a deck of cards since you got here? Used to sell them myself for a while. That's their newspaper. And—other things."

She was silent a moment, thinking about the boy who had tried to sell her the deck of cards, the card with Cumaq's picture, the boy shouting after her that he could get newer cards. "So that's it," she said. "It doesn't seem very, well, accurate."

"Not a lot out here is accurate," Charles said. "Sometimes I think accuracy is something invented by the Americans."

"Well, what about—" She hesitated. How much could she tell him without him thinking she was crazy? "Well, someone, a native, told me that death is different in this country. What do you think he meant?"

"Just what he said, I guess," he said. "Lots of things are different here. It's hard to—to pin things down. You have to learn to stop looking for rational explanations."

"I guess I'll never make it here, then," she said. "I'm a journalist. We're always looking for rational explanations."

"Yeah, I know," he said. "It's a hard habit to break."

She did a short interview with him—"How has the shortage of tourists affected your job as a guide to the ruins?"—and then she drove back to the city.

In the next few days she tried to find the shabby three-story building again. It seemed to her that the city was shifting, moving landmarks, growing statues and fountains, swallowing parks and churches. The building had vanished. She showed a taxi driver her directions, and they ended up lost in the city's maze for over two hours.

She went back to the airport, but the young man was gone and no one seemed to remember who he was. The old man who had sold poetry was gone too.

And finally her time in the city was up. She packed her suitcase, tried to call Jeremy one last time and took her plane to San Francisco. She tried to read on the plane but thoughts of Jeremy kept intruding. She would see him in three hours, two hours, one hour. . . .

He wasn't at the airport to meet her. For an instant she was worried, and then she laughed. He was always so concerned about her safety, so protective. Now that it was her turn to be worried she would show him. She would take a taxi home and wait calmly for him to get back. No doubt there was a logical explanation.

The apartment was dark when she let herself in, and she could see the red light blinking on their answering machine. Six blinks, six calls. For the first time she felt fear catch at her. Where was he?

"Hello, Mrs. Schwartz," the first caller said, an unfamiliar voice. She felt annoyance start to overlay her fear. She had never taken Jeremy's name. Who was this guy that he didn't know that? "This is Dr. Escobar, at the county hospital. Please give me a call. I'm afraid it's urgent."

The doctor again, asking her to call back. Then Jeremy's

brother—"Hey, Jer, where the hell are you? You're late for the game."—then a familiar-sounding voice that she realized with horror was hers. But she had tried to call Jeremy *last night*. Hadn't he been home since then? Then the would-be writer—she fast-forwarded over him—and another strange voice. "Mrs. Schwartz? This is Sergeant Pierce. Your next-door neighbor tells me you're away for two weeks. Please call me at the police station when you get back."

With shaking fingers she pressed the buttons on the phone for the police station. Sergeant Pierce wasn't in, and after a long wait they told her. Jeremy had died in a car accident. She felt nothing. She had known the moment she found herself calling the police and not the hospital.

She called a taxi. She picked up her suitcase and went outside. The minutes passed like glaciers, but finally she saw the lights of a car swing in toward the curb. She ran to the taxi and got in. "To the airport, please," she said.

At the airport she ran to the Cathay Pacific counter. "One ticket to—" Damn. She had forgotten the name of the country. She fumbled through her purse, looking for her passport. "To Amaz, please."

"To where?" the woman behind the counter said.

"Amaz. Here." She showed her the stamp in the book.

"I never heard of it," the woman said.

"I just got back this evening," Monica said. "On Cathay Pacific. Amaz. In the Far East. Do you want to see my ticket?"

The woman had backed away a little and Monica realized she had been shouting. "I'm sorry," the woman said. "Here's a list of the places we fly. See? Amaz is not one of them. Are you sure it's in the Far East?"

"Of course I'm sure," Monica said. "I just got back this evening. I told you—"

"I'm sorry," the woman said again. She turned to the next person in line. "Can I help you?"

Monica moved away. She sat on a wooden bench in the center of the echoing terminal and watched people get in line, check their gate number, run for their planes. She was too late. The magic didn't work this far away. It had been stupid, anyway, an idea borne out of desperation and something the crazy American had said at the ruins. She would have to face reality, have to face the idea that Jeremy—

A woman walked past her. She was wearing a gold five-pointed earring in one ear. Monica stood up quickly and followed her. The woman turned a corner and walked past a few ticket windows, her heels clicking unnaturally loudly on the marble floor, and got in line at Mexicana Airlines. Monica stood behind her. The glass windows behind them were dark, and the lights of the cars and buses shone through the windows like strange pearls. "One ticket for Amaz, please," the woman said, and Monica watched with renewed hope as the clerk issued her a ticket. Amaz had apparently moved to Latin America. Monica could not bring herself to see anything very strange in that. "One ticket to Amaz, please," she said to the clerk, her voice shaking.

The plane left almost immediately. She was very tired. She leaned back in her seat and tried to sleep. Two sentences looped through her mind, like fragments of a forgotten song. "Death is different in this country." And, "You have to learn to stop looking for rational explanations." She tried not to hope too much.

She must have slept, because the next thing she knew the stewardess was shaking her awake. "We've landed," the stewardess said.

Monica picked up her suitcase and followed the others out of the plane. The landing field was almost pitch-dark, but the heat of the day persisted. She went inside the terminal and had her passport stamped and then followed the crowd down the narrow corridor.

Jeremy came up to her out of the crowd. She dropped her suitcase and ran to him, put her arms around him, held on to him as if her life depended on it.

▽

AFTERWORD

D eath is Different," like "Cassandra's Photographs,"
started with a character—in this case Monica, who realizes that she doesn't need to have adventures vicariously
through men, that she can go out and live adventurously on
her own. Once I had the character the natural place to put
her was Amaz. I was happy to have the chance to revisit the
place, to see how it had changed since I had gone there with
Charles in "Tourists."

BREADCRUMBS AND STONES

M y sister and I grew up on fabulous stories. Night after night we would listen, spellbound, as my mother talked of kings and queens, of quests through magical lands, of mythical beasts and fantastic treasure and powerful wizards. As I got older I realized that these were not the tales my friends and classmates were hearing: my mother was making them up, piecing them together from a dozen different places.

She seemed like a queen herself, tall and pale, a woman made of ivory. When I was a child I was sure she was the most beautiful person I knew. Yet she changed when she went outside the house, when she had to deal with grocers and policemen and bank tellers. Her store of words dried up, and she spoke only in short formal phrases. Her accent, nearly nonexistent at home, grew worse. But she never lost her grace or became awkward. It seemed instead as if she changed like one of the heroes of her stories, turned from a living woman into a statue.

I rarely thought about my childhood. But now, as we waited at the hospital, my father, my sister and I, all these things went through my mind. My mother's condition was the same, the nurse had told us: she was sleeping peacefully. There was no reason for us to stay.

We stayed, I guess, because we couldn't think of anywhere else to go. "They've got her in a room with a terminal patient, a woman who's had three operations so far," my father said. He was angry and on edge; every few minutes he would stand and pace to the soda machine. "What kind of atmosphere is that for her?"

My sister Sarah and I said nothing. Was our mother a terminal patient too? We knew only that she had been in and out of the hospital, and that her illness had been diagnosed at least a year before my father told us about it. There were so many things we did not say in our family; we had grown used to mystery.

Finally Sarah stood up. "There's nothing we can do here," she said. "I'm going home."

"I'll go with you," I said quickly.

Sarah lived in a one-room apartment in the Berkeley hills. She had a couch that turned into a bed and a wall of bookshelves and stereo equipment, and very little else. She made us some tea on a hot plate and we sat on the couch and sipped it, saying nothing.

"Do you think she's been happy, Lynne?" Sarah asked finally.

"What do you mean?"

"Well, if she's—I don't think she's got much longer. Do you think it was all worth it? Did she have a good life? Did we treat her all right?"

"I don't know. No, I do know. She always tried to be cheerful for us, but there was something—something she kept hidden. I don't know what it was." We had been talking about her in the past tense, I noticed, and I resolved to stop.

"Was it us?"

"I don't think so." I thought of our father, an American soldier she had met after the war. Did she ever regret marrying such an ordinary man? "Maybe it was—maybe it's Dad. She felt she made a bad marriage."

"Maybe it was something about the war," Sarah said.

We had asked, of course, what had happened to her in the war. She had been born in Germany, but her parents had managed to place her with a Christian family and get her forged papers saying she was not Jewish. She looked like what the Nazis had considered Aryan, tall and blond, so the deception had not been difficult. She had worked in a glass-blowing factory, making vacuum tubes. Her parents had been sent to a concentration camp and had died there; we had never known our grandparents.

"Maybe," I said.

"Do you ever think—I sometimes wonder if I could have survived something like that. When I was twelve I thought, This is the age my mother was when she went to live with the foster family. And at sixteen I thought, This is when she started at the factory. . . ."

"No," I said, surprised. She had never told me any of this.

"And what happened to our grandparents. I think about that all the time, that something terrible is going to happen. That's why I don't have any furniture, because at the back of my mind—at the back of my mind I always think, What if I have to flee?"

"To flee?" Perhaps it was the unusual word that made me want to laugh, and that, I knew, would have been unforgivable.

"She hardly told us anything. I used to imagine—the most horrible things."

"You shouldn't think of things like that. She had it better than most."

"But why didn't she tell us about it? Everything I know about her life I heard from Dad."

"Because—Because she had to be secretive in order to survive, and she never got over it," I said. I had never spoken about any of this before, had not known I knew it. "Once when I was a kid, and we were in some crowded place—I think it was an airport—I tried to get her attention. I kept calling, 'Mom. Mom,' and she wouldn't look at me. And finally I said, 'Hey, Margaret Jacobi,' and she turned around so fast . . . I thought she was going to hit me. She said, 'Don't ever mention my name in a public place.' "

"I know. And she would never fill out the census. She hid it away that one time, remember, and a man came to the door. . . ."

"And she wouldn't talk to him. He kept threatening her with all these terrible things—"

"And then Dad came home, thank God, and he answered it."

"I thought they were going to take her away to jail, at least."

I was laughing now, a little nervously, hoping I could make Sarah forget her terrible thoughts. But then she said, "Why do these things happen?"

"What things?"

"You know. Cancer, and concentration camps."

But I had no idea. Why did she have to ask such uncomfortable questions? The best I could do was change the subject and hope she would forget about it.

The next week my father called and told me that my mother had asked for me. I hurried to the hospital and met him and Sarah at her bedside. But by the time I got there her eyes were closed: she seemed to be asleep.

"They had to give her a shot—she was in a lot of pain," my father said. "They told me she was getting better." He seemed barely able to contain his anger at the doctors who had given him hope. I could see that he needed to hold someone responsible, and I understood; I felt the same way myself.

My mother stirred and said something. "Shhh," I said to my father.

"Did you feed the dog?" my mother asked softly.

We hadn't had a dog in years. "Did you—" she said again, her voice growing louder.

"It's okay, Mom," I said. "Don't worry."

"Good," she said. "Sit down. I'll tell you a story if you like, but you'll have to be quiet."

We said nothing. Her eyes opened but did not focus on any of us. "The princess came to the dark fortress," she said. Her accent was very strong, the "th" sound almost a "d." "It was locked, and she didn't have the key. Did I tell you this story before?"

She had told us so many over the years that I couldn't remember. "No, Mom," I said softly.

"I'll tell you another one," she said. "They went to the woods." She stopped, as if uncertain how to go on.

"Who did?" I said.

"The children," she said. "Their parents took them to the woods and left them there. Their father was a poor wood-cutter, and he didn't have enough to feed them."

To my amazement I realized that she was telling the story of Hansel and Gretel. She had never, as I said, told us conventional fairy tales; I think she considered the Grimms too German, and she avoided all things German after the war.

"The woodcutter's wife had convinced him to leave the children in the woods. But the children had brought along stones, and they dropped them as they walked. The woodcutter told his children that he and his wife would go on a little ways and cut wood, and they left the children there. The children went to sleep, and when they awoke it was dark. But they followed the stones back, and so they came home safely."

I hadn't ever heard this part. The way I knew it Hansel and Gretel had dropped breadcrumbs. But all fairy tales were hazy to me; I had trouble, for example, remembering which was Snow White and which Sleeping Beauty.

"The woodcutter was pleased to see his children, because he had felt bad about leaving them in the woods. But his wife, the children's stepmother, soon began to complain about not having enough food in the house. Once again she tried to convince her husband to take the children to the woods. And after a while he agreed, in order to have peace in the house.

"The children overheard their parents talking, as they had done the last time, and they went to gather stones again. But this time the door to the back was locked."

She closed her eyes. I thought she had fallen asleep and I felt relieved: her story had made me uncomfortable. "The door was locked," my mother said quietly, one last time.

When I think of that summer I see my sister and me in her apartment in the hills, sitting on her couch and sipping tea. She was an elementary school teacher on vacation for the summer, and I had taken a leave of absence from my job to be available to my mother. By unspoken agreement we started going to her place whenever we left the hospital. We were trying to understand something, but since we weren't sure what it was, since our parents had chosen to reveal only parts of the mystery at a time, we had long circular conversations without ever getting anywhere. It was the closest we had been since childhood.

"What happened to Hansel and Gretel?" I asked Sarah. "The children drop breadcrumbs instead of stones the next time, and the birds eat the breadcrumbs so they can't find their way back, and then—"

"Then they meet the witch," Sarah said. "I've read it to the kids at school hundreds of times."

"And the witch tries to—to cook them—"

"To cook Hansel. Oh my God, Lynne, she was talking about the ovens. The ovens in the camps."

"Oh, come on. She'd never even seen them."

"No, but her parents had. She must have been trying to imagine it."

"That's too easy. It was the children who were threatened with the oven in the story, not the parents. And just because you try to imagine it doesn't mean everyone else does."

"I used to think they looked like those ovens in the pizza parlor. Remember? They took us there a lot when we were kids. Long rows of shelves, black and hot. I wondered what it would be like to have to get into one."

I thought of the four of us, sitting in a darkened noisy pizza parlor, laughing at something one of us had just said. And all the while my little sister Sarah had been watching the ovens, imagining herself burning.

"Don't tell me you never thought of it," she said.

"No, not really."

"You're kidding. It happened. We have to face the fact that it happened."

"Yeah, but we don't have to dwell on it."

"How can you ignore—"

"Okay, I'll tell you what I think. If I had survived something like that, the camps, or having been in hiding, I would be grateful. I would think each day was a miracle, really. It would be a miracle to be alive."

"And what about the people who died? The survivors feel guilty just for being alive."

"How do you know?"

"I have books about it. Do you want to see what the ovens looked like?" She stood and headed toward her bookshelves, and I saw, alarmed, that she had a whole shelf of books on the concentration camps.

"No, I don't."

She stopped but did not sit back down. "What must that be like, not to have a home?"

"She does have a home. It's here with us."

"You know what I mean. A whole generation was wiped out, a whole community. All their traditions and stories and memories and customs."

"She has stories—"

"But she made them all up. She doesn't even have stories of her own—she forgot all the ones her parents told her."

"Come on—those were great stories. Don't you remember?"

"That's not the point. She'd lost everything. Dad was always having to tell her about Jewish holidays and customs. She'd forgotten it all."

"She remembered Hansel and Gretel," I said, and for once Sarah had no answer.

A few days later my father called to tell me that my mother was better. She would stay in the hospital for more tests, but he thought that she would be going home soon. I was surprised at the news; at the back of my mind I had been certain she would never return. Perhaps I had absorbed some of Sarah's pessimism.

The day she came home I invited the family over for dinner. My place was larger than Sarah's, with a dining table and dishes and silverware that matched. Still, when I looked around the apartment to make sure everything was ready, I realized I had pared down my life as much as my sister had. I had no close friends at the software company where I worked, I had never dated any man for longer than six months, and I had not lived with anyone since moving away from my family. I never discussed politics or gave my opinion on current events. In Berkeley, California, perhaps the most political city in the United States, I had never put a bumper sticker on my car, or worn a campaign button, or come out for one candidate over another. These things were no one's business but my own.

I had even, I saw now, started to drift away from Sarah. My

sister's words came back to me, but they weren't very funny this time: What if I have to flee?

My parents had dressed up for dinner, as if they were going to a party. My mother wore an outfit I remembered, a violet-gray suit, a gray silk blouse and a scarf of violet gauze, but it was far too large on her. Her skin was the gray-white color of ashes, and her blue veins stood out sharply on her neck and the inside of her wrists. I had seen her in the hospital and was not shocked at the changes; instead I felt pity, and a kind of squeamish horror at what she was going through.

I don't remember much of that dinner, really, just that my mother ate little, and that we all made nervous conversation to avoid the one thing uppermost in all our minds. And that my mother said she wanted to hike through Muir Woods, a favorite spot of hers. Sarah and I quickly volunteered to take her, both of us treating her request as the last wish of a dying woman. As, for all we knew, it was.

It was sunny the day I drove my sister and mother across the San Rafael Bridge to Marin County and up Mount Tamalpais. The road wound up past the dry, bleached grass of the mountainside. Then, as we went higher, this began to give way to old shaded groves of eucalyptus and redwood. Light shot through the branches and scattered across the car.

We parked at the entrance to Muir Woods. It was a weekday and so the place was not too crowded, though the tourists had come out in force. We went past the information booth and the cafeteria, feeling a little smug. We did not need information because we knew the best places to hike, and we had packed a lunch.

There is a well-worn circular trail through the woods that brings you back to the parking lot, and there are paths that branch off from this trail, taking you away from the crowds. We chose one of these paths and began to hike through the trees. Squares and lozenges of light fell over us. The ground was patterned in the green and brown and gold of damp leaves and twigs and moss. We could hear a brook somewhere beneath us, but as we climbed higher up the mountain the sound faded and we heard only the birds, calling to one another.

After a while my mother began to lag behind and Sarah and I stopped, pretending we were tired. We sat on a rock and took out the sandwiches. When I gave my mother hers I brushed against her hand; her skin was as cold as glass. We ate in silence for a while.

"There's no good way to say this, I suppose," my mother said. Sarah and I stopped eating and looked up, watchful as deer. "You children had an uncle. My brother."

Whatever revelation we were expecting, it was not this one. "You would have liked him, I think," my mother said. "He loved children—he would have spoiled you both rotten. His name was Johann."

Uncle Johann, I thought. It sounded as distant as a character in a novel. "What happened to him?" Sarah asked.

"We were both adopted by a Christian family," my mother said, and I saw that for once she would not need prompting to tell this story, that she had probably rehearsed it over and over in her mind. "You remember, the one I told you about. And then when we were old enough we began to work in the factory, making the vacuum tubes. Once I dropped some of the liquid glass on my foot—molten glass, is that the right word? I still have the scar there." She pointed to her right foot. The scar, which I had never noticed, was hidden by the hiking shoe.

"Everyone laughed, I suppose because I was new at the work, and so clumsy. But Johann came to my side immediately, and put towels soaked in cold water on the burn."

She did not look at either of us as she spoke. It was as if she were compelled to tell the story to its end, without stopping. Yet her voice was level and calm, and I could not help but think that she might as well be telling us one of her fabulous stories.

"Johann was a little hotheaded, I think. At home he would talk about sabotage, about making vacuum tubes that didn't work or even about blowing up the factory, though I don't know where he would have gotten the dynamite. He talked about his connections in the Underground. We were together nearly all the time, in the factory and at home, and I knew that he had no connections. But I could not help but worry about him—the Germans were taking younger and younger men into the army as the war began to turn against them, and I knew that soon it would be Johann's turn.

"Near the end of the war, as more and more young men were drafted, the Germans brought in prisoners from the labor camps to work in the factory. We knew that these prisoners were probably Jews, and it made Johann angry to see how they were treated—they had to work longer hours than we did, and had less to eat at the midday break. He wanted to do something for them, to contact them in some way.

"We got into horrible arguments about it. You must understand that we hardly ever talked to our fellow workers for fear of giving ourselves away, and so the only company we had was each other. We had become like two prisoners who had shared the same cell for far too long—for a time we could not say anything without giving offense.

"I told him I thought these prisoners were better off than the ones in the camps, because by this time we had begun to hear terrible rumors about what went on in those places. I said that he could do nothing for them, that he would only raise their hopes if he went to talk to them, and that he would be putting himself in danger for nothing. And I pointed out that they didn't speak German anyway—they seemed to be mostly Hungarians and Poles.

"As I said, we couldn't speak to each other without causing pain. He called me a coward. He said—oh, it was horrible—he said that I had lived among the Germans for so long that I had begun to think like one, that I believed myself superior to these people. And—and he said more, too, of a similar nature.''

I noticed that my mother had said it was horrible, but that her expression and her tone still did not change. And that she did not stop telling her story but continued on as calmly as though she were reading it from a book. Her fingers picked at the sandwich, dropping pieces of it on the ground.

"So I didn't speak to him for a week. I had only my foster parents to speak to, and I—well, I was an adolescent, with an adolescent's certain, impatient opinions about the world, and I had started to hate my adopted family. They were Germans, weren't they? And so at least partly responsible for this war and the dreadful things that were happening. I had heard the remarks my fellow workers made about the Jews at the factory, and I thought my foster parents must feel the same way. So what if they had saved my life, and my brother's life? Perhaps I hated them for that too, for their courage and generosity.

"Was Johann right? I don't know. We might have been able to help these people, but I can't think how. Perhaps if everyone who felt the way my brother did had done something—I don't know.

"We used to walk each other home when our shift ended, but now I started going home by myself. I couldn't bring myself to speak to anyone. I felt that I was alone, that no one understood me. The war might not have existed, I was so deeply buried within myself.

"There was a young man at the factory, a German, who began to watch me as I worked, who always seemed to be next to me when I turned around. I thought he was a spy, that he knew my secret. You children, oh, you've lived such a pampered life—you have no idea what we went through. We had to suspect everyone, everyone. Then one of the women who worked near me said, 'I think Franz is in love with you.'

"Of course I hated him—I don't have to tell you that. He was a German. It's strange, isn't it? We had such strong feelings about each other, and we had never spoken a word together.

"When he saw that Johann and I had stopped walking home together he started to wait for me at the end of my shift. I tried everything I could to avoid him, but some days it just wasn't possible. I was terrified that he would make some remark about the Jews working in the factory, and that I would not be able to contain myself and somehow give myself away. After a week of this I was desperate to make up with Johann again, to have everything the way it had been before. I hadn't forgotten what he had said to me, but I had convinced myself that it didn't matter. Well, you've been an adolescent too—you know how quickly you can change your feelings about something.

"I managed to avoid Franz and I waited outside the factory when my shift ended. But Johann didn't come out. Soon all my fellow workers had gone home, and the new shift had started, and I still didn't see Johann. I went back inside.

"Did I ever tell you what the factory looked like? It looked like hell. Whenever people say anything about hell I always nod, because I know what they're talking about. The place was huge, with low ceilings and almost no light to work by, just the yellow flames of the gas jets. It was hot in winter and like a furnace in summer, with everyone's jet on all the time. We dipped into the big vats of liquid glass and blew our tubes, and that was all we did, eight and nine hours a day. We were allowed to sit down only at the midday meal.

"At first I couldn't find Johann at all. Then I saw that he was walking over to the part of the factory where the Jews worked, and that when the guard looked away he passed a note to one of the prisoners. The other man read it and then turned on his jet of fire and burned it. And neither of them had looked at the other.

"Johann grinned when he saw me and said, 'It's all taken

care of.' I wondered what he meant, but I was so glad he was talking to me again that I didn't really care. And maybe he had been right; maybe he could do something for these people.

"When we left the factory I saw that I hadn't gotten rid of Franz after all—he was waiting for me at the door to the factory, and he was smiling, as if he knew something. Had he seen Johann? But I felt something of my brother's confidence, and I put Franz out of my mind until the next day.

"Franz sat next to me during the midday break. 'What is your brother doing?' he asked.

" 'What do you mean?' I said. I am a very poor liar; I had always dreaded the thought of someone, anyone, asking me questions.

" 'I saw him the other day talking to the Jews,' Franz said. To this day I cannot stand to hear a German say the word 'Jew'—*Jude,*' they say, in that horrible accent."

She did not seem to realize that that "horrible accent" was her own as well. I said nothing.

"What was wrong with Johann? Franz asked. He leaned closer to me and raised his voice at the same time. I was desperate to ask him to speak quietly but I could say nothing, or his suspicions would fall on me. Was Johann a Jew-lover? Some kind of spy?

"I felt battered by his questions. He became more offensive. Why did I never leave my brother's side? Was I in love with him? Was I a Jew-lover as well? If I knew something about my brother's activities I had better go to the authorities and tell them, hadn't I?

"Then he said something I have thought about every day of my life. 'I might just go to the authorities with what I know,' he said.

" 'What do you mean?' I said. 'Don't be stupid. He hasn't done anything.'

" 'Good,' Franz said. 'You'll stop me, won't you?'

"It's obvious to me today that he wanted to—to blackmail me. That he wanted me to walk home with him, or he would report Johann. And probably he wanted more as well, wanted sex, though I tried not to think of that at the time. I was young, and very sheltered, and even the thought of having to speak to him made me shudder with disgust. So I convinced myself that that could not be what he meant, and that he had no proof against Johann. And, for all I knew, Johann had not done anything. So I avoided Franz, and a week passed, and I began to relax.

"Only once in all that time did Franz try to contact me. He walked by me and gave me a note, and I burned it without reading it. I thought that that would tell him I wanted nothing more to do with him, and that he would leave us alone.

"But the next day when we came to work the prisoner who had gotten Johann's note was gone. Johann noticed it first, and I felt him become stiff with fear beside me, terrified to go to his place in the factory. 'What?' I said. 'What is it?'

" 'You don't know anything about anything,' Johann said. 'Don't worry, I'll tell them that.'

" 'What's happened?' I said, but at that moment three men in the uniform of the Gestapo came into the factory, and Johann began to run.

"One man guarded the door, so the only place Johann could go was up the stairs. There were several floors above us—I think they were offices—but we were not allowed to go off the first floor and so I had never seen them. Johann must have run as far as he could go, until he was trapped, and then they brought him back down—" She was crying now, but her expression still had not changed. She wiped at her eye with her hand. "I saw him on a Red Cross list after the war. He had died in Auschwitz."

Sarah and I said nothing. We were not a family used to confidences, to strong emotion. I wondered how my mother could have kept this story from us for so many years, and what

I could possibly say to her. And I remembered Sarah's question—"Do you think she was happy?"—and I thought that nothing could be more irrelevant to her life.

"Does Dad know?" Sarah asked finally.

"I think so," my mother said.

You *think* so? I thought, horrified. How had she told him? With hints and misdirection, just as she had always answered our questions, until finally he suspected the worst? But my mother had become silent. We would get no more stories today. For the first time I thought she looked very old.

We began to walk back. Had Gretel, I wondered, come back to the forest with her daughter? Many years later, when she was an old woman and tired of secrets, had she taken her daughter by the hand and followed the old path? What could she have said to her?

"This is where our parents left us, in that clearing by the brook. And here's where we saw the cottage. Look there— the trees have come and claimed it. And this is where the oven was, this place where all the leaves seem burnt and dry. We saw these things when we were young, too young, I guess, and all we knew was terror. But there were miracles too, and we survived. And look—here is the path that you can take yourself."

It seemed to me that all my life my mother had given me the wrong story, her made-up tales instead of Hansel and Gretel, had given me breadcrumbs instead of stones. That she had done this on purpose, told me the gaudiest, most wonder-filled lies she knew, so that I would not ask for anything more and stumble on her secret. It was too late now—I would have to find my own way back. But the path did not look at all familiar.

AFTERWORD

As I said earlier, I've never been very good at writing to an editor's assignment. So when Ellen Datlow told me about an anthology of stories based on fairy tales she was co-editing with Terri Windling I promptly forgot all about it. Then one day I remembered that as a child I had confused the ovens of the concentration camps with the oven in "Hansel and Gretel," and I thought that something might be made of that.

But fairy tales are never as simple as they seem. Perhaps because of the primal nature of the tale I was writing about the story grew broader and deeper at every turn. I realized that instead of writing about a superficial parallel, as I had thought, I was exploring the ways in which parents abandon children: Hansel and Gretel, Margaret and Johann, and finally Lynne and Sarah. Because of this complexity—like most fairy quests, half planned and half discovered along the way—"Breadcrumbs and Stones" is my favorite of all my stories.

The Woman in the Painting

25 June 1858

My Dear Henry—

You will not believe what a treasure I found yesterday. As you know, I had been trying to finish the painting I began last January, but it grows no closer to completion, and indeed I sometimes feel that it will never be done, that I will still be attempting it when I have grown too old and feeble to hold a brush. And yesterday I had an additional problem: the light was poor, a sooty, sunless London day. As the painting proved impossible I resolved instead to take a walk to clear my brain, and I headed toward the shops in Leicester Square.

And that is where I saw her, in a milliner's shop. At first, as I gazed at her through the dusty window, I thought her quite plain, with pallid brown hair and a thin, ungenerous mouth. To be honest I don't know why I stared for so long, except that she posed a minor sort of mystery: She was not a shop-girl, and in some indefinable way I knew that she was not one of the ladies patronizing the store.

Then she turned and saw me. Do you know how some women seem to change their appearance in an instant? I cursed myself for thinking her plain. Her hair was not brown but long and thick and black; her mouth was red, her skin so white it seemed luminous.

I have thought about our first meeting several times since then, but I cannot explain that first glimpse I had of her. Perhaps when she turned to me my soul understood her as she truly is; perhaps (more likely, I admit) I had first seen her through a distortion in the glass.

I must have stared for several seconds, longer, I fear, than propriety allows. But when I came to my senses I saw that she was not offended. There was a dreamy expression on her face, a vague sort of confusion; everything in the store seemed equally a mystery to her, the hats, the shopgirls, the other ladies present. I yearned to paint her.

I went into the store, lifted my hat to her, and asked if I could be of assistance. She looked vastly startled, as if she had worked out that the store was inhabited only by women; my presence there threatened to pose a further mystery. Then her lips moved a little—I cannot describe so slight a motion as a smile—and she said, "You are very kind, sir."

When she first spoke to me she had a faint accent, a way of pronouncing her words as if she were more used to singing than speaking. Now, a day later, the accent is quite gone. I cannot account for this. Everything about her is a mystery.

She would have said more, I believe, but at that moment she collapsed into a dead faint.

Bustle, commotion, ladies stepping back in horror, shopgirls hurrying to offer her smelling salts. At length her eyes fluttered open—they were a deep blue—and she moaned a little. The confusion had returned to her eyes.

The shopgirls were concerned, of course, but when she managed to stand, aided by two or three of them, they could not think what to do with her. One suggested that she rest in a chair provided for the patrons of the store, but the others quickly demurred—the owner of the shop would return soon, and the owner, it seemed, was a terrible dragon.

And there matters would have stayed, had I not lifted my

hat a second time and offered to find the woman's family. The girls turned to me gratefully, and in a short time I was leading this extraordinary woman through the streets of London.

Not knowing what else to do, I took her to a good restaurant and watched, amazed, as she ate a meal large enough for several stevedores. Her problem, then, had been simple hunger, as I had hoped; I had feared consumption, or worse.

And there my tale ends. She dropped off to sleep on my couch as soon as I brought her back to the studio, woke briefly this morning for another of her gargantuan meals, and is at present sleeping again. I have been able to find out next to nothing about her; she does not seem to know who her family is, or where she came from, or what she did before her collapse. I recited several names to her—Mary, Elizabeth, Jenny—and she responded strongest to Jenny, so that is what I call her.

She seems a gift from the gods. I wanted nothing more than to paint her, and here she is, delivered to my studio as if by heavenly messenger. I have abandoned the painting I had struggled with for so long and have started several preliminary sketches, hoping to use her as a model when she grows strong enough.

I trust that you and Kate are well. I know you both will understand if I ask you not to visit my studio for a few weeks—I am anxious to begin the new painting, and I work best with no distractions. I will write you as often as I can; our mail system, the best in the world, will see to it that I keep in touch with you.

Your loving friend,
John

26 June 1858

Dear John—

I must admit that your letter disturbed me very much. For one thing, I would like the opportunity to examine this woman. I speak not only as a doctor but as one who has seen the ravages of consumption at close hand—for surely you remember when Kate's poor sister Anna died of the disease. From what you tell me it seems quite possible that this unfortunate woman, this Jenny, is also a victim of consumption. Like many laymen you seem to think that you have enough medical knowledge to make a diagnosis, and such a belief is dangerous, both to you and to her.

But you put yourself in moral danger as well. Surely you must see that it is quite impossible for her to live with you. If she is an honest woman who has lost her memory you compromise her to the extent that she may no longer be able to make her way in society. Even if you act the perfect gentleman with her your situation is one that is bound to cause talk. And no doubt she has friends and family who are frantic with worry about her—think of them, and of what the loss of their loved one must mean to them.

And if she is not a lady—well, then, in that case I fear you compromise yourself. In either circumstance you must stop your painting and make every effort to find this woman's family. Failing that, you must put her in a hospital. In any case, I would like to see her and make a diagnosis.

> Your most sincere friend,
> Henry

26 June 1858
Dearest John,

I would like to add my voice to that of my husband, to ask you to allow us to come call on you at the studio. Henry and I have never forgotten your kindnesses to us during the dreadful year when my sister was ill, and we would consider it an honor to be allowed to repay you.

> Your loving friend,
> Kate

27 June 1858

Henry—

It is not surprising that you abandoned painting when we were together at university. The surprise is that you became a doctor instead of a prating literal-minded clerk; you have the very soul of a clerk. Why must you constantly prostrate yourself before the god Propriety? There is nothing unseemly about my sharing the studio with this creature: she is ill, and cannot be moved for days, perhaps weeks.

You are my doctor, true, but you are not my conscience. Really, Henry, the accusations you make! I must confess myself surprised you did not go on to call me a white slaver. Please believe me when I say that she is as safe here as she would be in any house in England. And I am doing everything in my power to find her family.

And tell me, O keeper of my conscience, what would you have done with her? Where would you have taken her? She has still not remembered her family, or her occupation if she had one. I am afraid she is a prostitute, one of the many women who have come to London and have been unable to find work in more honest trades. And if that is the case then it is an act of mercy for me to use her as my model. Though society frowns on women who model for artists we both know that this is honorable work, and far more worthy of her than her former profession.

You will be happy to hear that I have started a new painting, one inspired by her beauty. She has lost the confused expression she had when I found her; she now seems regal, unmoved, as remote as an allegorical figure or an ancient queen. Of course I must paint her as Guinevere, waiting for Lancelot. I believe strongly that it will be the best thing that I have ever done.

Please do not come visit, as I cannot afford the time to receive you. I must take advantage of every minute of the day until the light fails. And even then, with the help of dozens of lamps, I am able to work, to paint in the background while She sleeps.

—John

28 June 1858
My Dear John—

I am sorry if my letter offended you—you must know that I was only trying to offer my help. If you will not let me see this woman I hope you will tell me more about her. What are her symptoms? Does she grow stronger or weaker? Does she speak of her family at all? What was she wearing when you met her?

I hope that you are well.

Your sincere friend,
Henry

29 June 1858
My Dear Henry—

I am happy to see that you have climbed down from your high horse, that you are able to discuss the matter of Jenny calmly. And you must know I never truly opposed you, my dear friend; of course she must be found lodgings as soon as possible. But, as I said before, she is far too ill to be moved now.

You ask about her clothes. They are of surprisingly good quality. I know next to nothing about women's clothing, but even I can see that hers are made of good fabric, with fine lace at the throat and wrists. Upon reading this you will, I know, return immediately to your earlier suspicions and tell me that she is a great lady, but I am now entirely convinced, for reasons I will tell you later, that this is not the case. It is far more likely, I think, that she had the patronage of some wealthy lord, and lost it again.

Besides, it no longer matters to me who she is. She is Guinevere.

She is also, unfortunately, quite mad, and this is why I do not believe she is a lady; no family of high birth would let their daughter wander the streets in her condition. She wakes several times a night and goes to the windows; once there she looks out at the stars for minutes, sometimes hours. If she were not so clearly a human woman I would think her an angel, longing for heaven. And she asks questions about the most ordinary things—What is a pen? What is a butter knife? She seems a blank slate, a canvas on which I may paint anything.

Yours,
John

30 June 1858
My Dear Henry—

I write you in a state of high excitement. Before I can continue, though, I must ask you not to repeat, under any circumstances, what I am about to tell you.

I would also ask you not to judge me. I know you are worried about the possibility that I might corrupt this woman, but I must assure you that she was as eager for what happened as I.

She is, as I mentioned before, ignorant about things of the world; there is no guilt for her in matters of the flesh. Unlike most women she showed no coy hesitation as she removed her dress; rather, she seemed curious as to what might come next.

I write you not to boast about my conquest but to ask your professional advice as a doctor. For I have to tell you that when she removed her undergarments it seemed for a moment that her parts were not formed as are those of other women. For the space of an instant I saw nothing but a smooth expanse of skin between her legs. And then this skin seemed to unfold as I watched, petaling like a flower, or opening like an eye. . . .

So quickly did this happen that once or twice since I wondered if I imagined it. But I know beyond a doubt that it did take place.

My question to you, of course, is—Is such a thing possible? Have you ever come across such a thing in your practice?

Yours sincerely,
John

2 July 1858
John—

No doubt you believe I should apologize for my sudden visit to your studio. I will not apologize, however. I believe I was right to call on you when I did, that your extraordinary letter absolved me of all blame. It is impossible for a friend of long standing to stand by while another follows a course harmful to himself and to others.

And now that I have seen the woman you call Jenny I know that I have a reason for my concern. You called her remote, disinterested, but having heard her story I could not see her as anything but a woman in the greatest distress. Several times, while you were not watching, I was certain that she looked at me with the most pitiable expression, as if she asked me to rescue her from the impossible situation which entangled her. She looked, in fact, a little like my wife Kate, though younger.

What have you done to her, to this innocent, unfortunate woman? I must confess that I cannot forget the contents of your last letter to me, and that I shudder whenever I remember how you used her. You must stop. You *must* remember that she is not in her right mind.

I even thought of severing all ties with you, of refusing to speak to you until the woman is returned to the bosom of her family. I feel, however, that her interests would be best served if I continued to press you to give her up. Kate and I would be happy to have her in our house until her family is found.

My father is ill; I am leaving for the country tomorrow to tend to him. Kate will remain in London. I urge you to write to her, to tell her how you are getting on with your search. It is unfortunate that women of good breeding cannot visit artists' studios alone, or I would have her call on you.

Yours most sincerely,
Henry

3 July 1858
Dearest Kate—

You must not believe a word your husband says about me. I am, in fact, healthier than I have been in years. I feel renewed, almost reborn. I am working harder than I have ever done in my life.

I have finished the painting of Guinevere, but I grew dissatisfied with it the moment it was done. How could I have thought her remote, unattainable? She is a woman like any other. I am painting her meeting with Lancelot—she will be the very personification of Carnality. It is my best painting so far.

I hope you are well, and that Henry will return soon.

Your sincere friend,
John

4 July 1858
Dearest Kate—

Did I call her Guinevere? She is Morgan le Fay, the temptress, the sorceress, the lamia. She has ensorcelled me; I cannot rid my thoughts of her.

I have started another painting. I am determined to capture her, to fix her forever on canvas *as she truly is*. I am devouring her. No—she is devouring me. But if I can capture one iota of her beauty my paintings will be the talk of London.

—John

5 July 1858
My Dearest Husband—

I must confess that I have visited John in his studio today. Please do not be angry—I am sending you his latest letter to me, and I am certain that when you read it you will understand my concern.

You told me that when you called on him he did not want to let you inside. I am afraid that he is now so obsessed with this woman that he is indifferent to visitors—he opened the door without asking for my name, murmured a few words and nodded absently, and then motioned me in. Once I was inside the studio, however, he seemed to forget my presence entirely, and paid no more attention to me than he did to his furniture—less, in fact, since he painted his furniture.

His studio was lit by dozens of lamps and candles, all of them artfully arranged to show his Jenny in the best light. Do you remember that horrible gargoyle candelabrum, the one he displayed proudly at a dinner party until we all begged him to hide it away? That was there, resting on the floor, the wax dripping slowly into its open mouth.

Against the wall I saw a half-finished painting of Eve offering the apple to Adam, and another of a sorceress luring a figure, possibly Merlin, into a cave. The canvas on his easel held the barest outline of a tall dark-haired woman. The colors were astonishing, vibrant and strong. He said in the letter I enclose that his paintings will be the talk of London, and I do believe that if he shows them they will not be soon forgotten.

I must tell you I was very alarmed by his appearance. His

face was pale, his eyes sunken; his clothes, which were stained with paint, were as rumpled as if he had worn them for a week or more.

If I was worried by him, however, I became even more concerned about the woman Jenny. You said that she seemed pitiable, uncertain. At first I did not find her so at all; she looked hard, all glittering surface, a little cruel. But after a while—No, I will tell you the story in the order in which it occurred.

She lay against his divan, dressed in white and green. Golden jewelry glinted against her neck and at her fingers. As he worked the sun came out, shining so brightly through his windows that I had to squint to see against it, but he did not pause to douse the lamps. I remember what you told me, that he is in great want because he has not sold (or indeed completed) a painting in quite some time, and I was alarmed at his profligacy.

He stopped for a moment and looked around him. He swore horribly—I will not repeat what he said. Then he looked at Jenny and said, "Where is my other paintbrush?"

She said nothing. I truly believe she did not know. He paced up and down the room, agitated. "Answer me!" he said. "What do you have to say for yourself? Nothing—I assumed so. You were nothing before I found you. Where did you put my paintbrush?"

I had to speak in her defense. "She doesn't know," I said, timidly enough. "Can't you see that?"

"Hold your tongue!" he said to me. "Don't defend her to me. You don't know what she is."

I could not think what to say to this. Before I could answer, however, he left the room, still cursing, to look for his paintbrush.

I took advantage of his absence to study the woman Jenny. And at that moment the most extraordinary thing happened. She seemed to—to change her shape. She was no longer the woman of his paintings, aloof, cold, cruel, but fragile, thin and pale. She looked like nothing so much as my sister Anna before she died.

I asked her her name and the name of her family. She seemed not to regard me at first, but gradually I thought she warmed to me; she even tilted her head to the side as Anna used to do when she wanted to concentrate on something.

I think it is true that she is quite mad. She told me that she had come from the heavens, that when night fell she could point out the very star that is her home. I asked her if she thought she was an angel.

"An angel!" John said, coming back into the room. I turned to him, startled by his sudden entrance. He laughed. "Where are the other angels, then, all the heavenly host?"

She shook her head. "Lost," she said. "All lost, and I have forgotten much—"

"An angel," John said, laughing again. "You do not know her, or you would not say such a thing. She is a very devil, a devil from Hell."

"She is nothing of the sort," I said. "She is a poor harmless woman, a lost soul. She deserved better than to be found by you."

"Nonsense," he said. "I rescued her. If I had not taken her to my studio she would have—well, you know what happens to women of her sort. She is lucky to be here."

He wiped his face, which was wet with perspiration. We were all terribly hot—the heat blazed from the windows, and the candles and lamps, as I said, still burned around the room. I forced myself to become calm.

"John, my good friend," I said, trying to speak in soothing tones. "How can you say she is evil? You know nothing about her, nothing at all, not even her station in life."

"She is a temptress," he said. "She will be the death of me yet."

"Come—look at her, see her how she really is. Don't you think she resembles my sister Anna?"

He turned to her—we both turned to her. And there, on

his divan, was the image of my poor dead sister. How could I have thought her cold, cruel?

His face changed in an instant. "Dear God," he said. He wiped his face again on his sleeve. Then he hurried to one of the pieces of paper scattered around the room and began to sketch.

I looked over his shoulder and saw a drawing of Anna, her large eyes, the pale skin with the two red spots of consumption on her cheeks. As I watched he drew several bold lines, and then several more—wings. He had made Anna an angel.

I remembered that he had regarded my sister as a saint, especially in the last terrible days of her illness. "I see," he said, talking as if to himself. "I see it all now. I will capture her yet—she will not escape me."

Once again I did not know what to say. I was certain that he was mad, as mad as she—a *folie à deux*. I turned and left quickly.

I agree with you that the woman should be placed in a better situation as soon as possible. Your suggestion that she live with us until her family is found seems to me a good one, and good-hearted as well—you are, as always, a charitable man.

I hope that you are well, and that your father is improving. I would like to have you home again, so that we may do something about this dreadful situation.

> Your loving wife,
> Kate

7 July 1858

Kate—

I cannot thank you enough for your insight into Jenny's character. There is a brilliance about her that is hers alone; when I fixed a strand of pearls at her neck they kindled into light, as if they caught fire from her. She is an angel—that explains the innocence I saw in her when I first rescued her. I need her, need that innocence, to start afresh, to be reborn. She makes me see everything in a new light.

—J.

20 July 1858
Dearest Henry—

These past two weeks I have felt the most terrible apprehension for John. I waited anxiously each day for the morning and afternoon post, but nothing arrived from him. My worry grew to such a pitch that I felt I must visit him again, despite your prohibition.

Accordingly I called on him at his studio today. (You must forgive my shaking handwriting—I am still terribly alarmed by what I saw there.) My dear Henry, I am sorry to tell you that the situation is worse than ever. He is emaciated, his face sunken, his eyes huge. Flies buzz around the remains of his meals, rotting meat and vegetables, and the room has a terrible smell. I do not think he has eaten in several days. And she—she is thinner and paler than ever. My heart goes out to her, poor creature.

The room was dim, shadowy—all of the lamps were out, and the candles were nearly extinguished, leaving pale clots of wax on the floor. The sun, which had burned so brightly the last time I visited, had gone behind a cloud, and a thin rain fell. Dusty fans and feathers and tin crowns lay scattered about the floor.

And yet there was a strange light in the room. I hope you will not think me as mad as he is if I tell you that the light seemed to come from her, from her lambent face and skin. She was still pale, still thin, her eyes huge—she seemed to be consuming herself, spending her life, as Anna did. I cannot tell you how horrible it was to see this woman suffering so—it was as if I were condemned to watch Anna die twice.

When I looked away from her I could see small lights gleam in the shadowy corners. Some of the light came from the facets of the paste gems with which he had draped her, but others—oh, how I longed to leave, to simply turn and run out the door!—I fear some of the other light came from the glint of rats' eyes in the darkness. They came out to eat the food, and neither John nor Jenny had the strength to chase them away.

Despite the odd light he continued to paint, pausing only once to coil a chain of gold around her arm. "She is ill," I said. "She must be seen by a doctor."

At first he did not seem to hear me. He moved away from her, overturning the gargoyle candelabrum at his foot, and studied his model. Then he said, "She is not ill, though she may seem that way to you."

"How can you say that? She—"

"She is changing, becoming something new. Haven't you noticed?—she appears in a new light from day to day." He lit a match; the light flared up briefly in the darkness. The smell of sulfur lingered for a moment in the room. He bent and lifted a candle, lit it.

"What do you mean?"

"She was remote, a queen of antiquity," he said. He began to pace. The candle lit his face from beneath, made his eyes into hollows, his eyebrows into spread wings. "Then she became carnal, a fleshy woman. And an evil sorceress, and an angel . . . I don't know how she does it, but she—she responds to me somehow. And to you as well—to everyone. You changed her into Anna, didn't you? Your husband thought she resembled you."

"What do you mean?" I asked again, backing away. Nothing I had seen in this room had prepared me for this lunacy.

"But what is she?" he asked. His pacing grew agitated. "She is mystery, an unknowable mystery. You feel it too, you must. She blazes like a fire, but what will happen if she begins to fade, to gutter out like a candle? I must discover the answer before she dies, before we both die. And I will discover it—I will burn her down to her core."

"You're mad," I said, and turned and fled.

My dearest Henry, I have thought of nothing but that poor woman since I left John's studio. I pray that your father regains his health soon, and that you return to me, and that together we may take Jenny from him and place her in our care.

Sometimes—sometimes I wake in the night, and see the stars from our bedroom window, and I wonder if John could be right. What if we each see in this woman what we want to see? It's true that she appeared to me as my sister, and to you as me, and to John, it seems, as every woman he has ever desired.

What if she did come from the sky, as she told me? What better way to ensure her safety among us than to appear as the thing we most love? But then who is she, what is her true appearance? What will happen if John does as he threatens and burns her down to her core?

> Your loving wife,
> Kate

27 July 1858
Dearest Henry—

I am sending you the last letter I received from John. I became alarmed even before I read it, and if you but glance at it you will see why. The handwriting is chaotic, unruly—as he says he wrote the last part completely in the dark.

After I read the letter I hurried to his studio. I found him motionless and dazed, but—God be thanked!—still alive. All his candles had gone out, and only a fitful light came in through the window. Heaps of things lay scattered across the room—in the dim light they were no more than shadows. There was no sign of Jenny.

I brought him home with me, not caring what the neighbors might think, and I fed him. After a little while he responded to my ministrations. He refuses to speak of Jenny—all I know comes from the letter I enclose.

Your loving wife,
Kate

K.—

I have no more food. I have no more candles. For our old friendship's sake I beg you to come to my studio and give me what you can.

And yet I am not in the dark, for the light that comes from her is strong enough to guide me, grows stronger as I watch. I do not know what she is. I know she is changing one last time, and that I am changing as well. Perhaps this last change is death.

Look!—She is—she is shedding everything, all the costumes and jewelry I gave her, all her disguises. She is shedding her skin as well, she is emerging—

And I see—I see Her. She flares, she shines! I know—I understand—But she is gone.

How can I tell you what I saw? I understand now that she was not unknown, but unknowable. She never changed at all, in all the time I knew her—it was I who changed in my efforts to understand her. She was everything, illumination. And my mind could not grasp what she was, and so I put a familiar face on it, called her Jenny, as you called her Anna.

Her light has gone out, extinguished like a candle. But it is enough for me to have understood her for a single second, for her to have illuminated the entire world for me. It is enough to know that for a moment I partook of mystery. Because I am truly in the dark now, with only my pictures and my memories.

—J.

AFTERWORD

T he Woman in the Painting'' grew out of an interest in the
Pre-Raphaelites. In the first draft the characters were actual painters and hangers-on; by the second draft I realized
that my story was saying rather terrible things about a group
of people who hadn't really been all that bad. If there are
libel laws in the afterlife my historical novels have already
given me far too much to answer for, so I changed these people to fictional characters.

DAILY VOICES

C ontinue driving until you see the freeway entrance, and then push the button."

Vivian tried not to feel depressed. It looked like she was going to work today. She had been hoping for a shopping trip, though she knew she had nothing to shop for. "Continue driving until you see the freeway entrance, and then push the button," the voice said again. The freeway, only a mile from her apartment, came up on the right. She pushed the large button on the dashboard of the car. "Get on the freeway and drive until you see the Elm Street exit, then push the button."

Dammit, she thought. There would be no surprises today. She was going to work. Dammit, dammit, dammit. She wondered if she should risk saying something out loud. There was no evidence the voice could hear anything she said. But cowardice held her as always. She knew she would say nothing. And what difference would it make if she did?

The voice came on again with the same instructions. The voice came on every thirty seconds, and the voice's instructions lasted about ten seconds. She had timed it on the dashboard clock. The drive to Elm Street took over ten minutes, so she would have to hear the same instructions twenty times. She wanted to scream. She wanted to press the ugly black button on the dashboard again and again, beating it with her fists. But she didn't dare.

Instead she stared at the clock on the dashboard, watching the second hand glide slowly around the clock-face. Eight more minutes. Seven. She wondered why she had a clock in her car, wondered if everyone had one or if it was unique to her. She had never really needed it except for timing things. And what about the other things on the dashboard: the mileage counter (at 02360.5), the pointer that showed her how fast she was going, the red lights labeled "battery" and "oil"? Did other people have those things too? She liked it when the red lights came on, because then the voice would direct her to a service station and she would get to take the bus home. The bus trip was the only time she got to hear other people and to pick up the clues she would spend hours trying to piece together.

She turned down Elm Street and pushed the button. The voice directed her to 820 Elm Street, #206. She parked the car and climbed the steps to the second story office. As she put her key in the door she could hear the voice inside the office start up immediately: "Turn on the lights and push the button."

Number 206 was a small windowless room with only a desk, a chair, a typewriter, a filing cabinet and a fan that was on all year, winter and summer. The fluorescent lights overhead stuttered as she flicked the switch and then stayed on. She went to the desk and pushed the large black button on the right hand side.

"Alphabetize the papers on the desk and file them in the filing cabinet, then push the button," the voice said. She relaxed a little. Alphabetizing wasn't too bad, was almost fun if you didn't mind the voice in the background coming on once every thirty seconds. It gave you time to think. She hated typing, because her back hurt her after an hour, and

238 ▽ LISA GOLDSTEIN

she hated tearing apart carbons because her hands got covered with the black carbon, but alphabetizing was all right. She sat down and started putting the papers in stacks.

The voice was the only thing she could remember. On her good days she thought there must have been a life before the voice, but on bad days she wondered if the voice had started when she was born and had never let her go. She could remember back only about a year, but there was really no evidence that the year before, or the year before that, or the year before that had been any different. Certainly she could not imagine what her childhood would have been like if the voice hadn't been there.

Sometimes she thought that somewhere along the line she must have made a bad bargain, and that this was the consequence. Whenever she thought that she would try and try to remember what that bargain had been, because if she could remember it she might be able to get free of it. But she could remember nothing before her one room apartment, her car, her work, and the voice connecting them all like beads on a string.

At other times she thought that everyone had a voice in her car, her home, her office, that that was just the way life was. The woman at the checkstand in the supermarket probably had one, and the man who fixed her car, and some of the people on the bus, the ones who seemed barely alive. Maybe, she sometimes thought, everyone forgets their life overnight. Maybe something went wrong and I'm the only one who remembers. That would explain the overelaborate instructions, the ones that go on and on until I'm ready to scream. If people really didn't remember they'd need instructions like that to get them through the day.

But as always the explanation failed to satisfy her. It didn't explain the others, the woman she had seen dancing (dancing!) in the street, the teenage boys with the loud radios, the couples arguing with each other or quietly holding hands, the woman she had once seen in her rear-view mirror crying quietly inside her car. And the coffee shops and movie theaters where people seemed to go, the billboards for vacations in Rio or Paris, parties in the apartment above hers, the fireworks she had once seen flower over the city like a blessing. And anyway, most people seemed to have a radio in their cars instead of a black button; she had looked.

She wondered what it would be like to go to a movie, to take a vacation. Sometimes when she put her key in the door of her apartment and heard the voice start up inside she wanted to run away and never come back. Sometimes when she saw couples kissing in the street she felt happiness and yearning and desire and loneliness, and other feelings she had no words for. She wondered if other people felt these things or if she was unique, or if they felt them more than she did, if their lives were a riot of sensations.

She felt a sharp pang of envy and put her head on the desk for a moment. Her life, the only one she had, was being wasted. "Alphabetize the papers on the desk and file them in the filing cabinet, then push the button," the voice said. She had almost forgotten it. It didn't do to become depressed, she knew, though she had moments of black depression several times a day. She hurried to finish and pushed the button. "Go to the cafeteria on the corner for lunch," the voice said, "come back and push the button."

She wondered what the voice would have said if she'd finished before lunch, if that would have made any difference. She wondered what would happen if she were to go somewhere else for lunch, but as far as she knew the cafeteria was the only place to eat in the neighborhood. She left the office—the door locked behind her—and went to the corner. "A tuna fish sandwich, please," she said to the woman behind the counter at the cafeteria. They were the first words she had spoken all day.

In the afternoon she typed itemized lists of things the company was shipping—auto parts, it looked like, though the last time she had typed a list it had been furniture. When she finished the voice directed her to her car and then to a gas station where she filled up her tank.

"Turn on to Second Street and then push the button," the voice said when she started the car. The voice was taking her to the freeway and then home. For once she didn't mind the instructions. She was tired and hungry and incapable of thought, and wanted only to go home.

She stopped at the light before the freeway. The man in the car next to her had his radio turned up loud and she listened to it eagerly, forgetting her tiredness. A song came to an end, loud and discordant. The announcer gave the title and then another voice came on. "They came from beyond the stars," the voice said, "and Earth trembled beneath their rule."

Who were they talking about? She watched the light anxiously, hoping that it wouldn't turn green. Were they talking about a movie? If it was a movie, she knew, then it wasn't real. But if it was real . . . "Coming to a theater near you!" the radio blared. The light changed and the car sped away.

It was a movie then. But suppose there were people . . . people from the stars . . . "Turn left on to the freeway and then push the button." Dammit. She had almost forgotten and gone straight, eager to follow the car with the radio. She turned left and went home.

At home the voice told her to make a hamburger, and after dinner directed her to the half-finished jigsaw puzzle on the coffee table. She wondered if the voice liked jigsaw puzzles because the instructions for the night never varied: "Find the next piece and push the button." This was the third puzzle she had done. The cover showed an open tin filled with different colored jelly beans. Before the jigsaw puzzles the voice had told her to embroider. Once it had directed her to buy a woodworking set, but the set had been so hard she had collapsed in tears. The voice's even, mechanical tone had started to sound sadistic. The next evening the voice told her to embroider. It had never mentioned the woodworking set again and she had thrown it out stealthily, piece by piece.

The puzzles were relaxing, like alphabetizing. She started to think about the commercial on the radio again. Suppose the voice had come from the stars, suppose people from the stars had taken her over, and others, and were about to . . . to . . . She couldn't think what. Or maybe *she* was from the stars, sent here to observe and report back about life on Earth. Only she didn't have the faintest idea what life on Earth was like.

She started to pick up a piece and then stopped. Could people live on the stars? There were probably books about it, but she couldn't afford a book. The voice kept careful track of her money. She stood and went to the window and back to the coffee table. The night was hot and she was strangely restless. The commercial had given her a new idea, her first new idea in a long time.

Finally she walked to the door and went outside. Behind her the voice said, "Find the next piece and push the button," but she ignored it. She looked up. Bright stars swam across the vast sky, a splendid and infinite array. She had never seen anything so beautiful, so much of a contrast to the finite, precisely-measured instructions of the voice. Her throat hurt to look at it. Finally after a long time she looked away.

A young man stood in front of the apartment next to hers, watching her. In the light from his apartment she could see that he was smiling. For a confused moment she wondered if she wanted to kiss him. Then he said, "It's really somethin', isn't it?"

She didn't understand what he meant. Of course it was something. Everything was something. What a stupid thing to say. She nodded, flustered, and went back to her apartment. The jigsaw puzzle was waiting, and she sat down to it with relief.

The next day there was a check for her on the desk at the

office. She looked at it carefully, as she had looked at the ten or twelve checks she had gotten over the year at the office, though they never varied. "Pay to the order of Vivian Stearns," the check said. Was that her name? Did most people have two names like that, or only one, or three or four? The woman at the supermarket, for example, had a nametag that said her name was Ruby.

She was glad to get the check because it meant the voice would let her off early to cash it. She typed for the rest of the morning and went to the cafeteria for lunch. "Hot, isn't it?" the woman behind the counter said. Vivian hesitated a long moment and then said, "It's really something." The woman nodded and gave her her tuna fish sandwich.

She went back to work feeling almost gleeful. So that was what the man last night had meant! She should have said, "Yeah, it really is," and then they could have had a long talk about the stars, and she could have asked him whether people lived on them, and then she could have invited him to her apartment—No, the voice was there. Well, maybe he would have invited her to his apartment, and she would have found out if he had a voice too.

She was sitting down to the afternoon's work—stamping papers—when she remembered the relief she felt last night back in her apartment. Why had she been so anxious to get away from him? A thought came to her—a horrible thought—and she said, "Oh, no," aloud, though she was usually so careful not to say anything the voice might hear. What if she had once had a life like everyone else's—dancing and movies and vacations—but it had gotten too complicated? What if she had gotten frightened, if she could no longer bear to talk to people because of all the ways they might misunderstand her and she misunderstand them, what if she had gotten more and more frightened, more and more confused, and finally, to simplify everything, she had set up the voice herself? What if she had arranged to work for a company, and to get paid by them, without ever seeing anyone?

Her heart was pounding now, and the blood throbbed in her ears so that she could no longer hear the voice. What if there was no bad bargain, no people from the stars—what if she had done it all herself?

The wave of dizziness passed and she heard the voice say, "Stamp the papers on the desk and push the button." Could that be her voice? She had always thought it was a man's, but she didn't know what her voice sounded like. Shaking, she looked at the check again. As usual the signature was illegible. The company name on the check was Aramco, and the address a post office box. Was there a way to find out who they were?

After a few hours the voice told her to leave the office and go to the bank. It was 3:30 by the clock in the car. She was glad to get out of the heat and into the air-conditioned bank. Two people behind her in line were talking quietly. "She said she had a miscarriage but I'll bet it was an abortion," one of them said.

"But why?" the other one said. "Why would she do that?"

"To get back at her husband," said the first one. "Because he had that affair. You remember."

As usual Vivian listened intently. Was that what had happened to her? A miscarriage, an abortion, a husband who had an affair, a screaming fight, driving off in the night with no destination in mind, crying in the car like that woman she had seen once? Life could be so horrible, so complicated. Would she take it back if she could? Did she really want to know?

When she reached the teller she decided that she did. She cashed the check, asked for a money order to pay her rent, and while the teller was filling out the money order asked, "Do you know—Is there any way to tell who sends me this check? I mean, where it comes from?"

The teller looked at her for a long moment. "Honey, you mean you don't *know*?" she said finally.

"I—No, I don't."

"You mean to tell me you don't know who you work for," the teller said.

Vivian nodded. She wished she hadn't said anything. Behind her the line stirred impatiently.

"I guess—Hell, I don't know." The teller thought a moment. "I guess I would go to this post office here and watch who goes to the box," she said. "The post office is just around the corner. There's no way I can tell you who they are—I don't have access to those records."

Vivian nodded again. "Thanks," she said finally. She picked up her cash and the money order and tried not to look as if she were running from the room. The two people next in line were still deep in conversation.

She drove home and, on the voice's instruction, put the money order in the manager's mailbox, Box #1. There was a Box #7, corresponding to the number of her apartment, but she had never seen anything in it. She wondered, as she did every month, what would happen if she didn't pay the rent, if she saved the money until she had enough to start over somewhere else, in an apartment without a large black button. Would they evict her? Once on the bus she had seen an advertisement that said, "Evicted? Legal Aid can help." She had wanted to copy down the phone number but hadn't dared. And no one else had been paying the slightest attention to the ads; maybe it was wrong somehow.

After dinner she could not concentrate on the jigsaw puzzle. "I guess I would go to this post office here," the woman at the bank had said. What if she just went? The voice would think she was taking an extraordinarily long time to find the next piece in the puzzle. But so what? She got up, went to the window, went back to the puzzle. The heat of the evening was stifling. She wished she had an air conditioner. Maybe she could take the fan home from the office. No, that was crazy. What was wrong with her? It was no wonder she needed a voice to tell her what to do—she was a freak, filled with wild emotions, not to be trusted to make her own decisions.

"Find the next piece and push the button," the voice said. And the next piece, and the next, and so on until she died. What *right* did the voice have? She deserved to know. She would go to the post office, she would confront them, him or her, and . . . and . . . And what? She couldn't think, could only hear the pounding of her heart. After I find this next piece, she thought. No, she thought. Do it now.

Before she could change her mind she picked up her purse and left the apartment. She looked up at the sky, the myriad stars, and felt a little safer. Nothing bad could happen to her beneath that bright canopy. She got in the car and turned the key.

When she heard the voice she thought she would die. It was true, then: the voice watched her at every moment, knew exactly what she was up to. She waited for her punishment. The voice repeated three times before she heard the words. "Go to Main Street and push the button," it said. The voice thought it was morning! She felt silly with relief. The voice thought it was morning and was sending her to the supermarket. The voice was stupid, stupider than she'd ever hoped. Escape was easy. Why hadn't she done this before?

She drove away from the curb before she realized the voice wasn't going to tell her what to do next. She had to figure out her own itinerary. She thought of all the streets in the city, most of which she had never seen, separating and coming together in a great maze. What if she just drove away, threading through the city endlessly, timing herself by the dashboard clock to return in an hour? What if she got lost? The thought made her giddy. Then she remembered her determination. She thought she could find the way to the bank, and the post office, the woman at the bank had said, was just around the corner.

The city looked strange at night, different, as though it

had another life. Two cars flashed their lights at her, on and off, on and off, before she realized she hadn't turned the car's lights on. She missed two turns and had to backtrack, once for fifteen minutes, spellbound by the dark night and the lights of the city, like stars scattered on Earth.

The post office was dark when she finally found it. No, she thought, despairing. I didn't know. It's not fair. She got out of the car to make sure. The post office was closed. She peered through the window, trying to see something in the gloom, then read the hours painted on the glass door, 9–5 Monday through Friday, 9–12 Saturday.

That teller must be crazy, she thought. How could I watch the post office during the day, every day this week? Doesn't she think I work? She went back to the car and sat for a long time. She felt frustrated, blocked at every turn. The voice was far too clever for her. So what if she had escaped it for a night? The voice would have her back. She was still a prisoner.

The depression came on her again, and this time she couldn't stop it by following the voice's instructions. She started the car and headed home. "Go to Main Street and push the button," the voice said. Shut up, she thought. Shut up, shut up, shut up.

The man from the apartment next door was outside again when she drove up. "Hi," he said when she got out of the car.

"Hi," she said.

"This heat is amazing, isn't it?" he said.

"Yes," she said. He seemed to want more from her. "It's really something," she said.

"You know, on nights like this I just want to get away," he said. "Just get into my car and drive. You know what I mean?"

She stared at him. He had said exactly what she was thinking. "Yes," she said. "Yes, I know."

"Where would you go?" he said. "If you could. Anywhere at all."

That was a hard one. She only knew the city, and the names of a few other cities she had seen while typing addresses. But which one should she say? Maybe a city from a billboard. She didn't want him to think she was stupid. He already thinks you're stupid, she thought. Most people don't take this long answering a simple question. Look at the expression on his face. She thought of their conversation last night and said finally, looking at the stars, "Up there?"

He laughed. "I'm with you," he said. "I'm Russ, by the way. Your new neighbor. And you?"

"Vivian," she said, since he had given only one name. Maybe he only had one.

"Okay, Vivian," he said. "I'll see you around."

"Bye," she said. She went into her apartment. "Find the next piece and push the button," the voice said immediately. She closed the door quickly, hoping he hadn't heard.

The voice got her to bed at eleven and then stopped. From eleven to seven in the morning was her time, time to think lazily and to dream. She usually fell asleep after about fifteen minutes. Tonight she wondered if she would sleep at all.

Lying there in the dark she called up a picture of Russ. Did he think she was good-looking? She had only one mirror, a small hand-held one, and what she had seen in it was discouraging. She was too pale, especially in comparison with the women on the billboards, and there was something else wrong with her face—it was too square, maybe, or too angular. The voice had never let her buy the advertised cosmetics and she didn't know what to do with them if it had.

He had liked her answer, though. What had he said? I'm going too. No, he'd said, I'm with you. She sat upright in bed as a new idea came to her. What if he had meant just that, that he was with her? What if he was from the stars, from the stars like she was, and he had come to take her home? In that case she had said exactly the right thing. But when would he take her? Tomorrow, maybe, or the next day. She saw a group of people on a large ship, standing and talking and laughing, and one of them saying, "But what are they like? What are people on Earth like?" And she would laugh and say, "They're so strange. You wouldn't believe it. They have expressions like, 'It's really something.' I mean, what does that mean?"

But the man—Russ—had taught her that expression. So he couldn't be from the stars, could he? She had invented the whole thing, and only because—because she didn't want to think about her other new theory. That she had set up the voice. That she was jailer and prisoner both. And that—even more terrifying—if she had set it up she could stop it. There was nothing to prevent her from never following the voice's commands again.

She drifted toward sleep. "I'm with you," the man had said. "I just want to get away. Just get into my car and drive . . . Where would you go?"

She awoke the next day feeling profoundly different. I did it, she thought. Last night. I really did it. I got away. When the voice told her to wear her brown suit she put on her red dress instead and pushed the button. The voice calmly went on to the next instruction. She cooked her egg for five minutes instead of three. I can do it, she thought. Look, I'm doing it.

She felt dizzy with freedom. I'm going to go, she thought. I'm going to escape. Today. She had to stop, to rest her head on the coffee table, before the trembling would go away. Maybe last night Russ had given her a message from the people who lived on the stars. Just get away, he'd said. It was a little like the voice's instructions, but not as specific. And probably Russ is just some guy who's moved next door, she thought, but I need to believe he's giving me instructions. Just for now. I don't know if I can make it on my own.

She stepped outside. I can go *anywhere,* she thought. At the thought she nearly turned and went back inside the apartment, but she forced herself to go on. When she passed Russ's apartment she wanted to stop, to knock on his door and see if he had more instructions for her, something more specific. Instead she went to the car and got in.

"Go to Main Street and push the button," the voice said as she started the car. She laughed out loud. She had known the voice was going to say that, but the voice hadn't known that she knew it. The voice was stupid, stupider than she was.

She turned the car around in a neighbor's driveway and headed toward Main Street. No, wait, she thought, panicking. What am I doing? Her hand reached out to push the button. "Turn left on Main Street and drive until Eleventh Street," the voice said, "and push the button." All right, she thought. I'll go to the supermarket and get on the freeway near there. She hoped she would do it. Panic was guiding her moves now, and she was no longer as certain as she was this morning. She gripped the steering wheel tightly.

"Turn left on Eleventh Street," the voice said, "park at the supermarket and push the button." She drove on, watching the supermarket come up closer and closer on the right. Her hands on the steering wheel were clenched, bloodless. Russ wants you to do this, she thought. No. *I* want to do this. She passed the supermarket and turned onto the freeway.

For a moment she thought the strange noise she heard was the voice. Then she realized she was crying, crying and laughing both. "Turn left on Eleventh Street," the voice said. She hit the button, hit it again and again, listening in wonder as the voice measured out day after day she would not have to live. She drove on, into the unimaginable future.

AFTERWORD

T he idea for "Daily Voices" came to me on a very long trip after my car radio had failed. I like stories in which some limiting paradigm is transcended, stories where the character, by redefining his or her obstacles, reaches some other level of reality.

A Game of Cards

The doorbell rang at seven. Rozal looked through the peephole and saw two guests framed as in a picture, a woman with short brown hair and a tall gangly man carrying a bottle of wine. Helen and Keith—they'd been at the house before. Rozal opened the door.

"Beautiful house," Helen said, coming in and slipping off her coat. Rozal nodded, not sure how to take this. Of course they knew the house belonged to Mr. and Mrs. Hobart.

She hung the coats in the closet; they had a faint perfume scent, and the smell that water brings out in wool. Was it raining, then? In the bustle that surrounded the preparations for dinner Rozal had not been able to go outside all day.

Helen paused at the framed mirror in the entryway and patted her hair. Keith scowled and grinned at his reflection, as if resigned to what he saw. The bottle of wine hung from his hand as though attached to it; he seemed to have forgotten it was there. Rozal watched as they made their way through the thick off-white carpet in the living room, leaving footprints as they went. The carpet had been vacuumed just minutes before the party and would have to be vacuumed again tomorrow.

She couldn't resist a quick glance in the mirror herself. Most Americans took her for older than her twenty-four years, but then most Americans looked far younger than their actual age. Her hair and eyes were brown and her complexion dark; they had called her skin "olive" at the immigration office, and she had looked the word up as soon as she got home, but she'd been none the wiser. She smiled at the reflection; she had not looked so healthy, so plump, in many years.

The doorbell rang and she hurried to answer it. A young blond woman stood on the doorstep, Carol, another frequent visitor to the house. As soon as Rozal hung up her coat she heard the bell again. This time when she opened the door she saw a good-looking dark young man, balancing on the balls of his feet in impatience. He had an amused, quizzical expression, as if he had put on a face to greet Mrs. Hobart.

Rozal had never seen him in the house before but she recognized him immediately from the movies she watched on her days off. He looked shorter than she would have expected. He said something to her in Spanish but she smiled and shook her head: no, she was not Spanish.

Mrs. Hobart had seated Keith and Helen and Carol on the sectional couch, and now rose to greet the new arrival. "Steve!" she said. "So glad you could make it."

"Drinks!" Mr. Hobart said, coming into the living room and clapping his hands. Carol called for something Rozal didn't catch. Keith stood to hand over his bottle of wine and Mr. Hobart pretended to be angry at him; somehow it had been both right and wrong for Keith to bring the wine.

At a signal from Mrs. Hobart Rozal hurried through the dining room to the kitchen for the appetizers. The kitchen was at least ten degrees hotter than the living room: both ovens were on and the cook had set a teakettle on the stove for tea. Rozal nodded to the cook, who sat on a high stool near the stove and fanned herself with a magazine, but the other woman seemed not to notice her. There was some question of status between her and the cook that Rozal did not quite understand.

Rozal took the tray of appetizers out of the refrigerator and went back to the living room. The party had already divided itself into groups: Mrs. Hobart was deep in conversation with Steve, waving her cigarette smoke away from his face, and Keith and Helen sat a little uncomfortably on the couch next to Carol. "And what do you do?" Keith asked. His face was too long, and his jaw and forehead protruded a little.

"Keith!" Helen said, and leaned to whisper something in his ear. Rozal offered them an appetizer, trying not to look amused. She had seen Carol come up to the house and talk to Mr. Hobart; money and small plastic bags were exchanged. "I thought she had something to do with video," Keith said, unrepentant. Carol laughed, and after a while Helen joined in.

Rozal returned to the kitchen for more appetizers. As she passed the wet bar that divided the kitchen from the dining room she heard a voice raised in anger, and she glanced around quickly. In the three months she had been with the Hobarts she had learned that though they rarely became angry it was best to pay attention when they did. But the shouting she heard was not directed at her. Mr. Hobart sat at the bar, speaking to someone on the phone.

"I just want to know where he is," Mr. Hobart said. "No, he isn't here—that's why I called you. Well, how the hell should I know where he is?"

Rozal hurried back to the living room and began to pass around the appetizers. "Thank you, Rozal," Mrs. Hobart said. The shouting from the bar grew louder; surely everyone in the living room could hear it by now. Mrs. Hobart raised her voice to cover it.

"No, she isn't Hispanic," she said. She laughed a little, but Rozal could see that she was getting worried. She glanced at her watch. "Why don't you ask her yourself? Rozal, Steve wants to know where you're from. Do you understand?"

"From Amaz," Rozal said.

"Amaz?" Steve asked. "Where's that?"

"Oh, you must have seen it on the news," Mrs. Hobart said. "There was a coup and then a counter-coup—no one's really sure who's running the country now. It was horrible. But Rozal managed to get out—she was one of the lucky ones."

"Yes," Rozal said. She had found a pack of cards somewhere on the long terrible road to the United States and they had told her what Mrs. Hobart was saying now, that she would be fortunate, she would reach her destination. "Great abundance," the cards had said, and she had certainly come to the land of abundance, a place where even the candy bars were encased in silver.

The doorbell rang and she set down the tray of appetizers and went to answer it. Peter Hobart, Mr. and Mrs. Hobart's son, stood in the doorway. By the streetlight behind him Rozal could see the rain she had sensed all day, coming down now in a black sheet like a slab of stone. She looked for Peter's wife but did not see her anywhere.

"John!" Mrs. Hobart called. "John, he's here."

Peter took off his leather jacket, revealing a pony-tail that fell nearly to his waist, and handed the jacket to Rozal. It shone like silk from the rain. Mr. Hobart came into the entryway as she was putting it away. "Finally," he said, "Don't you think you're taking the concept of fashionably late a little too far?"

"He wants to shout at me but he doesn't dare," Peter said to Rozal. "Not with all these people here."

Rozal smiled at him, not too wide a smile because her first loyalty, after all, was to her employers. Still, she couldn't help but like Peter; over the months she had discovered that most people did.

"We can start eating now," Mr. Hobart said, going into the living room. "My son has decided to grace us with his presence."

"Kill the fatted calf," Peter said. He did not follow his father but remained behind to whisper to Rozal. "I've got something for you, Rosie my love. You'll like it."

Rozal closed the door to the closet, pleased. She remembered the loud, dissatisfied tourists she had seen in Amaz, travelling in groups like fat geese, and she thought how lucky she was to be here, in this house, working for people as kind as the Hobarts. She had never heard that employers gave gifts to their servants. What could Peter possibly have for her? The pocket of his jacket had felt heavy.

The guests moved in an undisciplined group toward the dining room. "I'm sure everyone needs their drinks refreshed," Mr. Hobart asked, going behind the bar. "I would have asked before, but I was busy trying to find my son."

"Were you?" Peter asked. He sat at one of the two remaining places at the table; the other was probably for his wife. "There was no reason to bother Debbie—you know I always turn up sooner or later."

Rozal went to the kitchen and began ladling the soup. "Does Mr. Hobart hate his son?" she asked the cook.

The other woman looked at her so oddly that for a moment Rozal thought she had gotten a word wrong, and she went over what she had said in her mind. Then the cook said, "It's none of our business what they get up to. My job is to cook the food, and yours is to serve it, and that's all we have to know." Chastised, Rozal took the first bowls of soup out to the dining room.

"Looks wonderful," Keith said. "Is this Amaz cuisine? Amazian cuisine?"

There was silence for a moment; Keith had made another social error by not knowing that the Hobarts had a cook in addition to a maid. Rozal began to like him. "I'm sure Amaz cuisine would be wonderful," Mrs. Hobart said graciously. "We're stuck with plain old American tonight, I'm afraid. Does anyone object to lamb?"

Rozal went back to the kitchen for more soup. She had never heard of Amaz cuisine; since the drought and the disruptions on the farms most people had had enough to do just finding food to eat. A friend of hers, a man who had come to America with her, had opened a restaurant in the refugee neighborhood near downtown. He'd told her that no one here really knew what people ate in Amaz; he could serve anything he liked.

The talk at the table grew boisterous. Rozal knew that Mr. and Mrs. Hobart were in something called the "entertainment industry," and the idea of a business formed solely to entertain greatly appealed to her. But she could barely understand anything the guests said, with their talk of points and box office and percentages.

Steve began to talk about a movie he'd seen lately. Carol, seated next to him, was watching him intently. Keith tried to say something but Steve interrupted him, his voice growing angrier and louder. "You've got to look at the numbers!" Mr. Hobart said, pitching his voice to drown out everyone else's. "Look at the numbers!" Rozal wondered what numbers Mr. Hobart meant. She didn't think she could ask anyone; certainly the cook wouldn't know.

At last the meal ended, and Rozal went to the kitchen to prepare the tray of coffee cups. Loud laughter came from the pantry; Rozal looked through the doorway and saw Carol and Mrs. Hobart standing there. "He's gorgeous!" Carol said. "Wrap him up—I'll take him home! Did you invite him for me?"

"Of course I did." Mrs. Hobart waved the smoke from her cigarette away from her face. "You were complaining for so long about never meeting any good men that I thought it was our duty to find you one. Go in there and be charming."

"What's wrong with him? Is he married?"

"Never been married, as far as I know."

"What does that mean? Is he afraid of commitment? Oh, no—I bet he's gay!"

Mrs. Hobart laughed. "I don't think so. He was dating someone for six months—they just broke up."

"It's drugs, then."

"You'd know that better than I would."

"I don't sell the hard stuff, you know that."

"Listen—why don't you ask him yourself if you're so curious?"

"Oh sure. Excuse me, but do you have any antisocial habits I should know about? And by the way, you wouldn't happen to have any horrible diseases, would you?"

Mrs. Hobart shepherded Carol into the dining room, and Rozal followed them. "You don't know how lucky you are, being married," Carol said, turning back to her hostess.

The guests in the dining room seemed to have talked themselves out; Carol and Mrs. Hobart took their places in silence. Rozal could hear the rain beating on the roof. Peter leaned back in his chair. "Oh, yeah," he said. "I brought something you might be interested in."

Rozal set down a coffee cup and looked up at him, wishing she had some pretext to stay in the dining room. Or could this be the present he said he'd gotten her? As if in answer to her question he said, "Stay here, Rosie—you'll like this."

He stood and went to the living room. Mrs. Hobart exchanged glances with a few of the guests, her eyebrows raised above her china coffee cup. Mr. Hobart whispered something to her, and she said, "Well, I certainly have no idea. He never tells me anything, you know that."

Peter returned with a flat box the size of a book. "Oh . . ." Rozal said involuntarily.

He winked at her. "I thought you'd like this, Rosie my love," he said. "You've seen these before, then?"

She reached her hand out to touch the box, but Peter

had already turned to show it to Steve. "I found these in that new neighborhood downtown, where all the refugees live," Peter said. "They said it's the first time they've gotten a shipment of cards from Amaz."

"What are they?" Carol asked. "Are they like Tarot cards?"

"Apparently you're supposed to play a game with them," Peter said. "That's what the man who sold them to me said, anyway. Isn't that right, Rosie?"

Rozal shook her head, wishing she had the words to explain. "They say—they tell us what happen in my country. In Amaz."

"What do you mean?" Mrs. Hobart asked.

"Like on television. We have no television, so we read the cards."

"You mean like the news?" Carol asked.

"*Beka,*" Rozal said, so grateful for the word she reverted to her own language. "Yes. They tell us the news."

"Actually you're supposed to play a game with them," Peter said, frowning a little. "See? It looks like Bingo." He opened the box and took out little boards, which he passed around to everyone at the table.

Carol laughed, delighted. Keith turned his board over and studied the elaborate pattern on the back. "Come on, Helen," he said to his wife, who had not touched her board. "Let's play awhile." Helen looked around the table, seeming anxious that her husband not make another blunder, but when she saw the others collect their boards she relaxed.

Rozal looked on, feeling wretched. This was not the way you treated the cards at all. You had to read them for the latest news first; it was only when they became outdated, when all the timeliness had gone out of them and another pack was issued, that you played games with them. Or you told fortunes; she had been the best in her village for coaxing meaning out of the cards.

She ached for news of Amaz, something to counter the

rumors she and every other immigrant heard every day. Who had come to power while she had been struggling to find her way in America? Which faction had triumphed? Were the famines finally over?

Peter began to read the instructions. Was this the present he had promised her? She felt cheated, so bitterly disappointed that she could barely pay attention.

But Peter had said that a shipment of cards had come in. She could buy one the next time she went downtown to visit her friends. She relaxed and began to watch the game. It seemed odder than she could say to look on while these people, most of them strangers, played a game familiar to her since childhood.

" 'Announcer will take card from deck and read face,' " Peter read. Everyone laughed. "Rosie! Hey, Rosie, what does this mean? Look, it's written in Amazian, too. Here, translate this for us, will you?"

The language she spoke was called Lurqazi, not Amazian. She took the instructions from Peter but did not try to read them; she had had to leave school when she was eight. "You have to take the card from—from here—"

"The deck," Mrs. Hobart said, encouraging her.

"Yes, the deck, and read what it says. And then if you have that picture on your card you cover it with a stone. And if you have these pictures here—" She drew lines on the card with her hands, vertical, horizontal, diagonal.

"See, it's Bingo," Peter said. "Where do we get all those stones, though?"

"Poker chips," Mrs. Hobart said. "John, where did you put the poker chips?"

Mr. Hobart stood heavily; he had had a little too much to drink. Carol studied her card. "Look, there's a picture of a cactus here. And ugh, look—here's a snake."

Mr. Hobart returned with the case of poker chips. "Now what?" he asked.

"Now I take card from deck and read from face," Peter

said. "Okay. Okay, it looks like a house. Anyone have a house?"

"I do," Keith said.

"My man!" Peter said. "One poker chip for you—here, pass it down. And the next card—"

"No," Rozal said. Everyone turned to look at her. "Now you read the—here. Read what it says."

"Hey, look at this," Peter said, unfolding the instructions. "It's got—they look like fortunes. House, let's see. House—here it is. 'Beware of build on unstable land.' There you are, Keith—beware of build."

Everyone laughed but Helen. Now Rozal remembered that Keith and Helen had talked a little about their new house during dinner. The card must mean that they couldn't afford it. She glanced at Helen; the tightness around the other woman's mouth told her everything she needed to know.

These people weren't that different from the ones whose fortunes she had read in Amaz. They had the same hopes and fears and desires, and their bodies gave away what they tried so hard to hide with words. But she saw that they didn't understand the power of the cards, that they had no idea what they were doing. If she said something would they stop? She didn't think so.

"Okay, next card. Cactus. Hey, good one, Carol." Someone passed Carol a chip. "And the cactus means—"

"Don't tell me, I don't want to know," Carol said. "Prickly, right? Sharp and unpleasant."

"Cool water in a dry country," Peter said, reading.

Everyone turned to look at Carol, who blushed. "Not bad," Mrs. Hobart said. "Come on, do another one. I want to see what they say about me."

Rozal had sagged forward a little in relief. The cactus meant that the drought in Amaz had ended. She had seen it on Carol's board but that didn't mean that it would turn up in the deck. So—unstable land meant that the country was still in the hands of bad leaders, but at least the water had come, and the famine might end.

She glanced at the well-fed group at the table and saw that they had guessed none of this. They were only interested in what the game might say about themselves; they didn't realize that the cards held more than one meaning. A story they could not guess at unfolded all around them.

Peter drew another card from the deck. "Looks like—scales." He showed it to the rest of the party. "Scales of justice. Do you have that in Amaz, Rosie?"

Rozal nodded, unable to speak. Justice would come to Amaz, then. She was crying a little, and she wiped her eyes quickly so that no one would notice.

"Here!" Keith said, looking up from his board.

"Keith!" Peter said. "Who said you're supposed to win this game? I haven't gotten a single one yet."

Keith grinned. "Read it."

"Justice, balance. A wise man speaks unwelcome words."

"A wise man," Keith said, still grinning. "What do you know."

"What do they mean by unwelcome words, though?" Carol asked.

"You did tell me my last picture sucked," Mr. Hobart said.

Helen stirred, and with that gesture Rozal understood a great many things. Keith needed to write for Mr. Hobart's next picture; he had bought the house on the strength of his expectations and then had antagonized Mr. Hobart by speaking frankly to him. Helen, sitting beside Keith and squeezing his hand, meant to make certain he said nothing unpleasant the entire evening.

"I'm sorry, I shouldn't have—"

Mr. Hobart waved his hand. "No, no—you've groveled quite enough for that already. And look at Steve here—he's spent dinner telling me how much my current picture sucks."

"Yeah, but he's an actor," Keith said. "Everyone knows actors don't know anything."

He had meant to be charming, Rozal saw, but because there was some truth in what he said—Mr. Hobart listened to screenwriters far more than he listened to actors—Keith had managed instead to insult Steve as well as Mr. Hobart. Helen saw it too, and she tightened her grip on her husband's hand.

"Is that so," Steve said flatly. "Did you know I have a master's degree in philosophy?"

"No—look, I'm sorry. Do you really?"

"No," Steve said, and everyone laughed.

Keith sat back with relief. He thought the crisis had passed; he had missed the fact that no one had really relaxed. Mrs. Hobart lit another cigarette though her last one still smoldered on the saucer in front of her. Steve glanced at his watch and Carol looked at him anxiously, clearly hoping he would stay. The rain sounded loud on the roof.

"Whew," Peter said. "Next card. Or should I just give it up entirely?" Everyone called for him to continue. "Okay. The lion."

"Yo!" Steve said. "That's me—the lion. What does it say?"

Peter looked at the instructions and laughed. "Cruel," he said.

"What?"

"Cruel. That's all it says. Here, look."

"That can't be me—I'm a pussycat. It's got to be a mistranslation. Here, Rozal. What does this say?"

Rozal moved forward to take the instructions from his hand. There was a growl of thunder from outside, and all the lights went out.

Someone laughed; she thought it might be Peter. "Get the candles!" Mrs. Hobart said, sounding a little frightened. "Rozal, you know where the candles are, don't you?"

"Yes," Rozal said. She felt her way toward the kitchen.

Lightning jumped outside, briefly illuminating her way, and the thunder roared again. "Hey, it's the lion," Mr. Hobart said, behind her. "Just what the card said."

A few people laughed, but Rozal knew Mr. Hobart was right; the cards predicted small truths as well as large ones, current events and things that might not happen for years. A light glimmered ahead of her and she saw that the cook had managed to find the candles and light one. She took the silver candelabrum and four candles from the cabinet, lit the candles and set them in the candelabrum, and headed back.

"Can you read this by candlelight?" Steve said as she came up to the dining room table.

She took the instructions from him. *"Kaj,* cruel," she read. Perhaps she should lie and tell him it meant strong, or manly. But by the shivering light of the candles she saw Carol looking at him, wide-eyed, and she knew that she couldn't lie for Carol's sake. "Cruel, yes," she said.

No one spoke for a moment. Then Carol said, "What the hell—it's only a pack of cards."

Suddenly Rozal saw a brief glimpse of the future, something that had happened to her once or twice before when she read the cards. Steve and Carol would become lovers; she would be water in a dry country to him for a little while, until his temper and jealousy got the better of him. She wanted to warn Carol, but she knew the other woman wouldn't believe her.

The lightning struck again. Each face stood out as sharp and meaningful as a card. She saw the patterns and currents swirling among them and she knew from the way they looked at her that now they saw her for what she was, a fortune teller and wisewoman.

Peter took a long breath and turned over the next card. "Garden," he said.

"I've got that one," Mrs. Hobart said.

Peter squinted in the candlelight and read the instructions. "A shelter shaded by leaves, a place of protection," he said. Then he laughed, almost involuntarily. "Refugee," he said.

No one laughed with him. Everyone sat hunched over his or her board, drawn in tight against what might be coming. "Let me see that," Mrs. Hobart said, reaching out for the instructions.

"Refuge," said Keith, the writer. "They mean refuge."

"Oh," said Mrs. Hobart. "Oh, thank God."

"Next card," Peter said, speaking quickly as if anxious to finish. "Looks like a beautiful woman. Anyone have this one?"

"I do," Mr. Hobart said.

"Good. Beautiful woman, let's see. Here it is."

"Well?" Mr. Hobart said. "What does it say?"

Peter looked up at his father. His face was expressionless in the candlelight, all his good humor leached away. "I'm not going to read it," he said.

"What?" Mr. Hobart said. "What do you mean—you're not going to read it? Give me that."

"No."

"Peter—"

Silently, Peter gave his father the instructions, and in that motion Rozal saw twenty-five years of similar gestures between father and son. Mr. Hobart scanned the list of cards, looking for the beautiful woman.

" 'Treachery, betrayal,' " he said. " 'The woman does not belong to the man.' " He looked up at his son. "So? What does that mean? Why wouldn't you read that?"

"You know perfectly well."

"I'm afraid I don't—"

"Do you want me to tell everyone? I will if I have to. I've certainly got nothing to lose."

Mr. Hobart laughed. "Peter, if you've got something to say—"

"You slept with Debbie, didn't you? And you didn't even

have the decency to do it before we got married—you had to wait until afterwards—"

"Peter, you can't believe—"

"It was more fun to wait, more exciting, wasn't it? More of a conquest—see, the old man's not quite dead yet, not if he can interest his son's lawfully wedded wife—"

"Peter, stop that. You have no right to say those things—you have no proof—"

"Of course I have proof. She told me. She felt so bad about it that she finally came out and told me. Why do you think she isn't here tonight? She never wants to see your face again."

Mr. Hobart turned to his wife. "Janet, I never—You have to believe me—"

"Of course I believe you," Mrs. Hobart said. The gaiety was gone from her voice; she sounded almost as if she were talking in her sleep. "Peter, why are you saying these dreadful things?"

"I'm not saying anything, Mom," Peter said. "It's the cards talking. The cards just told you everything you need to know."

"It's only a game, Peter," Mrs. Hobart said. She reached for a cigarette.

The lights came on. All around the table people blinked against the brightness. One by one they dared to glance at each other, seeing in each others' faces a harshness that hadn't been there earlier. "Well," said Carol, pushing back her chair, "it's late—I've really got to go."

"Me, too—" "Thank you for a wonderful dinner—" "We'll see you again—" Rozal hurried to the entryway closet to get their coats.

As she went she saw a last picture of Mrs. Hobart, the smoke spiraling up from her cigarette as she stared bleakly at the board in front of her. It would take a while, Rozal knew, but after all the accusations were spoken, after Mr. Hobart had moved out and started the divorce proceedings, she would learn to be, finally, a shelter shaded by leaves, a place of protection.

Afterword

When I wrote about the cards of Amaz I didn't know that they had an analog in real life. But one day my friend Michaela Roessner showed me a deck of Mexican Loteria cards, and I saw to my amazement that something I thought existed only in my imagination was in fact very real.

In the instant Mikey showed me the cards I got the idea for "A Game of Cards"; I saw how the story could be written and how it would end. I wish they were all that easy.

SPLIT LIGHT

SHABBETAI ZEVI (1626–1676), the central figure of
the largest and most momentous messianic movement
in Jewish history subsequent to the destruction of the
Temple . . .

Encyclopedia Judaica

H e sits in a prison in Constantinople. The room is dark,
his mind a perfect blank, the slate on which his visions
are written. He waits.

He sees the moon. The moon spins like a coin through
the blue night sky. The moon splinters and falls to earth. Its
light is the shattered soul of Adam, dispersed since the fall.
All over the earth the shards are falling; he sees each one,
and knows where it comes to rest.

He alone can bind the shards together. He will leave this
prison, become king. He will wear the circled walls of Jerusalem as a crown. All the world will be his.

His name is Shabbetai Zevi. "Shabbetai" for the Sabbath,
the seventh day, the day of rest. The seventh letter in the Hebrew alphabet is zayin. In England they call the Holy Land
"Zion." He is the Holy Land, the center of the world. If he is
in Constantinople, then Constantinople is the center of the
world.

He has never been to England, but he has seen it in his
visions. He has ranged through the world in his visions, has
seen the past and fragments of the future. But he does not
know what will happen to him in this prison.

When he thinks of his prison the shards of light grow faint and disappear. The darkness returns. He feels the weight of the stone building above him; it is as heavy as the crown he felt a moment ago. He gives in to despair.

A year ago, he thinks, he was the most important man in the world. Although he is a Jew in a Moslem prison he gives the past year its Christian date: it was 1665. It was a date of portent; some Christians believe that 1666 will be the year of the second coming of Christ. Even among the Christians he has his supporters.

But it was to the Jews, to his own people, that he preached. As a child he had seen the evidence of God in the world, the fiery jewels hidden in gutters and trash heaps; he could not understand why no one else had noticed them, why his brother had beaten him and called him a liar. As a young man he had felt his soul kindle into light as he prayed. He had understood that he was born to heal the world, to collect the broken shards of light, to turn mourning into joy.

When he was in his twenties he began the mystical study of Kabbalah. He read, with growing excitement, about the light of God, how it had been scattered and hidden throughout the world at Adam's fall, held captive by the evil that resulted from that fall. The Jews, according to the Kabbalist Isaac Luria, had been cast across the world like sand, like sparks, and in their dispersal they symbolized the broken fate of God.

One morning while he was at prayer he saw the black letters in his prayer book dance like flame and translate themselves into the unpronounceable Name of God. He understood everything at that moment, saw the correct pronunciation of the Name, knew that he could restore all the broken parts of the world by simply saying the Name aloud.

He spoke. His followers say he rose into midair. He does not remember; he rarely remembers what he says or does in his religious trances. He knows that he was shunned in his town of Smyrna, that the people there began to think him a lunatic or a fool.

Despite their intolerance he grew to understand more and more. He saw that he was meant to bring about an end to history, and that with the coming of the end all things were to be allowed. He ate pork. He worked on the Sabbath, the day of rest, the day that he was named for or that was named for him.

Finally the townspeople could stand it no longer and banished him. He blessed them all before he went, "in the name of God who allows the forbidden."

As he left the town of his birth, though, the melancholy that had plagued him all his life came upon him again. He wandered through Greece and Thrace, and ended finally in Constantinople. In Constantinople he saw a vision of the black prison, the dungeon in which he would be immured, and in his fear the knowledge that had sustained him for so long vanished. God was lost in the world, broken into so many shards no one could discover him.

In his frantic search for God he celebrated the festivals of Passover, Shavuot and Sukkot all in one week. He was exiled again and resumed his wandering, travelling from Constantinople to Rhodes to Cairo.

In Cairo he dreamed he was a bridegroom, about to take as his bride the holy city of Jerusalem. The next day the woman Sarah came, unattended, to Cairo.

The door to his prison opens and a guard comes in, the one named Kasim. "Stand up!" Kasim says.

Shabbetai stands. "Come with me," Kasim says.

Shabbetai follows. The guard takes him through the dungeon and out into Constantinople. It is day; the sun striking the domes and minarets of the city nearly blinds him.

Kasim leads him through the crowded streets, saying nothing. They pass covered bazaars and slave markets, coffee houses and sherbet shops. A caravan of camels forces them to stop.

When they continue on Shabbetai turns to study his guard. Suddenly he sees to the heart of the other man, understands everything. He knows that Kasim is under orders to transfer him to the fortress at Gallipoli, that the sultan himself has given him this order before leaving to fight the Venetians on Crete. "How goes the war, brother?" Shabbetai asks.

Kasim jerks as if he has been shot. He hurries on toward the wharf, saying nothing.

At the harbor Kasim hands Shabbetai to another man and goes quickly back to the city. Shabbetai is stowed in the dark hold of a ship, amid sour-smelling hides and strong spices and ripe oranges. Above him he hears someone shout, and he feels the ship creak and separate from the wharf and head out into the Sea of Marmara.

Darkness again, he thinks. He is a piece of God, hidden from sight. It is only by going down into the darkness of the fallen world that he can find the other fragments, missing since the Creation. Everything has been ordained, even this trip from Constantinople to Gallipoli.

Visions of the world around him encroach upon the darkness. He sees Pierre de Fermat, a mathematician, lying dead in France; a book is open on the table in which he has written, "I have discovered a truly remarkable proof which this margin is too small to contain." He sees Rembrandt adding a stroke of bright gold to a painting he calls "The Jewish Bride." He sees a great fire destroy London; a killing wind blows the red and orange flames down to the Thames.

He is blinded again, this time by the vast inrushing light of the world. He closes his eyes, a spark of light among many millions of others, and rocks to the motion of the ship.

* * *

Sarah's arrival in Cairo two years ago caused a great deal of consternation. No one could remember ever seeing a woman travelling by herself. She stood alone on the dock, a slight figure with long red hair tumbling from her kerchief, gazing around her as if at Adam's Eden.

Finally someone ran for the chief rabbi. He gave the order to have her brought to his house, and summoned all the elders as well.

"Who are you?" he asked. "Why are you travelling alone in such a dangerous part of the world?"

"I'm an orphan," Sarah said. "But I was raised in a great castle by a Polish nobleman. I had one servant just to pare my nails, and another to brush my hair a hundred times before I went to bed."

None of the elders answered her, but each one wore an identical expression of doubt. Why would a Polish nobleman raise a Jewish orphan? And what on earth was she doing in Cairo?

Only Shabbetai saw her true nature; only he knew that what the elders suspected was true. She had been the nobleman's mistress, passed among his circle of friends when he grew tired of her. The prophet Hosea married a prostitute, he thought. "I will be your husband," he said. "If you will have me."

He knew as he spoke that she would marry him, and his heart rejoiced.

They held the wedding at night and out of doors. The sky was dark blue silk, buttoned by a moon of old ivory. Stars without number shone.

After the ceremony the elders came to congratulate him. For Sarah's sake he pretended not to see the doubt in their eyes. "I cannot tell you how happy I am tonight," he said.

After the ceremony he brought her to his house and led her to the bedroom, not bothering to light the candles. He lay on the bed and drew her to him. Her hair was tangled; perhaps she never brushed it.

They lay together for a long time. "Shall I undress?" she asked finally. Her breath was warm on his face.

"The angels sang at my birth," he said. "I have never told anyone this. Only you."

She ran her fingers through her hair, then moved to lift her dress. He held her tightly. "We must be like the angels," he said. "Like the moon. We must be pure."

"I don't understand."

"We cannot fall into sin. If I am stained like Adam I will not be able to do the work for which I was sent here."

"The—work?"

"I was born to heal the world," he said.

The moon appeared before him in the darkened room. Its silver-white light cast everything in shadow.

The moon began to spin. No, he thought. He watched as it shattered and plummeted to earth, saw the scattered fragments hide themselves in darkness.

He cried aloud. He felt the great sadness of the world, and the doubt he had struggled with all his life returned.

"It's broken," he said. "It can never be repaired. I'll never be able to join all the pieces together."

Sarah kissed him lightly on the cheek. "Let us join together, then," she said. "Let two people stand for the entire world."

"No—"

"I heard you tell your followers that everything is permitted. Why are we not permitted to come together as husband and wife?"

"I can't," he said simply. "I have never been able to."

He expected scorn, or pity. But her expression did not change. She held him in her arms, and eventually he drifted off to sleep.

*　*　*

With Sarah at his side he was able to begin the mission for which he was born. Together they travelled toward Jerusalem, stopping so that he could preach along the way.

He spoke in rough huts consecrated only by the presence of ten men joined by prayer. He spoke in ancient synagogues, with lamps of twisted silver casting a wavering light on the golden letters etched into the walls. Sometimes he stood at a plain wooden table, watched by unlettered rustics who know nothing of the mysteries of Kabbalah; sometimes he preached from an altar of faded white and gold.

His message was the same wherever they went. He was the Messiah, appointed by God. He proclaimed an end to fast days; he promised women that he would set them free from the curse of Eve. He would take the crown from the Turkish sultan without war, he said, and he would make the sultan his servant.

The lost ten tribes of Israel had been found, he told the people who gathered to hear him. They were marching slowly as sleepwalkers toward the Sahara desert, uncertain of the way or of their purpose, waiting for him to unite them.

When he reached Jerusalem he circled the walls seven times on horseback, like a king. Once inside the city he won over many of the rabbis and elders. Letters were sent out to the scattered Jewish communities all over the world, to England, Holland and Italy, proclaiming that the long time of waiting was over; the Messiah had come.

A great storm shook the world. Families sold their belongings and travelled toward Jerusalem. Others set out with nothing, trusting in God to provide for them. Letters begging for more news were sent back to Jerusalem, dated from "the first year of the renewal of the prophecy and the kingdom." Shabbetai signed the answering letters "the firstborn son of God," and even "I am the Lord your God Shabbetai Zevi," and such was the fervor of the people that very few of them were shocked.

* * *

The boat docks at Gallipoli, and Shabbetai is taken to the fortress there. Once inside he sees that he has been given a large and well-lit suite of rooms, and he understands that his followers have succeeded in bribing the officials.

The guards leave him and lock the door. However comfortable his rooms are, he is still in a prison cell. He paces for several minutes, studying the silver lamps and deep carpets and polished tables and chairs. Mosaics on the wall, fragments of red, green and black, repeat over and over in a complex pattern.

He sits on the plump mattress and puts his head in his hands. His head throbs. With each pulse, it seems, the lamps in the room dim, grow darker, until, finally, they go out.

He is a letter of light. He is the seventh letter, the zayin. Every person alive is a letter, and together they make up the book of the world, all things past, present and to come.

He thinks he can read the book, can know the future of the world. But as he looks on, the book's pages turn; the letters form and reshape. Futures branch off before him.

He watches as children are born, as some die, as others grow to adulthood. Some stay in their villages, farm their land, sit by their hearths with their families surrounding them. Others disperse across the world and begin new lives.

The sight disturbs him; he does not know why. A page turns and he sees ranks of soldiers riding to wars, and men and women lying dead in the streets from plague. Kingdoms fall to sword and gun and cannon.

Great wars consume the world. The letters twist and sharpen, become pointed wire. He sees millions of people herded beyond the wire, watches as they go toward their deaths.

The light grows brighter. He wants to close his eyes, to look away, but he cannot. He watches as men learn the secrets of the light, as they break it open and release the life concealed within it. A shining cloud flares above a city, and thousands more die.

No, he thinks. But the light shines out again, and this time it seems to comfort him. Here is the end of history that he has promised his followers. Here is the end of everything, the world cleansed, made anew.

The great book closes, and the light goes out.

In Jerusalem he preached to hundreds of people. They filled the synagogue, dressed in their best clothes, the men on his right hand and the women on his left. Children played and shouted in the aisles.

He spoke of rebuilding the temple, of finding the builder's stone lost since the time of Solomon. As he looked out over his audience he saw Sarah stand and leave the congregation. One of his followers left as well, a man named Aaron.

He stopped, the words he had been about to speak dying before they left his mouth. For a moment he could not go on. The people stirred in their seats.

He hurried to an end. After the service he ran quickly to the house the rabbis had given him. Sarah was already there.

"What were you doing here?" he asked.

"What do you mean?" she said. Her expression was innocent, unalarmed.

"I saw you leave with Aaron."

"With Aaron? I left to come home. I didn't feel well."

"You were a whore in Poland, weren't you?" he asked harshly. "Was there a single man in the country you didn't sleep with?"

"I was a nobleman's daughter," she said. Her voice was calm. He could not see her heart; she held as many mysteries as the Kabbalah.

"A nobleman's—" he said. "You were his mistress. And

what did you do with Aaron? What did you do with all of them, all of my followers?''

"I told you—"

"Don't lie to me!"

"Listen. Listen to me. I did nothing. I have not known a man since I came to Cairo."

"Then you admit that in Poland—"

"Quiet. Yes. Yes, I was his mistress."

"And Aaron? You want him, don't you? You whore—You want them all, every man you have ever known."

"Listen," she said angrily. "You know nothing of women, nothing at all. I was his mistress in Poland, yes. But I did not enjoy it—I did it because I was an orphan, and hungry, and I needed to eat. I hated it when he came to me, but I managed to hide my feelings. I had to, or I would have starved."

"But you wanted me. On our wedding night, you said—"

"Yes. You are the only man who has ever made me feel safe."

A great pity moved him. He felt awed at the depths to which her life had driven her, the sins she had been forced to take upon herself. Could she be telling the truth? But why would she stay with him, a man of no use to her or any other woman?

"You lied to your nobleman," he said carefully. "Are you lying to me now?"

"No," she said.

He believed her. He felt free, released from the jealousy that had bound him. "You may have Aaron, you know," he said.

"What?"

"You may have Aaron, or any man you want."

"I don't—Haven't you heard me at all? I don't want Aaron."

"I understand everything now. You were a test, but through the help of God I have passed it. With the coming of the kingdom of God all things are allowed. Nothing is forbidden. You may have any man, any woman, any one of God's creatures.''

''I am not a test! I am a woman, your wife! You are the only man I want!''

He did not understand why she had become angry. His own anger had gone. He left the house calmly.

From Jerusalem he travelled with his followers to Smyrna, the place where he was born. There are those who say that he was banished from Jerusalem too, that the rabbis there declared him guilty of blasphemy. He does not remember. He remembers only the sweetness of returning to his birthplace in triumph.

Thousands of men and women turned out to greet him as he rode through the city gates. Men on the walls lifted ram's horns to their lips and sounded notes of welcome. People crowded the streets, cheering and singing loudly; they raised their children to their shoulders and pointed him out as he went past.

He nodded to the right and left as he rode. A man left the assembly and stepped out in front of the procession.

Shabbetai's horse reared. ''Careful, my lord!'' Nathan said, hurrying to his side. Nathan was one of the many who had joined him in Jerusalem, who had heard Shabbetai's message and given up all his worldly goods.

But Shabbetai had recognized the fat, worried-looking man, and he reined in his horse. ''This is my brother Joseph,'' he said. ''A merchant.''

To his surprise Joseph bowed to him. ''Welcome, my lord,'' he said. ''We hear great things of you.''

Shabbetai laughed. When they were children he had told Joseph about his visions, and Joseph had beaten him for lying. Seeing his brother bent before him was more pleasing than Shabbetai could have imagined. ''Rise, my friend,'' he said.

In the days that followed the city became one great festival. Business came to a standstill as people danced in the streets, recited psalms to one another when they met, fell into prophetic trances proclaiming the kingdom of God.

Only Sarah did not join in the city's riot. He urged her to take a lover, as so many people in the city were doing, but she refused. When he called for an end to fast days she became the only one in the city to keep the old customs.

Despite her actions he felt more strongly than ever that he was travelling down the right road, that he was close to the fulfillment of his mission. He excommunicated those who refused to believe in him. He sang love songs during prayer, and explained to the congregation the mystical meaning behind the words of the songs. He distributed the kingdoms of the earth among his followers.

His newly-made kings urged him to take the crown intended for him, to announce the date of his entrance into Constantinople. He delayed, remembering the evil vision of the dark prison.

But in his euphoria he began to see another vision, one in which he took the crown from the sultan. He understood that history would be split at Constantinople, would travel down one of two diverging paths. He began to make arrangements to sail.

Two days before they were to leave Sarah came to him. "I'm not going with you," she said.

"What do you mean?" he asked. "I will be king, ruler of the world, and you will be at my side, my queen. This is what I have worked for all these years. How can you give that up?"

"I don't want to be queen."

"You don't—Why not?"

"I don't feel safe with you any longer. I don't like the things you ask me to do."

"What things?"

"What things? How can you ask me that when you tell me to lie with every one of your followers? You're like the nobleman, passing me around when you get tired of me."

"I did nothing. It was you who lusted after Aaron."

"I didn't—"

"And others too," he said, remembering the glances she had given men in the congregation. She *had* pitied him, and hated him too, just as he had always thought. "Do you think I didn't notice?"

"I've done nothing," she said. "I—"

"I won't grant you a divorce, you know."

"Of course not. If we're married you still own me, even if I'm not there. That dream you told me about, where you took Jerusalem as your bride—you want to master Jerusalem, make her bow to your will. You want to control the entire world. But have you ever thought about how you will govern once you have the sultan's crown? You want to be ruler of the earth, but what kind of ruler will you be?"

"What do you know about statecraft, about policy? I have been ordained by God to be king. And you—you have been chosen to be queen."

"No," she said. "I have not."

She turned to leave. "I excommunicate you!" he said, shouting after her. "I call upon God to witness my words— you are excommunicated!"

She continued walking as if she did not hear him.

He watched her go. Perhaps it was just as well that she was leaving. He had known for a long time that she could not grasp the vastness of the task he had been given; she had never studied Kabbalah, or had visions of the light of God. His work in the world was far more important than her private feelings, or his.

He and his followers set sail on December 30, 1665. Word of his departure had gone before him. His boat was intercepted in the Sea of Marmara, and he was brought ashore in chains.

He sits in his prison in Gallipoli and waits for the light. He has not had a vision in many days; perhaps, he thinks, they have left him. He wonders if they have been consumed by the great fires he has seen in the future.

What had gone wrong? He and his followers had been so certain; he had seen the signs, read all the portents. He was destined to be the ruler of the world.

He puts his head in his hands and laughs harshly. Ruler of the world! And instead he sits in prison, waiting to be killed or released at the whim of the Turkish sultan.

The light of God is broken, dispersed throughout the world. And like the light his own mind is broken, splitting.

There is a knock on the door, and Nathan enters. "How did you find me?" Shabbetai asks.

Nathan appears surprised. "Don't you know?" he asks.

Shabbetai says nothing.

"I bribed a great many people to get you here," Nathan says. "Are you comfortable?"

"I—Yes. Quite comfortable."

"The sultan has returned from Crete," Nathan says. "There are rumors that he will want to see you."

"When?"

"I don't know. Soon, I think. He is alarmed by the support you have among the people of Turkey." Nathan pauses and then goes on. "Some of your followers are worried. They don't believe that we can hold out against the combined armies of the sultan."

"Tell them not to fear," Shabbetai says. He is surprised at how confident he sounds. But there is no reason to worry Nathan and the others, and perhaps the visions will return. "Tell them that God watches over me."

Nathan nods, satisfied.

A few days later Shabbetai is taken by guards from Gallipoli to Adrianople. They pass through the city and come to a strong high wall. Men look down at them from the watchtowers.

Soldiers with plumed helmets stand at the wall's gate. The

soldiers nod to them and motion them through. Beyond the gate is a courtyard filled with fountains and cypress trees and green plots of grass where gazelles feed.

They turn left, and come to a door guarded by soldiers. They enter through this door and are shown before the sultan and his council.

"Do you claim to be the Messiah?" a councilor asks Shabbetai.

"No," he says.

"What?" the councilor says, astonished.

"No. Perhaps I was the Messiah once. But the light has left me—I see no more and no less than other people."

The sultan moves his hand. The councilor nods to him and turns toward Shabbetai. "I see," he says. "You understand that we cannot just take your word for this. We cannot say, Very well, you may go now. Your followers outside are waiting for you—you have become a very dangerous man."

"We are prepared to offer you a choice," the sultan says. "Either convert to Islam or be put to death immediately."

The light returns, filling the room. Shabbetai gasps; he had begun to think it lost forever. The light breaks. Two paths branch off before him.

On one path he accepts death. His followers, stunned, sit in mourning for him for the required seven days. Then Nathan pronounces him a martyr, and others proclaim that he has ascended to heaven.

His following grows. Miracles are seen, and attested to by others. An army forms; they attack the Turks. A long and bloody war follows. The sultan, the man sitting so smugly before him, is killed by one of his own people, a convert to what is starting to be called Sabbatarianism.

After a decade the Turks surrender, worn out by the fighting against the Sabbatarians on one side and the Venetians on the other. Shabbetai's followers take Constantinople; Hagia Sophia, once a church and then a mosque, is converted a third time by the victorious army.

The Sabbatarians consolidate their power, and spread across Europe and Asia. First hundreds and then thousands of heretics are put to death. Holy wars flare. Men hungry for power come to Constantinople and are given positions in the hierarchy of the new religion.

Finally, using the terrifying tools of the far future, the Sabbatarians set out to kill everyone who is not a believer. The broken light that Shabbetai saw in his vision shines across the sky as city after city is laid waste. Poisons cover the earth. At the end only a few thousand people are left alive.

Shabbetai turns his gaze away from the destruction and looks down the other path. Here he becomes a convert to Islam; he changes his name to Aziz Mehmed Effendi. The sultan, pleased at his decision, grants him a royal pension of 150 piasters a day.

His followers are shocked, but they soon invent reasons for his apostasy. Nathan explains that the conversion was necessary, that the Messiah must lose himself in darkness in order to find all the shards of God hidden in the world.

Over the years his followers begin to lose hope. Sarah dies in 1674. Two years later he himself dies. Several groups of Sabbatarians continue to meet in secret; one group even survives to the mid-twentieth century.

He turns back to the first path. Once again he is drawn to the vision of annihilation. An end to breeding and living and dying, an end to the mad ceaseless activity that covers the earth. Perhaps this is what God requires of him.

He remembers Sarah, her desire to lie with him. She thought him powerless; very well, he will show her something of power. Flame will consume her descendants, all the children he had been unable to give her.

The moon spins before him, fragments into a thousand pieces. He understands that his vision is not an allegory but real, that people will become so strong they can destroy the moon.

His head pounds. He is not powerless at all. He is the

most powerful man in the world. All the people he has seen in his travels, the bakers and learned men and farmers and housewives and bandits, all of them depend for their lives on his next word.

He thinks of Sarah again, her tangled hair, her breath warm on his cheek. If he lets the world live all her children will be his, although she will not know it. Every person in the world will be his child. He can choose life, for himself and for everyone; he can do what he was chosen to do and heal the world.

The light blazes and dies. He looks up at the sultan and his men and says, calmly, "I will choose Islam."

AFTERWORD

The story of Shabbetai Zevi has fascinated me ever since I first came across it. If he hadn't converted to Islam, of course, we would have another world religion.

I showed this story to the Sycamore Hill Writers' Workshop and to my own writers' workshop in the Bay Area. Both groups seemed to like it, but after I made some of the changes they had suggested I realized that I could not imagine it in any of the existing science fiction markets. This complete inability to write for a market has been a recurring problem throughout my career. I would not recommend blithe disregard for the marketplace as a way to go to any beginning writer; in my own case, however, I don't seem to be able to help it. Therefore, this story appears here for the first time.

SMILIN' JACK

and the

Daredevil Girl Pilot

A New Story Based on the
Famous Comic Strip by

ZACK MOSLEY

Authorized Edition

WHITMAN PUBLISHING COMPANY

RACINE, WISCONSIN

TABLE OF CONTENTS

LIST OF ILLUSTRATIONS

Jack Martin Had Never Seen So Much Fog

SMILIN' JACK
and the Daredevil Girl Pilot

CHAPTER ONE

THE MYSTERY GIRL

A gray, shadowy mist floated between the cabin of the plane and the little red and green lights gleaming on the wing tips. Fog, clouds and mist: this was the worst weather Smilin' Jack Martin had seen in many a hop in his speedy, custom-built cabin ship.

An ocean of murk crowded between Nashville and Memphis—maybe it ran all the way north to St. Louis, perhaps over the whole Mississippi valley. Jack had never seen so much fog stuffed into one place.

Somewhere under the plane—and Jack knew from his instruments that he was right side up—was the world. But it wasn't wise to try to land on it during a night like this. It was unwise to do anything except try to fly out of the fog or let the fog get out of the way of the flier.

But certain things might make landing a necessity— one was Jack's gasoline supply.

To all of Jack's senses it seemed he was alone in the universe with a drying gas tank. His instruments told him he was at five thousand feet, high enough to be safe from hills, but comparatively low if his gas ran out. He might come down quickly, and the world is unkind to planes without gas on foggy nights.

"I ought to have better sense," Jack upbraided himself. "The weather report said I'd meet bad weather over Tennessee, but I never thought it would be as bad as this."

To preserve his self-confidence, Jack reminded himself that his flight was not due altogether to a lack of good judgment. "Downwind" Jaxon had told him to stop in Omaha, on his way West to be inducted as a Coast Guard officer. To go off to war without saying good-bye to an old pal like Downwind was unthinkable. So Jack had flown out of his way in spite of bad weather reports.

"This fog is just what the Japs ordered—regular Fifth Column stuff," Jack decided. "It's likely to wreck one perfectly good Coast Guard reservist."

It couldn't be helped, so Jack quit beefing. The fog was getting thicker anyhow. Nashville had reported zero-zero, which meant the only thing to be seen there was fog, on the ground and in the air.

If that was the way it was, Jack couldn't land in Nashville. Maybe Memphis!

Smilin' Jack lifted his "mike" to his lips.

"Smilin' Jack callin' Memphis!" he said. "Callin' Memphis! How's your weather, Memphis? Come in, please."

The receiver emitted a coughing *pwop* as Jack cut the transmitter and waited for the reply.

"Hello, Smilin' Jack," it came. "Memphis is zero-zero-X. Can't even see the boundary lights 'cross the field here."

Wasn't the fog ever going to let up? Jack glanced at his fuel tank gauge and groaned aloud. It was zero-zero-X, too, like the ceiling and visibility at Memphis.

"Thanks, Memphis." Jack spoke again in his transmitter microphone. "I'll try up north—probably at Cairo."

Cairo, Illinois, might as well be Cairo, Egypt, as far as being within range of Jack's fuel supply, but he might make it if the tail wind shoved him hard enough. He hung up the microphone. Soup! This stuff wasn't soup, it was solid granite. This thick fog could have been cut into blocks and used to build courthouses and libraries!

The compass swung around as Jack headed northward. He listened to the faint buzzing sound in the radio receiver. That would be the St. Louis beam.

No it wasn't a radio-beam buzz. It was a humming sound—almost musical. What was the matter with that radio? Was it "going haywire," or was the beam catching boogie-woogie?

The noise in the receiver grew louder.

"Da-da-da de-dee-dah! Ump-pum-de.   De-dee-day! Floogie-woogie floy floy."

Now what in the world was the matter with that radio beam? Was the radio gummed up by this soup? Once more came the refrain:

"Da-da de-dee! Gogie-wogie floy-floy-flogie."

Of course it might be an angel. A modern angel though! Maybe Jack himself was crazy. Maybe the beam was all right. But it certainly didn't sound all right.

"Da-da-hut-sut! Da-da—"

Jack had to put a stop to this before he went completely off his *mental* beam. But wait a minute, there was a human note to that sound. It wasn't a beam at all, but somebody singing! It was a girl!

Jack growled and picked up his mike.

"Listen, Miss Floy-floy!" he said sternly. "Get off this wave band with your floogie-woogie. I've got things to do to keep from wrapping up my plane."

"Oh!"

The singing ended with a startled gasp. There was a slight pause and then came the station identification in a melodious contralto.

"Oh, I'm so sorry!"

"You ought to be!" Jack spoke before he thought.

"It's my transmitter," came the voice again, apologetically. "It slipped out of its regular wave band and I didn't even know it was on. I was just humming to myself—it's so foggy up here—"

"Up here? Are you flying, lady?"

"Why, of course, silly! Did you think I was sitting in my plane on the ground? I'm flying and I felt so alone in the world, I guess I just got to singing to keep from feeling lonesome—"

"Lady," Smilin' Jack said, with considerable restraint, "your transmitter is still on. And I've got my opinion about anyone that goes for a joy ride in soup like this. Now if you'll just turn that little switch and get off the air, I'll get on the radio beam so I can get out of trouble.

Every minute you wait means that my gasoline is getting that much lower. I'm in plenty of trouble."

"Trouble? Oh, I'm so sorry! Maybe I can help you."

"Yes, lady, you can help by getting off the air. Now will you please—"

"But where are you? Your signal is strong. You must be awfully close. If I could only find you I could help you."

"Help me?"

Say, maybe she could. She certainly couldn't hurt much.

"Well, it won't hurt to try. I'm north of Memphis on the St. Louis beam. If you can help me out, you can sing the rest of the night, Miss Floy-floy."

"So generous of you—Mr.— Grumpy!"

"I'm Smilin' Jack Martin!"

"*Smilin'?* You certainly don't sound smiling to me, but keep talking. I'm getting your signals clear now and you ought to be pretty close."

"Don't run into me. My landing lights are burning, but you won't be able to see them very far away."

"That's fine. Just keep talking. I think I'm real close now."

"Lady, do be careful! You're likely to smash into me. Your signals are awfully loud."

"Oh, I see your lights! Here I am, over to your right!"

Jack turned his head around and his eyes widened in complete amazement as he saw, almost at the tip of his wing, another machine flying in the same direction as his. A cabin monoplane, with sleek lines and a powerful motor—an expensive job!

But this was only half of what Jack saw. The cabin was brightly lighted and a girl was at the controls of the other plane. An angel after all, thought Jack. And a modern one indeed! Even at this distance he had a revelation of a soft, smiling face and glorious hair. The girl smiled and waved at Jack.

"Don't gawp, Smilin' Jack," came her voice over the radio. "I'm a perfectly natural phenomenon—a girl flying a plane. Now then, if you're in trouble, we can't waste time. You said your gasoline was low."

"Low! Lady, the gauge said the tank was empty fifteen minutes ago. I don't understand how the motor keeps going. It's likely to stop any minute now."

"Well, I know where there's a little landing field near here—"

"There was one at Memphis, but it was too foggy to use," Jack said.

"Oh, but this one is behind a hill and there's an updraft that usually makes it clear even on foggy nights. The field has lights and it's large enough for your plane. Can you follow me?"

"If I can't, I don't deserve to be rescued," Jack said. "What do you think this is, my first solo?"

"I'm banking right, Smilin' Jack!"

With a wave of her hand the girl put the plane into a turn. Smilin' Jack followed the maneuver with admiration in his eyes. This girl was a crack pilot and she handled those controls like a veteran.

Precision flying was one of Smilin' Jack's specialties and he had no difficulty in holding his aircraft within sight of the girl. She was going down now. Suddenly the planes came into a hole in the fog.

"Here it is, Smilin' Jack! The updraft clears away the fog here!"

Below his plane, Jack saw the lights of a farmhouse perched on the side of a hill.

The girl gunned her motor, running the prop at low pitch so that it gave a resounding roar, loud enough to awaken farmers for miles around.

"That's my signal," the girl explained by radio. "Mr. Dayfield will turn on the airport lights from his house."

As she spoke, floodlights suddenly flashed on directly below the planes. They lighted a small "postage stamp" size field on the gentle, sloping approach to the hill.

"This is my private field," the girl explained, "but you can use it. You've got to stop quickly, though, or you'll go through the fence into Mr. Dayfield's garden."

She was circling now, and preparing to land. Jack lowered his flaps and checked his speed. His troubles weren't over yet, for the field was tiny and Jack's craft had a high landing speed. He side-slipped and dropped toward the lighted field.

As the wheels of Smilin' Jack's airplane touched the ground, his motor coughed and died—the last drop of fuel was gone. Jack applied his brakes and flipped his tail around so that the plane came to a stop not twenty feet from the fence that cut the flying field off from the farmer's garden.

But the girl, who had been headed for a landing, zoomed upward and disappeared into the fog on the other side of the field.

"So long, Smilin' Jack!" came her voice in Jack's earphones. "Sorry, but I can't stop. I've got a date on the West Coast tomorrow!"

"Thanks a million!" Jack shouted into his own microphone. "You've saved my life, Miss Floy-floy—say! What in the dickens *is* your name?"

Her reply was a melodious laugh.

"I'll tell you some other time!"

"Hey! Wait!" Jack called. "You can't run off and leave me like this. I owe you a lot. I want to contact you again later so I can really thank you. What's your name?"

"I can't stop now, Smilin' Jack!" she called back. "Mr. Dayfield will sell you airplane gas and put you up for the night and that should solve all of your current problems. So I'll toddle along. Seventy-three!"

"Don't go away!" Smilin' Jack pleaded. "Hello . . . hello . . ."

No reply came over the receiver. The girl was gone. She had switched off her transmitter. Who was she? What was she thinking of, flying around in a foggy night like this? She could at least have given Jack her name.

But Jack couldn't figure out the answers just sitting there. The farmer was coming through the gate onto the airfield. Mr. Dayfield, she said his name was. Jack

Jack Landed on the Tiny Field

climbed from his plane to meet him.

"Howdy, son!" the farmer hailed. "Foggy night, ain't it?"

"Your fog-proof field certainly was a lifesaver for me," Jack said. "I'm plumb out of gasoline and if that girl hadn't shown me the way here I'd be cracked up along the river."

"Oh, so Betty brought you here?" he asked. "I thought I heard another plane but I reckoned she was already well on her way to the West Coast—a friend of hers cracked up in a plane out there a few days ago."

"Betty? What's her last name?" Jack asked.

"Betty Brown—she goes to Charterfield Girls' School in Memphis when she ain't gaddin' around the country in her flyin' machine," Mr. Dayfield said. "Well, what shall I do for you? Do you want a place to stay for the night?"

Jack considered the question. If he got enough gas he could fly out of the fog.

"No, just give me some gasoline. I'm flying to Omaha."

The farmer motioned toward a gasoline pump at the edge of the field. Jack walked to the pump and picked up a can. He'd have to get enough gas to taxi to the pump.

"Where's Miss Brown going on the West Coast?" Jack asked.

"Valley Ridge. What do you want to know for?" There was a twinkle in the farmer's eyes as he asked the question.

"Oh, I thought I might run across her some day and thank her for saving my life."

"Oh, is that it?"

In a few minutes Jack had refilled the plane and he was ready to start.

The engine caught and Jack waved to the farmer. Then he took off, his thoughts centered on his recent narrow escape.

At least Jack knew her name was Betty Brown—the girl, not the escape—and she lived in Valley Ridge, California. There might be more than one Betty Brown there—probably there were thousands of them in the United States—but only one particular one he had to find. Jack felt sure he would find her.

First, though, he had to stop in Omaha to see Downwind.

When Jack landed at the airport the next morning, he found Downwind had been waiting all night for him.

"What kept you so long, old-timer?" the red-haired Downwind Jaxon asked.

"The worst fog I've ever seen!" Jack explained. "And I ran out of gasoline right in the middle of it, but—"

"Humph! So you let weather get the worst of you, eh?" Downwind grinned. "That's the first time a little soup ever got in your way. You're slippin'."

"It was more than 'just a little weather!'" Jack insisted. "Honestly, Downwind, it was terrible! If it hadn't been for Betty—"

"Betty?" An understanding glint crept into Downwind's eyes. "Oho! Now I see what grounded you. Betty! Now there's an excuse for being late. You ain't slippin', Jack. I apologize."

"Don't get me wrong, Downwind!" Jack laughed at his friend's kidding. "Betty saved my life and then sailed away without even letting me get a good look at her. But I think I can find her on the coast—"

"Oh, sure!" Downwind grinned. "We'll just wire Tojo and Hitler to hold up the war a couple of months until you locate Betty and thank her for saving your life. Shucks, Jack. You got other things to think of. There'll be plenty of cute little de-icers on the Coast. Just thank them and what's the difference? Betty got as much kick out of saving your life as you got out of having it saved."

"Not quite, Downwind," Jack laughed. "Well, perhaps you're right. This is war and there's a lot of nasty business to be done. I can look up Betty after the war, when she'll probably be married to some dodo who tended the anti-aircraft gun in her front yard."

"Sure! You can repay her by sinking a couple of Jap subs. What does she look like?"

"Why, I'm not sure because I didn't get a good look, but I could recognize her plane anywhere and her voice is one I'd know in a million—melodious, low, beautiful —like—well—like an angel's—"

Suddenly a plane's motor roared and across the field a small cabin ship taxied for a take-off. Jack's mouth dropped agape and he stood staring at the plane.

"Downwind!" Jack cried. "There's Betty Brown's

plane now! It's taking off from this airport."

Jack broke into a run across the field, but the swift little cabin plane already was sailing upward into the air. Smilin' Jack waved and shouted, but the plane nosed west without even a circle around the airport.

Jack slowed down to a walk, then dejectedly returned to Downwind who was standing with his hands on his hips, looking disgustedly at his pal.

"I thought you weren't interested?" Downwind asked.

"Kid me if you want to, Downwind," Jack replied, "but with me a debt of gratitude can't go unpaid. I was simply trying to thank her."

"Well, Jack, it's been nice seein' you again. I know that I'd lose your friendship keeping you here when you ought to be flying out to California to thank an angel-voice," Downwind said. "Your plane's oiled and gassed and if you hurry you might pick up the angel trail near Salt Lake. So long, pal. Sink a sub or two for me."

Grinning sheepishly, Jack shook Downwind's hand.

In virtually no time at all, Smilin' Jack was in his plane winging his way toward the Rockies. But Jack and Downwind had underestimated the speed of the small cabin plane. Jack did not sight it all the way to the Coast, although he sent his own ship along at a three-hundred-mile-an-hour clip most of the way.

In the early afternoon Jack set his plane down on a field near the navy airport in San Diego. He reported at once to Commander Young, who was in charge of Jack's Coast Guard squadron.

"Oh, yes, Martin," the officer said. "We sent for you because we need you on a special job—something out of the ordinary for the Coast Guard. You are to report to Mr. Stevens, but he was called out of town today and he won't be back until tomorrow. Why don't you just take some time off, and see San Diego and report back here tomorrow—that's when you're scheduled to be here anyhow."

"Good idea," Jack said. "How far is Valley Ridge from here?"

"Valley Ridge?" The commander eyed Jack strangely. "About fifty miles. Why do you ask?"

"I know a young lady there," Jack said. "I thought I'd call on her."

"Oh!" the commander nodded understandingly, and quickly gave Jack the proper directions.

Later in the afternoon Jack landed his plane at a pretty little airport just outside the town of Valley Ridge.

Several other craft were on the field, but one of them attracted Jack's attention immediately. It was a small cabin monoplane with a powerful motor.

There was no mistaking that plane! It was exactly like the one Betty Brown had flown. Since this was Valley Ridge, the plane should be hers—

CHAPTER TWO

IN DUTCH

Jack bounded out of his own plane and started toward the other craft. On the far side he saw a small figure approaching—a girl with black hair, sparkling eyes and pretty teeth. She was swinging a helmet on her arm as she approached the plane. Jack mentally noted that she was more beautiful than he had expected.

Jack walked around the plane and came face to face with the girl. He touched his cap and smiled. The girl's eyes searched him curiously, apparently failing to recognize him.

"Beg pardon," Smilin' Jack said sheepishly, "but aren't you Miss—er—Miss Floy-floy?"

Her eyes widened incredulously. The astonishment which swept over her face lasted only a moment; it was replaced by a warm smile. Betty laughed aloud and, at the sound of her voice, Smilin' Jack knew he had made no mistake in the girl's identity.

"Smilin' Jack!" she exclaimed. "How did you get here so quickly? I never thought we'd meet again—or at least not so soon!"

"I was afraid we wouldn't meet very soon," Jack admitted, "and I wanted so much to see you again—to thank you for saving my life. But I recognized your plane the minute I landed here, Miss Brown."

"Oh, you know my name? But of course Mr. Dayfield told you."

"Yes, he told me and he said you lived in Valley Ridge," Jack explained. His eyes turned admiringly toward Betty's sleek plane. "Some job you have there."

"Custom built. Father had it made for me," she said.

"Your father—"

"I'd offer you a ride," Betty went on, not giving Jack a chance to ask who her father was, "but I'm terribly upset right now. A friend of mine has been in a bad accident and I flew clear out here from Memphis to see him. Now that I'm here I understand that no one will be permitted to visit him for several days—"

"Him? Your brother?" Jack asked. "Or your father?"

"Neither," Betty replied. "My fiancé."

Jack glanced quickly at her left hand. For the first time he noted that there was a diamond on her ring finger. Someone else had discovered Betty before Smilin' Jack.

At the sight of the diamond, Smilin' Jack became speechless. He wanted to ask questions. He wanted to see Betty again. He had a thousand things to say. But he found that he could say nothing.

With considerable effort he thanked her again for saving his life and watched her climb gracefully into the cockpit of her plane. As the little ship rose briskly into the air, Jack suddenly realized that Betty was gone, leaving him very much alone in the center of a vast airport.

Not quite alone, however, he instantly became aware.

From the side of the field, two men appeared, walking snappily toward Smilin' Jack. They were strangers, so Jack turned to go back to his plane.

"Hey, wait a minute, buddy!" one of the men, the taller of the two, called. "We want to talk to you!"

The shorter man broke into a run and Jack noted a glint of metal in his hand. As the man came closer Jack saw that he held a gun.

"Say!" Jack blurted angrily. "What *is* this?"

"Don't try anythin' funny, Powder!" the short man barked. "I've got you covered an' I'll blast you out by the roots if you make one false move."

Perplexed, Jack waited for the men to reach him, unable to understand what part he played in this melodrama.

The taller man stood in front of Jack and flashed a badge which he held in the palm of his hand.

"FBI," he said, as if that explained everything. "Come along with us, Powder. This is the end of the line and you're under arrest—we've been looking for you a long, long time. We thought we'd find you when Miss Brown dropped in."

So Betty Brown was mixed up in this too!

"Come along, Powder!" the G-man told Jack again, with finality.

"Say!" Jack exclaimed suddenly. "What did you just call me?"

" 'Powder.' Would you rather we called you *Mister*

Pellet?" the short G-man asked sarcastically.

" 'Powder' isn't my name. You've made some mistake. I'm Smilin' Jack Martin."

"Aw, tell that to the Marines!" the taller man scoffed.

"Listen! I'll tell it to the Coast Guard instead. I've an appointment with Mr. Stevens tomorrow and he'll wring the FBI's neck for this!"

"Ho! I'll say you've got an appointment with Mr. Stevens," the short G-man chortled. "Only he hasn't anything to do with the Coast Guard. He's our chief in the FBI."

Confused, upset and considerably angry over his unjustified arrest by the federal officers, Smilin' Jack went along with his two captors to a small car. He was ordered into the back seat with the taller G-man and the machine whisked him away toward the business section of Valley Ridge. Halting beside a three-story building, Jack was taken from the car and led up a stairway to a tidy little office on the top floor.

Here they waited silently in a small reception room. The G-men watched Jack much as a cat eyes a goldfish in a bowl. After a short delay a connecting door opened and a well-groomed man walked briskly into the room.

"Hello, boys," he greeted the two G-men. "What have you got here?"

The newcomer was about average height, with sleek black hair and a closely cropped mustache. His sharp eyes seemed to pierce Jack with a glance. After inspecting the prisoner, he looked inquiringly at the men who had taken the aviator into custody.

"We finally caught him, Mr. Stevens," said the taller man, nodding his head at Jack. "He was at the airport talking to Betty Brown. We recognized him from his pictures."

"Yeah, chief," the smaller man added. "This is Powder, all right."

"Powder?"

There was a note of incredulity in the voice of the man addressed as Mr. Stevens. Was this the man Smilin' Jack had been called by the Coast Guard to meet? What did the FBI have to do with the Coast Guard Reserve?

Stevens' eyes were scanning Jack more closely than ever. Nodding approvingly at something he saw, he let his lips curl into a pleased smile.

"You'll do, all right," he said. "What's your real name, young man?"

A new note in Stevens' voice made Jack feel easier.

"I'm Smilin' Jack Martin, Mr. Stevens," Jack said. "I was called from the East by the Coast Guard—"

"Smilin' Jack Martin!" Stevens interrupted. "This is better than I expected." He turned to the two G-men and waved them toward the door. "All right, boys. Leave this man with me. I'll take care of him."

The shorter man's mouth flew open in surprise.

"But he's dangerous, chief!"

"If I need help, some boys in the next room can handle him," Stevens said. "You did a nice piece of work, both of you."

"What's nice about it?" Jack asked himself—but not aloud—as the two men left.

Stevens watched them go and then turned to Jack.

"Well, Smilin' Jack," he said, "you've got your credentials with you, I suppose?"

Jack reached inside his pocket and brought out his pilot license and Coast Guard Reserve papers which he handed to Stevens.

"I tried to show them to your two officers," Jack said, "but they wouldn't give me a chance."

"They're both new to the FBI and a little green—but hard workers," Stevens explained, glancing at the credentials, satisfying himself and handing them back to Jack. "Yes, I guess you are Smilin' Jack, all right."

"I had an appointment for tomorrow with a Mr. Stevens," Jack said. "But I thought it was in the line of duty with the Coast Guard—not the FBI—"

"I'm the Mr. Stevens you were sent to see," the sharp-eyed man declared. "Sorry my men made the mistake of misinterpreting you, but it gives us a whole day's start on our program."

Jack mopped his brow with his handkerchief. Being arrested by federal agents in wartime was no fun, even though Jack knew he could prove his innocence.

"I'm still in the dark!" Jack said, smiling.

"Your resemblance to a man called Powder is remarkable," Stevens said. "But how does it happen you know Betty Brown?"

Betty Brown! Why was *her* name always cropping up?

"Your Resemblance to Powder Is Remarkable!"

Why was *she* being watched by the FBI?

"Oh, I only met Miss Brown yesterday," Jack explain-ed. "She helped me out of some trouble in a fog near Memphis. I heard she lived in Valley Ridge and I hopped over here to thank her. I met her just as she was leaving, at the airport."

Stevens nodded slowly.

"You'll have to give us the details so we can check your story, Jack," Stevens said. "You see, we can take no chances. Miss Brown is one of the reasons we sent for you. You see, she is a spy suspect!"

The words slapped at Jack's ears like a crash of thunder.

"Why—why it can't be true!" Jack exclaimed. "She's not the type."

"Unfortunately spies often do not look the type," Stevens said. "We may be wrong and we haven't much evidence against her except that she associates with oth-ers whom we are certain are spies. We have been watch-ing her, and through a slip-up my men arrested you be-cause you looked like one of those known spies. Luckily, the man you resemble already is in custody, although my men do not know it. We've been keeping that fact a secret for a very special reason."

Mr. Stevens paused while Jack digested the words.

"As long as you're here now," the FBI man went on, "I think we can get down to business. You're the only man we could find—in the Coast Guard, the Army, the Navy and the Marines—who can do this very special job—"

"You flatter me, Mr. Stevens," Jack said. "I take some pride in my work, of course, but I'm surely not the best pilot in the world—the armed forces are full of men as good as or better than I."

"It isn't your ability as a flier, Jack," Stevens explained. "It's your appearance. You see, your picture in the Coast Guard files led to your selection for the job I have for you."

"Yes?" Jack wondered vaguely if this was a gag about his well-known smile.

"Yes."

A humorless twist of his lips flicked beneath the little close-cropped mustache. Mr. Stevens was all business. There was no fooling now. Something very important was afoot, for he was talking to Jack in tones unmistakably serious.

"Come—I'll give you an idea what's to be done," Mr. Stevens said, opening a small closet door and taking his hat from a shelf.

The FBI operative led the way through the corridor and down the rear stairs. He motioned for Jack to get in a small car that was parked behind the building. The car swung out of the driveway onto a boulevard.

"This spy ring we're investigating," Stevens began, as he drove the car, "has been operating in both North and South America. We haven't been able to bag the leaders but we did shoot down one of the higher-ups—a fellow named Dave Pellet, who is called 'Powder' Pellet."

"The man that looks like me?" Jack asked, suddenly guessing the answer.

Stevens nodded.

"Yes. Powder wasn't badly hurt, but we managed to convince the physician on the case that he shouldn't see visitors. In that way we have kept his arrest a secret. He's in the hospital now, but he doesn't know he's guarded. We're going to see him, you and I."

The car swung up the drive of a large brick building. Stevens stopped the machine and climbed out, followed by Jack.

As they entered the building, the familiar odors of a hospital assailed Jack's nostrils.

Riding an automatic elevator to the third floor, the two men followed the hallway to the extreme end of an ell of the building, where Stevens stopped and opened the door.

Jack stepped into the room. To his astonishment, the room was empty.

"Say, what *is* this?" Jack asked in surprise. "A joke?"

"Sh-h!"

Stevens put his finger to his lips and moved softly across the room to a small panel. He opened the panel, exposing a little glass window.

"Powder is in the next room," Stevens explained. "We had this line-up glass window put here so we could keep our eyes on him without being seen. It's one-way glass: we can look through it without his seeing us."

"Oh!"

Jack had heard of this kind of glass. He looked through the panel. On a hospital bed in the next room lay a sleeping man who was about Jack's age, build and height, except that his hair was curly, while Jack's was straight, and it was also blond while Jack's hair was dark. The sleeping man's face was paler than Jack's wind-tanned skin, and he wore a small mustache.

Jack turned to Stevens.

"Do I look like him?" Jack asked.

"Not exactly," Stevens explained, smiling. "But your measurements are the same. That can mean a great deal. Your eyes are the same color, your ears and nose the same shape as his, you are approximately the same age, height and build. I've conferred with several Hollywood make-up artists and showed them your picture. They say that you can be made into a perfect twin of Powder in no time at all."

Jack peered through the glass again.

"He's just a rat as far as I can see," he remarked with a shrug of his shoulders. "One of those handsome rascals who are no earthly use except to cause trouble. I've known a lot of men like him—you can pick them out the minute you see them—but I never thought I looked like one."

"You really don't, Jack," Stevens said. "After all, it is largely the expression that makes the character show up in your face. The expression on Powder's face can be mimicked by you with a little practice and then the movie make-up men will do the rest."

"So I'm to do some undercover work in this spy ring, disguised as Powder?" Jack asked.

"You've guessed it," Stevens said. "Now that you've had a look at Powder, let's go back to the car where we can talk without being overheard. I'll tell you more about what you're to do. If you accept—?"

"Don't kid me," Jack cut in simply.

A few minutes later, as the car whizzed along a country road, Stevens explained the assignment he had planned for Smilin' Jack.

"Powder didn't have an ordinary accident," Stevens explained. "Our men shot down his plane. He was knocked out and didn't have time to destroy certain documents which identified his connection with the spy ring and gave us some important plans. Among the papers we found was a letter instructing him to meet 'The Head' three weeks from today off the coast of South America. This man referred to as 'The Head' is, we believe, the chief of the spy ring."

"Whew! That would be a haul if you caught him."

"*When* we catch him, Jack."

"It's our chance to wreck the enemy's entire espionage system, providing we learn The Head's future plans and where his bases in this hemisphere are," Stevens said. "That's why we want you as an undercover operative to meet The Head, learn these things and let us know before we arrest him. It's likely to be the most dangerous job you've ever tackled, Smilin' Jack."

"You're wasting time," Jack returned shortly.

Jack felt cold chills running up and down his spine—not from fear, but from the realization that here was a task which had odds against success from the very start. Literally millions of obstacles lie in the path of any man who tries to impersonate another. An impostor can easily be detected in spite of the most perfect disguise.

But although Smilin' Jack realized he was taking a long shot, his chances were no worse than many an American soldier was taking without complaint on the fighting front. Any service a man could perform for his country in this day of grave peril was a simple duty that he could not hesitate in undertaking.

"You're our man, Smilin' Jack," Mr. Stevens asserted. "Now I'll take you back to my office where we'll map our campaign from start to finish. We'll do everything in our power to make you a perfect twin of the man you're to impersonate."

"Yeah," Jack said with his ready smile. "Including going to a beauty parlor for a bleach and a permanent wave. That's gonna be hard to take, mister."

Stevens chuckled, but there was little mirth in his face as he turned to Jack with a serious expression in his sharp eyes.

"Yes, Jack, but there's something that may be harder to take," he said. "There's a mark on Powder's left hand —a symbol of some sort that appears to have been burned in the flesh with a branding iron."

Jack nodded.

"Okay," he said.

"Perhaps we can duplicate the mark with acid," Stevens continued, "but it won't be fun."

"Well," Jack said slowly, "I hope I can take it. What has to be done, must be. Just one slip-up in my disguise and I'd be a dead duck."

In this business there could be no half-way measures. He had to do everything possible so that his disguise would be perfect. The more perfect the disguise, the more chance the desperate plan had of succeeding.

CHAPTER THREE

LIFE AND DEATH REHEARSAL

The days that followed were busy ones for Smilin' Jack.

The branded symbol—a flaming sun crossed by a flash of lightning—was successfully burned in acid. But the wound was so painful that Jack could not use his left hand for some time.

Then came those uncomfortable trips to the beauty parlor for a permanent wave and a hair bleach. Jack's mustache sprouted and the make-up artists set to work trimming his hair-line and applying padding to his clothing so that nothing was left undone to make Jack resemble Powder.

Stevens and a corps of experts who studied Powder day and night brought up new things each day for Jack to master. For instance, Powder had a taste for a special brand of strong cigars. Jack himself rarely smoked cigars. Learning to enjoy Powder's kind of tobacco was almost as much punishment as the branding ordeal.

Records were made of Powder's voice during his conversation with his nurse and his physician. Jack listened to these records and spent hours copying Powder's enunciation, pronunciation and inflection.

"That guy uses better English than I do," Jack admitted to Stevens.

"Well, that's about the only improvement you'll get out of this masquerade," Stevens said with a small smile.

"Skip it," Jack retorted.

As his hand started to heal, Jack moved into the hospital room adjoining Powder's, so that all of his spare time could be spent studying the spy and his mannerisms.

"You have to talk, walk, eat and sleep like Powder," Stevens stressed.

This was more difficult than it sounded. Powder seemed to like the very foods that Jack detested. Powder plucked his eyebrows and Jack found that this was a painful operation. Powder slept with his mouth open and snored, and learning to snore is no easier than breaking the habit.

But, one by one, the problems of learning a lifetime of habits in a few days' time were overcome. Jack worked hard to copy the numerous distasteful characteristics of the spy. He spent hours memorizing the personal items found among Powder's effects and studying out clues to Powder's individuality. The one thing that bothered Jack was the lack of data as to the spy's associates and past.

"I wouldn't let it worry you too much, Jack," Stevens pointed out. "Men in Powder's line of business don't talk much about their past life or their associates. He's probably pretty much of a stranger to the men he directs."

Eight days of constant rehearsing had completely changed Smilin' Jack's manner and appearance. Jack was walking up and down the hospital room practicing his

Jack Became More Like Powder Every Day

role when Stevens, watching near by, spoke sharply:

"Powder, come here!"

Jack turned quickly without thinking.

"Yes? What is it, Mr. Stevens?" he asked.

Stevens smiled appreciatively and Jack grinned from ear to ear. He *was* Powder—he had answered to the name unhesitatingly. The disguise was perfect.

"Atta boy, Jack!" Stevens exclaimed. "I was just testing you. You responded as if Powder were the only name you're ever known. You're Powder to a T, now!"

Jack was pleased by this praise, but still not confident.

"I'm glad you think so," he said, speaking in Powder's voice. "But that's only your opinion. I'd like to test my disguise on someone who has known Powder. I may be Powder to you, but would I pass muster with someone else—say his doctor or nurse?"

"I've been thinking about that kind of test, Jack," Stevens said with a nod. "The doctor and nurse wouldn't be very good judges, since they haven't known Powder long. There's a better way. It's a test that we've saved until last. If you pass it, you'll be able to pass as Powder anywhere."

"I'm ready for it," Jack said.

"We're going to allow Powder's girl friend to visit him," Stevens said. "Do you think you could fool Betty Brown?"

"Betty!"

Jack had been so busy that he hadn't figured out the obvious answer to Betty's flight from Tennessee to the

Coast and her reference to her sweetheart hurt in an airplane crash. Powder was Betty's fiancé!

"Don't get excited, Jack," Stevens said. "You've got a job to do. You mustn't let yourself think that because she saved your life once it isn't cricket to spy on her. She may be an enemy of our country and responsible for the deaths of others, even though she saved your life. The stakes we play for are high."

"Are you going to arrest her?" Jack merely asked quietly.

"We haven't got the goods on her yet," Stevens admitted. "Maybe later, after you meet The Head, we'll have our evidence."

It was a difficult task—spying on someone who had saved your life, but Jack did not question the necessity of going on with it.

"What has to be done, has to be done," Jack agreed somberly.

"I knew you'd see it that way, Jack," Stevens said. "Now we'll get ready for this final test. You'll take Powder's place in his room this afternoon and we'll let Betty Brown know that Powder is 'out of danger' and she can visit him."

Stevens went through his plan detail by detail, making sure that Jack understood every phase of the part he was to play. At first Jack would pretend to be asleep. The girl would enter the room. Her first glimpse of the sleeping man would be a test of Jack's general disguise. Then he was to awaken and talk to her. This would test his ability to impersonate Powder's voice and actions. If Jack passed both parts of the test there would be nothing to fear when Jack met The Head, Stevens pointed out.

"What do you mean, 'nothing to fear'?" Jack asked. "The girl will see me only a few minutes, and part of the time I'll be pretending to be asleep. But when I'm with the spy ring, I'll be under observation several days at least."

"Yes," Stevens replied, "but The Head is a man, after all—he may not have studied you as closely as this girl has."

Right after the noon lunch, Powder was placed on a stretcher and moved to another hospital room, while Smilin' Jack donned pajamas and took the place of the spy in the bed.

Jack was slightly nervous.

"Stage fright," he explained to Stevens. "I haven't felt this way since I took part in my high school class play."

"I'm not worried about you, Jack," Stevens replied. "You'll calm down. Remember—everything depends on how completely you fool Betty Brown!"

If only this were some other girl than Betty Brown!

"Come, Jack!" Stevens spoke sternly as he noted the worried expression on Jack's face. "Pull yourself together."

Jack laughed nervously.

"What would she think of me if she discovered I was paying her back for saving my life by causing her arrest?"

"A spy deserves no mercy, Jack," Stevens said. "If she's

guilty, she'll get none."

Jack had made his decision. He wasn't going to back out now. Besides, if Jack didn't go through with the plan, Betty—if she were a spy—might cause the death of thousands of American soldiers and sailors who were fighting for bigger stakes than Smilin' Jack's life. His own life was insignificant in comparison to the importance of succeeding in carrying through this impersonation.

No, Jack wouldn't back out now. He would go on. Everything depended on the success of this masquerade. This was war. Jack's own feelings and all personal considerations were submerged in the national war effort. It was every man's duty to do what was needed to win the victory for United States of America.

Too, what if Betty was not a spy after all? It was hard to imagine her plotting against her own country. If she was not guilty, Jack could perhaps prove her innocence by doing his job well.

"Don't worry about me, Mr. Stevens," Jack assured the FBI chief. "I'll not let you down."

Jack's nervousness vanished. He was calm. His senses were alert. He would do his best to be the precise duplicate of Powder.

"Good boy!" Stevens said, clasping Jack's hand.

The FBI chief left Jack alone in the room. A gentle spring breeze fluttered the curtain at the window.

Faintly at first and then louder, Smilin' Jack heard the click of high-heeled shoes coming down the hospital cor-

ridor. The heels stopped in front of the door. Jack heard
a hand placed on the door. The knob turned softly.

Betty Brown was entering the hospital room.

Jack's head was on the pillow. He closed his eyes as the
faint squeak of hinges told him the door was opening.

This *had* to be good. All the effort he had expended
during the preceding eight days would be wasted unless
his disguise as Powder Pellet fooled Betty Brown.

The girl stepped into the room. Jack hoped she could
not hear the loud thumping of his heart.

Three soft footsteps tapped from the doorway to
Smilin' Jack's bed. His eyes remained closed. He dared
not risk even a peep at the girl who stood, he was sure,
looking down at him.

"Powder!"

Betty's voice came softly, almost in a whisper, but it
still was the melodious contralto that Jack had first heard
while flying in the fog near Memphis.

The calm expression on Jack's face as he feigned sleep
did not change. With trained self-mastery, he kept his
eyes closed.

"You poor, poor boy!" Betty spoke gently as she bent
over the bed. Her hand touched his forehead. Jack felt
the band of the diamond ring, the ring that had been
given to her by Powder Pellet.

Why should such a sweet, pleasant, refreshing girl fall
for a scoundrel like Powder, and why should she become
a traitor to her country— that is, if Betty were actually
a spy?

"You were hurt so terribly!" she whispered sympathetically.

Betty had been in the room long enough now to notice anything wrong with the disguise. The first part of the test had been successful, but the most severe part would come in a moment.

Again her hand stroked Jack's brow.

"Why—you're perspiring!" she exclaimed almost aloud. "Your fever must be broken! You're getting well! I'm *so* glad!"

Jack could have told Betty without medical prompting that the perspiration was not the result of a broken fever. But had hospital attendants taken Smilin' Jack's blood pressure at that moment, probably they would have started to feed him oxygen—or maybe they would have run for an air-raid shelter. Jack's blood pressure was—*he* felt— at the exploding point!

The first test had run long enough now. Realizing that he had passed it with flying colors, Smilin' Jack opened his eyes and looked full into the soft blue orbs of Betty Brown at his bedside. He smiled weakly.

"Betty!" he whispered, in perfect imitation of a sick man.

This weak voice, however, was not altogether acting. Jack really felt weak.

"Oh!" Betty exclaimed, half reprimanding herself. "I woke you up."

She returned Jack's smile.

"But I'm glad you did!" Jack said quickly.

He wondered if he had the proper inflection in his voice. Everything depended on whether the girl would see through the disguise or not.

"I'd be angry to learn that you'd been here and I hadn't seen you," he went on.

"This is the first chance I've had to visit you, Powder," Betty explained. "They wouldn't let me in before—they said you were hurt too badly. But you seem normal again. You're getting well, aren't you?"

"I had a bad shock," Jack said. "The doctor was afraid visitors might run up my blood pressure."

As if Jack's blood pressure was low right now!

Betty pulled a chair up to the side of the bed and sat down. She glanced anxiously toward the door.

"A message came for you today, Powder," she said. "I opened it—I thought you wouldn't mind."

Jack's heart was thumping like a bass drum. Would Betty incriminate herself by what she was about to tell him?

"That's all right," Jack said. "Wh-what did it say?"

"It was from The Head," Betty said.

She *was* incriminating herself—she must be involved personally.

"About the meeting?" Jack asked, quietly.

"Yes, Powder," Betty whispered. "Since your plane was cracked up, you won't have to fly to meet him. He'll send Jim in a seaplane to meet you on the shore directly west of Belvu. Will you be ready to make the flight in another week?"

"I could leave now," Jack said, "but the doctor says I'll have to stick around a little while."

"Good. I'll wire father and he'll tell The Head."

So Betty's father was in on it too. That placed Betty in this ring deeper than ever.

"I won't see you again, Powder," Betty said. "I'm leaving tonight. But after your job is done, we'll see each other again."

"Sure!"

Jack gulped, realizing that the next time he saw Betty Brown might be at her trial as a spy against the United States.

Betty clasped Jack's hand.

"Now let's talk about something else besides business," she said.

"Sure!" Jack exclaimed. "Nothing would suit me better —right now."

But at that moment the door opened again and a nurse appeared.

"I'm so sorry, Miss Brown," the nurse said. "But your time is up. You'll have to leave now. Doctor's orders."

"Not even another minute?"

The nurse shook her head.

"His condition still isn't quite satisfactory for a long visit," the nurse said.

"Oh, well!"

Leaning forward Betty planted a kiss on Jack's cheek, and then turned away. She paused at the door to look back again at Jack with a good-bye smile.

"I'll be seeing you!" she said.

"Yes," Jack answered, as Betty disappeared through the door. "We'll see each other again, never fear."

The door closed softly behind the girl. The nurse nodded at Jack and left the room.

Jack raised up in the bed. He had passed a test which he almost hoped he would not pass. Nothing stood in his way—there was nothing to prevent his "repaying" Betty for saving his life by exposing her as a spy: an extremely distasteful duty, but still his duty.

As Stevens came from the next room through a connecting door, Jack swung his feet out of bed.

"Great work, Jack!" the FBI operative exclaimed. "You were perfect! I watched the whole thing through the one-way glass panel and you handled the situation like an old trouper! Even Powder's mother would have been fooled by the act you put on. And we learned some things from it, too!"

"Thanks," Smilin' Jack said drily. "Are—are you going to arrest her?"

"Not right away," Stevens said. "Her arrest might tip off The Head that we're onto his plans. Later, perhaps we may."

Tossing his dressing gown over his broad shoulders, Jack hurried into his own room where he quickly dressed. Attendants wheeled the real Powder back into the room Jack had just vacated.

"Powder's about well enough to be taken to a detention camp," Stevens said. "But we'll hold him here until you've studied him awhile longer. Then you can go to Belvu to keep Powder's rendezvous with this seaplane."

"I'm ready to go any time," Jack said.

The telephone extension in Jack's room rang. Stevens picked up the receiver:

"Yes—yes, this is Stevens.—Yes.—Okay."

The FBI man hung up the receiver. His face was grave as he turned to Jack.

"We were having Betty Brown followed," he said. "But our shadow got caught in a traffic jam on the way to the airport. When he got to the flying field she was gone."

"Well?"

"What if she saw through your disguise and didn't let on?" Stevens asked pointedly. "Perhaps she's gone to warn other members of the ring. If she has, your life isn't worth a plugged nickel!"

"Whew!" Jack exclaimed.

He hadn't thought of this obvious possibility. He had been patting himself on the back as having completely fooled Betty. But she might have been masquerading too. A clever spy wouldn't reveal everything that passed through her mind.

"Are you still willing to take the chance, Jack?" Stevens asked, fixing his gimlet eyes on the aviator.

The assignment, perilous enough without the added complication, afforded new dangers now. There was no way of knowing how much Betty Brown had guessed during her interview with Jack in the hospital. There was a possibility that she had guessed nothing, and an equal chance that she had seen completely through Jack's disguise. But the first chance offered an opportunity to trap the spy ring. It was worth taking.

"I'm no quitter!" Smilin' Jack said firmly.

CHAPTER FOUR

THE KISS OF DEATH

The following days passed slowly, but at last the zero hour arrived. It was time for Smilin' Jack's rendezvous with the seaplane at Belvu.

Stevens issued last minute instructions to Jack as he took him by car to the little coastal town in southern California.

"Your trip may take you into neutral countries of South America," he said. "As you know, some of the South American countries are not at war with the Axis and your conduct in those nations must be guided accordingly. You'll be entirely on your own. You must act on your own initiative in those lands, for the United States has no legal power to endorse your actions outside of its national boundaries."

"I understand," Jack acknowledged. "If I'm caught, I can expect no aid from Uncle Sam."

"And you must keep in mind that the entire success or failure of this mission depends on you. If you fail, it may cost the lives of many boys overseas. If you succeed, valuable lives will be saved."

"I don't intend to fail."

"You *must not* fail," Stevens said with determination. "I believe in you, Jack. Nothing must stop you from learning the set-up operated by The Head so we can bring his gang to justice. Once you have landed him, the whole ring will be crushed. That's worth a severe defeat on the battlefield for the enemy."

Jack nodded as he realized that there was an implication that if *he* were defeated, it would mean a defeat for the United States. This was a desperate game and the stakes were high. One man's life meant nothing in the total score. Jack could not hold his own life highly—nor must he hesitate even though it placed a woman, the woman who had saved his life, behind prison bars.

Stevens let Jack out of the car on the outskirts of Belvu. As Jack sauntered through the torrid little village, he could not get over the feeling that he was being watched. Nerves, he supposed.

He passed through the town and went to the beach where the sea lashed a rocky shore. A small cove a couple of miles north of the town seemed to be the logical place for the seaplane to land. Just before dusk Jack arrived at the spot. Seating himself on a rock he watched the sun sink into the western ocean. Dusk faded into twilight and twilight into night. Jack waited, listening to the roar of the waves.

Then, faintly above the sound of the beating surf, Smilin' Jack heard the familiar hum of an airplane motor. The seaplane was coming!

Jack was on his feet, straining his eyes toward the sea. Then he caught a glimpse of the plane's lights as it hit the surf and taxied toward the shore.

The Plane Hit the Surf and Taxied Toward Shore

The pilot—Jim, Betty said his name was—apparently was thoroughly familiar with every inch of the coastline, for he avoided the treacherous rocks expertly and brought his plane to rest on the edge of the beach.

Tensely and cautiously, Smilin' Jack made his way forward to where the plane idled its motors. Here was another test of his disguise that might unexpectedly result in discovery. Jack could never be sure of continuing success in his impersonation of Powder. Besides, Betty might have suspected something at the hospital and the pilot might have orders to finish Jack off, instead of picking him up.

A gruff voice sounded from the plane. "Hold it!"

Jack halted in his tracks. A flashlight gleamed in the cockpit and its beam fastened itself on Jack.

"That you, Powder?" the voice called.

"Yeah!" Jack answered huskily—the strain was beginning to tell on him.

The flashlight traveled from Jack's head to his shoes while the pilot looked him over.

"Uh-huh!" came the voice. "No mistakin' that handsome face, you old rascal. Heard you cracked up."

"Not much—guess I was lucky," Jack said. "It kept me in the hospital awhile, but doc said it was mostly shock."

"Did you get rid of everything before you crashed?" the pilot asked.

"Sure—Jim—" Jack decided to risk the name; and when there was no reaction he felt safer. "—Think I was born yesterday?"

"Come on over here," Jim ordered.

The voice was a little gruffer. Had Jack made a miscue? Maybe this man wasn't Jim.

With leaden feet Jack moved toward the flashlight.

"Far enough!" the pilot commanded as Jack reached the side of the seaplane. "Lemme see your left hand."

Smilin' Jack almost whistled his sigh of relief. He was certainly glad now that he had undergone the painful branding of the symbol on his hand: the secret mark of the spy ring!

Jack thrust his left palm into the rays of the flashlight. The pilot gave it a cursory inspection and nodded.

"Yeah. That's okay. I just wanted to make sure—The Head's orders, you know, old man."

"Sure, Jim. I understand." Jack felt much relieved.

"We can't take any chances nowadays," Jim said. "It ain't like the old days when all we did was shanghai bums for Death Rock."

The reference went over Jack's head, and Jack grunted noncommitally.

"Nope. We can't take chances."

"All right, toss away that foul-smellin' cigar—same old brand, I see—an' jump in. We've got a lot of flyin' to do," the pilot said.

As Jack boarded the seaplane he saw Jim putting away a forty-five automatic. That cannon had been trained on Jack during the first interview. One false move and it would have ended his part in the American war effort. Jack was more than thankful for the long hours he had spent in learning well how to impersonate the man known as Powder.

After holstering the automatic, Jim turned to his passenger.

"We're gonna take it slow and easy," he announced. "The Head said you'd probably be so weak from the hospital that you couldn't stand makin' this trip in one jump. Anyhow, we've got to do most of our flyin' at night to avoid patrol planes. We'll stop at the usual hide-outs in Mexico and South America, an' meet The Head at sea in about three days."

"It ought to be a nice, pleasant trip," Jack said.

Jim laughed.

"Same ol' Powder—always cool, never afraid of nuttin'. But don't worry. Old Jimmy can get us past Panama without no trouble."

Getting "past Panama" was an item Jack hadn't thought of. Uncle Sam maintained a constant patrol of fighter planes in the vicinity of the Canal Zone. They were almost certain to be stopped unless they wanted to risk a little machine-gunning from faster and better planes.

Jim gunned the motor and the seaplane began taxiing out to sea.

Through the night the seaplane flew. Hour after hour passed without incident. The noise of the motor dinned in Jack's ears until at last the first streaks of dawn appeared in the east. Then the airplane settled down along the coast of Mexico.

Among the trees was a large building, constructed of logs and carefully camouflaged. The building was filled with drums of oil. This was a secret seaplane and submarine base maintained by Fifth Columnists!

Jack made a mental note of the landmarks around the place. Later, if he got through his trip safely, the information would be communicated to American authorities who would see that the place was put out of operation.

The most dangerous part of the trip lay ahead. The flying through the area near the Panama Canal would mean constant peril. Patrols, warships, listening devices of all kinds could detect the approach of any aircraft— and all unidentified planes were warded off, by force if necessary.

But Jim seemed not to worry about the future. As the plane took off at dusk on the second leg of its southward flight, Jack noticed that Jim was climbing steadily.

At eighteen thousand feet, Jim signaled for Jack to begin using oxygen. The plane went still higher. It passed the twenty-thousand-foot level and continued to climb. Finally it leveled off at twenty-five thousand feet.

As nearly as Jack was able to determine his position, the plane was still about one hundred and fifty miles north of the Panama Canal when it reached its top level. But listening devices can easily detect planes that far away. Posts at the canal already were aware of the approach of the seaplane! Air-raid alarms were sounding and interceptor pilots were scrambling into their planes.

Jack was as sure of these preparations as if he were

taking part in them!

Gunners were manning anti-aircraft cannon. The Canal Zone defenders were on the alert. No doubt every military establishment in the zone knew that "an unidentified aircraft" was flying southward toward the lifeline of the United States Navy.

Jim had opened the throttle wide—the plane was traveling at least 300 miles an hour. At this speed, the seaplane would pass the Canal in about thirty minutes—not a long time, but time enough for interceptor planes to get high into the air.

Jim flipped off his lights now and flew in total darkness, still keeping his altitude.

Jack watched below. As the moon peeped out from behind a cloud, he caught a glimpse of the silvery ribbon of the Panama Canal cutting from southwest to northeast across the isthmus. No planes were visible yet, but they probably were in the sky, flying dark to intercept the strange aircraft.

A searchlight stabbed into the sky. Then another! There seemed to be a line of bars of light blocking the path of the seaplane. To fly into one of these beams meant death from anti-aircraft guns below.

Toward this network of destruction, the seaplane carrying Smilin' Jack flew at top speed.

Suddenly Jim leaned forward and cut the engine. Silence closed in over the plane.

The searchlights stabbed frantically into the sky, seeking to find the silent intruder. Jack's heart bounced up into his throat as those long silvery arms wove closer and closer to the seaplane.

Above the whisper of the seaplane's propeller, Jack heard the roar of fighter planes below, trying to locate the seaplane. But Jim was still flying at high altitude and his craft was only a tiny, almost invisible speck in the sky.

Jim's speed and altitude would enable him to glide for miles, silent as an arrow.

In a few minutes the seaplane had dodged through the bars of light. Jim started the motor and the seaplane raced for safety over the South American republic of Colombia.

The most dangerous leg of the journey had been completed.

"Nice work, Jim!" Smilin' Jack muttered as Powder would have said it.

But his words were drowned out by the roar of the seaplane's motors. Jim never heard the words, nor did he know that he had done Uncle Sam a great service by dodging the air defenses of the Panama Canal. It might have been better for the enemy spies to have had a less able pilot than Jim that night.

At dawn the seaplane settled down along the coast of the South American nation where another enemy base was located. Smilin' Jack made a second mental note of the location which would aid in the final round-up of enemy spies. This series of Axis bases from California to the Pacific coast of South America was undoubtedly designed to serve for more than underground railway stations for spies.

Submarines could be refueled there, for instance—enemy subs that were prowling the seas to sink merchantmen carrying supplies to the forces of the United Nations.

Jack also learned some useful facts about Jim. The pilot, he learned, was one of those unscrupulous, worthless airmen who sell their services to smuggle contraband merchandise and fly dope into the United States in peacetime.

No respectable aviation company would have hired a man of Jim's type, and his record barred him from Army service. With flying as Jim's only art, he had sold himself to The Head—another peacetime smuggler as well as an international Axis spy—for a job. Jim had been willing to betray his native country for a few dollars that he might never have a chance to spend.

After eating and resting at the coastal base, the plane took off in daylight, flying west this time over the waters of the Pacific.

Late in the day a small yacht was sighted. Jim cut his speed and circled the ship, which seemed to be at anchor. Then he signaled for Jack to buckle his safety belt for a landing.

The seaplane glided toward the waves. It struck the rough surf and taxied through the waves toward the ship.

A crane on the deck lowered a hook, which Jim fastened to a ring just behind the motor. Slowly the seaplane and its two passengers were lifted from the water and placed on the deck.

Jim turned to Jack and grinned.

"Well, Powder," he said. "We made it!"

"Good enough!" said Jack, not forgetting to use Powder's tone of voice and inflection. "Part of the way I had my doubts."

"Aw, it was easy!" Jim said in self-deprecation.

The pilot hopped to the deck and Jack followed him. A ship's officer was hurrying toward them as Jack hit the deck.

"Hello, Powder!" the officer greeted. "The Head is expecting you, but he sent word that he won't be able to see you until tomorrow."

"Okay," Jack said. "I'm pretty tired anyhow."

Jack was thankful for a chance to rest before subjecting his disguise to another test. The following day he would be refreshed and ready to pose as Powder before The Head, astute and shrewd chief of the espionage ring.

Stretching his muscles, wearily, Jack turned to the officer.

"Where's my cabin, sir? I'd like to turn in."

"I'll show you," the officer said. "It's No. X-13. Just follow me."

The officer led him to a gangway leading to the lower deck. Before he reached the steps, a small figure pushed up from below and rushed past the officer toward Smilin' Jack.

"Powder!" a girl's voice screamed in delighted surprise.

The shrill cry was followed by happy laughter as the figure collided with Jack. He felt small arms twine about his neck and a kiss planted on his cheek. He caught the fragrance of a familiar perfume that somehow reminded him of the hospital at Valley Ridge.

The girl stood back, surveying Jack.

"Powder!" she exclaimed. "It's so good to see you again!"

At last Jack knew the voice as the girl spoke in her normal tone. He saw her familiar face as she stood away from him.

Betty Brown was on the yacht!

"Betty!" Jack said, beaming with happiness that was not altogether feigned. "So you beat me here!"

"I had a week's leeway, Jack!" she explained. "I would be a pretty poor flier if I couldn't have made it with such a head start. But the way I got held up at the Panama Canal made me think I'd never get here."

"How *did* you get through?" Jack asked.

"Why, father did it, of course!" Betty exclaimed, almost as though "Powder" should have known that without asking.

Jack would like to know more about Betty's father. Who was he? How did he manage to smuggle Betty in a strange plane past the Panama Canal?

"Well, Powder," Betty said. "Don't just stand there staring at me!"

"Huh?" Jack said, jarred out of his thoughts.

"I meant, aren't you going to kiss me?"

"Ah—"

Jack hesitated.

"Powder!" the girl's voice rang out complainingly.

"Your Cabin Is X-13," the Officer Said

"Aren't you glad to see me? You act so strange—so cool!"

If he was not careful, this girl would be suspicious enough to see through the disguise. Jack couldn't let himself fail now. He had to act just as Powder might have acted. He had to behave as though he were in love with Betty Brown, even though she might be a deadly enemy.

Everything depended on Jack now: he couldn't afford to miss any bets. He had to kiss her.

Impelled by necessity but with considerable inward reluctance, Smilin' Jack pulled Betty toward him. He took her in his arms and delivered what seemed to him to be a kiss of death.

Certainly it was a fake caress—a Judas kiss!

Betty stood back.

"For a minute I thought you didn't care," she said, laughing. "Well, I suppose you're tired out from your long trip. Oh, I almost forgot, Powder, you're just out of the hospital. How selfish of me to keep you from getting some rest!"

"I didn't mind," Jack said.

The strange part about it was that he wouldn't have minded the kiss under ordinary circumstances, but he did mind the circumstance that it was not Smilin' Jack but Powder whom Betty thought she had kissed.

"I'll show you to your stateroom now, sir," the officer spoke.

"If you'll excuse me, then—"

"Of course, Powder," Betty said. "I'll see you later."

Jack followed the officer below deck. He was shown to a small stateroom numbered X-13.

"I hope you're not superstitious, Powder," the officer said, glancing at the number significantly.

"Well," Jack said, "if I were, I probably couldn't do anything about it."

"That's right," the officer agreed. "The Head ordered me to assign you to this cabin."

The Head had a nice way of making his guests feel comfortable, apparently. Glancing up the corridor, Jack saw that *all* of the cabins were numbered thirteen! They were distinguished one from another only by the letter of the alphabet which preceded the number.

Well, it looked as though members of this particular spy ring were not a superstitious lot.

CHAPTER FIVE

THE HEAD AND THE CLAW

Smilin' Jack did not see Betty at breakfast the next morning. In fact, except for one or two members of the crew, he was alone at breakfast.

"Not much adoin' here in the mornin'," the steward told Jack. "Like the owls, we live mostly at night."

"Owls or wolves?" Jack asked, in a manner that the steward did not fully grasp. "Wolves roam at night, too."

"Ha, ha! Very good, sir!" the steward said with a laugh. "Ah, yes—*wolves.*"

After breakfast, Jack walked the deck. So far his trip had been productive and his disguise had been impenetrable. No one seemed to suspect that he was anyone but Powder—and Powder apparently held a position high up in the ring.

Jim, who had flown Jack from the United States, had certainly not seemed in the least uneasy during the brief stops at enemy bases. Jack, in fact, had been able to make observations at the bases that would lead to their capture or destruction as soon as he was able to communicate with Mr. Stevens.

What big plans were afoot, Jack wondered, that had caused this meeting at sea? After Jack had learned these plans, he could begin preparations to escape to the mainland and contact American officials at some South American consulate. After that the whole spy ring could be smashed.

Yet there remained one unpleasantly distasteful aspect of the whole business. What about Betty Brown? How had she gotten mixed up in this band of international criminals? Had she been brought into its circle by Powder, or had she been a member before her acquaintance with him? To look at her, one would never suspect her of even the most casual associaiton with such a man as Powder.

When the spy ring was rounded up, Betty would be arrested along with the others. No matter how innocent she might look, if she were guilty she would deserve punishment for being a traitor to her country.

Traitor! The word seemed wholly foreign and outlandish when applied to Betty.

"She simply can't be a spy!" Jack resolved, rather foolishly--since all evidence pointed to her as one of the gang.

Jack had been so busy thinking that the soft-footed steward's approach was unnoticed. When he saw the man at his side, Jack gave a start.

"The Head sends his compliments and asks you to come to his cabin," the steward announced.

"Thanks, steward."

First tossing away his cigar—the black, foul-smelling brand that Powder preferred—Jack obeyed orders.

Jack felt no particular fears as he entered the luxuriously

furnished cabin that served as The Head's quarters. Jack already was confident that his disguise would fool the spy chief. His chief concern was that he would be asked something he could not answer. But Jack consoled himself with the reminder of Agent Stevens to the effect that men of Powder's caliber rarely discussed their past.

Jack's eyes became accustomed to the darkened room as he entered the door and came face to face with the man known as The Head. He was almost visibly startled by the weird appearance of the notorious international spy.

Jack had no idea what sort of looking man The Head would be, but he had expected something quite different from what he saw.

No canny cleverness appeared in the face; there was no importance or dignity in the features. The face was neither intellectual nor distinguished. The Head was uncommonly insignificant—to look at. He was an absurdly tiny man —completely bald, with large, Oriental eyes, and a weak, pusillanimous mouth. As he sat behind a large, highly polished desk he looked like a mere toad of a man. The drooping eyelids concealed a languorous stare.

"Did you send for me—Chief?" Jack asked, in Powder's inflection.

"Yes, Powder!"

The weak voice seemed insultingly intoned, until Jack realized that this was the man's natural way of speaking. He apparently looked upon other human beings with the condescension that a whale might feel for a mollusk, his diminutive stature notwithstanding.

"I am very glad to see you," The Head began in a voice that seemed to say that he would have been just as happy if Jack were never seen by anyone again. "Your accident did not seem to hurt you seriously. You're looking better than I ever saw you before."

A chill ran up Smilin' Jack's spine—did The Head already suspect the masquerade?

"Thanks, Chief. They fed me well at the hospital."

Outwardly Smilin' Jack gave not sign of his uneasiness.

"And of course Betty was there to see you often!"

Jack was about to answer when he noted a tiny twist to The Head's mouth. The spy was trying to trap him! The spy knew that Betty had *not* been permitted to see Powder often.

"Well, the doctor wouldn't let her in to see me very much, Chief," Jack said. "Afraid it might run up my blood pressure."

The Head smiled, toying with a sharp letter opener. At last he chuckled, mirthlessly, and touched a button on his desk. A door opened at the side of the cabin and through it came a huge, waddling bulk of a man.

The newcomer was even more grotesque than the shriveled dwarf-like man known as The Head. Naked to the waist, he was, so to speak, modeled on gorilla lines. His skull was bald, like The Head's, but its shape was like the nose of a bullet. His beetle brows were surmounted by black, scowling grooves of flesh. His nose was bashed to one side as though it had been forced to follow the twisted lines of his mouth.

"It is well that you answered truthfully, Powder," The Head said. "I was afraid that some of your papers might have fallen into the hands of American counter-espionage agents and that you were a disguised impostor sent here to learn some damaging details of our organization. For that reason I had your old friend The Claw in the next room, ready to use his little hook—"

The Claw laughed derisively, and raised his right arm. Instead of a hand, Jack saw an ugly metal hook fastened to the stump of his amputated lower arm.

"Glad to see you again, Claw," Jack said, forcing a smile —as he hoped Powder would have smiled.

"Ugh!" The Claw grunted non-committally.

"He is still unfriendly toward everyone but me, Powder," The Head remarked with a certain smugness. "It is somewhat of a disappointment to him that he did not get to sink his claw into you."

Smilin' Jack laughed in order to conceal the shudder he felt.

"Well," The Head continued, "I suppose we'd better get down to business. Your job, as you may have expected, has to do with flying."

"I thought so." Jack nodded. "Seemed likely, anyhow."

"Have you ever flown one of the new model patrol bombers the American navy uses in the Pacific?" came the question.

"Why, no—those ships are pretty well-guarded secrets!"

"They won't be for long," The Head said knowingly. "But I see no reason why you couldn't fly one—you could

The Claw Raised His Right Arm

familiarize yourself with the controls in a short time. After that, flying a patrol bomber is like flying any other kind of craft."

"Yes," Jack said. "I could fly one, I suppose."

"I am stealing one of the patrol bombers," The Head announced. "Two of my agents in the American navy arranged to be on one of the bombers during a test flight. They 'disappeared' last night, and by spreading some oil on the ocean and planting some pieces of wreckage they should have fooled the navy into thinking they crashed at sea. Instead, they simply dumped other members of the crew overboard—so the bomber now is flying here to meet me. You are to fly it on to one of the Japanese-held islands."

The boldness of The Head's plan left Smilin' Jack almost stunned. Actually to steal a patrol bomber from under Uncle Sam's nose! But The Head wouldn't get away with it: already Uncle Sam was "in the know," for Jack was acting for Uncle Sam. Once Jack was at the controls, he could fly back to the mainland—

"The Claw will be your companion on the trip, Powder," The Head added with an evil smile. "Now, I know you are very anxious to talk to Betty. She is on the forward deck. Good morning—Powder!"

Jack was not altogether sure of his success as he emerged from his conference with The Head. The master spy either was unduly cautious or he suspected something. Smilin' Jack only hoped he would have an opportunity to communicate with Stevens before The Head trapped him and revealed that he was indeed not Powder—but a trusted agent carrying out a mission for the U. S. A.

Betty was waiting for Jack—she ran to meet him as the aviator left the cabin.

"I was wondering how long you were going to talk business with Mr. Ghindi," Betty said.

Mr. Ghindi—that probably was The Head's name. Jack made a mental note of it for future reference.

"Pretty *bad* business, Betty." Jack spoke slowly. He was on thin ice and he watched Betty's eyes as he spoke. "Don't you sometimes wish you'd taken up *another—* kind of business?"

"Why, Powder!" Betty laughed. "I think it's the most fascinating business in the world. But I guess it's in my blood. My father has been in this business in South America for fifteen years."

The girl was absolutely sincere: she enjoyed being a spy! She came from a *family* of international spies. Jack could hardly credit his own ears.

"Well, Powder," Betty said, taking Jack's arm. "Here we are on my yacht in the middle of the Pacific—"

So it was Betty's yacht!

"—just as we planned," she finished warmly.

"Yes," Jack said, wondering what the girl was driving at. "Just as we planned."

"Shall we go ahead with the schedule today, or later?"

"Right now!" Jack said.

"Now? The same old Powder! Always impetuous! But I couldn't get ready before afternoon. A girl can't get married like she'd buy a new dress, even though we planned this elopement."

Marriage! Elopement!

It suddenly dawned on Jack what Betty had been talking about. She and Powder had planned on being married during this meeting with The Head—combining business with romance. What kind of cold-blooded, heartless creature was this daredevil girl, mixing "love" with betrayal of her native land.

Betty was soon busy formulating a program. They could be married during the afternoon with the captain officiating and Mr. Ghindi as best man. The stewardess could be matron of honor. Jack's head spun at the swiftness with which events were following one another in his new role.

"Mr. Ghindi said that there may be submarines in these waters and we're only to send one message apiece," Betty went on.

A message! That was the answer. If Jack could send a message to Stevens he might get United States naval planes here in time to foil the theft of the patrol bomber.

"Let's send the messages now!" Jack suggested. "Then we won't have anything to think about after the ceremony."

"Oh, Powder! I've never seen you so flustered! But maybe it would be a good idea. Who are *you* going to tell?"

"Well," Jack said slowly, "I've an old friend back in Valley Ridge—Stevens—I guess he ought to know."

"All right. I'll send mine to father and you let your friend know."

Jack hoped that he could make Stevens understand so Stevens would get the navy on the job before the wedding ceremony could take place.

"Come on," Jack said. "Where's the radio room?"

"Oh, I'm so *thrilled!*" Betty said, excitedly, as she led the way to the top deck.

Jack quickly collected his thoughts. He would have to tell Stevens that the PB craft—patrol bomber—was being stolen and where to find it. Jack didn't know their latitude and longitude, but he did know they were somewhere near Peru. He would have to send a message that would say one thing but *mean* something else. He could use the letters PB as initials for Stevens name! P. B. Stevens! That would warn Stevens right away to be on the alert.

Betty led the way into the radio room.

"What are you going to say, Powder?" she asked, with a natural feminine curiosity.

"Oh, something to kid him along," Jack said.

First picking up paper and pencil, he began to write slowly, making sure he was saying two things at once. At last he finished and handed the message to Betty, who read:

" 'P. B. Stevens, 444 East Twelfth Street, Valley Ridge, California. Perfect elopement remedies unsoundness. Smile! And check—it's not lost but stolen love. Thief is Betty Brown in the middle of Pacific. Powder!' "

Betty blinked, her forehead in furrows. "It isn't **very** coherent, but maybe he'll understand it. Why don't you just say: 'Eloped with Betty'?"

"He's a newspaper man," Jack said. "That first sentence is written headline style because he probably wouldn't understand any other kind of lingo."

"I guess it is sort of clever," Betty conceded dubiously. "You go ahead and write one for my father while I hunt up the captain. He'll have to okay the messages— it's some sort of war regulation Mr. Ghindi explained to me."

As Betty left, Jack checked an impulse to overpower the radio operator and send a message himself. But the odds were against him. The radio operator was armed and Jack could hardly take him by surprise.

That cryptic message to Stevens *had* to get through.

"Couldn't you start sending this now—to save time?" Jack asked the operator.

The radio officer turned to Jack and picked up the message.

"Did The Head see this?" he asked.

"No—" Jack began.

"But I'll be pleased to read it now," came a sarcastic voice from behind Jack.

Jack whirled to come face to face with the little man, who extended a tiny arm and jerked the paper from the radio operator's hand.

"I was telling a chum about Betty and me getting married," Jack explained. "He's the kind of screwball who'll

Betty Led the Way to the Radio Room

get a wallop out of that scrambled radiogram."

The Head did not reply. His right hand went inside his coat and an automatic appeared from a shoulder holster. With the weapon pointed at Jack, The Head's lips parted in an evil grin.

"Even your innermost thoughts could not be hidden from me, Powder," he said. "I have suspected you since you first came aboard. Somehow you did not act altogether like the real Powder—perhaps it was your manner, or it may have been that you did not look *dissipated* enough."

Another shadow blacked out the door. It was The Claw coming into the room. His ugly hook was lifted and there was a grin of evil anticipation on his vicious face.

"Shall I throw him to the sharks, Chief?" he asked eagerly.

The Head holstered his pistol.

"Not yet," he said. "I want to read this interesting message addressed to 'P.B. Stevens.' 'P.B.' could not possibly refer to *patrol bomber,* could it, Powder?"

Smilin' Jack was silent. A thousand times as he had rehearsed his role as Powder, he had foreseen the possibility of being discovered as a masquerader. He had wondered if he would be afraid. He was angry at being in the power of such an insignificant little scoundrel.

Outwardly Jack was calm, composed, waiting for a chance.

The dwarfed man was not giving Jack a chance, however.

"You needn't tell me, Powder," he went on. "I can guess. Now that first sentence intrigues me: *'Perfect elopement remedies unsoundness.'* At first glance I'd say it was nonsense, but isn't it a coincidence that the initials of those four words are P-E-R-U, *Peru,* the country nearest our location in the Pacific!"

Jack compressed his lips tightly. The Head was no dunce—he was doing a good job of deciphering the message.

"And there are other acrobatics with words in this odd message. For instance: *'Smile'!* What does that mean? It might not be intended to be set off by itself. Perhaps it is part of the next sentence: *'Smile and check.'* Could that mean something?"

To Jack it meant something, but to The Head it did not. To Jack it was his own name, "Smilin' Jack," as closely as he could have said it in a message likely to be censored. Stevens undoubtedly would have read it "Smilin' Jack" as he deciphered it.

"The meaning escapes me," The Head went on. "I must congratulate you for making part of the message undecipherable. But the rest is quite clear: *'It's not lost but stolen.'* Referring to the plane, not to 'love" as you wrote in the message. *'Thief is Betty Brown in middle of Pacific.'* That is redundant. You've already told your friend you were off Peru and it is nonsensical to incriminate Betty Brown. I resent your attributing my feats to others. But perhaps you wanted to tell your friend that Betty Brown's yacht was involved. Yes, that is probably what you meant, although I did not know that you had learned the yacht belonged to her. Powder knew this, but you didn't. You see, I know you are not really Powder."

Jack lunged forward, but his charge toward The Head was checked sharply by a pressure in his shoulder. The Claw had fastened his hook into Jack's clothing and the point was pressing against Jack's skin.

"Lock him in the hold, Claw," The Head ordered. "We'll keep him there until we reach the next coral reef. Then we'll plant him on it—to die!"

"Chee, Boss! I could do it much better!"

"Much messier, too, no doubt! No, Claw. Do as I say, and do it now!"

Jack was marched through the door. As he emerged on deck he saw Betty running toward him.

"Powder!" she cried.

The Head stepped between Jack and Betty.

"It is fortunate for you, Miss Brown, that Powder did not send that message," he said. "It wasn't the kind of message you thought it was."

"You—you mean Powder's a—a spy?" Betty stammered.

"The message would have given the enemy a great deal of valuable information, Miss Brown," The Head said, glancing swiftly from under lowered eyelids at Jack.

"I—I can't believe it!" came the girl's low, troubled sob.

"March!" The Claw ordered, pricking Jack's shoulder

with the hook.

Jack stumbled toward the gangway. It was harder than ever for him to believe that Betty was a member of this unprincipled band of plotters and killers.

CHAPTER SIX

PUZZLING EVIDENCE

With The Claw's sharp hook menacing Jack at every step, the American aviator walked down a narrow, ladder-like stairway to the dark and smelly hold of the yacht.

Here the tropical heat, abetted by the boilers in the engine room, made the atmosphere stifling and stagnant.

Sometimes pushing and sometimes prodding, The Claw hurried Jack forward of the engine room to a small room fitted with a barred door.

"De brig," The Claw announced, catching Jack's shoulder with his hook and holding him while he removed some keys from his pocket with his left hand.

The lock turned and the door swung open on rusty hinges.

"Nuttin' like a cell wit' hot an' cold runnin' rats," The Claw chortled. "Take it easy, Powder. Don't try t' jerk away: dis claw ain't made of rubber."

With that, The Claw pushed Jack into the cell. Still holding his prisoner to prevent a sudden break, the bullet-headed giant examined the room to make sure there were no bits of iron or wood that could be fashioned into crude weapons or tools of escape.

Assuring himself that the only objects in the room were a mattress for a bed and a battered chair, The Claw flung Jack to the floor and made his exit. He locked the cell door and removed the key. Then he paused for a moment to gloat over the prisoner.

"Lockin' you up ain't my way of handlin' you," The Claw said with a snarling laugh. "You're lucky. I could fix you up with my claw, but The Head is a pig. He wants to have all de fun."

Smilin' Jack sat in the chair and rubbed his shoulder where the hook had gouged his flesh. He heard The Claw's footsteps retreat down the passage to the ladder leading to the upper deck.

Alone, Jack peeled off his coat and unfastened his tie and collar. It was suffocatingly hot and this was only the beginning. Jack did not doubt that The Head planned to put him ashore on some coral reef, without food or water. If that wasn't The Head's plan, something worse was in store.

"I've got to escape somehow," Jack vowed.

Not only was his own life at stake, but the information he had gained had to be communicated to American authorities on the mainland.

Jack began a survey of his surroundings. The one porthole in the cell was barred and bolted shut—no chance to escape from that. The bulkhead was strong.

He tried the door. It rattled, but it was solid. The lock was large but Jack didn't have anything to use to pick it. There wasn't a loose bit of metal in the cell and Jack had nothing of that kind on his person.

Escape seemed absolutely impossible.

Jack sat down on the dirty mattress to consider his plight. He might try to overpower his jailer when the next meal was served. But even if he did, what chance would he then have to escape from the ship? The yacht probably was miles from land.

A rat scratched in one corner of the cell. The Claw had not understated his suggestion that Jack would have rodent companionship in his prison. There was another scratching noise—

Jack turned his head. The sound seemed to come from above. Were the rats crawling on the ceiling, too?

A grill was overhead. The noise came from there—the opening from the ventilator!

"Da-da-de-dee!"

No rat made that sound.

"Powder! Can you hear me?"

Betty was calling Jack through the ventilator.

"Betty!" Jack called softly. "Yes, I can hear you—"

"Lucky thing I know more about this ship than they do. What are they doing to you?"

Jack hesitated. How far did he dare to trust Betty? She was a trusted member of this spy ring. Yet—she might not be—perhaps she could help.

"Betty," Jack asked. "How deeply are you mixed up in Mr. Ghindi's—The Head's business?"

"Why, you know as well as I, Powder. You know he's been associated with my father for years—just as you have—"

Betty's father, then, was the boss of the ring and The

The Claw Locked the Door and Took the Key

Head was his associate.

Betty had broken off suddenly in her reply to Jack. Now her voice came again through the ventilator, but she was not speaking to Jack.

"I was trying to find out, Mr. Ghindi, just why you have locked up my fiancé." The Head had arrived on the scene.

"That is quite easy to explain, Miss Brown," replied the Head's voice. "Your fiancé was a spy. He was preparing to turn over your father's secrets to a friend on the mainland. The message he wrote, presumably telling his friend of your elopement, was in code—"

"Powder!" Betty's voice rang through the ventilator. "I can't believe it. Tell me the truth!"

Jack was silent, thinking. If Betty's father were one of the chiefs of this spy ring, then Betty was in it too.

"I thought there was something fishy about that radiogram!" Betty said. "You *are* a spy! And to think I would have married you!"

An object rattled down the ventilator and dropped to Jack's feet on the floor. Jack picked it up. It was the diamond ring.

Without replying to the girl, Jack dropped the ring into his pocket. He heard her leave the ventilator in company with The Head, who apparently had overheard her conversation with Jack and had interrupted it. Betty Brown, the girl with the soft contralto voice, was a Mata Hari unmasked—a woman no man loyal to his country should ever trust.

While Jack was eating his noon meal, which a sailor had brought to the brig, the engine stopped. The rattle of anchor chains sounded at the bow. Something was afoot.

Pushing his plate aside, Jack stood up and peered from the porthole. On this side of the ship was only the rolling ocean. No land was in sight.

Jack quickly dropped to his chair again and picked up the remains of his lunch as he heard footsteps in the passageway. Then he saw a gigantic blob of darkness silhouetted against the bars of his cell.

"Just wanted to make sure you was all right," came The Claw's growl.

"I'm not cooked yet," Jack said with attempted cheerfulness. "Say, Claw, what's the idea of stopping here?"

"Worried?" The Claw asked. "No, Powder, we ain't reached that coral reef yet. We're just waitin' for that PB to show up. If you listen maybe you'll be able to hear the motors when it comes 'longside."

The Claw rattled the door to make sure it was tightly fastened and then he turned to go.

"Well, as long as you're still salted down okay, I'll move along," he said.

"I'm doing quite well—thank you—under the circumstances," Jack replied. "But I do much better when you're not around."

The Claw laughed unpleasantly.

"My my! Wotta cheerful disposition," he said as he walked away.

As soon as Jack heard The Claw go up the ladder to the deck, he moved his chair to the window. A moment before, when he stood beside the port, one of the bars had seemed loose. He examined the bar with care. Only a single, rusty bolt held it in place. He needed something to cut that bolt.

A smile spread over Jack's face as he remembered he had something! In his pocket was the hardest substance in the world—a diamond. It could cut steel like a file! It would even cut glass!

Jack dug into his pocket. A look of dismay crossed his face as he found the pocket empty. Then he felt the ring in his other pocket and the old smile reappeared.

Holding the diamond to the light, Jack marveled at its size and beauty. But there was no time to waste. He set to work cutting the bolt that held the bar across the porthole.

For almost an hour he worked, making slow headway. It was hard to hold the ring firmly. Then he heard the hum of motors in the distance. The four-motored patrol bomber was arriving just in time to fit into Jack's plan.

If Jack could get out of the porthole soon after the plane landed, he might find it temporarily unguarded. That patrol bomber would be just the thing for him to use in his escape!

The metal bolt and the tiny ring burned and numbed his fingers, but Jack kept on working. At last the bolt was worn almost in two. With a supreme effort, Jack twisted it off. Then he caught hold of the rusty bar and, throwing all of his weight on it, bent it back to the bulk-head. Luckily it was a small, narrow bar.

Now only a pane of thick glass separated Jack from the open air. Jack might use the chair to smash the glass, but the sound possibly would be heard on deck.

The diamond must be used to cut away the glass.

The roar of the four-motored bomber was deafening now, and suddenly Jack caught his first glimpse of it through the dirty porthole. A moment later it landed gracefully on the sea and taxied toward the yacht.

"What a plane!" Jack said admiringly as he gazed at the craft through the porthole.

But there would be time to feast his eyes on the plane later. Jack redoubled his efforts to cut the glass. The ring had dug a deep scratch around the glass now and Jack was ready to remove the pane.

Picking up his discarded coat, Jack spread it against the glass. Then he pressed against the center of the glass with the palm of his hand. There was a sharp crack as the glass broke. It fell outward and dropped with a faint splash into the water of the ocean.

For several precious seconds Smilin' Jack stood in front of the opening, gulping refreshing lungfuls of cool air. But he could spend little time enjoying this luxury. Quickly he turned his full attention to escape. The Claw might return on another inspection trip at any moment and the open porthole would be quickly discovered.

With his coat wrapped around his hand, Jack pried loose the remaining bits of glass from the frame of the

porthole. When he had finished, he stripped off the remainder of his clothing.

To measure his chances, he thrust his head through
the opening.

It was the smallest porthole he had ever seen, but there
was a chance he could make it. At least it was worth a
try.

He wormed one shoulder through with only a little
difficulty, but the second shoulder was a problem. At last,
squirming and twisting, and at the cost of some skin, he
made it.

Bracing his muscular arms against the side of the ship
he drew his chest through the opening.

"Lucky for me I don't have a big waistline," he thought
grimly.

Inch by inch he eased his body, glistening with perspiration, through the small opening. Then he stopped,
his hips stuck fast.

A momentary panic swept over Smilin' Jack as it seemed that he could not move either forward or backward.

"Good night!" he muttered. "I'm in for it now. I'm
caught."

He rested a second and then strained with all his
might. His body moved a fraction of an inch as the frame
of the porthole gouged deep into the flesh of his hips.
Every move he made scraped off some skin. But he had
to go on. He worked and struggled painfully.

Perspiration flowed from every pore in his body and it
was this moisture that did the trick. Slowly at first and

then faster his body slid through the opening. The sharp edges of the porthole cut less deeply and Jack was freeing himself. Suddenly his body slipped forward and he plunged headfirst into the water beside the ship.

The cooling dive put new energy into his muscles, even though the salt bit at the bleeding scratches made by the sides of the porthole. He was free!

Jack rose, gulped in a lungful of air and then sank under the waves again. Swimming under water and rising only to gasp air, he moved toward the patrol bomber which was being refueled at the stern of the yacht.

One man, undoubtedly one of the two spies who had stolen the naval aircraft, was on the wing holding the hose in the fuel tank.

"Lucky there's only one to deal with," Jack thought as he came up on the far side of the plane.

His arm shot up and caught the wing strut. For a moment he rested and then drew his body out of the water. A slow stealthy climb brought Jack to the wing.

The man on the wing heard the noise as Jack pulled himself to his feet, but before he had a chance to realize what was happening or give a cry of alarm, Jack had lunged forward with his fists swinging. A left-right, one-two blow to the jaw sent the spy staggering off the wing and into the water.

The shout of alarm released by the falling man was echoed aboard the yacht.

"Powder's escaped!" shrieked a voice from the bridge. "Get guns!"

Diving into the cockpit, Jack slammed on the starters and throttle. The engine caught instantly. Four propellers churned the air. The craft swung around, but it did not seem to move.

It was anchored!

Suddenly there was a crash of glass as a rifle bullet smashed through the cabin of the bomber. Jack would be riddled in a second or two by the shooting from the deck of the yacht.

Grimly Jack grasped the controls of the aircraft and swung it around so that the back-wash from the propellers of the four motors swept the deck.

The firing suddenly ceased as a miniature hurricane swept across the yacht. Good shooting was impossible in the teeth of that gale.

The maneuver gave Jack a chance to locate and release the anchor control. The patrol bomber shot forward like an arrow across the water. In a few more seconds it began to lift and skimmed upward into the air.

Jack glanced back, feeling safe for the first time since he had been made a prisoner by The Head. But Jack's troubles were not ended.

The crane on the yacht was lowering one of the two seaplanes to the water in preparation for pursuit.

Jack's position now was serious. He was familiar with the seaplanes and he knew that they had six synchronized machine guns in the wings. Without a gunner to fight off the smaller and swifter machine, Jack would be at the mercy of his pursuer.

RAT-TAT

RAT TAT-TAT

The Seaplane Tailed the Larger Plane

With this realization, Jack checked his climb. There was no time to gain altitude now—he had to put as much distance as possible between himself and the seaplane.

The seaplane came skimming over the water. In a moment it took the air and tailed the larger and slower craft. It seemed to gain with the speed of a bullet, in spite of the fact that Jack had his throttle wide open.

All chances of escape were fading. In a few more minutes the white web of tracer bullets would begin weaving a death trap for Smilin' Jack.

But danger breeds ideas. The instinct of self-preservation is strongest when it is needed most.

Smilin' Jack's brain did a ground loop and landed with a three-point idea.

Jack's hand went forward throwing the robot pilot into operation. The American's face was set grimly as he released the controls of the craft. It was sailing straight ahead, a perfect target for bullets from the little hornet on its tail, but Jack was willing to take a chance that the pursuer would hold his fire in hopes Jack would surrender. The patrol bomber was much too valuable a military prize to destroy if it could be captured in one piece.

"If this trick doesn't throw 'em off my tail, the surprise will!" Jack muttered to himself.

He left the cockpit and moved along the catwalk to the tail turret. Crouching behind the machine gun in the turret he trained it on the seaplane.

The pursuer was creeping closer. It was near enough now to turn loose with its six "stingers" and riddle the larger craft to shreds.

Jack's finger squeezed the trigger of the turret gun. A deafening roar rattled in his ears. The smell of powder swept into his nostrils. A chain of empty shell-cases dropped from the tail of the bomber.

The spray of bullets struck the seaplane with crippling force. The little machine seemed to shudder with the impact. It wobbled from its course. Desperately it tried to come out of its uncontrollable slip. Then a black streamer of smoke began to rise from the engine and red tongues of flame licked at the fuselage.

The pursuing craft suddenly went completely out of control and fell like a wounded duck straight toward the waters of the Pacific Ocean.

Striking the sea with a tremendous crash, it turned over on its nose and settled on the waves with roaring flames climbing up the frame of the cockpit.

A feeling of pity swept over Jack for the man inside that plane, even though the pursuer might have been ready to send Jack to a similar fate. More than likely the pilot was Jim, the man who had flown Jack to meet the Claw. It was the end of a long career of dishonest flying—dope running, smuggling, and, finally, betrayal of his country.

"He deserved it," Jack said grimly.

CHAPTER SEVEN

A MYSTERIOUS ENCOUNTER

Having made good his escape, Smilin' Jack had only a vague idea where he was, but he knew there were many islands in this part of the Pacific. If he could find one of them inhabited, he would land and get in touch with American authorities on the mainland.

There were two reasons for not using the radio on the patrol bomber until he was in a friendly port: The Head still had another seaplane, faster and more maneuverable than the big ship, and there might be other enemy planes within striking distance.

Jack's job was to get the bomber back to America or, failing that, to destroy it so that it would not fall in enemy hands. He hoped that he would be within range of rescue when the time came to destroy the plane if that last recourse became necessary.

When an island shoved its head above the horizon Jack nosed the bomber toward it. Leeward of a jungle-fringed shore on the southeastern end of the isle was a lagoon. From the air the place looked uninhabited, but there might be some people living there. At any rate, Jack could replenish his fresh water supply and rest a while before flying northward and eastward toward the United States.

Jack donned clothing he found aboard the plane: a

pair of dark blue trousers, a light shirt and some shoes stored in a locker. There also was food—iron rations—but the water was low.

The bomber circled the lagoon. It was small and apparently rarely used, but it looked sufficient to harbor the bomber, unless hidden reefs were under the water. Still, a seaplane with a very small draft might glide safely over water so shallow as to be dangerous for a ship.

Down, down, Jack nosed the plane. He sideslipped to check his speed and then straightened out. The bottom of the ship touched the waves and then rested on the water, skimming toward the sandy beach that ran to the water's edge from the jungle.

"I'm goin' to make it!" Jack beamed as these words sang triumphantly in his brain.

But hardly had the words left his mouth when there was a grinding crash. The forward motion ceased abruptly and the plane swung around. From below, salt water surged into the cockpit.

The patrol bomber was sinking!

In spite of the plane's shallow draft, Jack must have hit a submerged reef as he tried to beach his ship on this lonely island. The rocks apparently had torn away most of the bottom, and the inrushing sea water could not be stemmed.

Dropping the controls Jack clambered out of the cockpit just ahead of the rising water. He took stock of the situation quickly. The shore was not far away and he could make it. The doomed bomber was useless to Jack and equally lost to the enemy.

Without further delay Smilin' Jack plunged into the ocean and struck out for shore.

As he struck the water he remembered sharks, but it was too late to change his mind. The thought seemed to put strength into his muscles as he breasted the waves. Each ripple of the ocean around him seemed to be a fin charging toward him; each tug of the ocean on his body seemed to be the current caused by the closing of saw-toothed jaws.

Then Jack's feet struck bottom. He pulled himself, wet and bedraggled, up on the white sands. Looking back he saw only a ripple where the giant bomber had been a few minutes before. His only means of transportation was on the bottom: Jack was shipwrecked three thousand miles from home.

"Now I know how Robinson Crusoe felt," Jack muttered to himself.

But Crusoe was lucky. He had rescued tools and supplies from his ship before it sank. Jack didn't have even a hammer.

All he could see of the island was utterly desolate. His eyes swept the beach.

Wait a minute—what was that?

Something seemed to move near the fringe of palm trees. It dived into a clump of brush at the edge of the beach. Jack tensed. The figure had looked human. If it was friendly, why did it hide? If it was a foe, why didn't it attack? An attack, at least, would be relief from a disturbing uncertainty.

The swaying brush ceased moving. A deadly silence settled over the beach.

Was the figure a native? Jack recalled reading somewhere that while cannibalism was generally believed to be stamped out, it might still persist among some primitive savages in out-of-the-way places. The American aviator had visions of himself going into a pot to provide a feast for a king with a bone ornament in his nose.

Well, cannibals or not, Jack had to find out—he could stand the suspense no longer. Cupping his hands he shouted toward the thick curtain of vegetation:

"Hi, you! Come out of that brush!"

Again the branches of the shrubs stirred as something moved. Something was there—an intelligent something that could understand the English language.

A piece of driftwood lay on the beach. Jack stooped, picking it up as he advanced to find out what was hiding in the shrubs. He went forward determinedly, half crouching, ready to meet any sort of attack.

The stirring of the green leaves grew violent.

"No, no!" came a startled cry from the undergrowth. "Fat Stuff he come out. He surrender!"

The brush parted and from the undergrowth stepped a puff-cheeked, pot-bellied man.

A native? Yes. His brown skin and black hair were unmistakably those of an islander. A cannibal? No. There was a pleasantly good-natured gleam in the man's countenance, even though the fellow's eyes rolled with fear and his mouth was agape with fright.

But these first impressions were swept away by another feature that struck Jack with the force of a blow.

This man wore the striped clothing and monkey hat of a convict!

"Who—what—?"

The native did not seem to hear Jack's words. An expression of relief enveloped the man's whole body as he noticed Jack's wet clothing and bedraggled appearance. Possibly this fat, puff-cheeked native had expected something quite different. At any rate, the hunted look vanished and the gape of his mouth narrowed into a grin.

"Oh!" the native exclaimed. "You stranger here."

"You're a convict!" Jack said accusingly. "Where did you escape from?"

The hunted look returned.

"Don't sendum Fat Stuff back to Death Rock prison!" he pleaded.

"Death Rock prison?" Jack had never heard of the place.

"Fat Stuff no likum work in sulphur mine. Fat Stuff likum fish. Him no likum work at all."

This man who called himself Fat Stuff looked harmless, yet many criminals had innocent baby-faces and disarming ways. Fat Stuff might be a convicted murderer. Fat Stuff had lost his jacket, but the striped trousers were enough to prove that he had been in a prison. Aiding a prisoner to escape would make Jack a criminal too, but he did need help—badly.

"We'll talk that over later," Jack decided. "Right now you can be of help to me. Where's the closest settlement on this island?"

Fat Stuff shook his head.

"No go there," he said. "Limehouse throwum you in prison too. Him need convicts. Him short."

"That's ridiculous, Fat Stuff—if that's your name," Jack said. "I haven't done anything to be thrown in prison for—unless—say, what country owns this island?"

Fat Stuff shrugged his shoulders.

"Death Rock owned by man. Him toss everybody in jail who come here."

Fat Stuff spoke earnestly and convincingly, but the meaning his words conveyed was too outlandish. In any civilized community (except one ruled by Nazis or Japs) men aren't imprisoned for no reason at all. The oversized native probably was fabricating the tale.

"I've got to get something to eat and find a radio station," Jack went on. "I'm in no position now to capture a fugitive from justice. I'll make a bargain with you. Direct me to the settlement and I'll go there alone. I'm not promising that I won't tell the authorities where I saw you, but I'm unarmed and I could hardly be expected to bring in a desperate convict without the proper—er—equipment."

Fat Stuff listened and smiled.

"Good bargain," he agreed cheerfully.

"*No* bargain!" came a new voice.

From the palm trees behind Fat Stuff a white man

appeared. His long, angular body was impeccably dressed in a linen suit and on his head was a tropical sun helmet. A hypocritical smile flicked underneath his long
and pointed nose in his dish-face. He held an automatic
rather carelessly in his hand, pointed in the general direction of Jack and Fat Stuff.

Still smiling cynically the newcomer stepped out on
the beach and approached Jack and the native. Fat Stuff
trembled violently.

But the newcomer's eyes were not fixed on the escaped
convict—they were fixed on Jack.

"My word!" he exclaimed. *"Powder!"*

Smilin' Jack's heart sank. The name Powder carried
with it certain unpleasant implications. If anyone ever
deserved to be behind prison bars it was Powder Pellet.

The dish-faced white man stopped half a dozen paces
from Jack. He still held the automatic carelessly, but
Jack caught a cruel look in the man's eyes hinting that
he would not begrudge using it—with care.

"So you finally decided to come back to see Limehouse, did you?" the white man asked. "I suppose The
Head sent you. How'd you get here, anyhow? Your
clothing's all wet—maybe you swum!"

Limehouse laughed mirthlessly.

"I came by plane, Limehouse," Jack said, in Powder's
voice. "But it struck a rock in the lagoon and sank."

Limehouse's evil grin broadened.

"Now isn't that too bad! If this gun should go off accidentally, our friend The Head would never know you

Limehouse Held the Automatic Carelessly

landed here at all."

Limehouse's two references to The Head gave Smilin' Jack an inkling that this man, whoever he was, had at one time associated with the international spy. Limehouse therefore would not be above shooting just for the fun of it.

"But I don't think I shall kill you yet, Powder," he went on, allowing the muzzle of the automatic to drop slightly. He turned to the native. "Well, Fat Stuff, your freedom didn't last long."

"What did I do for-um go to prison?" Fat Stuff asked plaintively.

"Do? *Do!*" Limehouse roared with laughter. "You got caught, that's what. Jim caught you, just like Powder caught so many on the mainland. Only difference between Jim an' Powder is, Jim knocked over natives. He got easy ones. Powder used Mickey Finns to nab sailors on the mainland."

"You take-um me back?" Fat Stuff asked, with a panicky look in his eyes. "I die sure!"

"Lie down on the beach, Fat Stuff," Limehouse ordered curtly. "Keep quiet. One false move an' I'll plug you, even if it'll make me another man short."

Limehouse's references to Mickey Finns and being "short" bewildered Jack. Something very strange was going on—something unholy.

Fat Stuff was prone on the beach now, and Limehouse turned to Jack.

"You know, Powder," Limehouse began, "there's a

mite of unfinished business 'tween you an' me."

Jack's heart sank. Whatever had taken place between Limehouse and Powder was a closed book to Jack, who had not even known of this man's existence a few minutes ago. Bluffing might serve, but Limehouse might catch on at any time that this was not Powder Pellet standing before him.

"Unfinished business?" Jack asked, stalling.

"Don't act so innocent, Powder," Limehouse said sneeringly. "I'm referring to that diamond ring you stole from the countess. Big as a forty-five bullet. Where is it?"

"Oh!"

Jack knew where that diamond was. Limehouse had given him a hint, after all. The diamond was in the clothing he had left behind on the yacht—in the ring Powder had given Betty to seal their engagement.

"Where is it?"

There was a threatening undertone in Limehouse's voice, but Jack was unshaken.

"I got bumped on the head when the plane hit the reef," Jack said. "It's hard for me to remember."

"Maybe it would make you remember if I put you on Death Rock awhile," Limehouse spoke sharply. "You needn't think you've fooled me, Powder. I know you and The Head have had a falling out. He sent a message to me earlier today telling me the whole story. I sort of figured you'd wind up here because I know you've got a nice little cache of treasure hidden on the island. Money, jewelry and other little trinkets you stole from the men you shanghaied for Death Rock!"

Here was a new revelation concerning the man that Betty Brown had expected to marry. He was engaged in shanghaiing men for Death Rock—whatever that might be.

"The Head's comin' here soon, Powder," Limehouse went on. "What he has in store for you ain't none of my business, but it's plenty of yours."

Cold perspiration broke from Jack's pores. The Head might have any number of horrors in store for the man he believed to be Powder.

"Now I'm a reasonable man, Powder," Limehouse went on. "I don't like to see my friends suffer. Just show me where your treasure is, an' I'll forget I ever saw you."

So Limehouse wanted to be bribed! The scoundrel must think Jack was easily duped to offer such a proposition. From Limehouse's manner, it was not hard to guess that murder was a trifling thing to him. As soon as Jack uncovered a treasure, Limehouse would shoot and forget that he ever saw anyone called "Powder."

On the other hand, if Jack didn't appear to agree to the plan, The Head would make matters much more complicated.

"Okay," Jack said. "You can have the treasure."

Limehouse turned to the heavy man lying on the sand.

Slowly the huge native rose to his feet.

"Turn around!"

Fat Stuff groaned, as Jack watched the proceedings

without realizing at first what they meant.

"Sorry to do this, Fat Stuff—but where a fortune is involved one can't let everybody in on it."

Jack suddenly realized that Limehouse was about to kill this friendless native.

"Wait!" Jack cried. "I've a better idea."

Limehouse lowered the gun slightly.

"Well, speak fast—I'm in a hurry to get my hands on that gold."

"That's just it," Jack said. "It's possible we may not find the treasure."

"Maybe you'd rather let The Head play with you?" Limehouse suggested.

"No, but I'm not sure I know the exact spot," Jack said. "And someone may have found it already. Why not keep an ace in the hole? Leave Fat Stuff tied here and then you can collect the reward on him if I don't turn up the treasure."

Limehouse, to Jack's surprise, seemed to consider the proposition. Jack had been stalling, hoping for a chance to make a break or to overpower this beady-eyed man. But the suggestion, advanced by Jack in the face of uncertainties, seemed to be well taken.

"M-m-m!" Limehouse said. "Something in what you say. I'm short of prisoners an' even a worthless slob like Fat Stuff can't be spared very well. Yes, Powder, thank you for lookin' out for my interests. Fat Stuff *will* be an ace in the hole. But remember, in case you're looking out for any tricks, The Head will pay a fancy price for you, too."

Limehouse took some handcuffs from his pocket and put them on Fat Stuff's wrists. Then, with Limehouse forcing his two prisoners to walk ahead, they entered the jungle. A short distance away they came upon an old model touring car. Into this he forced Fat Stuff; then the native's legs were tightly bound with rope, which Limehouse found in the car.

From a trunk on the side of the car Limehouse pulled out a pick and shovel which he tossed over his shoulder.

"Lead the way, Powder!" he ordered, pointing the pistol at Jack.

Without the slightest idea where he was going, Smilin' Jack plunged into the jungle. The task was difficult. He was supposed to know this area but he had never visited it before.

For several minutes they walked through thick undergrowth.

"Just a minute, Powder," Limehouse called. "You needn't try to stall. I know the treasure is somewhere around here. I followed you a couple of times, but you always eluded me here. You know where the gold is. Show me."

Jack had to do some fast thinking and unrehearsed acting.

"Oh—why—sure—it's been so long since I was here, I didn't recognize the place!" Jack stammered, looking around. "There it is!"

Jack pointed toward a giant palm tree about a hundred feet ahead.

"There's the place. We start there and walk a straight line toward that tall peak—"

A glimpse of a basalt spire through the trees gave Jack his lead, and he strode from the foot of the palm on a line toward it.

"—ninety paces—then a right turn—"

Jack could hardly keep this up very long. If he could only stall Limehouse until after dark, he'd have a much better chance to escape. It was already late afternoon—night could not be far from falling.

"Yes, yes!" Limehouse said impatiently. "What next?"

"Now fifty paces to—to that sharp rock!" Jack spotted the rock just in time.

"Yes, yes—is that where the treasure is?" Limehouse asked eagerly.

"—Ah—no," Jack said. "We have to wait till after dark and line this rock with the North Star—and then—"

A cunning gleam came into Limehouse's eyes.

"Dark, hey? Powder, if you're plannin' a double-cross you're just as good as in The Head's torture chamber right now!"

Limehouse was pointing the gun directly at Smilin' Jack's heart.

Jack knew he couldn't stall much longer.

"Well, maybe I can find it without the North Star," Jack said. "Yes—that way is north."

Jack counted off twenty-five paces from the rock and asked for the shovel. There was nothing else to do but to start digging in the spot he had selected entirely at random.

The eager and impatient Limehouse stood to one side with the gun pointed at Jack as the hole grew deeper and deeper—and the shadows grew longer and longer.

"Better hurry," Limehouse said.

Jack had to do something. A desperate plan began forming in his mind. The next time the shovel blade struck a rock—

The blade rang against a buried chunk of lava.

"Look!" Jack exclaimed. "I've found it!"

Limehouse sprang forward for a look. As he came close to Jack the shovel came up, hurling loose sand full in the face of the man holding the gun.

Ducking a bullet which crashed into a tree behind him, Jack sprang from the hole and dashed for freedom.

Momentarily blinded by the sand, Limehouse roared with anger. He tried to brush his eyes clear, and then, howling with rage, fired aimlessly at the hazy figure of Smilin' Jack he saw darting into the jungle.

Only a few more steps and Jack would be completely out of sight, but the bullets were whizzing close to him, panging off rocks and burying themselves in the palm trees.

The automatic crashed again. This bullet accidentally struck its mark. With a scream of pain, Smilin' Jack stumbled and fell in the grass of the jungle.

A moment later he rose. His leg felt as if it had been kicked by a mule, but he knew it was only a flesh wound.

Desperately, Jack tried to drag himself into the dense undergrowth of the jungle. Each move cost him pain, but he had to get away before Limehouse spotted him.

Limehouse, however, had heard Jack's cry, and, before Jack could hide, he had run toward the spot where Jack had fallen.

"Oh!" he cried spotting Jack crawling into the brush. "There you are! You can't double-cross *me* an' get away with it!"

Limehouse's arm shot down, seized Jack's shoulder and jerked him back from the brush. Jack looked upward into the muzzle of the automatic.

"Say your prayers, Powder!" Limehouse snarled. "An automatic is about to be emptied in your face!"

CHAPTER EIGHT

DEATH ROCK

For a moment Smilin' Jack stared unflinchingly into the barrel of the pistol. It held steadily for a second and then seemed to turn away from Jack's gaze.

"Well?" Jack asked, stubbornly. "What're you waiting for? Get it over with. It'll be better than meeting The Head again."

Limehouse's mouth twisted sideways in an abortive smile.

"No," he said studiously, "shootin' is too easy for you, Powder. I'd enjoy turnin' you over to The Head, to die by inches. Then you'll realize how foolish you were not to lead me to the treasure, you double-crosser."

Limehouse rose and jerked Jack to his feet. The wound pained Jack considerably, but he did not utter a sound.

"But before The Head gets you, I think I'll give you a taste of my own revenge," he said. "I'll put you in Death Rock to rot for awhile with some of the men you shang-haied from the mainland. No doubt that will help you decide to take me to the buried gold."

The name of Death Rock sounded bad enough. Jack had heard enough to realize it was some sort of a prison. Fat Stuff must have escaped from there. But why were men shanghaied for this prison? Even the hardest-hearted warden in the world does not solicit prisoners, nor have them kidnaped so that his prison will be full. There was something deeply and wickedly mysterious about Death Rock.

But what made it appear less savory than ever to Smilin' Jack was the fact that Powder, the man Jack was impersonating, had assisted in kidnaping prisoners for this undeserved punishment. The wrath of these unjustly incarcerated men might lead to a terrible revenge if they recognized Powder as the villain responsible for their plight.

Limehouse released his hold, and Jack, weak from pain, dropped to the ground.

Limehouse pulled back Jack's torn trouser leg and glanced at the wound.

"Bad luck, Powder," he said. "The wound ain't serious. It would be lucky for you if it was."

Then Limehouse pulled a handkerchief from his pocket and handed it to Smilin' Jack.

"Bandage your wound," he ordered. "It'd make me sad if you cashed in your chips before we got to Death Rock prison."

Night was falling rapidly now, bringing the darkness Jack had needed for his escape, but escape no longer was possible since Jack had a painfully wounded leg. As inhuman as Death Rock prison was painted by Limehouse, medical treatment at least would be given there, Jack reasoned.

Jack's leg was growing stiff as he managed to get to his

feet at last. Limehouse refused to aid his prisoner, pre-
ferring to watch Jack's agony as they retraced their steps
through the jungle to the car. When, at last, they reached
the machine, they found Fat Stuff fast asleep. The native did not let his troubles keep him awake.

"You two will bring a nice reward," Limehouse gloated as Jack climbed laboriously into the car. "An escaped
prisoner brings as large a premium as a new one. You,
Powder, will bring a double reward. You are both a new
prisoner and a man on whom The Head has placed a
price."

Jack turned the words over in his mind. The statement
that rewards were paid for new prisoners sounded
strangely like slavery. But slavery had no proper place
in the modern world. This must be a place outside the
pale.

Limehouse tied the arms of the two prisoners and took
the wheel of the car. The machine followed the jungle
road until it reached a barren chain of hills along the
eastern shore. Here the road began a winding ascent. The
hills grew steeper until they rose precipitously out of the
sea, seeming to form a rampart against the lashing waves
of the ocean.

The highway itself seemed to be only a ledge carved
in the side of the vertical cliff.

For several miles the car chugged up the steep road,
then at last it came in view of several buildings surrounded by a high wall on which searchlights gleamed.

"There it is!" Limehouse exclaimed. "Home, sweet

"There Is Death Rock Prison!" Limehouse Said

home—Death Rock prison! The inferno of the South
Sea Islands—the hotel where guests enter vertically an'
come out horizontally."

Even at a distance the prison had a bleak and cruel
look. The moonlight and the glow of the searchlights
created a ghastly illusion of something unreal, as in a
nightmare. The buildings were perched on the side of the
mountain, with the sea directly below and high cliff walls
above. The only approach was along the narrow highway on which the car was traveling.

The car stopped in front of the gate. Limehouse untied
his prisoners and, brandishing his gun, ordered them out.

A challenge came from a tower at the gate and Limehouse shouted an answer:

"It's all right, guard!" he called. "Open up. This is
Limehouse returnin' with a couple o' prodigal sons."

A gruff voice shouted indistinguishable words behind
the wall and a moment later the huge gate swung open.
Jack caught a glimpse of a barren courtyard, patrolled
by armed guards beyond.

"Okay, you birds," Limehouse said. "Get goin'."

Fat Stuff pulled Smilin' Jack's arm over his shoulder.

"Lean on Fat Stuff," he told Jack. "Him help you
walk."

"Thanks, Fat Stuff," Jack said.

As they approached the gate, Limehouse turned to his
prisoners and remarked tauntingly:

"Well, boys, you'd better take a deep breath—this is
your last chance to breathe free air."

Jack heard Fat Stuff growl deep in his chest. But the sound was not loud enough for Limehouse to hear.

The huge gate clanked behind them as they passed into the prison courtyard. Jack underwent a feeling of helplessness as he realized that escape now was cut off. His life was sealed among the living dead of a South Sea island prison: a concentration camp of the vilest kind.

Limehouse directed them toward a large central building, and the two men were taken through a corridor to a large office where a light was burning.

"We'll see the commandant now," Limehouse said. "Then I'll be sure of gettin' full credit for you two."

Guards seized Jack roughly and, paying no attention to his wound, fingerprinted him and then thrust him stumbling into a room where a bald, foreign-looking man in uniform sat at a desk.

Limehouse, with a self-satisfied grin on his ugly face, was standing near by.

"This is the new one, sir," Limehouse explained. "Maybe you recognize our ol' friend an' former helper— Powder Pellet."

"Ah! So it is!"

"You are making a serious mistake," Jack said. "As a matter of fact, I am not Powder Pellet. If you will communicate with the nearest United States consulate I can quickly establish my identity. My name is not Pellet. I am Smilin' Jack Martin, an American aviator."

"Ha, ha!" Limehouse laughed. "You are surely smarter than that, Powder. You admitted to me that you were Powder."

"My employer has placed a price on your head," the commandant said.

"Your employer? Isn't this a government prison?"

"Ah, yes," the commandant said. "A certain South American official furnishes us with convicts to work our mines. We lease the labor, as it were, Mr. Pellet. But the government official is too humane. He does not wish to see the scum of the earth he sends us, die. Therefore we have to replace the men who die with live ones. There always is an opening here for new talent, as you well know."

"He ought to know," Limehouse laughed. "Powder has brought plenty of shanghaied men here in his airplane."

Now Jack was beginning to understand. The Head owned this island and leased convicts for labor, through the connivance of some corrupt politician. Unhealthy conditions at the prison made the lives of the prisoners short and in order to avoid the cutting off of his labor supply, The Head had taken upon himself the replacement of men who had died. Fat Stuff had been kidnaped probably from a near-by island. Powder, whom Jack was impersonating, had shanghaied men from South American ports. More than ever, Jack sensed the monstrous nature of the man known as The Head.

"But I am not Powder!" Jack insisted.

"You lie!" shouted the commandant. "Your features

and the brand on your left hand are proof enough for anyone that you are Powder Pellet."

Fat Stuff now entered and offered his support for Jack. The commandant seemed to notice for the first time that Jack was wounded.

"He resisted arrest an' I had to plug him," Limehouse explained.

Fat Stuff looked expectantly at Jack.

"Take him to the hospital and then throw him in the bull pen with the rest of the convicts," the commandant said with a smile. "Powder ought to find some of his *old friends* there. Men he brought here!"

Fat Stuff helped carry Jack to the hospital.

"Your name not Powder, but Jack?" he asked.

Smilin' Jack nodded.

"Very strange," he said. "Powder not popular here. It will be hard to make others believe."

"I hope we can," Jack said, resolving that, somehow, he must survive whatever was in store for him at Death Rock.

"Jack, why you no tell commandant how Limehouse try to make you tell of buried treasure?" Fat Stuff asked.

"What's the use, Fat Stuff?" Jack asked. "My word would be worthless against Limehouse's. Besides, the commandant might have a few greedy ideas himself and try to make me tell *him* where the treasure was hidden."

The prison doctor quickly confirmed that Jack's wound was of a minor nature. The injury was cleaned and treated, and Jack was placed in the infirmary.

In this hospital ward Jack began to learn more about the nature of Death Rock prison. As he had suspected, the prisoners were farmed out to a syndicate owned by The Head. The prisoners were employed in sulphur mines, where convicts died by scores in the scorching heat and unhealthy atmosphere.

The government was doubtless unaware or unwilling, because of political corruption, to take cognizance of these conditions. Jack suspected bribery. At any rate The Head was required to return only the number of prisoners each year corresponding with the number whose terms had expired. Inefficiency, or crookedness, seemed to cause the proper officials to overlook the fact that the prisoners who returned seldom had features or fingerprints corresponding with the men whose names they bore. Even in the United States such corruption was not unknown, as was revealed when the guilty officials were brought to justice.

The Head, of course, was allowed a small "loss" in prisoners due to death. But he was forced to resort to kidnaping tactics in order to prevent an investigation as to the treatment of the convicts in his charge. The convicts themselves knew of the conditions and considered their chances of freedom virtually zero.

After about three days of treatment, Jack's leg had almost healed and Commandant Trefwitz ordered the prisoner transferred to the "bull pen."

As he was being escorted to the pen, Jack caught sullen looks from other prisoners. Snarling taunts were hurled at him from evil, distorted faces behind the bars of cells.

"What a reputation Powder is giving me!" Jack thought to himself. "Nearly every man in this prison is his enemy!"

But the feeling could hardly be condemned. The real "Powder" had evidently brought by violent means many of these men to this island of living death.

"Lookie what's here, boys!" came a cry as Jack was thrust into an enclosure filled with other convicts.

A degenerate-looking being thrust his features close to Jack's.

"Remember me, Powder?" he said. "Remember that doped whisky you fed me in Chiclavo?"

A snarl sounded behind Jack and a wizened little man came charging toward the American with doubled fists.

"Let me at him!" he cried.

The first convict suddenly thrust his body between Jack and the smaller man.

"Wait, Lizard!"

Lizard tried to fight off the larger man.

"Let me at him, Slab!" he cried. "I'm gonna get even wit' him for de time he slugged me in Guayaquil an' brought me here!"

"Take it easy, Lizard," Slab cautioned. "If we start a rumpus an' th' guards hear us, they'll turn scaldin' water on us sure!"

Another sprang forward and helped Slab check Lizard's murderous intentions.

"We'll have a much better chance to settle with Powder when we're back in the mines," Slab said hoarsely, casting an evil glance at Jack.

"Yeah," said his helper. "De guards ain't so watchful t'ere. Ya can do anyt'ing ya like to Powder den. But remember one t'ing—" the convict glanced around the room "—no fair killin' him till we've all had our toin at gettin' even wit' him!"

Jack's heart sank. If the sulphur mines didn't get him, his fellow prisoners would.

Later in the day Limehouse appeared with an armed guard and called Jack from the bull pen.

"The commandant desires your presence in the courtroom, Powder," Limehouse announced. "He told me to inform you that you are convict No. M-6000. It's a lucky number—the last man who had it wasn't here very long."

Sensing from the ugly inflection that M-6000 had not been released, Jack retorted:

"He must have had a drag to get such a distinctive number."

The unscrupulous prison official chuckled mirthlessly.

"I'll take some of that insolence out of you, No. M-6000," he said. "I'll make a lot of changes in you. Those pretty curls will go first—you won't look so handsome with your head shaved."

Jack smiled to himself. When his blonde hair was shaved away, his scalp would sprout locks of quite a different color—chestnut brown. "Powder" would become a different person than Limehouse expected.

Commandant Trefwitz sat silently on the bench as Jack was taken into the court room. He cleared his throat and addressed the prisoner in a stern tone:

"I've examined the records in your case, M-6000. I find that you have no credit marks and your recent attempt to escape demands the addition of another ten years to your sentence. The time must be spent at hard labor in the sulphur mines."

A malevolent laugh came from Limehouse as he took Jack by the arm.

"Same as a death sentence!" he said. "Ten years in the furnace of a South Sea sulphur mine."

"I might fool you," Jack said grimly. "I might be able to stand the heat."

"Oh, but the heat ain't all that gets you, my dear friend," Limehouse spoke, mockingly. "There's also the sulphur dust—but you'll find out. Now we'll see about some new clothing, more in keepin' with your position."

Jack was taken to the prison tailor shop.

Without ceremony, trousers, shoes, and coat were handed to Smilin' Jack and he was ordered gruffly to try them on. Limehouse, enjoying himself to the utmost, passed taunting remarks with each move Jack made.

"Ain't that a nifty single-breasted, three-button number," the guard said. "Stripes are so becomin' to you!"

Jack scowled.

"Now if you don't mind, may I retire to my suite in th' blockhouse and curl up with a nice leg-iron?" he asked.

"Not so fast, my good man," Limehouse said with a curious gleam in his eye. "I've been savin' the best till last. You haven't visited the prison beauty shop yet."

Farther down the corridor was another room in which half a dozen barber chairs were in use. Jack awaited his turn and at last was turned over to a barber of French nationality.

"Oh, Le Mieux," Limehouse spoke to the barber, "our friend, Powder, wants one of your streamlined, air-conditioned head shaves."

Le Mieux smiled.

"Ah! Powder, is it? *Oui, oui,* Monsieur Limehouse! I weel geeve heem ze door-knob special!"

Dressed in his prison stripes, Smilin' Jack seated himself in the barber chair. Le Mieux moved to one side and jerked Jack's right arm up on the arm rest of the chair. There was a quick snap and metal bracelets were fastened on the arm. Le Mieux then fastened the left arm.

"What's the idea of the handcuffs?" Jack demanded.

Limehouse chuckled at the question.

"An old custom here, my friend," the prison guard explained. "They are just in case you should suddenly become fond of Monsieur Le Mieux's razor and try to grab it."

Le Mieux seemed to like his work. His razor lifted aloft and cut a swath down the center of Smilin' Jack's hair.

CHAPTER NINE

CONVICT REVENGE

Possibly because there was such a contrast between Smilin' Jack's rather handsome head and his own vastly different contours, Limehouse seemed to take an unholy delight in watching Le Mieux at work.

"Ah! Right down th' old fairway!" the guard exclaimed, as the barber cut his first groove down the center of Jack's hair. "Your technique is superb, Le Mieux."

"By the way, Limehouse," Jack spoke to the guard, "just why are you cropping me? I noticed some of the other cons—Fat Stuff, for instance—still have their hair."

"A very good question, Powder," Limehouse said, lighting a cigaret. "This service is only for special guests— the ones who are most likely to try to check out without permission. I know Fat Stuff got away once, but he ain't likely to fool us again. But you are dangerous, Powder. The haircut is a tribute to your abilities."

"I still don't see—"

"Ah, but it is quite simple," Limehouse continued. "Did you ever notice how a billiard ball shines when you turn a flashlight on it? Well, supposin' you don't like our hospitality and try to make a break. Just think how a guard's marksmanship would be aided when the prison searchlights beam upon your glistenin' dome!"

Le Mieux quickly finished his job. Jack looked into a mirror to see his head clean and shining—a perfect reflector for a prison searchlight.

Assigned to a cell, Jack spent the night tossing in his bunk. Ten years, plus whatever time was still unserved on M-6000's sentence, remained between him and freedom. From what he had already heard in the bull pen and in the prison infirmary, no man could live that long in the South Sea sulphur mines. Tomorrow he would begin his work in the pits.

Jack had just been able to doze off to sleep when a bell in the cell block rang, announcing the beginning of a new prison day.

With the other prisoners, Jack was herded into the dining room where he was given a breakfast of soggy wheat cakes and coffee. Then he was marched into the bull pen where a hundred or more other convicts were being loaded into trucks for transport to the mine.

Jack noticed that several other convicts, among them Slab and Lizard, who had cast vengeful glances at him the preceding day, were in the group. There also was Fat Stuff, who grinned at his new-found friend.

The sulphur mine was in a deep hollow on the other side of the hill that formed a rampart of the island against the sea. A pit had been opened in the rock and guards were stationed on the rim. These guards carried rifles and their features were those of men who enjoyed seeing fellow beings suffer.

Limehouse seemed to be a supervisor of the guards. He

Jack Set to Work With Fat Stuff

often left the rim to move about in the pit forcing convicts to work harder and to watch for infractions of pris
on rules.

Jack was handed a pick and set to work with Fat Stuff,
loosening the sulphur in the floor of the pit.

The morning dragged slowly. At noon the men were
given only a small meal of thin broth and dried crusts of
old bread.

"Dangerous to work on a full stomach," Limehouse
explained as he dished the food out to Jack.

During the afternoon Jack began to grow exhausted.
He noticed other convicts ready to drop. No wonder men
died like flies in this sulphur mine!

Fat Stuff was weak, but he kept swinging his pick.

"Whew!" he said. "Minin' much hard work. No fun,
Jack!"

"You said it, Fat Stuff," Jack replied grimly.

The sulphur was embedded in rock just as it had been
spewed, centuries before, from a volcano on the island. It
was necessary for the sulphur to be separated from the
lava before it was loaded into a banking machine which
hoisted the mineral from the pit to the ledge above the
mine.

"For a man that hasn't done any harder work than
jiggle a control stick during the past few years, this is
certainly no picnic," Smilin' Jack said as he ceased swinging his pick.

Fat Stuff straightened up and rubbed his lumbar re-
gion.

"O-oh!" he groaned. "Fat Stuff back hurtum much!"

You and I are in the same boat," Jack spoke. "And I used to think I was tired after a double round of golf—*whew!*— I've just got to rest a second."

But as Jack leaned on his pick, there came an angry cry from across the pit.

"Hey, you loafers! Get to work."

Running toward Jack and Fat Stuff was Limehouse, swinging a blacksnake whip! The whip came down with a crack and the leash bit deeply into Smilin' Jack's back.

There was to be no rest in this mine. Jack bent his back and went to work.

"There'll be no loafin' on this job!" the guard announced, with his evil eyes on his newest convict.

Jack caught a glimpse of Lizard and Slab grinning with amusement at his suffering. They were more or less toughened to the heavy labor which was tearing and blistering Jack's hands.

Almost frying in the terrific heat, Jack continued his work in the dust-filled sulphur quarry. As he began to think the night would never come, a shrill whistle blew, signaling that his day's work was finished.

Just nine years and three hundred and sixty-three days left to go!

"You can stop work now, Powder!" came the tantalizing voice of Limehouse. "I hope the work isn't too hard for you—you look a little tired. But you'll feel better after a hearty meal. This is special diet day."

From experience, Jack knew that Limehouse's little

jokes were full of cruel irony and he was not surprised at the "special diet." It consisted of one slice of bread and a cup of water.

Limehouse took a cruel joy in torturing his prisoners. Although the bullet wound in Jack's leg had not fully healed, he was allowed no shortened hours because of it. His only rest was ten minutes each hour, when the water boy brought some lukewarm water to drink.

Limehouse, too, seemed to look the other way when convicts sought to play their little pranks on Jack. In the role of "Powder," who richly deserved such treatment, Jack could hardly find it in his heart to resent these attempts at vengeance.

Foremost among the pranksters were Slab and Lizard. Once, during the noon lunch period, Jack removed his prison shirt to cool his perspiring chest and shoulders. An instant later the shirt had disappeared. Jack suspected Slab as the thief, but he had no way of proving it—not that it would have helped to be able to prove it.

A few minutes later Fat Stuff noticed Jack laboring shirtless in the hot tropical sun.

"You can't stand that, Jack," Fat Stuff said sympathetically. "Where your shirt?"

"Some louse stole it," Jack replied. "Limehouse won't issue another today. Gosh! This heat is getting me down. I already feel dizzy."

Fat Stuff shook his head.

"Sun burn you up. You die with sun sickness," the native warned. He unbuttoned his own shirt and handed it to Jack. "Here, wear my shirt."

Jack smiled, but waved the proffered garment aside.

"No thanks, Fat Stuff," he said. "I wouldn't take th' shirt off another man's back!"

"No bother!" Fat Stuff insisted, pressing his shirt on Jack. "Here, you take it. Sun no bother me. Me grow up naked in tropics!"

The offer, thus explained, was more than Smilin' Jack could refuse. What Fat Stuff had said was true. The South Sea islander, accustomed to the heat of the tropical sun, could withstand it. Jack on the other hand, had been born in a much different climate, and he was not physically adapted to bear up under the sun's rays without protection.

"You're a big fat Samaritan!" Jack said warmly. "I'm certainly glad I accounted for Jim, the man who brought you here."

"You gottum Jim?" Fat Stuff asked, his eyes widening with happiness.

"I'm pretty sure he was the pilot of the seaplane I shot down when I escaped from The Head," Jack said with a nod.

"You wantum my pants, too?" Fat Stuff asked. "You can havum all my clothes—anythin' you want. Fat Stuff, him your friend for life!"

"I'm your friend too, Fat Stuff," Jack said.

Limehouse was coming toward them with his whip, and Jack quickly donned the shirt and set to work. The pick which Jack wielded was blistering and tearing his hands. The very touch of the wooden handle on Jack's raw palms was maddening torture. To swing the pick was excruciating agony.

Limehouse knew about Jack's hands and he communicated this to the other prisoners, who seemed to enjoy Jack's suffering. Such a fate, they harshly shouted, was too good for the man who had shanghaied so many "prisoners" for Death Rock.

Hour-like minutes piled up their pains until at last it was time for the water boy in the all-too-short rest period the convicts were allowed out of each heavy hour of forced labor.

"Water!" the cry came from parched throats through cracked lips.

Jack put aside his pick and seized the dipper. He gulped down the tepid liquid that seemed to sizzle in his parched throat. Jack sat down and closed his eyes after drinking. He was too tired to notice Lizard and Slab hovering near by. He was too tired to care what mischief they were plotting against him. Even their dirtiest trick would be worth a minute of heavenly rest from that torturing pick.

"Time's up, Powder!" Lizard called out to Jack. "Better get back to work. Limehouse is comin' wit' his whip!"

Jack scrambled to his feet only to perceive that he might have taken a little more time than his ten-minute period for rest.

He reached down for his pick.

Suddenly, from behind Smilin' Jack, a brown hurricane came charging forward. Fat Stuff's body struck Jack and knocked him aside.

"Don't touch pick!" the South Sea islander cried.

Lizard sprang forward, swinging his fists.

"Why, you dirty little meddler!" he cried.

"Fat Stuff see you pour acid on Jack's pick handle!" the native said.

Lizard swung his fist.

"I'll teach you to spoil my revenge!" he said.

The blow landed on Fat Stuff's chin, sending the islander into a heap on the ground.

Jack, picking himself up off the ground, lunged toward Lizard. A single punch, launched from Jack's shoe tops, struck Lizard on the chest. The ugly convict staggered back and then caught himself.

"Dis is what I been waitin' for!" he yelled.

But Jack was ready. He might not be able to swing a pick, but he could fight. His fist swung again. This time the blow caught Lizard on the point of the chin and the convict sank to the ground.

"Stop it, you varmints!" came a coarse voice.

Limehouse, holding his ever-ready automatic, came charging on the scene. He caught Jack by the coat and held him. Another guard, armed with a sub-machine gun, held the other convicts at bay.

"Powder started this riot!" Slab whined as he lifted his friend Lizard to his feet.

Limehouse shook Jack.

"I know! I saw him start it," Limehouse said. "Well,

Powder, accordin' to our penal code, incitin' a prison riot adds two more years to your term, plus the loss of one meal a day for a month."

After one week of work, Jack had "gained" more than one hundred weeks on Death Rock.

Jack's punishment began that night. He was sent supperless to his cell after the prisoners returned from the mine. But Fat Stuff remembered that Jack was penalized for helping him and the native smuggled a crust of bread to Jack.

Jack nibbled at the crust while Fat Stuff explained how he knew Lizard had put acid powder on the pick handle to burn Jack's raw hands.

"Me hear Slab an' Lizard talk," Fat Stuff explained. "Lizard an' Slab hate 'Powder.' Wantum get even."

"Their reaction is understandable," Jack said, "I can't blame them, but I wish I could make them believe I am not 'Powder.' I've tried to explain, but no one will listen."

"They think you lie," Fat Stuff asserted. "But I believe."

"I certainly owe you a lot, Fat Stuff," Jack said warmly. "I don't suppose I'll live long enough to get out of here and repay you, but some day maybe I'll get a chance. You're a real guy."

"You sockum Lizard," the native returned. "You real guy, too."

"By the way, Fat Stuff," Jack asked. "What is your real name?"

Fat Stuff's face blossomed with his infectious grin.

"Real name is Euah-layi-kamil-aroari-yuin-bai-balijaoyra-a-mulung," he said in a sing-song voice.

"Quite a mouthful," Jack said. "Just what does it mean?"

"It mean—Fat Stuff."

Jack, in spite of his misery, grinned—until his cracked lips hurt.

Although Jack resolved to seize the first opportunity to escape that presented itself, there seemed to be no possibility of getting away from the prison. Life on Death Rock was short and uncertain. Clouds of suffocating dust rose day after day in the hot, sun-baked sulphur pit, irritating and burning throats and lungs of the men who labored under the watchful eyes of armed guards.

Jack was growing toughened to the work and he grew more accustomed to the heat, but the sulphur dust seemed to bother him more each day.

Jack's summary dealing with Lizard had helped him in more ways than one. Many of the convicts grew more friendly and seemed to take stock in Jack's tale that he was not Powder. Certainly Jack's powerful blow that felled Lizard had been a far cry from the dandified actions of the man they had known as Powder.

Besides, Jack was one of them, coughing in the sulphur dust, roasting in the sun, unjustly deprived of freedom. Misery made him their fellow.

The slightest breeze made the pit almost unbearable by stirring up the dust that covered the ground. When the wind was strong men coughed from morning until night.

Jack, seized with a coughing spell one day, grew so weak he could hardly hold his pick.

"What trouble, Jack?" Fat Stuff asked.

"That sulphur dust!" Jack coughed. "My lungs feel like they're on fire!"

Even Fat Stuff was coughing.

"Mine, too," the native said. "Sulphur dust much bad for breathe."

A few feet away a convict fell on the ground. Limehouse and an armed guard rushed to his side.

"Poor devil!" Jack said, loudly enough for Limehouse to hear.

The supervisor of the guards sprang to his feet with the ever-ready whip in his hand.

"He's just dead!" Limehouse roared, brandishing his whip. "Another weaklin' who couldn't stand the gaff. Get back to work, so us guards can return to our posts on the bank, where the air is fresh!"

The coughing prisoners went back to their killing labor.

Jack swung his pick silently, thinking. How *could* he get out of here?

Unless he escaped soon, he would die just as that other poor prisoner had died. If Jack died without communicating with headquarters in the United States, all the discoveries about the espionage ring and the Fifth Column bases on the West Coast would never be known by the intelligence corps. Each day of delay might mean losses of ships from submarines fueled at the secret bases.

While Jack pondered one day on some desperate means of escape he heard the first faint drone of a familiar buzz. The sound came from high above the clouds of sulphur dust that filled the air of the pit. But the noise was easily recognizable.

"Maybe I'm going nuts with the heat, Fat Stuff," Jack said in a low voice to his friend. "Maybe I'm having delusions—but I think I hear a plane."

Fat Stuff listened.

"You no nuts," he said, speaking without moving his lips. "It *is* plane."

"Are there planes on this island?"

"Many planes base here on island. Other planes fly over. Me see-um 'Merican warplane with star on wing on patrol sometimes."

An American patrol plane! Jack was closer than he thought to headquarters. If he could only signal the craft—possibly it was a patrol bomber like the plane The Head had tried to steal.

The small spark of hope fanned to a flame in Jack's mind. Once Jack was able to signal the men at the controls of that plane, he could bring about his release—or at least pass on the information he had learned about the spy ring. But Jack would have to work stealthily. If Jack was caught signaling the plane, he would be placed in solitary, where it would be impossible to communicate with the outside world.

Signaling would be a problem with the sulphur dust clouds in the air, which hid the pits like a smoke screen.

If Jack could escape, even for a short time, and get out at sea in a small boat, he might attract the naval plane's attention. But there would be another danger then, too. Other planes based here, which Fat Stuff had spoken of, could only be enemy planes. They would attack the patrol bomber. The reason no attack had been made on the bomber thus far was probably because the island was more valuable as an espionage base than as a base for air attack.

As Jack's mind centered on these thoughts, a whip cracked in the air behind him. Limehouse was approaching with an unpleasant gleam in his eye. Jack resumed his digging. The guard laughed.

"Much as I hate to interrupt the work you love so well," he began, "I must ask you to stop. The Head has asked me to bring you to his office. His wishes are most urgent."

Jack turned in his tools and followed Limehouse from the pit to a station wagon, which bumped him over the mountain road to the prison. A few minutes later the prisoner, covered with yellow dust, was escorted into an office in the administration building.

The dust-free air, the soft Oriental rug, the lavish furniture, all seemed to belong to a forgotten world of dreams.

"Wait here," Limehouse ordered, closing the door of the office.

Jack stood, silently waiting. A movement on the other side of the room caught his ears. He turned to see a figure rising from a chair—a girl with brown hair and soft,

To Jack's Surprise, a Plane Flew Over the Island

dreamy eyes.

"Betty!"

She had been facing the other way—she turned at the sound of Jack's voice. In spite of his shaved head and prison uniform, she recognized him.

"Powder!"

CHAPTER TEN

UNEXPECTED COMPLICATIONS

Instinctively the girl started toward him, then halted, her eyes wide with horror as the details of the change in him struck home.

"Powder!" she exclaimed. "Those convict stripes! Your hair! What has happened to you?"

Her question revealed her complete ignorance of the events since Jack had left her yacht. Betty's position in the spy ring had never been clear to Jack, and while all the evidence pointed to her being in league with The Head, he could never fully convince himself that she was heart and soul in that role.

The girl's actions now were too genuine to support the belief that she had been in The Head's confidence regarding the living doom of Death Rock. Nor had The Head told her "Powder" was here.

"The stripes and haircut mean that I'm now wholly within The Head's power," Jack announced. "I'm being held here because he regards me as a very dangerous enemy."

"Why should you be an enemy, Powder?" she asked. "I never could believe you were a spy—I don't believe you shot down Jim Roderick, The Head's pilot, in cold blood as The Head said you did. Yet you are in prison—"

143

"I shot Jim to keep him from killing me," Jack said. "He deserved it. Murder was a minor crime for him."

"Then it is true!"

"Why should you seem so shocked?" Jack asked. "Aren't you a spy yourself?"

"A spy? A spy against my own interests? Why, that is perfectly foolish!" Betty's eyes flashed indignantly. "Besides, my father runs his business on strictly ethical lines—while other firms may spy against him, he doesn't stoop that low!"

Suddenly Jack knew the truth. He knew now that Betty Brown, in calling Jack a spy, might not be speaking of the same kind of espionage that Jack referred to. The name "Brown" suddenly struck a familiar chord in Jack's memory.

"Betty," Jack asked suddenly, "are you the daughter of Old Man Brown—Isaac J. Brown—of South American Airlines?"

"Powder! Have you gone crazy? You worked for my father for years! You know who I am!"

That was it. Old Man Brown, fireball ace of the first World War, was almost a legendary figure in aviation. Jack slowly recalled that Brown did have a daughter. She was born in South America when Brown was starting his airline on a shoestring.

During the armistice years between the World Wars, Brown's aviation empire grew. There had been hints of Nazi backing, but no one believed that the cigar-chewing, gruff executive of the line could be "run" by anyone, even a pack of wolves like the Nazis.

But Jack was beginning to realize that somehow under cover operatives of Hitler's Nazi cohorts had wormed their way into Brown's confidence. They had used the line for their own ends, including possibly the transporting of shanghaied men to Death Rock. Unscrupulous pilots, men without countries, men loyal only to money, had been imported to work on the line. Powder and Jim had been of this type.

Perhaps Old Man Brown had been fooled by these men. Trusting implicitly in his executives, such as The Head probably was, he had allowed them free rein, not suspecting that they were using him as a blind for their own Fifth Column activities against the United Nations.

Jack recalled once that Betty had spoken of "the game" being in her blood. That her father had "been in the business fifteen years." Jack had thought she was referring to international spying and that Betty was the daughter of a spy. She had been talking about *aviation.*

The term "spy" as used by Betty did not refer to treacherous espionage against the United States, but to shady business methods. Many firms "spy" on other firms. Commercial spying is a highly paid profession, but not a criminal one.

Betty had not known the real activity in the Pacific that had resulted in the use of her yacht by The Head. Some trumped-up story had satisfied her, while the true objective was the theft of the American naval patrol plane.

"Listen, Betty!" Jack said. "If you'll only believe me, I can explain everything. But tell me one thing—why are you here?"

Betty looked deeply into Jack's eyes, searching for the answer to a question that was unspoken, yet clearly shown in her expression. She seemed puzzled, baffled, completely at a loss.

"Sometimes you don't act like the old Powder I used to know," she said. "You seem changed—a different man. I can't understand you—"

"I *am* a different man, Betty," Jack said. "I am not—"

Smilin' Jack suddenly checked himself. What was he saying? While The Head suspected that Jack was not really Powder, he had no real proof. Putting Betty alone in this room with Jack might be a trap. The Head undoubtedly sought to learn something by this ruse. Instead, Jack decided to tell something The Head might not want told.

"Listen, Betty," he said. "I am not a commercial spy. But The Head, who probably is a trusted official of your father's airline, is worse. He is an international spy, an enemy of our country. He tricked you into obtaining the use of your yacht to steal an American naval plane. Your father thinks The Head is working for you, but instead he is working for the Axis Powers—for the Nazis in particular."

A connecting door of the office swung open suddenly. In the doorway stood The Head, leveling an automatic pistol at Smilin' Jack. Behind the dwarfed little man was a huge, grotesque figure, The Claw, sharpening the hook on his right arm with a file.

"That's enough, *Mister* Powder!" snapped The Head.

The Claw crowded forward. He tossed the file aside and seized Jack by the coat, holding the hook menacingly in the air.

"Shall I give him the facial, Chief?" he asked. "I could do a better job than you could do with that popgun!"

"Let him alone, Claw!" The Head ordered.

He turned to Jack:

"My dear Powder," he began, "your assertions are illtimed and ill-advised. I would suggest that you remember that you are completely in my power. Remember also that Miss Brown is now at my mercy. I own this island and the prison guards are quite obedient to my orders. True, some of the prisoners were convicted in the courts of a South American government, but that government is kept by my paid agent from being very curious about them or how they are treated here. Through my agents on the mainland I am able to alter penal records to conform to my purposes. It happens that some of these prisoners are women. Miss Brown might easily find herself among the forgotten convicts on this island—"

"You wouldn't dare!" Betty said defiantly, her eyes blazing.

The Head was expressionless. She turned to Jack.

"I'm beginning to understand, Powder. Strange, I never saw The Head in his true light before. Now I understand many things that struck me only as being odd. I realize why you were imprisoned aboard my yacht and why you are wearing stripes now." Then, to The Head, "My Father will kill you if you harm me, Mr. Ghindi!"

The Head smirked.

"Unfortunately, your father is not in a good position to do that," he said. "He is on the mainland many miles away. You are helpless here—any move he makes against me might result in your—ah—suffering. Should he try anything rash, he might suddenly find himself surrounded by men who are more loyal to me—for reasons they know best—than to the head of the firm that employs them."

Deep chagrin swept over Smilin' Jack. Instead of hampering The Head, as he had expected to do by telling Betty what sort of man he really was, Jack had jeopardized Betty's safety.

The Claw shifted uneasily as The Head threatened Betty.

"You ain't gonna hoit th' girl, are you, Chief?" he asked anxiously.

"Mind your own business, Claw!" The Head snapped.

"You'll never get away with this!" Jack told The Head. "You don't dare kidnap Betty Brown, as you've kidnaped me and the other poor devils held on Death Rock!"

The expression on The Head's face was as immobile

as the walls of his prison. Jack could not tell whether the threats against Betty were bluff or not.

"Miss Brown," The Head said, turning to the girl, "against my orders you went for a flight in the seaplane today."

Then it had been the seaplane, not a patrol plane, Jack and Fat Stuff had heard while working in the prison mine.

"And," The Head continued, "you saw a warship in waters off this island. Due to my foresight, the radio in the plane wasn't working, but you came back to your yacht to radio American authorities, because you recognized the warship as a Jap cruiser. Too bad, Miss Brown, but you now know too much. Put yourself in my position —if I allow you freedom you will ruin me. But I will not kill you, Miss Brown, because I owe your father so much for allowing me to use his business as a center for my espionage ring—although he was stupidly unaware of the fact."

"So that's why you told me I could notify authorities in prison of the warship and they would communicate with the American consul—"

"Yes, Miss Brown," the Head continued suavely. "I decided not to kill you. Your death would net me nothing. Besides, Mr. Trefwitz tells me we are short of women prisoners on this island. I shall notify your father that you have gone to visit friends in the United States for a time. Your disappearance will follow—and the assumption will be that your plane fell into the sea."

Jack restrained himself with difficulty. But he realized he could do nothing then—The Claw was too eager to use his hook on Jack, and The Head was too likely to pull the trigger of his automatic.

"You—you're a Nazi!" Betty gasped. "Only a Nazi could be so cruel!"

The Claw shifted uneasily on his feet, glancing anxiously at The Head and then at the girl. At last he spoke.

"Maybe we better not put the girl in the women's prison, Chief," he said. "It makes women old. She's pretty. She hasn't done nothing—"

"I'll decide, Claw. You need only *follow* my orders!" The Head spoke sharply. Then he turned to Betty. "Your opinion of me does not matter in the least. My actions are above the opinions of ordinary people."

"Isn't there something—anything—?" Betty began, and looked beseechingly at Jack. "Why couldn't you have told me before?"

"Powder—and I'm pretty well convinced this man is an impostor and not the real Powder we once knew— this man thought you were a spy, in league with us. While he would be unwilling to put you behind the bars of this prison, not so long ago he was working quite diligently to put you inside an American penitentiary."

"Who are you?" Betty asked Jack, in amazement.

"It does not matter who he is," The Head went on quickly. "But I think he can serve me. What do you think of having this lovely young woman sentenced for the remainder of her life on Death Rock?" he demanded

Betty Looked Beseechingly at Jack.

of Jack.

"It would be the most terrible crime you have ever committed," Jack said with cold fury in his voice.

"It is within your power to prevent it, Powder," The Head explained calmly. "Due to your rash actions and my own inefficiency and overconfidence I lost the new patrol bomber that my agents stole from the United States. Limehouse tells me that it sank in the lagoon at the other end of the island and the sea probably has torn it to pieces on the bottom of the lagoon by now. But I believe that if you communicated with your chief—the man who directs your spying—he would send a bomber to rescue you."

"I would be only too glad to let the United States know where I am," Jack said.

"You answer too quickly, Powder," The Head continued. "But you underestimate me if you think I was not prepared for that answer. No, your message will say nothing about this island. There is another island some distance from here where the bomber will land to 'rescue' you. When it arrives, the crew will be overpowered or slain, and I will have the plane. In return for this small favor, I will agree not to confine Miss Brown in the women's prison. Instead, she will live in a comfortable little cottage by the sea until the war is over."

Betty turned to Smilin' Jack and shook her head, to tell him to refuse.

"And you, Powder," The Head went on, "will be taken out of the sulphur mines until the period of your sentence is up."

"Do you think I would put any faith in your promises?" Jack asked. "How long do you think I'd live after you had your hands on the patrol bomber?"

"How long do you think you'll live in the sulphur mines, with your lungs encrusted with yellow dust?" The Head asked.

"I would live longer than I would with my spine tinted yellow!" Jack returned angrily.

"And you will leave this sweet, lovely American girl to rot in the Death Rock prison laundry?"

"I won't rot and I won't be in your prison long," Betty said. "You won't get away with this as easily as you think."

"I will give you one last chance, Powder!" The Head said, his cold eyes resting on Smilin' Jack's face. "What is your decision? Will you follow my orders?"

"I'll answer for him! He won't!" Betty exclaimed hotly.

The Head still was looking at Jack. He disregarded the girl's reply.

Jack turned toward Betty. To think of her lovely face streaked with agony, her fingers cracked from working over steaming washing machines—

"Hurry! Make your decision!" The Head urged.

On the other hand, if the enemy copied the American bomber, cities in the United States would be bombed. Thousands of girls like Betty Brown would be torn and twisted in death—

"Go jump in the ocean!" Jack said finally.

"My, my! Your friend certainly isn't the one for gallantry!" The Head taunted Betty. "He'll trade you for a bomber any day."

"If he hadn't, I'd have as low an opinion of him as I now have of you!" Betty declared.

"And he'll suffer because he has! Back to the mines for you, Powder. And as for you, Miss Brown—Claw, take her to the prison laundry."

The huge, one-armed giant hesitated. His bestial eyes blinked a dim-witted revolt. His twisted nose twitched in distaste for his job.

Then, so surprisingly that it startled friend and foe alike, tears ran down his cheeks and his voice exploded with a sob:

. "I—I j-j-just c-c-can't d-d-do it, Chief" The Claw cried. "She-she's s-s-so p-p-pretty! I j-j-just c-c-can't."

As the bullet-headed beast began to weep, The Head's expression showed fury—the first violent emotion Smilin' Jack had ever observed on the usually motionless features. A purple rage swept from brow to chin. The dwarf's hands clenched and unclenched as he sought to control himself in the face of this rebellion in the man who had once obeyed his smallest command.

"Do you know what it means to refuse me, Claw?" The Head thundered in hoarse rage. "Do as I say!"

"I—I c-c-can't!" sobbed the Claw.

"For the last time—"

"K-K-Kill m-m-me, Chief. But I—I c-c-can't!"

The Head's eyes burned as he glowered at the blubber-

ing giant. Then, somehow, he seemed to regain control
of himself. His face grew calm, as before. A dangerous
expression shot into his eyes. Smilin' Jack felt sorry for
the moronic giant who cried like a schoolboy at the
thought of destroying beauty.

The Head stepped forward. Quick as a flash, he seized
The Claw's right arm. He twisted suddenly, and the
hook came loose from the leather covering on the stump
and fell to the floor.

"Limehouse!" The Head called.

The door swung open and the ugly face of the guard
appeared. As Limehouse's eyes took in the scene, he
seemed to understand what had happened. Smilin' Jack
and Betty, both pale, stood straight and determined. The
Claw, disarmed of his sharp hook, had slumped into a
chair where he sat with tears running down his cheeks.

The Head turned to The Claw.

"No, Claw, I won't kill you. After all, you have done
me many favors and I shall reward you by letting you
live. You may have a chance later to win your freedom.
I'll let you think over your disobedience in the sulphur
mines, working at Powder's side."

Limehouse came further into the room, a look of ex-
pectancy on his sleek face.

"Yes, Chief?" he asked.

"Send Miss Brown to the prison laundry to be dressed-
in," The Head ordered. "The Claw is to be dressed-in
also, at the men's prison. Powder is to be taken back to
the mines."

Limehouse's eyes danced as he snapped handcuffs on The Claw's wrist. The Head's chief lieutenant had fallen from favor, and it was easy to see that Limehouse coveted the post.

Limehouse snapped a second cuff to Jack and then prodded the two toward the door, where he was met by a matron from the women's prison who had been summoned to escort Betty to a cell.

As Jack and The Claw were escorted through the courtyard to the station wagon which was to take them to the receiving gate of the mine, the tears ceased streaming from the giant's eyes and a sullen look of hatred spread over his countenance.

"After all I've done for him, he asks me to do that to a lady!" The Claw muttered. "I'm a gentleman, I am. I don't mistreat no dames!"

CHAPTER ELEVEN

THE SELF-APPOINTED BOSS

With ironic justice The Claw was locked with the other prisoners in the bull pen that night. Jack wondered whether such disloyalty to The Head as that displayed by The Claw was a permanent thing. Perhaps The Claw would now be on Jack's side. His low mentality made him of small value in formulating plans to escape, but where brawn and brute courage were needed, The Claw might come in extremely handy—as an ally.

Yet Jack hesitated to trust this misshapen monster of a man. The influence The Head had exerted over The Claw might be so deeply instilled in the brute that any action on Jack's part to divert him to other purposes might drive him back to The Head. It would not be wise to rely on him too heavily, but Jack still might find him useful.

In Fat Stuff, of course, Jack had someone he could fully trust. That loyal soul was incapable of scheming against a friend.

"There's a new girl prisoner, Fat Stuff," Jack revealed as they lay on the board that served them for a bed in the bull pen.

"Um? Pretty girl not stay pretty very long here," the native said.

"We've got to get out—and get her out!" Jack declared, vehemently.

"Um! New prisoner Jack's sweetheart, maybe?"

"No, Fat Stuff," Jack said with a shake of his head, "but Betty—that's the girl's name—saved my life once and here's my chance to repay her. If we can escape, we'll see that she gets away, too."

"You havum plan to escape now, Jack?" Fat Stuff asked practically.

"I'm working on something, but I'll need your help."

"You work on something; I work on something; everybody work on something, but nobody escapes," Fat Stuff said simply. "Me think hard at night while I sleep, but no better think come out than when I wake up."

Through the days that followed, while The Claw adjusted himself with the resignation of an animal to the man-killing routine, Smilin' Jack proceeded carefully to impress upon the one-armed man that "Powder" was trying to be his friend. He did this by performing small services. Slowly these little favors began to have their effect, and Jack noted that the other convicts made no more attempts to play their vengeful little tricks while The Claw was around.

During this time, while other convicts slept at night, Jack was busy, working with two bits of metal on the concrete floor of the bull-pen. At last, three days after The Claw had been sent to the sulphur mines with Jack, the plan for escape was ready to put into execution.

It was dusk, with the day's work finished. Convicts

coughing the yellow dust from their lungs, were allowed a few minutes relaxation before retiring. In this period the men were allowed to converse in the big enclosure, and they seized this opportunity for passing news from man to man.

Tonight, Jack moved to one end of the bull pen. The guards were far away, out of earshot.

"I've got something to say to you boys," Jack suddenly announced to the men near him.

Startled expressions crossed the faces of the convicts. Powder, the most unpopular man in the whole prison, was addressing the others as equals. Lizard guffawed and nudged Slab.

"Shut up, Lizard!" Jack said quietly, but with authority in his tone.

Lizard swung around and faced Jack sullenly.

"Who do ya t'ink ya are?" he asked. "I can laugh if I wanna."

"Not while I have something to say," Jack declared.

Knowing that only an overbearing manner would be effective, Jack abandoned his usual good-natured disposition. Stern insistence upon discipline was understood by these men, bullied by guards and mistreated as an everyday experience.

"Just what have *you* got to say?" Slab asked, backing up his partner, Lizard.

"I was about to announce that there are going to be some changes around here," Jack said, looking squarely at the two convicts. "The Head and Limehouse may run the prison on the surface, but I intend to run it on the inside."

"Huh?"

Jack's brazen announcement, made with deliberate calm, caught the prisoners off balance.

"Now if there's any objections from some of you boys," Jack continued, surveying the group with cold calculation, "I'm willing to argue. But before anyone gets rash, I'd like to point out that I'm fairly handy with my fists—and Fat Stuff isn't all fat, but he has quite a bit of muscle. Besides, I've got another friend here—the man you know as The Claw."

All eyes turned toward The Claw, a miserable newcomer in their midst. Although The Claw had been closely associated with The Head, he was unknown to the prisoners. The Claw, whose duties were those of bodyguard for The Head, had not been seen inside the prison often enough to be recognized as a former lieutenant of the man at the top.

But The Claw was not the formidable figure he once had been. His iron hook—the weapon that lent a vicious touch to the giant's ferocious manner—was gone. The Claw, seated on the floor, was weeping.

"Ho, ho!" Lizard laughed, recovering from the first shock of Jack's announcement. "Looky! Who's afraid of dat big slob! Th' baby's bawlin'!"

Slab reached out, seized Jack by the coat and drew him close, the black eyes of the convict's distorted face burning into Jack's. Slab raised his fist menacingly.

The Claw, Seated on the Floor, Was Weeping

"Why, you fresh guy!" Slab roared. "Who do you t'ink you are—tellin' us you're gonna be de big shot here?"

"Yeah!" Lizard echoed, stepping close to Slab. "If th' screws wasn't so clost, we'd take a poke at ya! Tryin' to scare us with a big slob of a cry baby!"

Jack deliberately raised his foot and stamped down on Slab's toes.

"OW!"

The convict emitted a gasp of pain and released his hold on Jack.

Slab closed in, but as Jack stepped back, his cold eyes met those of the convict. Uncertain what to do, Slab hesitated.

"Not so fast!" Jack said. "The Claw hasn't been in his right mind since a friend of his let him down. Besides, he isn't quite all there. Limehouse took an important part of his character when he removed the hook he used to have on his right arm."

It hadn't been Limehouse who had removed The Claw's hook, but Jack believed it best not to stress The Claw's prior association with the hated operator of the prison mine.

"He still don't scare me," Slab said, trying to get up enough courage to tackle Jack in an exchange of blows.

"I think, with the proper accessories, The Claw can be quite frightening, even to such men as you, Slab," Jack announced with a half-smile.

Reaching beneath the board that served as Jack's bed, the aviator withdrew two pieces of metal—one a sharp spear and the other a saw-like blade with a sharp edge. During the nights while other convicts slept, Smilin' Jack had filed them from a chisel and a spoon by rubbing them on the concrete floor of his cell.

"These may be crude instruments," Jack went on, "but they're sharp and they fit The Claw's socket perfectly."

Smilin' Jack turned and thrust the saw-like blade into the socket on the leather covering fixed to the stump of The Claw's right arm. At the sight of the blade where his old hook had been, a transformation took place in the blubbering face of the giant. Tears vanished and his eyes glistened with happiness. The Claw's crooked mouth widened into a grin of unholy glee as he became master of himself once again.

Jack watched, uncertain what reaction might take place. Would The Claw show loyalty to Jack, who had fashioned him a new weapon for his crippled arm, or would The Claw's dull mind revert to habitual subjugation to The Head?

Rising sullenly to his feet, The Claw turned his eyes on the circle of convicts, as if he awaited an opportunity to spring on one of them. The prisoners moved back, murmuring uneasily.

"Call him off, Powder!" Slab pleaded.

Others echoed the plea, and The Claw turned to Jack.

"You want me to fix 'em, Powder?" he asked.

Jack shook his head in negation.

"Not now," he said. Then he addressed the group: "I'm The Claw's friend because I've restored his self-confidence. He's my loyal partner now. Is there any man who still doubts who's running this show?"

As Jack spoke, The Claw moved his jagged weapon in an arc toward the shrinking convicts.

"None here, *boss!*" Slab croaked hoarsely.

"You're *It,* far as I'm concerned," muttered Lizard abjectly.

"Okay!" echoed another voice. "You're the big shot."

Jack surveyed the mob of hardened men with a smile. The first part of his plan had succeeded. By capitalizing on the strength of The Claw and by using his own wits, Smilin' Jack had welded these beaten men into a semblance of unity. These men were tough and as long as Jack had The Claw and Fat Stuff to back him up, he could lead them. Jack had a plan—an idea suggested to him on his trips from the cell-house to the mine when he occasionally caught glimpses of brilliantly plumed birds on the island.

"Move around and pretend not to be listening to me while I explain my plan," Jack said. "The boys at the other end of the bull pen are making enough noise to keep the guards from hearing what I say."

Jack was not afraid of the guards. He had waited for a time when a certain pair of guards were on duty. These two, he felt, might be bribed, and he was counting on their help on his plan. Already Jack had hinted to these men that they might earn some "easy money." He had promised them a "cut" from a "graft" from the outside if these two guards "played ball." The guards were "playing ball" now by allowing Jack and his fellow convicts to converse without being overheard.

"What're you up to, Powder?" Slab asked.

"Now we're gettin' down to business," Jack said. "The thing I'm thinking about is what every man here is thinking about! *Escape!*"

Jack barely whispered the word, but the stir among the convicts indicated that all had heard it.

"The most essential thing is money!" Jack announced, glancing around at the prisoners for the reaction he expected.

It came.

"You're right, Powder," Slab said, "but money don't grow on leg irons!"

"True and wisely spoken, Slab," Jack replied, as though approving Slab's wisecrack. "But money does grow on this island. It grows on tropical birds and I know how to pick it. Boys, we're going to *feather* our nest!"

Slab's piggish eyes glinted with a new admiration for the man he knew as "Powder."

"*Feather?*" he asked.

"Right!" Jack said with a nod. "That's the exact word for what we're going to do. Many of the beautiful birds that inhabit this island paradise—" he paused and grinned as he noticed the sour looks of his fellow prisoners, "—perhaps I should simply say 'island'—have valuable plumage, much sought by importers in the United States."

"Hm-m-m!"

Slab and the other prisoners were thinking. Whether the idea sounded crazy or not, it had an angle. These men were desperate, willing to gamble on anything that afforded hope of escape.

"We'll catch the birds," Jack continued. "I'll buy the feathers of the birds you catch. I think I've spotted a guard who, for a cut of the profits, will deliver them to a man on the outside who'll pay a fair price for our industry."

"There's just one catch in the idea," Lizard said. "How're we gonna catch the birds when we're in a cage ourselves?"

Smilin' Jack laughed.

"Quite simply," he explained. "We can bribe certain guards to let us pluck birds as we go to and from timber camps and the sulphur mines. I've been watching these guards and they're not above a little easy dough. They couldn't be and work for a shanghai joint like Death Rock!"

Slab was scratching his hairless head. Lizard was stroking his chin. All of the convicts within earshot were thinking deeply.

"It may be a disgrace to me perfession," said one of the convicts. "I've robbed everyt'ing from delicatessens to armored trucks, but stealin' tail feathers from boids ain't beneat' me, if there's a chance in it to bust outa here."

A mumbled cheer indicated others were willing to

gamble also.

"Okay, boys," Jack said. "I think I can make arrangements with the 'screws' to start work tomorrow. Remember—the guy that squawks will have to explain to The Claw!"

"Nobody's gonna squawk," Slab said. "We'll see to that."

"Say, Powder!" Lizard blurted out, "we been treatin' you plenty dirty—an' maybe you deserve it—but get us out of here an' everyt'ing's square."

"I'll do my best," Jack promised.

As the convicts drifted away to discuss the plan in small groups, Smilin' Jack sought out Fat Stuff. Whether the plan afforded a good chance to escape or not, Jack was sure of one thing—he no longer had to fear that these men would try to get even with the man they knew as Powder.

Fat Stuff saw a good chance to obtain further loyalty from the men unjustly and cruelly imprisoned at Death Rock.

"Why not ask Claw to tell others you not Powder?" he asked.

Jack considered the idea and then shook his head.

"The Claw isn't quite right in his head, Fat Stuff," Jack said. "He's not very smart—my real identity means nothing to him. In fact, I doubt if the big ox fully realizes that I'm not Powder Pellet."

"Well," Fat Stuff decided, "me gonna try to catch birds so we get plenty money for escape."

Jack had hopes for the ultimate success of his extra-ordinary plan, but even the cleverest of plans to escape would have long odds against it in this prison. But once Jack had his chance, he would play it to the limit and he would try his best to free Betty Brown at the same time from the women's prison on the island.

"Say, Fat Stuff," Jack asked, "where is the women's prison located?"

Fat Stuff understood.

"Thinkum about pretty girl Betty, eh?" he asked. "Woman prison on separate island—Devil Kitchen—just off coast of Death Rock. Me there once."

"Why were *you* there?"

"Cells for solitary confinement also on that island," Fat Stuff said.

A cell door clanged and a hoarse voice shouted:

"Break it up!"

Jack turned and saw the satanic features of Limehouse, who was just entering the bull pen. For an instant Jack was alarmed. What if Limehouse had some secret listen-ing device concealed so that he had overheard Jack's plan to raise funds for a prison break?

But Limehouse seemed to pay no attention to Jack or to any special prisoner. Limehouse had entered the bull pen simply for "amusement." The guard seemed to en-joy visiting the unhappy convicts, bullying them in their helplessness. There walked a perfect Nazi, a born Gestapo henchman, Jack thought grimly. Adolf Hitler's Storm Troopers were just of such pitiless mold.

As he moved across the pen, one of the convicts, a man known as Eagle Eye, failed to hear his approach. Limehouse swung his foot and kicked the man roughly out of the way.

Eagle Eye turned around, fire blazing in his eyes.

"Guard or no guard," he said coldly, "you kick me like that again, Limehouse, an' you'll be sorry."

Limehouse's smug smile did not change.

"So?" he asked. "Well, I'm curious, Eagle Eye. Let's just see what you'll do to make me sorry."

As he spoke, the prison guard swung his foot, catching Eagle Eye on the side of his hip, knocking the unfortunate prisoner back against the bars of the pen. The brutal blow was the typical kind of heartless cruelty that Limehouse enjoyed. He practiced his little malevolences with impunity, for no one dared report him to higher officials of the prison—who perhaps would not have interfered anyway.

For a second Eagle Eye crouched where he had fallen, glaring up at Limehouse, who was laughing tauntingly at the helpless man, confident that the convict had no chance to do him harm. His was a coward's courage.

Then Eagle Eye sprang. With the speed of a striking serpent he launched a wicked blow from his shoe-tops. Limehouse tried to protect himself, but the attack was so swift he had no time. The prisoner's fist caught him on the tip of his pointed chin, jerking his head back and dropping him to the floor with a thump.

A cry of unholy glee rose from the prisoners. As Limehouse landed in a limp sprawl, twitched once, and then lay motionless. Shouts of dismay came from the other guards. The convicts backed away and stood in sullen, muttering groups.

A bell jangled. Guards streamed into the bull pen with whips and guns to quell what seemed to be a riot. Eagle Eye was buried under a pile of guards who pounced on him unmercifully. Quickly Limehouse was carried out to be revived.

"Wow!" Smilin' Jack whispered to Fat Stuff. "At last Limehouse got a dose of what was coming to him. I surely wish we had that man Eagle Eye in our organization. He'd help us no end."

Fat Stuff shook his head dejectedly.

"We never see Eagle Eye again," he said with a solemn sigh.

"Why, what'll they do to him?" Jack asked.

"Mebbe givum year in dungeon, or solitary—one bad as other worse. If Limehouse neck brokum, Eagle Eye get guillotine—but he no such lucky."

This information had a sobering effect on Smilin' Jack, as he realized that the minor atrocities piled upon the prisoners by the guards would have only one effect on a normal, red-blooded man. Sooner or later a man with courage would rebel against constant heckling. Eagle Eye's actions and fate might someday be Jack's own. Jack had to escape before he was placed in an escape-proof dungeon!

There was more than Jack's own future at stake. There

was a gigantic spy ring operating against the United States that could be smashed once Jack was free to notify authorities at home. And then there was—Betty.

Nothing must stand in the way of Jack's escape.

CHAPTER TWELVE

A BREAK FOR FREEDOM

In his appraisal of the prison guards, Jack was uncannily accurate. Most of them were the scum of humanity, picked up in the cesspools of humanity by The Head to perform his lowest deeds. One or two of them had been prisoners themselves, shanghaied to the island by underlings of The Head and then given posts to guard other unfortunates after they had completed their unjust terms. Their lot was not much better, and they could be tempted easily by any promise of gold.

With the explanation of riches to come from plumes of island birds, Jack found several guards willing to aid him. These guards accepted feathers collected by the convicts, and, since they themselves lacked the intelligence and organizing ability to carry on the business without Jack's help, they quickly accorded the American aviator privileges that gave him time to make plans for escape.

Limehouse's injury at the hands of Eagle Eye aided Jack, for it was doubtful if Limehouse, had he been present, would have permitted Jack some of the privileges he got. Limehouse seemed to have a personal hatred for Smilin' Jack—or rather, "Powder"—and Jack assumed this was in retaliation for fancied wrongs Limehouse had endured at the hands of Powder in the past. Perhaps the unfound treasure had something to do with it.

But Limehouse had suffered a slight concussion from the blow landed by Eagle Eye and the prison guard was confined to the hospital while Jack and his fellow convicts were exchanging plumes of tropical birds for privileges in the bull pen.

During this time Jack worked under cover, examining the locks and automatic guarding devices of the prison. The gates of the big pen were operated by electricity from a central control station in the cell block. To prevent the complete locking of the doors, it was only necessary for Jack to adjust the motor mechanism so that the doors were partly closed, instead of shut completely.

A single guard barred the way to freedom once the convicts made their way past the doors of the bull pen. He carried keys that would unlock outer doors. Then the main gate could be rushed.

A liberal collection of feathers—meaning greater spoils to divide—would make guards outside the cell blocks less observant of what went on.

With the plans formulated, Jack called his fellow unfortunates together. Every convict was assigned a task. Fat Stuff, familiar with the island, would act as a guide through the jungle. Slab and Lizard would overpower the guard in the bull pen. Out of the twenty convicts in the block, most of them should get away—and the odds were not too great that all would escape.

But The Claw received the news of escape quite differently from what Jack expected.

"We gotta get the girl out too," he said.

"The girl?" Jack asked.

"Yes, Betty Brown. Unless she goes, I not go."

"Listen," Jack said. "No one wants to get Betty out of prison more than I do, but we can't take the risk now. Once we are free, I know I can spring her from the outside and put The Head and his gang in prison in our places. But we've got to get away ourselves first."

"Then I stay!" The Claw announced decisively.

Jack needed The Claw. He was not so sure that as Powder he would be safe among the other convicts without the protection of the huge one-armed giant.

Suddenly Jack had an idea. His hand slipped under the board used by The Claw for a bed. In a second he had the two sharp tools he had fashioned for The Claw's arm socket concealed under his coat.

"All right," Jack said. "You can stay. Maybe you can get Betty out yourself, from the inside."

"No," The Claw announced. "If you go, I go, but I'll stop at the women's cell-house and get Betty out."

"How?" Jack asked, watching The Claw closely.

The giant smiled and reached under his board bed. Jack watched him closely. A look of dismay crossed The Claw's face as he found his substitute "claws" missing.

"They're gone!" he whispered hoarsely. Tears began to well into his eyes. "They're gone! Without them, I'm no good!"

"You can have them again, Claw," Jack said.

"You know where they are?" The Claw's eyes flashed and his left hand moved toward Jack.

For a moment Jack expected an attack, but he stood his ground. His gray eyes flashed into the dim eyes of the giant. For a second The Claw hesitated, his self-confidence gone without his "claw." In that hesitation, The Claw lost.

"Well?" Jack asked. "Do you go with us?"

Slowly The Claw nodded.

"I go, but I come back for the girl," he said, with a crafty look in his eyes.

When Jack left The Claw that night, he felt gravely uncertain that he could trust the man. But to try to escape without him would be suicide, for hatreds still smoldered among the prisoners for the man who had stolen the freedom of so many.

Jack managed to "doctor" the cell lock mechanism and everything was prepared. It was a long chance, but the only one. Limehouse would be out of the hospital before long—and then opportunity for escape would be gone.

Through the day, the men worked silently in the sulphur mines. The very quietness of the prisoners should have aroused suspicion among the guards, but these men were not conscientious overseers.

At night the men were led back to the cell block. Jack no longer had to go without his night meal, which had been taken away by Limehouse as punishment for his fight with Lizard. But tomorrow he would be free and he could eat to his heart's content of the fruit and berries that abounded in the jungle.

The "lights out" warning came at last. The convicts settled back on their boards, listening to the footsteps of the guards outside the cells. Not one of the guards suspected that the doors of the cell-houses were not completely locked.

Time wore on. The guards ceased their stealthy patrol.

Slowly Jack rose from his bunk. He tried the door. It slid back. He stepped out into the bull pen. Along the tier of cells other doors opened and silent figures dressed in stripes emerged.

At the end of the big enclosure was a guard—sleeping. Lizard and Slab crept forward.

A dull thud came to Jack's ears. He felt no pity for the guard, dozing at his post. This guard, like many of the others, had often indulged in petty cruelties to torment the prisoners: he got his deserts.

Lizard returned and pressed some keys into Jack's hand.

"Follow me!" Jack whispered.

A few minutes later the group of convicts reached the court. They followed shadows, keeping out of sight of the beams of searchlights that lighted the prison yard.

They reached the gate. Jack pulled back the bolts and pressed forward.

The gate was locked!

A groan came softly from the other convicts.

"We're not stumped yet, boys!" Jack said.

He felt underneath his coat. The jagged, saw-edged blade he had made for The Claw was there.

"Come here, Claw!" Jack said.

The burly giant stepped forward.

"Here's your claw for being a good boy. Do you think you can pick the lock with it?"

"Sure!" The Claw said, beaming as he felt the weapon in the socket of his artificial wrist once more.

Huddled in the shadow of the wall, The Claw inserted the rude prong into the keyhole. The scraping of metal came audibly to Jack's ears, but apparently the sound was too faint to be heard by the guards on the walls. There was a muffled *click*.

"There!" cried The Claw hoarsely.

The gate swung open.

"Make a break for it, boys!" Jack shouted. "Don't all go in the same direction!"

The convicts streamed through the gate.

One man stumbled into the path of a searchlight beam. A startled cry sounded on the wall. A rifle cracked and the convict fell forward on the ground.

A siren began to wail on the wall. The escape had been discovered!

But Jack and Fat Stuff were well out of the gate by now.

"Follow me!" the native called to Jack.

They plunged into the underbrush and made their way down the steep side of the mountain toward the sea.

Someone was following. Jack turned to see three figures bobbing in the darkness behind him. They were gaining, but there were no commands to halt. These men were convicts too, not guards.

After stumbling down the steep sides of the hill, they reached the beach. Fat Stuff led the way along the sand until they reached the section that was thickly covered with jungle.

"We pretty safe here," Fat Stuff announced, puffing. "We rest."

Jack sat down and the three other convicts joined them. They were The Claw, Lizard and Slab.

The situation in which Jack now found himself was not altogether to his liking. It was going to be three against two.

"When we go back to get Betty?" The Claw asked as he sat down beside Jack.

"I told you, Claw, that Betty will be released from the prison, but we're not in the clear yet ourselves," Jack said.

A non-committal grunt came from the giant.

As they rested they heard distant cries and shouts, and then they faintly heard the baying of bloodhounds. The pursuit of the escaped prisoners was on.

"Can we get away from them?" Jack asked Fat Stuff.

"Island pretty big," the native said. "We follow river near here—gettum bloodhounds off scent."

"Let's get goin'!" Slab suggested.

All that night the escaped prisoners made their way through the jungle. Thorny vines plucked at their clothing and their legs grew tired, but the baying of the distant bloodhounds kept them moving.

At last Fat Stuff brought them to the bank of a small stream that flowed from the hills through the jungles to the sea. They stepped into the cool, refreshing water and followed it upstream for half a mile before stepping out on the bank on the other side.

From there on the sound of pursuit grew fainter. By morning they had reached a spot deep in the interior of the island.

Here they sat down to rest, at last.

"How're we gonna get off this island?" Slab asked. "We ain't got a boat."

"There are natives at the south end with outrigger canoes," Jack said. "The canoes are small, but there have been a number of remarkable journeys made in them. In fact, natives covered the whole Pacific in those canoes before the white man came."

Slab rose to his feet and walked toward some berries growing on a vine near by.

"I'm dyin' of hunger," Slab said. "I'm gonna eat some of these berries."

But Fat Stuff ran forward and caught Slab's arm before the sunken-faced man had a chance to pick them.

"No, Slab!" the native cried. "No eat! Poison!"

Slab sat down with the rest, his eyes still fixed hungrily on the berries.

For awhile they slept. Then they arose and prepared to march southward to the native settlement.

Slab found some fruit before they had gone half a mile and he plucked it joyfully. Again Fat Stuff stopped him with the warning that it, too, was poison.

The jungle seemed to have berries and luscious fruit on every tree, but each time Slab sought to eat some, Fat Stuff stopped him with the warning:

"No eat, Slab. Poison."

At last Slab spotted some purple grapes on a vine that ran up a tree.

"There's stuff I *know* ain't poison!" he said. "Them's grapes."

"No eat, Slab! Poison!" Fat Stuff warned again.

Lizard turned accusingly toward the native.

"Say!" he growled. "I think you're tryin' to starve us, Fat Stuff! You and Powder want to give th' rest of us th' slip an' get away without us. You say every fruit we see is poison."

"Yeah!" Slab growled. "You can't fool me no longer!"

With a vicious shove, Slab pushed Fat Stuff aside and plucked the grapes. He thrust them piggishly into his mouth and gulped them down.

"No! No eat! Poison!" Fat Stuff cried, rushing toward Slab.

Again the escaped prisoner thrust the native aside.

He devoured another bunch of the grapes, and started on a third, when he hesitated.

"I feel kinda funny!" he said, staggering.

Slab tried to catch himself on the trunk of a tree, but he slipped and fell. A moment later he writhed and then

Fat Stuff Led the Way Through the Jungle

lay still as the others tried in vain to revive him.

Jack bent over the still figure and felt his pulse. He listened to his chest, then moved away.

"Fat Stuff was right," Jack said. "Those grapes were poison. Quick, too. Slab is dead."

"Me try stop him," Fat Stuff said apologetically.

"It was his own fault," Lizard said coldly. He turned to Fat Stuff. "Lead us outa this blasted jungle. Find us some food that ain't poison!"

"Ugh!" growled The Claw. "Hurry. Me hungry."

The Claw and Lizard were going mad from hunger, but Jack felt safter now. Neither of the other two would try anything as long as only Fat Stuff knew which food to eat. And they found no berries or fruit that were edible as they went on through the jungle.

All that day they made their way slowly and painfully southward. At nightfall Fat Stuff found a bush with a few plum-like objects hanging from the branches.

"We eat this fruit," Fat Stuff announced. "Me know this fruit is not poison."

There were only two apiece for the hungry men.

On the morning of the third day they set out once more. They felt reasonably certain now that they had eluded the bloodhounds, but the menace of hunger grew. Edible fruit was scarce in the jungle. When bushes of wholesome berries were found there was barely enough to go around.

The Claw and Lizard were growing weak, while Jack was barely able to keep his legs moving. Fat Stuff's reserve seemed greater than the others, but even he devoured food eagerly whenever he found it.

Toward noon of the third day they reached another stream. Jack plunged in, leading the party toward the opposite bank. But as he made a second step, something caught him by the ankle and held him fast.

As Jack struggled to break away from what was holding him, his other foot was caught. The more he struggled the deeper he sank.

Jack was horrified at the realization of what had befallen him.

"Help!" Jack gasped as the water reached his armpits. "Quicksand!"

Fat Stuff ran toward the bank of the river ready to plunge into the water to help Jack.

Suddenly there was a growl and The Claw stepped forward, blocking the native's path.

"Let me past!" Fat Stuff cried. "Me gotta save my friend!"

The Claw brandished the knife-like weapon on the stump of his arm.

"How'd you like to have me puncture that fat body of yours?" he asked. "There's too many of us now! There'll be more to eat after we get rid of Powder!"

"Yeah! Let him go!" Lizard said. "I never did get even with him for tossin' me into that prison! Now I can watch him die!"

After shoving Fat Stuff aside, The Claw stood beside Lizard on the bank of the stream, while Jack slowly sank in the treacherous sand. The water reached Jack's chin and was crawling higher.

Absorbed in the struggles of the man they knew as Powder, The Claw and Lizard failed to notice Fat Stuff slip away.

The water reached Jack's mouth. In a moment it would be over his nostrils. Grimly and stoically Jack faced his fate.

But Fat Stuff was not giving up. He had climbed a near-by tree and from a limb he was lowering vines to Jack, helplessly caught by the sucking sand.

The Claw spotted the native as the vine was lowered to Jack. The aviator caught the vine and began slowly to pull himself up, out of the grip of the quicksand.

Lizard shrieked with anger as he saw that Jack was about to escape. The Claw's massive left arm swept upward and caught a limb of a near-by tree. The limb snapped and the giant tore it loose. Then he swung the long pole toward the vine.

The stick landed with a *whack* across Smilin' Jack's straining knuckles.

CHAPTER THIRTEEN

A JUNGLE VILLAGE

Vindictively, furiously, The Claw brought the branch down across Smilin' Jack's knuckles again and again as the aviator gripped the vines grimly, trying to pull himself out of the quicksand. Lizard jumped up and down on the bank, screaming with excitement.

The pain in his fingers was severe, but Jack held on desperately. He felt his feet pulling loose from the mire —a few more tugs and he would be free of the sand—if he could keep his hold despite The Claw's smarting blows from the pole.

The Claw viciously whacked at Jack's knuckles, but suddenly the attack ceased. A brown-skinned figure came zooming out of a near-by tree, swinging on a low hanging vine.

It was the South Sea Islander. He skimmed straight toward the two men on the bank of the stream. His feet struck like twin battering rams, bowling Lizard and The Claw to the ground like tenpins.

Exerting his final ounce of strength, Jack drew himself free of the quicksand. Using the vines for support, he dragged himself to the opposite bank of the stream.

"Come on, Fat Stuff!" he cried.

Fat Stuff, chortling with glee at Jack's escape and his

successful surprise attack on the two who had sought to
get rid of Jack, swung across the stream on his vine.

"Follow me!" Fat Stuff said, plunging into the jungle
with Jack at his heels. "We lose 'em."

But Lizard already was on his feet. Instantly he caught
the swinging vine that Fat Stuff had dropped. Quickly
he swung across the stream, shouting for The Claw to
join him.

"Can't let 'em get away!" Lizard cried. "That native
bloke is the only guy as can get us out of this jungle!"

The Claw, badly jarred from the punch of Fat Stuff's
naked heels, rose painfully and seized the vine. He swung
himself across the stream and trotted doggedly after
Lizard.

Jack and Fat Stuff, aware of the pursuit, were trying
to increase the distance between themselves and their
treacherous companions. Fat Stuff's pace was slackening,
however, as his huge body began to demand rest from
his exertions.

"Hurry!" Jack urged. "Keep going! They're gaining
on us."

"Fat Stuff—too fat!" the native panted. "No can—run
fast."

Alone, Jack might have outdistanced them, but he
couldn't desert this faithful follower now. Jack seized
Fat Stuff's arm and tried to hurry him along, but the
islander shook his head.

"No use, Jack!" he said. "Go on. Me can't go. Look
like—me in—for much trouble."

"If *you're* in for it, we're *both* in for it," Jack insisted. "I'll stick by you, Fat Stuff, because you've stuck by me."

In a spurt of his second wind, Jack dragged the native into some brush which looked like a good hiding place. He had to conserve his energy now if he was going to meet and oppose The Claw and Lizard, both half-crazy from hunger and bitterly seeking revenge.

The two double-crossing pursuers came into view.

"They're in the brush!" Lizard shouted, spying the swaying vines where Jack and Fat Stuff had crawled to cover.

The Claw brandished the jagged blade on his arm. His eyes rolled with villainous intent.

"No use," cried Fat Stuff. "They find us!"

But Jack said, "You take Lizard. I'll handle The Claw!"

As Jack's head rose above the undergrowth, The Claw bellowed like a maddened bull. On spotting the aviator his bloodshot eyes actually saw red.

Fat Stuff instinctively shrank back as the two convicts came toward them, but Jack stubbornly stood his ground.

Something compelling in Jack's attitude caused The Claw to change his course—to attack Fat Stuff instead of the determined American. But as the Claw dived for Fat Stuff, Smilin' Jack went into action with a flying tackle.

The aim was sure. Jack's lunge caught The Claw just as he charged on Fat Stuff. The tackle threw The Claw to the ground, but it didn't knock him out. As Jack sprang forward to land a knockout blow, The Claw—on his back—kicked hard, his huge feet catching Jack on the chest and sending him staggering back.

With the wind knocked from his lungs, Jack gasped for breath. The Claw sprang to his feet and closed in toward Fat Stuff.

"Wait, you dope!" Lizard shouted from behind the giant idiot. "Don't bump off our guide!"

Reluctantly, The Claw turned toward Jack.

"There! That's the ticket!" Lizard shouted approvingly. "Anythin' you do to Powder is okay by me!"

By now Fat Stuff had his fright under control. When he saw The Claw going after his friend, he leaped to the fray. With his head down, Fat Stuff charged like a steamroller straight at the great bulk of The Claw.

The Lizard sprang like lightning into Fat Stuff's path.

"Get back, you big tub of lard!" Lizard warned murderously.

But Fat Stuff was taking no orders from Lizard. He didn't even slow down. Like a deadly reptile Lizard snapped into action. He aimed a lethal kick right at the center of Fat Stuff's midsection.

"Oof!"

Fat Stuff grunted pitifully as the cruel blow landed. He staggered back and his usually calm features were warped with pain turning into rage.

"You dirty fighter!" Fat Stuff cried.

The overweight native sprang like a tiger on Lizard. The two closed in, rolling over and over in the brush.

Now Jack faced The Claw alone. Keeping a cautious eye on the deadly blade on The Claw's wrist, he waited for the attack. It came with calculated deadliness, but he was ready. As the blade swished at him, the aviator ducked. Before The Claw could recover his balance, Jack caught the arm and grappled with the savage giant.

Jack would have preferred not having to pit his strength against this particular foe. The Claw was much the more powerful physically and had the added advantage of his weight. And Jack couldn't spar, using his naked fists against a knife. First he had to get the knife out of the way and then hope to land a knockout blow.

The Claw tripped Jack, but as Jack fell he pulled his opponent to the ground with him. The saw-like knife was raised to strike—Jack, with all his reserve strength, strained to hold back the blow. But the weight of the giant was too much: the deadly knife, razor sharp, moved closer and closer to Jack's throat.

In a desperate convulsive twist, Jack wriggled aside to escape the knife. But his head struck something immovable behind him. He could wriggle no farther—a heavy log blocked his movements.

Nearer and nearer to Jack's throat the saw-toothed knife descended. In a few short seconds it would sink home. In this crammed instant of eternity Jack's brain was racing at top speed. His body tensed, sending a final surge of strength against the upraised arm.

Then suddenly all the force restraining the giant arm was released. All that had barred The Claw from sinking his knife into Jack's body was pulled away. The knife descended with a rush, out of control.

But Jack's throat was not where the knife landed.

Instead, Jack had jerked his head aside just far enough —in spite of the log. He rolled out of the way of the descending blow with the wiriness of a trained wrestler. The knife struck the log behind Jack's head instead. It sank deeply into the wood and stuck.

Roaring with rage, The Claw jerked his arm to pull the blade out and it came loose from its socket.

The Claw stared dumbly at his disarmed member. Suddenly he realized that Jack was on his feet, ready now to use his fists in a more evenly matched battle.

"Now," Jack said, "for once in your life you've got to fight like a man—you yellow-livered gorilla."

The Claw was suddenly and almost pathetically afraid.

Shrinking back, he was on the point of running. Deprived of his weapon, he was as helpless as a babe. The sharp hook had been his badge of courage. Now, with only an empty socket on the leather-covered stump of his arm, he became craven and contemptible. The Claw shrank back from the flashing fists that already were beginning to land punishingly on his face and body.

Trying to cover, The Claw ducked his head. As he did so, Jack's fist swung upward and landed with crushing force on the monster's chin. The Claw groaned and sank to the ground, knocked completely out.

Jack glanced over his shoulder just in time to see Fat Stuff, who had been struggling with Lizard, land a telling blow on the back of Lizard's head. The punch ended that battle: Lizard dropped like a rock.

Fat Stuff looked with astonishment at his prostrate foe.

"Me no know me such a fighter!" the native exclaimed. "Someday me take boxin' lessons—self-defense!"

Jack grinned.

"Well, if you ask me—you don't need many lessons. That was a sweet K. O. you gave Lizard."

"Sweet for me. Sour for him." Fat Stuff chuckled. "The Claw look like him enjoy nice sleep, too. You good punch man also, Jack!"

"Well, let's get out of here before we have to do it all over again," Jack urged. "Where do we go from here?"

"Maybe find native village," Fat Stuff said, leading the way into the jungle once more.

They struck a path and the going became easier. The path led, Fat Stuff said, to the native village.

"Funny the natives stay on this island, with The Head likely to kidnap them for his prison," Jack said.

"Natives help Head catch escaped convicts!" Fat Stuff explained.

"What? And you're taking me to their village?"

"We go to village, but we take native boat without native see us," Fat Stuff elucidated happily.

Darkness fell, but they did not stop to rest. Night was the best time to commandeer one of the native boats.

The path grew wider and finally led into a moonlit clearing. Fat Stuff held up his hand. Ahead, scattered through the clearing, were a dozen native huts, perched on stilts to protect the occupants from tropical insects that crawled on the ground.

"Now we get real food!" Fat Stuff sighed. "An' a boat."

"We'd better be careful. Maybe someone's on guard." Fat Stuff shook his head.

"No guard, but native light sleeper. You stay here. Fat Stuff look for food."

The islander slipped away towards a near-by native hut. Soon he returned, bearing several parcels of food wrapped in green leaves.

"Sh-h!" he whispered. "Hold food—wait here. Me look for boat."

Again Fat Stuff drifted away into the shadows. Jack began to take stock of his surroundings. From the floor of a native hut not a dozen paces away hung a little cord. The cord would serve nicely to tie up the food packages so they could be carried more easily.

Creeping to the hut, Jack grasped the cord. He gave a quick jerk, trying to break it off.

Suddenly a scream rang out inside the dwelling.

The cord jerked itself out of his hand and disappeared through a crack in the floor.

It wasn't an ordinary cord! It was *human hair!*

"What you do, Jack?"

Fat Stuff had reappeared and was tugging at Jack's arm, trying to drag the aviator back into the jungle. But, as Jack turned, dark figures poured in a flood from other native huts.

"Oh-oh!" Fat Stuff groaned. "You makum much trouble now! Come—we gottum get 'way fast."

"No use, Fat Stuff!" Jack said, noting that the figures coming from the huts were natives armed with spears. "We're surrounded. What did I pull, the fire alarm?"

"You pull girl's hair," Fat Stuff explained. "Native custom. When girl wantum date with boy friend, her sleep with hair hanging through floor. Boy see hair. Him pull an' girl come out for date."

Jack had pulled the hair—but not gently. No wonder the response was a scream!

Guttural voices sounded threateningly on all sides. Suddenly a feminine voice called from the hut, and from the doorway emerged a native girl, clad in a sarong. She came down the ladder and looked at Jack. She turned to the natives, shook her head and spoke.

"She say you not her boy friend," Fat Stuff translated her words. "She say you stranger."

"Well, tell her I made a mistake. I don't want a date. I just want to go."

Fat Stuff spoke quickly to the girl, who shook her head once more.

"Her say she no let us go. She makum money by returnin' convict to prison."

"But they wouldn't do that to you!" Jack exclaimed. "You're a brother South Sea islander."

Fat Stuff wagged his head in denial.

"True an' not true," he said. "We same race, but not same tribe. We both in same boat, Jack. My tribe all time war their tribe. Fat Stuff no popular here."

Brown arms of native warriors seized Jack and Fat Stuff roughly. They were bound and trundled into an empty hut where they were left for the night.

In the morning the native girl brought them food.

"At least they treat us more humanely than The Head and Limehouse," Jack said.

Soon after their breakfast, Jack and Fat Stuff were marched along a path toward the other end of the island. The trail avoided the jungle, so they were able to make much more rapid time. By early afternoon they had reached the prison gate, which was opened by the smirking Limehouse.

"Well, well!" the guard exclaimed. "If it isn't Powder an' Fat Stuff! Welcome back to dear old Death Rock prison!"

Limehouse sent a guard with the natives to the administration building where they were to receive their reward. Then he escorted the two prisoners into the office of The Head.

The dwarfed spy blinked as he saw the American aviator again.

"You are always causing me trouble, Powder," The Head said. "I think it would be best if I killed you."

Jack did not answer. He stared straight at the little man, his jaw set firmly with determination not to weaken at any threat made by this international outlaw.

"But death would be too easy and it would rob me of a great deal of pleasure. I have other plans for you," The

Head went on in a pitiless monotone.

The Head was watching Jack closely, but if he expected any change in the American's expression, he was disappointed.

"Haven't you anything to say?"

For the first time since he was brought into the room, Jack spoke.

"My companion, Fat Stuff, should not be blamed for this escape." Jack said. "I engineered it and I persuaded him to accompany me."

"Is that true, Fat Stuff?" The Head asked.

"I not say," Fat Stuff replied.

"Virtually an admission," The Head said. "Well, since you were *forced* to go along with this renegade, I'm going to let you off with a short term in solitary."

The Head seemed to smile as he shifted his half closed eyes to Jack.

"But as for you, Powder—in view of your *very bad* prison record—I shall sentence you to five years in solitary confinement in Devil's Kitchen," he announced.

"*Oh!*"

The gasp came from feminine lips. Jack turned to see Betty Brown standing in the court room, her eyes aghast at the fate she had just heard meted out to "Powder Pellet."

CHAPTER FOURTEEN

Betty Brown, still pretty in spite of her drab prison dress and pale face, moved swiftly across the room and stood in front of The Head.

"Aren't you human at all?" she asked. "Five years in the Devil's Kitchen! Most convicts can't live even *five weeks* there!"

She glanced at Jack. Much was changed in him since she saw him soon after her arrival on the island. His hair had been shaved then, and he was dressed in a new convict's uniform. Those prison stripes now were soiled and dirty from his futile attempt to escape. His hair was growing out again—not blond as Powder Pellet's had been, but the dark hair of Smilin' Jack Martin.

As she noted the changes, Betty looked at Jack in puzzlement. Then she turned to The Head to repeat her plea.

"You *can't* send him there!"

"There is one way to keep Powder away from the Devil's Kitchen," The Head said, speaking in his usual sarcastic tone. "Once I offered him his freedom if he would help me get a bomber here, but he refused—"

"I still refuse," Jack cut in unhesitatingly.

"Perhaps a week or two in the Kitchen will change your mind," The Head said. "You are still unacquainted

196

with that part of our prison where the cells are hewn from solid rock on a barren cliff. You can't escape from there, for the Kitchen is an island itself—separated from Death Rock by a narrow strait. Confinement in these rock ovens breaks a man quickly. A month will rob you of your mind—more than a month may kill you. Yes, maybe after you have tasted the ovens of the Kitchen, you will come round to my view."

"It's torture!" Betty said. "It's a punishment he doesn't deserve."

"I'm not so sure, Miss Brown," The Head said. "This man is a spy—he is not Powder, the man you once promised to marry."

Betty turned to Jack again, trying to place him in her mind.

"Where have I seen you before?" she asked. "You look familiar. I know it is not just your resemblance to Powder—"

Jack shook his head, trying vainly to halt the girl. But it was too late. A look of recognition sprang into her eyes.

"I know!" she cried. "In the fog near Memphis—at the airport in Valley Ridge. You are Smilin' Jack!"

"Ah!" The Head said, a note of satisfaction in his voice.

"And yet you doubt that he should be treated as a spy? Don't you know, Miss Brown, that it is an age-old custom in war for spies to pay with their lives when they are caught?"

Betty had been caught neatly in The Head's trap.

"You brought me here to make me give him away!" she said accusingly.

The Head smiled lazily and shook his head.

"No, Miss Brown," he told her calmly. "I was not aware that you and—ah—Smilin' Jack had met before, but your recognition makes the task simpler. I brought you here to urge you to dissuade him from sacrificing his mind and his life on the Kitchen. A word from you might persuade him to lure an American bomber here. Since you two know each other, perhaps it will be easier for you to convince him that—it would be best!"

Betty closed her lips tightly. It was easy to see that it was a struggle for her not to plead with Jack to save himself the torture of solitary confinement in the oven prison cells of Devil's Kitchen. But there was more at stake than one man's life—

"It is unnecessary for her to say anything," Jack said. "No matter what she said, I'd still refuse to help you—or any enemy of my country."

"Then it will be as you wish," The Head said, nodding to Limehouse. "You shall go to the Kitchen. And you, Miss Brown, will go there too, to comfort him. Oh—you needn't fear. You'll not be confined in a cell to lose your beauty and your mind. I have use for you later to force your father to let us employ the facilities of his airline to help our cause. But you will be near enough to see Smilin' Jack lose his smile, lose his mind—and lose his life. Then, perhaps, you will be more willing to persuade your father to help us."

The Head signaled Limehouse, who seized Jack's arm and turned him toward the door.

"Come along with me, Mr. 'Powder', or whatever your name is," he grunted. "The speedboat is ready to take you to the Kitchen."

A short time later a swift motor launch operated by a prison guard sped over the water toward a towering, precipitous rock standing off the coast of Death Rock Island. In the boat, guarded by Limehouse, were Smilin' Jack and Fat Stuff. Betty would be brought over later with a group of women to do the cooking and chores for prisoners in solitary confinement.

"The Head has made me special guard on the Kitchen," Limehouse said. "He ain't takin' no chances on your escapin' this time."

"Me hear no one ever escapum from there," Fat Stuff muttered.

"Yeah," Limehouse said, lighting a cigarette. "But there is always a first time, an' we don't care to let Smilin' Jack have that honor."

As the launch approached the isle, Jack saw a winding road running up from a wharf toward which the boat was making. Along this trail were small guardhouses, each watching over a tier of cells scooped out of the ledge of the perpendicular rock spire.

Escape was hardly possible under such close guard. Even if a man did manage to get out of his cell and past the guards, there remained the strait to swim in order to reach the main island. After that there was an ocean barring the way to freedom on the mainland.

"Thinkin' of swimmin' away from the Kitchen?" Limehouse grinned evilly as he watched Jack's eyes. "Let me remind you that even if a con did escape the Kitchen, he'd never reach the main island. The water here is lousy with sharks. They would rip a guy to ribbons in thirty seconds."

The boat came alongside the wharf, and Limehouse gruffly ordered his prisoners to disembark. As the boat swung around and headed back to Death Rock, Jack and Fat Stuff were ordered to march up the winding road.

The road was steep, and Jack already was exhausted from his exertions during the escape, but Limehouse allowed no rest.

From point to point the path branched off along ledges of the rock. Here were small steel cages, only a couple of feet above the ground and unprotected from the sun's glare, that marked the cells of solitary prisoners. The rest of each cell was solid rock, hewn four or five feet below the surface. With the hot sun beating down all day on the cells, it was easy to see how they became roasting ovens for the men inside.

Limehouse did not stop on the lower levels of cells. He sought to torture his prisoners by marching them up the path to the top tier, just below the flat summit of the rock.

Fat Stuff was ordered into one cell and Jack was placed in the next. It was dusk and too late for a meal, and the convicts were told that any clamor of protest would result in no breakfast.

A block of stone for a chair and a mattress on the rock floor were the only "furniture" in the cell. The small room, scarcely six feet by four, was hardly big enough for a man to turn around in—and it was unbearably hot, although the sun was sinking in the west.

Jack, exhausted from his ordeal, managed to drop off to sleep, but he was awakened at dawn by the arrival of guards with weak coffee and dried bread—breakfast.

Before Jack had finished the paltry meal, the heat of the day had set in. By noon the tropical sun was blazing through the iron grate above the ground. Jack was alone, with nothing to take his mind off his sufferings And his sentence was five years.

"Nothing to do—not a soul to talk to," Jack muttered to himself. "If a guy doesn't die from the heat here, he'll go nuts, all right, just from talking to himself."

Through the day Jack sat. Curious thoughts came to his mind. He likened himself to the hero of Jack London's "Sky Rover," the story of a convict who played at self-hypnotism in San Quentin. Jack tried to hypnotize himself, but in vain. However, there was one thing he could do—Jack recalled that in that story convicts communicated with other prisoners by tapping on the walls.

Jack sprang to his feet and removed one shoe. He tapped slowly on the wall of his cell. Fat Stuff was next door. He ought to hear the tapping.

No reply came.

Suddenly Jack realized why. Fat Stuff couldn't read or write—he couldn't spell messages even if he wanted to!

Jack had no space in which to walk the floor of his cell. "A person never realizes what a bore he is until he's alone with himself continually," Jack decided.

Suddenly Jack tensed. Faintly, to his ears, came the sound of music:

"Da-da—*de-dee-dah!* Ump-pum-de-dee-dah!"

Was Jack losing his mind? Was he hearing things?

The voice came nearer.

"Betty!" Jack gasped, pushing his face close to the bars.

"Sh-h!" the girl whispered. "I'm bringing you your lunch, but I can't talk to you."

Through a small opening in the cage, Betty pushed some food—a kind of porridge—and water.

"You're an angel!" Jack said. "Even seeing you at meal time is going to make my stay in this cell a lot easier to take!"

"O-o-o-h—if I had th' wings of an angel," Betty sang, "over these prison walls I would fly-y-y—"

Smiling, Betty moved on about her task of feeding the prisoners. Jack, however, did not eat the food. Instead, he was thinking of the words to the song. They ran through his mind again and again.

"Fly! With wings! That's the answer!" Jack whispered hoarsely to himself. "I'm no sailor—I'm a pilot. I won't go by sea, but by air. I'll fly—some way. I'll get wings!"

Seating himself on his pallet he ate slowly, absorbed

Jack Caught a Glimpse of a Plane on Dawn Patrol

in thought. By degrees a plan formed in his mind—a desperate plan, one that depended on sheer daring for success. But Jack's position was desperate and only a desperate plan could succeed. One day of suffering in the Kitchen proved that he could not last long here. If his mission for Uncle Sam was not to fail, he had to escape *now!*

Through the hours of darkness Jack tossed on his hard bed. He didn't know how he'd escape, but he would. Once away from this island, he could terminate the careers of The Head and his gang. He could obtain the release of men unjustly held in confinement. An American destroyer or a few bombers could take the island and blast its torture chambers to bits.

Dawn was breaking while Jack still studied his problem. Then faintly from the northwest came the sound of airplane motors. Jack caught a glimpse of the craft—a U. S. Navy bomber on dawn patrol.

A wild idea flashed into his mind. Wings of an airplane did not always need a motor.

"A glider! That's it! If I can get out of this cell I might be able to build a glider. I could launch it when one of those patrol bombers flew over. I could attract the crew's attention, land on the water and they'd pick me up."

Footsteps interrupted Jack's train of thought. Someone was coming.

"Hello, Powder!" came a raspy greeting.

Limehouse stood outside the cell.

"I hope that bomber didn't make you homesick."

Jack stood at the bars of his prison, looking up at Limehouse.

"A lot of difference it would make to you if it did!" Jack replied. "Say, how often do the bombers fly over?"

"What do you care?" Limehouse taunted. "You're not goin' out to meet one. But those bombers won't bother you much longer."

"What do you mean?"

"Death Rock ain't United States territory an' The Head has sent word to the gov'ment official in his pay in South America protestin' against the bomber flyin' over this island. He'll get the American ambassador to change the patrol route—prob'ly in a week or so."

Limehouse laughed tauntingly. The prison guard delighted in tormenting his prisoners. He wanted Jack to know that even the sight of friendly airplanes was to be taken away.

Jack tried to keep his face from showing his anxiety. The news meant that if he were to escape he had to do it within a week's short time.

Limehouse continued to torment Jack and the other prisoners in the tier of cells. Pulling a package of cigarettes from his pocket, Limehouse thrust one into his mouth, knowing how the men in the cells longed for a forbidden smoke.

Taking a small lighter from his pocket, Limehouse deliberately snapped it to light the cigarette. But the lighter failed to work. Jack concealed a smile. Limehouse tried again to make the lighter work—again it failed, and again he tried.

The prison guard's temper mounted as he felt himself humiliated by his own cigarette lighter. With an exclamation of disgust, Limehouse flung the lighter to the rocky ledge, turned on his heel and strode away.

Jack let his mind revert to his own problem. This problem was much more pressing than a cigarette lighter that failed to work. Jack was studying how the heat, reflected from this rocky mountain spire, would warm the air, thus producing a thermal updraft which could easily lift a small glider high into the air.

But Jack didn't have a glider and his cell was obviously much too small in which to build one. Jack's foremost problem was to get out of his cell to build such a glider. If he could only make a rude key, but he had no metal.

No metal?

An object glinted on the rock ledge in front of Jack's cell—the discarded cigarette lighter! Metal, if Jack could only reach it, fully eight feet away! Jack's arm stretched through the bars, hopelessly.

A pole or something! But there was nothing in the cell to extend Jack's reach. The metal tantalized Jack, glistening there in the early morning sunlight.

Then a thought struck him. He removed his jacket. Holding onto one sleeve he tossed it at the lighter, trying to sweep it toward the cell. But the jacket was too short.

"My pants!"

Removing his striped trousers, Jack tied them to the sleeve of the jacket. Again he tried to toss them over the lighter. Everything depended on accuracy. His first aim was bad. His second touched the lighter, but failed to budge it. The job would require skill and dogged persistence. Again and again he tried.

At last, success! A loose thread on the trousers caught the lid of the broken lighter. Slowly Jack pulled it toward him, bringing it within arm's reach.

He seized it hastily and drew it into the cell.

"I've got it!" he cried in a hoarse whisper of triumph.

Peering out through the bars, Jack made sure his actions had gone undetected by the watchmen in the guardhouse at the end of the ledge. But no one was abroad at this time of the day. The heat was growing intense and guards preferred the cooler shade.

Jack put on his trousers and set to work. Knocking the lighter apart, he used his stone seat to straighten out the metal. Then he began working the edges of the flattened tube against the rock.

For hours he sat, grinding the metal against the jagged edges of the stone seat. Slowly and painstakingly he was transforming the bit of metal into the semblance of a key.

This key would open the way to freedom!

There was enough silicon in the rock to give it an emery surface. The task would be tedious and painstaking, but eventually the job would be finished and Smilin' Jack would have a skeleton key with which to unlock his cell.

As the afternoon wore on and the heat grew less intense, guards paid their regulation visits to the cell. Jack hid his handicraft. The soiled bed was removed, the prisoners were taken out for exercise, and Jack was given a change of clothing.

Every time the guards unlocked Jack's cell, the aviator studied the contour of the key, fixing it in mind so that he could adapt his bit of metal to the general form.

Betty arrived with the evening meal just before sundown.

"I'm going to try to escape," Jack whispered to the girl.

"Jack! They'll kill you!" Betty spoke in a low voice that could not be overheard by the guards who were watching her serve the meal to the prisoners.

"No they won't, and if I don't escape I'll die!" Jack said. "I need clothing—not men's clothing but silk clothing."

"Are you going to dress like a woman, Jack?" Betty asked. "You might masquerade as Powder, but not as a girl. You're too big—"

"Never mind what I need clothing for," Jack said. "Where can I get silk dresses—"

"Limehouse has a daughter," Betty whispered. "She lives in his house—up on top of the mountain."

"Get a move on!" one of the guards shouted at Betty.

Betty quickly rose and moved away.

After dinner, the prisoners were left alone by the guards. Jack used this opportunity to file on his key, duplicating as closely as possible the original he had seen used by the guards.

Through the night he scraped, keeping his ears alert for sound of the guard's footsteps.

When dawn arrived, Jack had a crude key.

"Locks have been picked with much simpler objects," Jack said. "If this doesn't work I'm stuck here for the rest of my life."

Gingerly Smilin' Jack reached his arm through the bars of his cell.

"If it does work I'm still stuck—stuck with the problem of how to build a glider out of thin air!" he added.

The key slipped into the lock. The crucial moment had come!

CHAPTER FIFTEEN

A WEIRD CONTRAPTION

The makeshift key fitted but it would not turn. Jack withdrew it from the lock and filed some more. Trying again, he turned the key with difficulty. There was a sharp click and the door was open.

"It works!" Jack gloated in a throaty whisper.

He closed the door, but it would not relock. Again it was necessary to file and again he was successful. Now the key was perfect. It would lock and unlock the door. But it was daylight now. Soon the guards would be stirring and the construction of the glider would have to wait until after dark that night.

But from what could he fabricate any sort of glider at all?

Hiding his key under the rock seat in his cell, Jack went through the day's routine. Having made some headway, Jack found the heat not so unbearable now, nor did Limehouse's visit rankle him so much. Jack would be free before long—he hoped!

That night, Jack thought quiet would never descend on the tiers of cells. A prisoner on the level below was screaming and guards were trying to quiet him. But at last there was silence and Jack removed his key from its hiding place.

The door opened again without difficulty. What now? The trail down the side of the rock spire was so heavily guarded Jack could not expect to reach the base without discovery. He had to find the materials for his glider somewhere up above.

Slipping along the cells, past sleeping prisoners, Jack followed the trail. He avoided guardhouses by creeping behind and around them. The guards were dozing, believing that all prisoners were securely locked in their cells. Even if one did escape his cell, there wasn't a chance for him to reach safety across the shark-infested strait between the Devil's Kitchen and Death Rock.

At last Jack reached the top of the rock. A shadowy, barred structure loomed ahead of him in the light of the new moon. At first Jack thought he had run across a special cell of some sort. Then, as he crept closer he saw that the bars were not of steel, but of bamboo.

The "cell" was an old bamboo arbor constructed on top of the rock, possibly in a futile attempt to grow grapes or other vines.

Jack's heart beat rapidly. That bamboo would be just the thing for making longerons and wing spars for a glider!

"Why, I'm as good as sprouting wings right now!" Jack exclaimed to himself triumphantly.

But the problem was not so easily solved. There was wing fabric to consider. Jack already had an idea of what he could use for wing fabric. Betty had told him that Limehouse had a daughter. Girls mean clothes—clothes for a young woman ought to include lots of silk.

Silk would be the solution to Smilin' Jack's wing-fabric problem.

Following the path down from the top, Jack made his way toward the row of cottages which housed members of the families of the guards. The large, two-story house at the end undoubtedly was Limehouse's, for he was in charge of the guards on Devil's Kitchen.

The house was dark. Everyone was sleeping. Jack crept cautiously toward it, knowing that if he should arouse anyone in the house, he would be cruelly punished. Limehouse was not the kind of a man to miss an opportunity to punish with a vengeance.

A figure moved in the shadows. Jack tensed. Someone was coming.

Into the moonlight came a tiny creature. Not a man, but a small monkey—undoubtedly a pet of Limehouse's daughter.

"Scram!" Jack whispered.

The monkey disappeared into the house through an open window.

Smiling, the American aviator followed the monkey. Under cover of darkness he made his way into the house. Upstairs a door was ajar, and Jack peeked through the door. Limehouse was snoring in a bed in that room.

Restraining his desire to repay Limehouse for some of the things he had done, Jack tried the room across the hall. The scent of perfume told Jack that this was the place he sought. The room was occupied by Limehouse's daughter.

Moonlight streaming through the window revealed the door of the clothes closet. Jack pulled it open and stepped inside.

"Boy!" he thought as he ran his hands over the garments.

Limehouse's daughter had more clothing than a Fifth Avenue gown shop!

Jack grinned to himself as he filled his arms with silken dresses. Limehouse would certainly boil if he knew he had unwittingly provided for Smilin' Jack's escape.

Jack, with an armload of clothing, turned to go when suddenly a hand fell on his shoulder!

He was caught! This was the end.

Jack waited. A tender little finger stroked his ear.

It was the monkey Jack had met outside the house. The animal had followed him to the girl's room.

Jack sighed in relief, but to his dismay a coat hanger fell from the rack and clattered to the floor.

The girl's gentle breathing ceased.

"Who's there?" came a timid voice from the bed.

Jack's heart almost stopped. The girl had awakened.

"Who's there?" the girl repeated. "I know I heard someone!"

Jack heard the movement of the girl in the bed. If she turned on the light, escape would be impossible.

Jack's only hope was to answer the question in a way that would relieve the girl's fears. How? A sudden idea came to his mind.

Laying aside the clothing, Jack reached down and stroked the monkey, which had jumped to the floor at the sound of the girl's voice. His fingers tickled the creature's ribs. A startled squeal came from the monkey.

The simian, like human beings, was ticklish.

Squealing, the monkey ran across the room and hopped on the girl's bed. A sigh of relief came from her as her fears subsided.

"Oh!" she exclaimed. "So it was only you, Ringtail. What a bad little monkey you were to frighten me so! Now be quiet so I can go back to my dreams."

As the girl talked sleepily to Ringtail, Smilin' Jack slipped quietly out of the house. He made his way past Limehouse's door to the downstairs rooms. There he managed to find a sewing basket and a kitchen knife. But the thread in the sewing basket, while it would serve some purposes, was not strong enough for others. He needed wire or heavy cord at least. There seemed to be none in the house.

Leaving the place, Jack strolled through the shadows to the end of the row of cottages occupied by guards. At the far end was a little shed, from which came a buzzing.

"The electric dynamo!" Jack exclaimed. "There ought to be wire there!"

There was, in large quantities. Jack took as much as he thought he would need and then hurried away. A light-sleeping guard might interrupt Jack's plan and he did not care to take the risk of being seen by delaying within view of the guards' homes.

He found the top of the rock deserted as before. He set to work, laboring by the light of the stars. First he notched the bamboo ribs taken from the arbor. Using the kitchen knife he cut them into proper lengths.

The ribs were tied with wire to the main spar and the outline of the glider began to take shape.

Then, in the midst of his work, Jack heard a noise behind him. Turning quickly, Jack saw a shadow on the ground. But Jack was not upset this time. He recognized the shadow.

It was Ringtail, the monkey, come to pay another visit.

"Stick around, little fellow," Jack greeted the monkey. "Any kind of companionship does a fellow good in this forsaken place."

Through the night Jack worked, and when the first tint of dawn appeared on the eastern horizon, he hastily hid his tools and materials in a crevice and rushed down the trail to his cell. He reached the cell just as dawn was breaking, but he got there ahead of the guards making their morning rounds.

Jack hoped that the whittlings from his bamboo poles would not be found during the day and arouse suspicion.

"All I can do is to pray that no one blunders up on the mountain top," Jack said to himself as he slipped the key in the lock of his cell and closed it for the day.

He hid the key under the rock seat in his cell. As long as he had that key he had hope.

Jack went through the routine of the daylight hours, sweltering in the heat of his oven-cell, occasionally snatching bits of sleep as he waited for night to come.

Limehouse missed his usual round that day, and this struck Jack as ominous.

Late in the afternoon Betty appeared with the rations. She stooped beside Jack's cell.

"Jack!" she whispered. "What have you done?"

For a moment Jack's heart sank. Had his plan to escape been discovered?

"Done?"

"Someone has taken all the silk dresses Limehouse's daughter had!" Betty exclaimed. "There's a terrible commotion in the cottages."

"But what have I to do with it?" Jack asked, not daring to tell Betty the truth for fear of being overheard.

"You asked me about silk dresses day before yesterday," Betty said.

Smilin' Jack grinned and Betty winked.

"Tell me about it, Betty," he pleaded.

Betty glanced over her shoulder. The guards were busy abusing a prisoner and they weren't noticing her.

"When Laura—that's Limehouse's daughter—woke up yesterday morning she noticed some of her dresses missing," Betty related. "She told Limehouse, who blamed the convicts and threatened to search every prisoner here from head to foot.

"When Mrs. Limehouse heard of the theft of her daughter's dresses, she laid out her husband for letting someone steal the clothes from under his nose. Limehouse ordered a search of the women prisoners—that's how I happened to hear the story. But of course nothing was found.

"No one seemed to consider that a man might have taken the clothes—besides, the male prisoners here are all in solitary—locked tight in their cells. The only other solution was that women were stealing from each other. Mrs. Limehouse accused the daughter of another guard. Laura accused the wife of the pier guard. The wives have been fighting all day. The whole place is in an uproar. How on earth did you do it, Jack, and what are you up to?"

Jack was chuckling softly at the news, even though he realized that it would lead to worse punishment than ever if he were caught.

"I haven't time to tell you now, Betty," he said to the girl. "But I will some day, if everything works out. You'd better be moving along now, before the guards notice how long you've been talking to me."

"They won't notice," Betty laughed. "They've got troubles of their own. But—I—I hope your plan works, Jack! And *do* be careful!"

With those words, Betty moved away from the cell. Jack watched her go, hoping that, before long now, he would escape and bring rescuers here to release her and Fat Stuff.

The theft of Laura's clothing caused such a stir on Devil's Kitchen that the guards were too occupied to abuse the prisoners that day. In fact, the cells were scarcely visited and Jack managed to get in considerable sleep.

Had time not been so pressing, Jack would have enjoyed doing a little further sabotage of the prison guards' morale, but he had to escape before the route of the patrol plane was changed.

Jack heard the plane come over every morning, but it might shift its course at any time.

As soon as the cells were quiet when night came again, Jack removed his rudely fashioned key from its hiding place and opened his barred door.

Hurrying to the mountain top, he again set to work on his glider. The rude materials and tools were difficult to handle, but Jack's experience as an aviator overcame the handicaps. Besides, he *had* to work fast. The time left for him to succeed in making good his escape grew less each day that passed.

There were other possibilities, besides lack of time, that haunted him.

"Even to hope that this chicken coop will fly is a strain on a fellow's imagination," Jack muttered as he worked with the kitchen knife.

The moon, which had been shining brightly, was dimming beneath clouds that suddenly covered the sky. Soon after midnight it began to rain.

Ordinarily Jack would have welcomed rain as bringing relief from the suffocating heat. But now the rain meant delay in the completion of his glider.

He pulled his framework to the crevice and lowered it out of sight, hanging its tail on a projecting rock. The crevice furnished a safe hiding place unless a thorough search were made. But Jack had to pray that there would be no thorough search. There was no other hiding place available.

Jack ran back toward his cell as the rain fell, drenching him to the skin. He fervently hoped no rain would fall the next night, because, if it did, he might never get his glider completed before the patrol plane ceased flying near Death Rock.

The rain ceased as Jack locked himself in his cell. He was damp, but comfortably relieved from the heat.

Gazing from the barred doorway he saw he had a visitor. Ringtail, the monkey, was squatting outside. With a squeak of joy, Ringtail sprang through the bars, landing on Smilin' Jack, splattering mud over his prison uniform.

"You little pest!" Jack exclaimed, seizing Ringtail and thrusting him back outside the cell again. "If the guards see that mud on me, they'll get wise that I've been sneakin' out."

Jack managed to scrape off the mud with his hands, but as he did so he noticed that there was mud on his shoes also.

"Good night!" Jack exclaimed as a new thought dawned on him. "That means tracks!"

Suddenly Jack realized that he had left a trail from his cell to the top of the mountain and that this trail led directly to the spot where he had hidden his makeshift glider.

In a flash Jack was out of his cell. Once more he climbed past the guardhouse and up the trail to the top of the mountain. He cut a small length of bamboo from the arbor and, using it as a trowel to cover his tracks he started down, and erased each track as he went back to the cell.

It was a laborious job and a long one. He barely finished before the rising of the sun. The building of his glider was more than a simple construction job!

Before the guard appeared for the morning check-up, Jack heard the patrol bomber pass overhead again. Tomorrow morning he hoped to be in the air to meet it: a strange flier in a stranger aerial contraption!

"And I'll be there—if everything works out!" he vowed, lying down on his lumpy mattress.

The excitement caused by the theft of the girl's dresses still had not died down on this second day. Again the convicts were spared the usual harsh treatment as the guards quarreled and bickered among themselves.

Jack saw Betty again, but she was being watched by her guard and there was no time to exchange more than a greeting. Jack had hoped to be able to tell her that he planned to escape that night. But he didn't dare risk it.

When Jack left his cell that night, however, he did not go directly up the trail. Instead, he crept to the cell next to his and tossed a pebble inside.

"Fat Stuff!" he whispered.

A grunt came from within the cell. A moment later Fat Stuff's round face peered through the bars.

"Jack!" Fat Stuff's sleepy eyes opened wide as he saw his visitor. "What you do? How you gettum out your cell?"

"Sh-h!" Jack whispered, fearful lest other prisoners learn he was outside his cell. "I haven't time to tell you now, Fat Stuff, but I'm going to try to make a break for it tonight. Maybe I'll be back for you later."

"You not takum me?" Fat Stuff asked with disappointment in his voice.

Jack shook his head.

"Can't," he said "It hurts to think I have to leave you, but it's impossible to take you now. So I came to say good-by—wish me luck, and I'll return for you, old-timer."

Tears dripped from Fat Stuff's eyes. His chubby hand came through the bars to clasp Jack's.

"Good luck an' good-by, Jack." he said quietly.

"Don't give up hope, Fat Stuff." Jack told his friend as he shook the chubby hand. "If I get away it won't be good-by for long. I've a scheme that may set you free."

With those parting words, Jack slipped off into the darkness and made his way past the guardhouses to the summit of the rocky mountain. He took his framework from its hiding place. With needle and thread he set to work stretching the silken dresses taut over the wings and tail.

When Smilin' Jack thought of the beautiful gliders he had seen at Elmira and then looked at his creation, he groaned aloud.

"It sure gives me a sort of pancake-landing feeling in the pit of my stomach," he said to himself. "But this is the best I could do with a girl's dresses, wire and bamboo. I wish this glider were strong enough to take Fat Stuff along, too, but it'll be a miracle if it even carries me."

Jack stitched the final silk piece in place and stood back to survey the product of his labor. It was finished. The first streaks of dawn were appearing in the east and it would soon be time for the dawn patrol.

Everything depended on the trial flight. If it failed, there could be no more.

CHAPTER SIXTEEN

WAITING FOR THE DAWN

Realizing that daylight would come in a very few moments, Jack tried to dismiss a feeling of uneasiness as he waited for the distant drone of airplane motors which would herald the approach of the patrol bomber.

What if The Head's protest to the government of the United States, through the bribed official, already had resulted in altering the course of bombers passing near Death Rock? If the patrol failed to arrive, guards quickly would discover Smilin' Jack missing as they made their early morning check-up of the prisoners. After that Jack would surely be apprehended, for the guards would comb every inch of the Rock.

The first flaming segment of the sun appeared over the horizon in the east. Too late to turn back now, Jack thought, for he couldn't possibly reach his cell without being observed by the awakened guards.

Where was that patrol bomber? Why on earth didn't it show up? It was late!

Jack made a few final adjustments after an inspection of his makeshift glider. Then he pulled it close to the edge of the precipitous mountain. Alongside the glider ran the crevice which had afforded him a hiding place for the machine. There would be no time to hide it now, if the guards discovered Jack was missing. He might hide there himself, but the crevice was deep and filled with jagged rocks. A slip of his foot and he might crash a hundred feet to his death in some cavern below.

Jack stood beside his improvised flying machine, ready to take off the moment the Navy plane appeared.

Already the heat of the tropical sun was beginning to make itself felt, but Jack welcomed the heat today. It meant that currents of air were rising from Devil's Kitchen and these currents would help lift the glider into the air.

This high rock was ideal for glider flying.

But Jack's worry was not about flying. It was about the tardy bomber. He sat down and waited. He stood up and waited. He walked in circles and waited. He simply waited. But still no patrol bomber appeared.

The sun now was up. Guards already were beginning their rounds of the Kitchen's torture cells. In a few minutes Jack's escape would be known and Limehouse, enraged to the exploding point, would run the gamut of punishments when Jack was caught. Nothing would be too severe to inflict on this prisoner who had escaped a second time. Jack resolved not to be caught if he could help it—he'd take off in his glider anyway and try to remain aloft until the Navy craft appeared. Even a crash into the sea was better than recapture.

There was still no sign of the awaited plane.

Jack crept to the rim of the summit of the rock to look down on the activities of the guards below. They

Jack Waited Impatiently for the Plane

were making their morning check-up now, visiting cells,
rousing prisoners with the customary harsh treatment.

Limehouse was there, awakening the men in Jack's
own tier of cells. From Limehouse's actions, Jack judged
that the chief guard was still ill-tempered because he had
found no clues concerning the disappearance of Daughter Laura's dresses. If Jack were caught, that mystery
would be explained and Limehouse would have his culprit.

Limehouse was working along the cells from the opposite end from which Jack's was located. Jack's empty
cell would be the last to be visited. This was a break, but
Jack was afraid it would not be enough. Even though
Limehouse delayed visiting the cells in the tier for several minutes, that time would be needed for Jack to get
into the air once he saw the patrol bomber.

Ten minutes before his escape was discovered was
about the most Jack could expect.

Limehouse was in his bitterest mood. At one cell he
flew into a rage, probably because of some imagined "insolence" on the part of a half-crazed prisoner. The chief
of guards reached inside the cell and struck the helpless
man.

From cell to cell Limehouse continued his abusive
activity. At last he reached Fat Stuff's rock chamber, the
second from the last one and the cell next to Jack's.

Limehouse called for the prisoner to appear. Apparently there was no answer, for Limehouse knelt and
peered inside. Fat Stuff was unusually slow to awaken

this morning. Limehouse picked up a rock and threw it into the cell. Still the chubby native failed to arouse himself. Limehouse threw another missile.

"Good old Fat Stuff!" Smilin' Jack muttered as he watched the scene on the ledge below. "He's trying to give me extra time by delaying Limehouse. As long as Limehouse keeps trying to awaken Fat Stuff and as long as Fat Stuff keeps stalling, I've got a chance!"

Limehouse was growing angrier and angrier as Fat Stuff apparently refused to wake up. The guard impatiently rattled the bars of the cell. Thus failing to arouse the sleeping islander, Limehouse took his keys from his pocket and unlocked the door. Limehouse shouted loudly for Fat Stuff to get up.

"Rise an' shine or I'll beat you to a pulp!" Limehouse yelled at the top of his lungs.

But even this threat seemed not to have a great deal of effect on Fat Stuff, who apparently had decided it would take more than shouts to get him up this morning.

Limehouse climbed into the cell. A moment later he reappeared, dragging Fat Stuff out after him.

Limehouse was scolding, raging, pouring abuse on the unfortunate islander. But Fat Stuff was taking it all, standing there stolidly, letting Limehouse rave. Limehouse raised his fist and pounded it into Fat Stuff's face.

Jack's blood boiled as he witnessed the bullying actions of the guard. Some day Limehouse would pay dearly for those cowardly blows.

But Fat Stuff now had stalled as long as he could. There was a limit to even Limehouse's ability to hand out cruelties. Tired of punishing Fat Stuff, he shoved the chubby islander back into his cell. The door was closed and locked behind him.

"Now I'm in for it," Jack said as Limehouse turned to visit the cell from which Jack had escaped.

Once more Smilin' Jack glanced into the sky, hoping for a sign of the Navy patrol bomber winging toward the island, but the sky still was clear. There was not even the buzz of an insect to be heard and mistaken for the roar of a plane's motors.

Limehouse strode to Jack's cell. Stopping in front of the cell, Limehouse shouted for Jack. There was no answer. For the second time the guard lost his temper. He knelt by the bars and shouted. Still no answer. Without realizing that the cell was empty the guard tossed a handful of rock through the bars, at the same time calling a third demand for "Powder" to "rise an' shine."

There was still no answer. None could come from an empty cell.

Limehouse strained his eyes peering into the semi-darkness of the cell. Even from the top of the mountain, Jack could see incredulity course through the body of the angry guard as he saw nothing in the cell. Limehouse always had regarded his solitary confinement cells as escape-proof.

As Limehouse stared, the incredulity was replaced by

the realization that one prisoner, at least, had found a way out. Limehouse sprang to his feet.

Jack's escape had been discovered and the patrol bomber still had not appeared.

Limehouse cupped his hands in front of his mouth. His voice, shrill with excitement and rage, echoed from the rock prison:

"Guards! Guards!"

Two men ran from their station in the near-by guard-house. As they reached Limehouse, he pointed and gesticulated wildly at Jack's empty cell. The guards apparently could not believe him, for they knelt and looked inside, then rose shaking their heads, unbelievingly.

It was impossible for a man to escape from a cell in the Devil's Kitchen!

One of the guards kicked the door. To the further amazement of the three men, the door swung open.

The rage of Limehouse and his men magnified itself a thousand times. Limehouse stamped his feet on the ground. Where did "Powder" get a key? His voice roared in rage so that it could be heard to the top of the mountain:

"Sound the general alarm! He's got to be somewhere on this island. He couldn't possibly get away! Rout out all the guards! We'll find that culprit, or I'll break every guard on duty!"

The two guards sprang into instant action. They raced back to the guardhouse. A moment later the wail of a siren gave the alarm, notifying all guards on the Kitchen that a prisoner had escaped.

Jack's position on top of the mountain was perilous. He might easily be spotted as he watched the activities below. He left his post and hurried back to his glider, ready to take off. Vainly he searched the sky for the thousandth time. But no patrol bomber flew this course today.

The guards were searching every nook and cranny now for a trace of the escaped prisoner. Probably some of them already were on their way to the summit.

The hot sun was climbing in the sky and warm currents of air were tugging at the silken fabrics of Smilin' Jack's home-made glider.

For a few moments Jack was tempted to risk a take-off. Gliders might be kept aloft indefinitely in suitable air currents, but not Jack's makeshift affair. He would be lucky if it flew at all, but he had hopes born of desperation. In Jack's case it was all or nothing. If he took off too soon, those planes secretly based on Death Rock might shoot him down while he soared waiting for the bomber. Or, if the glider failed to stay aloft, sharks in the ocean would tear him to pieces when he came down in the sea.

On the other hand, to remain on the rock meant certain capture. All of Jack's studied plans would come to naught.

Was it worth the risk? Should he take off?

The decision was taken out of Jack's hands at that moment. A sharp cry came from the path up the cliff.

Wheeling, Jack saw Limehouse topping the summit.

The guard saw the glider and gaped at the sight of the multicolored silks stretched over a framework of bamboo. He trained an automatic pistol at Jack and roared:

"So you're the dirty thief who stole my daughter's clothes! You'll get the guillotine for this!"

Limehouse stumbled up the last few steps of the path. Jack was tempted to spring into the glider and take off, but such a move could only be fatal. Before Jack could leap, Limehouse would riddle him with bullets.

Limehouse's first flush of anger subsided. Realizing the prisoner was at his mercy, the guard decided to get a little personal revenge before returning Jack to his cell.

Approaching slowly, keeping the pistol pointed at Jack, Limehouse appraised the workmanship of the glider. A nasty little smile crept over his face.

"Well, well!" he spoke. "An aviation expert! Wonderful guy, ain't you?"

Chuckling at his sarcasm, Limehouse moved toward Jack. His expression was taunting, his eyes were narrow slits, hiding cruel, jeering gleams.

"I don't suppose you had any idea of usin' this little flyin' machine in an attempt to make connection with the American dawn patrol today, did you?" the guard asked.

Smilin' Jack saw no reason to reply. His eyes watched every move Limehouse made, seeking a chance to turn the tables. If Limehouse would only shift the muzzle of the gun for a brief instant!

But Limehouse was cautious. Even when he stopped

to pick up a length of bamboo for a club, the aim did not waver. Hefting the club, Limehouse still kept the gun trained. He advanced toward the glider, raising his cudgel, ready to land a wing-shattering blow.

"My heart bleeds to think of havin' to destroy such a work of art," he said sarcastically. "But our little institution is rather old-fashioned. We frown upon convicts becomin' air minded."

The club was poised for a blow, but as Limehouse spoke he forgot for a second to keep the pistol aimed. This was the chance Jack waited for! He dived at the prison guard, desperation propelling him with such speed that he was upon the surprised prison official before Limehouse could fire.

Limehouse squeezed the trigger, but the bullets whistled wildly wide of their mark as Jack drove his fists into the guard's body with punishing force. Limehouse rocked back on his heels. He dropped the club as he strove to maintain his balance. Jack caught the wrist of the gun hand, giving it a wrench.

Howling with pain, Limehouse's fingers released their grip on the pistol. The automatic clattered to the rocks, bouncing and sliding and finally crashing into the deep crevice where Smilin' Jack had hidden the glider during its secret construction.

Jack's sudden attack threw Limehouse on the defensive. The guard quickly regained his footing and directed a blow which landed harmlessly on Jack's shoulder. The two men grappled. Limehouse brought up his knee, seeking to plant it in the pit of Jack's stomach with crippling force. Again Jack was wary. He had expected such tactics from Limehouse. Swinging his fist, Smilin' Jack managed to land a prodigious blow which checked the attempt to disable him.

Limehouse roared and attacked with redoubled fury. He butted and kicked, but Smilin' Jack skillfully dodged. Another blow with Jack's free hand sent Limehouse sprawling. Jack dived on top of his foe, mauling the prison guard with his fists, trying to land a knockout punch.

But Limehouse was tough. He was hard to put out of action. Locked in a desperate struggle, the two men rolled over and over on the ground, approaching closer and closer to the edge of the crevice.

Below the fighting men came cries of other guards, rushing up the trail at the sound of the pistol shots. Jack had to finish his antagonist before reinforcements arrived.

Jack was tiring rapidly. His long confinement, his lack of good food and the grueling heat of the solitary cells had robbed the aviator of his stamina. Limehouse, on the other hand, had been hardened by his daily duties. Limehouse fought confidently, fully aware that Jack's imprisonment had sapped his endurance.

But there was a factor that Limehouse overlooked: Jack's mind was keener and quicker than the guard's. Jack's brain had been trained as an aviator to act in split seconds.

The two men hung on the rim of the crevice. Limehouse tried to push Jack over the brink, but Jack slipped away and sprang to his feet. Limehouse came after him—again the two men locked arms. Limehouse pushed Jack backward toward the glider, hoping that Jack would fall and smash the machine, and perhaps injure himself in the wreckage.

But for a slight second Limehouse left himself open. Jack landed a blow that toppled them the other way. They landed at the brink of the yawning crack in the rock. Jack's foot slipped over the edge and hung down in the death-trap of a hole. Summoning all his energy, Limehouse tried to shove Jack the rest of the way, but desperation sent a flood of new energy into Jack. Pushing the guard back, Jack landed a powerful left which knocked the warden momentarily aside. When Limehouse closed in again, Jack was on his feet, crouching like a professional boxer moving in for a knockout.

Disregarding additional punishment from Smilin' Jack's fists, Limehouse charged with his head down, butting Jack backward toward the rim of the pit. With the quickness of a cat, Jack caught himself and counterattacked.

Deadlocked, the two men stood toe to toe, sparring at the edge of the deep ravine. Jabbing and ducking, Jack wove in and out, parrying blows and sparring. This tricky sort of fighting was not Limehouse's style. He saw that Jack would be an easy victor if something wasn't done quickly. Jack's steady rain of blows had landed a neat score of bruises. One of the guard's eyes was closed; his face was swollen and bloody.

Slowly Limehouse retreated from the edge of the precipice. His good eye gleamed with a new cunning. Suddenly his hand flashed inside his coat and whipped out a long, sharp knife.

Limehouse's mouth opened with a nasty grin. He chuckled with evil anticipation as he closed in toward Jack, ready to use the knife on his opponent.

Jack realized the desperate nature of his situation. He was tired, panting and at the verge of exhaustion, and his foe had a weapon far more effective than Jack's bare fists.

Jack slowly retreated as Limehouse advanced. Back, nearer and nearer to the ravine, the two men moved. Limehouse held the knife ready to plunge it into Jack.

Suddenly Limehouse sprang, the weapon upraised. Jack was at the edge of the ravine, unable to retreat farther.

Even as the guard sprang, Jack's alert senses caught the sound of something he had been waiting for—the four-motored drone of a seaplane. The patrol bomber was coming, but Jack, locked in this desperate battle, could not get to the glider.

Realizing there was only one way out of the trap, Smilin' Jack whirled and sprang.

His body flashed across the abyss, barely reaching the other side. Catching his balance, Jack turned and faced Limehouse, who was ready to jump.

CHAPTER SEVENTEEN

THE FLYING WARDROBE

Limehouse, eyes glittering as he anticipated the finish of his opponent, launched himself across the chasm. He landed on the other side and braced himself for Jack's rushing attack.

The knife slashed viciously at Jack's chest, but the aviator quickly twisted his body so that the blade missed him. Jack retaliated with his fist, striking Limehouse squarely on the chin, rocking him back on his heels.

The guard staggered, attempted to catch his balance. But Jack's blow had landed unchecked. The force had driven Limehouse back so that his feet slipped in the loose rock on the brim of the ravine.

Desperately Limehouse tried to catch himself as he toppled backward through the crevice. From his lips came a scream of horror which ended with the thud of his body on the rocks below.

Limehouse had been swallowed up by the very rock which he had used to cause the doom of other men.

But Jack had no time to consider the ironic justice of his enemy's fate. The patrol plane was a growing speck in the northern sky. At its speed it soon would pass the island. There was no time to lose. Besides, other guards were steadily climbing the trail in response to the alarm given by Limehouse's pistol shots.

Negotiating the crevice with another leap, Jack ran to his home-made glider. Here was the moment on which all depended.

The sun was high enough to warm the eastern side of the mountain. The thermal updraft would do the rest.

Lifting his glider with tired muscles, Jack stood just in front of a bent piece of bamboo which was to serve as a seat. He held the glider above his head.

If the construction were scientifically correct, the make-shift flying machine would float gracefully in the air. Otherwise, Jack would end in much the same manner as Limehouse had met his fate a few minutes earlier.

Drawing a deep breath, Jack started to run.

"Here goes nothing!" he muttered.

He had a rough idea of how the Wright brothers must have felt when they made their first flight at the beginning of the century.

The wings of the glider caught the air as Jack reached the edge of the precipice overlooking the sea. A cry sounded behind. A gun cracked and a bullet whizzed past Jack's head. The guards had reached the summit and were trying to stop the fantastic escape.

Jack sprang over the edge of the precipice. The taut silken dresses strained in the air. The nose wobbled and pointed downward.

Something was wrong. The glider was in a dive. It had the gliding angle of a brick!

Jack realized what was amiss. The tail was too light.

Already he had swung his legs through the bent bamboo pole in the center of the wing, where he had intended to ride. The weight of Jack's body was sending the glider headlong toward the sea.

Hooking his knees over the pole which served as a seat, Jack leaned back, catching hold of the spars with his hands about midway between the wing and the tail. The shifting of the body weight threw the center of gravity toward the rear. The nose came up and the glider floated.

Although the glider now was soaring, Jack's troubles still were not ended. He needed all of the lessons he had learned at Elmira glider meets in order to fly this craft.

The makeshift machine actually was floating downward, but the thermal updraft from the sun-blistered rocks was strong enough to lift him faster than he fell.

There were no ailerons to steer the craft, but Jack had attached wires from his seat to the tips of the wings. He was able to make slight turns by warping the wing tips with these wires. In this manner he made the craft circle in the updraft so that gradually he rose higher and higher above the rock island.

Guards on the summit and ledges of Devil's Kitchen had spotted him and were firing madly. But their aim was bad, and Jack was slowly drifting out of range for accurate shooting.

Far away Jack saw the bomber turn in its course. It had been attracted toward the island by the sight of the weird flying machine.

Jack's one chance now was to bring the glider down

Jack Shifted His Weight to Steady the Glider

on the water so the bomber could land and pick him up before—he hoped—the sharks got him.

The glider settled downward as Jack sent it out to sea. As the craft approached the water, Jack swung forward and dived head first into the ocean. The glider splashed and floated gently on the waves.

The bomber circled the spot, and then came gently down on the water, taxiing toward the spot where Jack swam. A hatch opened and a man tossed a life preserver and rope to Jack.

A moment later, Jack was being pulled aboard the craft.

"Fellow, you sure executed an amazing feat!" exclaimed the young ensign who pulled Jack aboard the airplane.

The naval officer's eyes looked pityingly at Jack's striped prison uniform.

"—but I'm afraid it's our duty to return you to the prison from which you just escaped!"

Jack shook his head. He'd clear up everything in a few minutes.

"Listen, old man, I'm no convict!" he said. "Take me to your captain and I'll spin my yarn. This is important —as important as a big battle!"

"Bring the castaway in here!" came a voice from the cockpit.

It was a strangely familiar voice.

Jack entered the cockpit and the voice came again as a welcome roar.

"Smilin' Jack! You old son-of-a-gun!"

Seated at the controls and smiling broadly was "Downwind" Jaxon!

"Why, you old lady killer!" Jack cried, recognizing his pal.

Downwind grimaced as he saw Jack's prison uniform.

"So they finally caught up with you, eh? You old moth-eaten tail skid!"

Jack suddenly recalled that there was much important work to be done.

"Listen, Downwind," he said. "I was doing some undercover work and I've uncovered the biggest spy ring in this hemisphere. Better take off right away before the crook in charge of that prison gets on your tail!"

"Eh? So that's it, eh?" Downwind said. "What do you think we've been patrolling this island every day for? Say, Jack, this place has been under suspicion for a long time, but we haven't been able to crack the mystery—"

"I think I can explain."

An elderly, gray-haired man in civilian clothes appeared at the cockpit door.

"A man by the name of Powder Pellet, who is held in California, made a statement regarding some strange activities here. While I believe they are unfounded, I am anxious for the matter to be cleared up."

"Let me introduce you, Jack," Downwind said. "This is J. Q. Brown, owner of South American Airlines—"

"Not Betty's father!" Jack exclaimed.

"Eh? You know my daughter!"

"You bet I do and if you think there isn't anything fishy going on at this island you've got another guess coming!"

Briefly Jack explained what had happened.

"I had no idea!" Mr. Brown said. "I trusted Mr. Ghindi implicitly. I didn't suspect he was misusing my trust to carry on such nefarious schemes."

A sailor called from the forward machine-gun turret:

"Planes taking off from Death Rock!"

Downwind sprang into action. The huge bomber roared and swept across the waves, gathering speed for a take-off. As it left the water tiny pursuit planes were speeding toward it from the prison island.

Turning the controls over to the co-pilot, Downwind barked orders to the men in his command. Machine guns were manned; the radio operator was contacting headquarters ashore to send the vital information Jack had gained to naval authorities at once, in the event that the battle should go badly.

The radio operator reported that a carrier was near-by. It was sending help, but the bomber would have to hold off the enemy until that help arrived.

Then the first wave of pursuit planes reached the bomber. The rear machine gun clattered and the leading fighter plane ducked as tracers wove a pattern across its nose.

Jack, eager to do something, found a place to watch in the gun blister just aft of the control cabin. He caught glimpses of the pursuits diving and dodging, trying to come at the huge bomber from all directions.

One enemy pursuit swept close enough for Jack to catch a glimpse of the man in the cockpit—even behind the goggles, Jack recognized the dwarfed savage little man:

The Head himself.

The pursuit ship circled and came back. Fire spat from the wings. Bullets splattered into the huge bomber. The machine gunner in the turret groaned and clapped his hand to his shoulder.

"Here, son!" Jack cried, springing to help the wounded gunner. He dragged the man away from his seat. "Patch up your wound. I'll handle this Emma Gee."

The gunner groaned his thanks as Jack took his post and trained the fifty-caliber weapon on the plane carrying The Head. The craft floated in his sights and Jack squeezed the trigger.

The gun sang a song of death as white streaks of the tracers sped true toward the mark. The little pursuit ship shuddered as bullets shredded its vitals at the rate of five slugs a second.

The enemy pursuit ship nosed downward with red tongues of flame licking upward through the fuselage. Out of control it spun downward toward the sea.

That was the end of The Head.

Another plane swam into view and Jack was busy again. The machine guns of the bomber were taking a deadly toll of its attackers. The pursuits grew wary as

two more ships crashed in flames. A third limped homeward badly damaged.

A sailor shouted joyfully from the rear turret.

"Uncle Sam's coming!"

Off to the north the sky was black with navy planes.
Nearly two score of Uncle Sam's best bombers and fight-
ers were coming to the rescue. But they were hardly
needed. Already the sea under the big bomber was litter-
ed with wreckage and the rest of the pursuits were struggling homeward.

The bomber wheeled about, making its way toward
Death Rock, leading the bombers to attack the citadel of
The Head's spy ring.

But on the turret of the prison tower a white flag was
being run up on the mast. Without The Head, the underlings of the ring were surrendering for lack of leader-
ship. They sensed that bombs from Uncle Sam's naval
planes would not strike gently.

The planes landed in the prison airfield. Pilots, battered from the recent engagement with Downwind Jaxon's patrol bomber, quickly surrendered, while Jack, Mr.
Brown and Downwind went immediately to the prison
headquarters to accept the surrender of the prison
officials.

"This is most embarrassing!" Commandant Trefwitz
exclaimed as he came face to face with Mr. Brown.

"I'll say it is!" Mr. Brown exploded. "You'd better trot
my daughter out here before I wring your dirty neck!"

"Bring Fat Stuff, too!" Jack added.

Within a few hours some drastic changes were being made on Death Rock and Devil's Kitchen. Guards now were the prisoners and several hundred convicts who had been kidnapped by hirelings of The Head were released. Only criminals actually sentenced by the government courts were held in cells, but these men were to be transferred back to the mainland to serve their time under more humane conditions. A message would be sent to apprehend the corrupt official in the governmental capital responsible for the ghastly conditions in the prison.

Within a short time an American cruiser anchored off the island. U. S. Marines landed to get the situation well in hand.

Smilin' Jack, dressed in a borrowed naval uniform, greeted Betty Brown after her father had brought her from the Kitchen.

"You look more like yourself now, Jack," Betty exclaimed joyously.

"I'm glad I don't look like 'Powder' any more!"

"I hope you never look like that man again, Jack," Betty declared, flushing. "I've got my right senses back again. I can't understand why I was so misled about the man. He had been working for my father for years, I thought—although he was actually working for The Head. He really could act like a gentleman if he wanted to. And to think, all of that time he was making his money shanghaiing unfortunate men to the living death of this island—"

"That's only a small part of it," Downwind said as he

arrived on the scene in company with Fat Stuff, who also had been released. "Did you ever see this beauty before?"

Downwind fished a gleaming object from his pocket.

"My engagement ring!" Betty exclaimed.

"I found it in The Head's safe," Downwind said. "But I recognized it from the description Powder gave to the FBI in California. That ring was stolen from a man Powder kidnaped and brought here to die—"

"That was the ring I used to cut the glass porthole and escape from the yacht," Jack said. "The Head must have found it in the clothes I left on the yacht."

"A thief, too!" Betty cried, aghast. "He didn't even mention that he had found it!"

"The stone is worth a small fortune," Downwind went on. "The American government will see that it is returned to the rightful heirs. But there's a big treasure on this island that Powder will never get to spend. It is made up of a lot of money and jewels he took from the men he kidnaped. While some of it may be returned to its owners, undoubtedly much of it will never be claimed. I think Jack ought to have some of it as a reward for bringing The Head down—"

"It's hardly fair to give me a reward. Give it to Fat Stuff," Jack said. "If it hadn't been for Fat Stuff, I might have died in the prison."

"Me buyum war bonds," Fat Stuff said simply, and grinned.

"We'll see what can be done about it," Mr. Brown said.

"But you seem to know a lot about my island that I never suspected, Downwind—"

"Powder made a pretty full confession," Downwind explained, "but the story was so wild we hesitated to act on it without corroboration—which Jack was good enough to give us."

"I understand," Mr. Brown nodded. "You hated to interfere for fear of upsetting our Good Neighbor policy by offending the country which owns this island. I think that government will be highly pleased with Uncle Sam's work in clearing up this twentieth-century slave trade on Death Rock."

"What's next, Downwind?" Jack asked.

"Well, I just got a radiogram from headquarters. I'm to bring you back to San Diego—there's another job for you to do."

"When do I leave?"

Downwind seemed to study, and then he winked at Jack.

"I wouldn't think of leaving before tomorrow," he said.

Jack grinned and took Betty by the arm.

"Did you ever see a South Sea island by moonlight?" he asked.

"Why, of course, Jack!" Betty said.

Jack looked blankly at Betty and said:

"Shucks, I thought I could show you something new—"

"Oh, but it's something I never get tired of!" Betty exclaimed. "I love to watch it from my plane when I'm flying at night!"

"If there was ever a daredevil girl pilot," Jack said enthusiastically, "you're one in a million!"

But in the back of Smilin' Jack's mind there was the pressing thought that moonlight romance was not for him—back in San Diego another assignment was waiting, and he yearned to learn what it might be.

WHITMAN
GIRLS' FICTION

ADVENTURE—THRILLS—MYSTERY

Follow your **Favorite Characters** through page after page of **Thrilling Adventures**. Each book is a complete story.

Joy and Gypsy Joe

Joy and Pam

Joy and Her Chum

Joy and Pam at Brookside

Judy Jordan

Judy Jordan's Discovery

Polly's Business Venture

Polly in New York

Polly at Pebbly Pit

Polly and Eleanor

Rose's Great Problem

Helen's Strange Boarder

The Outdoor Girls on a Hike

The Outdoor Girls on a Canoe Trip

The Outdoor Girls at Cedar Ridge

The Outdoor Girls in the Air